GAME CONTROL

Lionel Shriver is the author of eight novels, as well as a journalist for the *Guardian*, the *New York Times*, and the *Daily Telegraph*, among many other publications. An international bestseller, *We Need to Talk About Kevin* won the Orange Prize for Fiction in 2005, and has been translated into more than twenty languages. A *New York Times* bestseller, *Time* magazine top-ten pick of 2007, *Entertainment Weekly's* Book of the Year and rising to number two on the Canadian bestseller list, *The Post-Birthday World* has already secured eleven foreign translation deals.

Lionel Shriver lives in London and New York City.

Acclaim for *Game Control*:

'Shriver manages the discussion very well; she counterpoints the mawkish with the calculated, shows how a disgust for poverty becomes a disgust for humanity itself.... *Game Control* moves towards an enjoyable and deft conclusion with the same tact and wit that makes Shriver an able and human commentator on our poor muddled white guilt.' Anne Enright, *The Sunday Tribune*

'*Game Control* brings to life in dramatic form the polarized views of recent debates on population growth and economic development. It is the perfect novel for anyone interested in the present and future of the human population, the environment, and development. It combines a thriller plot, a delicate love story, a believable ghost, and impressive technical accuracy in demography and AIDS epidemiology—all in a prose style by turns lyrical, ironical, humorous, and moving.... Lionel Shriver adds her own wild ideas, ideas that might best be concealed from some of the real participants in population debates lest they prove too tempting to resist.... *Game Control* is a novel about people as well as an adventure of ideas and action. It brings Lionel Shriver's novelistic gifts to her careful research into stacks of articles from *PDR*. It would make excellent reading for an undergraduate course on population, development, and the environment.' Joel Cohen, Director of Rockefeller University's Laboratory of Populations, *Population and Development Review*

Acclaim for *The Post-Birthday World*:

'*We Need to Talk About Kevin* was a mo[...]
exciting and exhilarating.' *Sunday Exp[...]

'Before it was co-opted and trivialized by chick lit, romantic love was a subject that writers from Flaubert to Tolstoy deemed worthy of artistic and moral scrutiny. This is the tradition into which Shriver's novel fits. In 50 years, we'll still be wild about Harry. And a lucky handful of readers may stumble across *The Post-Birthday World* and wonder why they've never heard of it.' Voted Number One Best Fiction Book of 2007, *Entertainment Weekly*

'A wise and moving novel, touching us most deeply when it shows us how finite our lives are, and how infinite we want them to be.' *Daily Telegraph*

'A playful, psychologically acute, and luxuriously textured meditation on the nature of love.' *The New Yorker*

'Shriver chalks her narrative cue with relish and, once the story gets underway, it's hard to take your eyes off the green baize.' *Tatler*

'Brutally wise, viciously funny and at times unflinchingly cruel.' *Sunday Telegraph*

'Complex and nervy, Shriver's clever meditation will intrigue anyone who has ever wondered how things might have turned out had they followed, or ignored, a life changing impulse.' *People*

'The writing is continually engaging, the 1990s period detail rich, and the novel itself is a compelling take on the desire to have more than one opinion, or passion, at a time.' *New Statesman*

'Hugely entertaining . . . tackles the duelling human needs for passion and security with fierce, witty honesty.' *Vogue*

'Irina is a thoroughly compelling character, an idiosyncratic yet recognisable heroine about whom it's impossible not to care.' *New York Times*

'This almost chicklit plot is transmuted to literary gold by the sheer quality of Shriver's writing, the thoughtfulness and accuracy of her observations on life and relationships, and some sublime structuring. . . . For the last five hours I didn't stop reading for a moment; the last author who achieved that was probably Enid Blyton.' *Daily Mail*

'It's extremely clever but the cleverness never overwhelms the emotional power of the whole. As a reader you're both impressed by the form but still completely enthralled by Irina's inner life and passions. . . . one of the best novels I've read in ages.' *Daily Express*

'Unflinching.... One certainty is that Ms Shriver is not interested in fostering illusions about love.... *The Post-Birthday World* is disturbing because it seems real: Irina's wavering and soul-searching are not the comic vacillations of Bridget Jones, and the choices she makes are not the pragmatic decisions of an emblematic woman ambitious to 'have it all'....' *Wall Street Journal*

'A compulsive, clever, wise and witty novel.' *The Times*

'Shriver shows us her character in a double light—her emotional strengths and occasional moral weaknesses are thrown into sharper relief. Shriver also tells us something fascinating about the emotional life and its betrayals.... One of the reasons why all this works so well is that everything Shriver shows us, in either version of Irina's life, is rooted in the concrete and the mundane, whether it be the convenience stores of Mile End or the feel of blankets on a transatlantic flight.' *Time Out*

'With its gimlet view of the vagaries and varieties of human love and its inventive double story line, Shriver's eighth novel is a piercingly funny follow-up to her tragedy-laden 2005 Orange Prize winner, *We Need to Talk About Kevin*.' *Elle*

'Shriver is a terrific, intelligent writer.' *Bookseller*

Acclaim for *We Need to Talk About Kevin*:

'This is an important book ... here is a fierce challenge of a novel that forces the reader to confront assumptions about love and parenting, about how and why we apportion blame, about crime and punishment, forgiveness and redemption.' *Independent*

'One of my favourite novels ... the best thing I've read in years.' Jeremy Vine

'This superb, many-layered novel intelligently weighs the culpability of parental nurture against the nightmarish possibilities of an innately evil child.' *Daily Telegraph*

'Urgent, unblinking and articulate fiction.' *Sunday Times*

'Cleverly balances the grand guignol and the mundane.' *Guardian*

'Shriver keeps up an almost unbearable suspense ... It's hard to imagine a more striking demolition job on the American myth of the perfect suburban family.' *Sunday Telegraph*

'Shriver has skilfully hit the bulls-eye on two best-selling targets in the American market: the fear of rampage killings by teenagers at school, and the guilt of working mothers . . . ' *TLS*

'An awesomely smart, stylish and pitiless achievement. . . . Franz Kafka wrote that a book should be the ice-pick that breaks open the frozen seas inside us, because the books that make us happy we could have written ourselves. With *We Need to Talk About Kevin*, Shriver has wielded Kafka's axe with devastating force.' *Independent*

'One of the most striking works of fiction to be published this year. It is Desperate Housewives as written by Euripides . . . A powerful, gripping and original meditation on evil.' *New Statesman*

'A great read with horrifying twists and turns.' *Marie Claire*

'Pitch-perfect, devastating and utterly convincing.' Geoff Dyer

'It is a book about the dangerous distance that exists between what we feel and what we are actually prepared to admit when it comes to family life. (. . .) It is a book about what we need to talk about, but can't. (. . .) Shriver's satire on child-centered families captained by adult buffoons whose intellectual, not to mention erotic, life is in pieces, could not be more timely.' *Guardian Weekend*

'Harrowing, tense and thought-provoking, this is a vocal challenge to every accepted parenting manual you've ever read.' *Daily Mail*

'An elegant psychological and philosophical investigation of culpability with a brilliant denouement . . . although (Eva's) reliability as a narrator becomes increasingly questionable as she oscillates between anger, self-pity and regret, her search for answers becomes just as compulsive for the reader.' *Observer*

Acclaim for *A Perfectly Good Family*:

'Pondering her dilemma in a wry and self-deprecating voice, Corlis analyses her parents and her childhood. . . . The novel is a penetrating study of family life in which a looming Gothic mansion and an ironic ending add a dose of the surreal to a domestic drama.' *The Daily Telegraph*

'Choice is the driving force behind this eloquent and painstaking novel . . . Shriver sets up and controls a tense triumverate with admirable precision and a keen understanding of the hastily formed alliances and subtly accorded trade-offs involved in family exchanges. . . . Choice, Shriver underlines, is enslavement as well as liberation, and *A Perfectly Good Family* is a fine illustration of that point.' *The Guardian*

'One of [Shriver's] most unambiguous successes is her portrayal of feeling — of the odd, inconstant emotions and the sense of distorted guilt that accompany bereavement. Her characters joke and slip into hysteria, and remain detached from their loss, but slowly, through their wisecracks and silences and attempts to deny it, grief slips out in delayed, upended moments which are unexpectedly expressive.' *Times Literary Supplement*

'The book is refreshingly free of the confining narcissism that marks so many contemporary "domestic" novels. Moreover, Shriver evinces a far sharper sense of irony than, say, Anne Tyler, but much greater subtlety than, say, Jane Smiley. There is no contrived warmth in *A Perfectly Good Family*, but there is no incest, either. The end result is a novel with a plausibly familiar moral centre, perfectly balanced between satire and melodrama — in short, the literary ideal.' *The Scotsman*

'Shriver brings a vicarious originality to the plot. . . . A story that laconically deflates every human pretension about love or money. Like the author, the sister has spent enough time in England to view the proud prejudices of middle America at a quiet remove. In depth and colour, in narrative confidence, this is a fine novel.' *The Mail on Sunday*

'A typically clever and astringent fourth novel [sic] from this North-Carolina-born, Belfast-based (and female) writer. . . . Southern melodrama wittily blends with hints of allegory, as liberal America itself decays.' *New Statesman & Society*

Also by Lionel Shriver

The Female of the Species
Checker and the Derailleurs
Ordinary Decent Criminals
A Perfectly Good Family
Double Fault
We Need to Talk About Kevin
The Post-Birthday World

LIONEL SHRIVER

game control

HARPER

Harper
An imprint of HarperCollins*Publishers*
77–85 Fulham Palace Road,
Hammersmith, London W6 8JB

www.harpercollins.co.uk

This paperback edition 2009
1

First published in Great Britain by
Faber and Faber 1994

A catalogue record for this book is
available from the British Library

ISBN: 978 000 727112 2

Set in Minion by Palimpsest Book Production Limited,
Grangemouth, Stirlingshire

Printed and bound in Great Britain by
Clays Ltd. St Ives plc.

To the
NAIROBI PRESS CORPS
whom I can thank for
my most barbaric opinions,
and none of whose number
ever batted an eye
at the premise for this book.

*The most dignified thing for a worm to do
is to sit up and sit still.*

HENRY ADAMS

Contents

GAME CONTROL

1

The Curse of the Uninvited

'Not on the list,' the *askari* declared grandly.

'Perhaps . . .' the other voice oiled, deceptively polite, 'one of the organizers . . . Dr Kendrick?' Exaggerated patience made a mockery of good manners.

With the bad luck that would characterize the next five days, Aaron Spring was just passing the entranceway. *Swell*. The last thing any population conference needed was Calvin Piper.

The Director bustled brusquely to the door. 'It's quite all right,' he assured the African with a sticky smile. 'This is Dr Piper. Is there some problem with his registration?'

'This man is not on my list,' the *askari* insisted.

'There must have been some oversight.' Spring scanned the clipboard. 'Let's enter him in, so this doesn't happen again.'

The Kikuyu glared. 'Not with that animal.'

Reluctantly, the Director forced himself to look up. Wonderful. A green monkey was gooning on Calvin's shoulder, teeth bared. Spring slipped the *askari* twenty shillings. That was not even a dollar, but the price of this visit was just beginning.

The interloper looked interestedly around the foyer, as if pointing out that he had not been here for some time and things might have changed.

'So good to see you.' Spring shook his predecessor's limp hand.

'Is it?'

'You're just in time to catch the opening reception. What happened with your registration, man?'

'Not a thing. What registration?'

1

'There must have been some mistake.'

'Not a-tall. I wasn't invited.'

Spring winced. Piper had a slight British accent, though his mother was American and he'd spent years in DC. The nattiness of Piper's tidy sentences made Spring's voice sound twangy and crass.

The Director led his ward through the sterile lobby. The Kenyatta International Conference Centre was spacious but lacked flair – wooden slatted with the odd acute angle whose determination to seem modern had guaranteed that the architecture would date in a matter of months. Kenyans were proud of the building, the way, Spring reflected, they were so reliably delighted by anything Western, anything they didn't make. All the world's enlightened élite seemed enthralled with African culture except the Africans themselves, who would trade quaint thatch for condos at the drop of a hat.

'Couldn't you at least have left the monkey home?' he appealed.

'Come, Malthus is a good prop, don't you think? Like Margaret Meade's stick.'

God rest her soul, Spring had always abhorred Meade's silly stick. 'Just like it.'

Spring hurried ahead. Having assumed the leadership of USAID's Population Division six long, fatiguing years before, surely by now he might be spared the pawing deference the Director Emeritus still, confound the man, inspired in him. He reminded himself that much of his own work that five years had been repairing the damage Piper had done to the reputation of population assistance worldwide. And by now Spring was well weary of his own staff's nostalgic stories of Piper's offensive mouthing off to African presidents. Why, you would never guess from their fond reminiscences that many of those same staff members had ratted on this glorified game-show host at their first opportunity. All right, Spring was aware he wasn't colourful – he did not travel with a green monkey, he did not gratuitously insult statesmen, he did not detest the very people he was employed to assist, and his pockets did not spill black, red and yellow condoms every time he reached for his handkerchief.

Behind his back Spring vilified Piper, but perhaps to compensate for going all gooey face to face. Here was a character whose politics, having veered so far left they had ended on the far right instead, Spring deplored as uncompassionate and irresponsible. Spring aspired to despise Piper, but he would never get that far. He would only be free to dislike the urbane, unruffleable, horribly wry has-been once sure that Piper adored and respected him first – that is, never.

And Piper made him feel fat. Piper was the older although he didn't look it, and was surely one of those careless types who never gave a thought to what they ate, while Spring jogged four joyless miles a day, and had given up *ice-cream*.

'You ruined that Kuke's day, you know,' Calvin was commenting about the *askari*. 'He loved barring my way. You get a lot of *wazungu* rolling their eyes about Africans and bureaucracy, how they revel in its petty power – but how they don't understand it, wielding stamps and forms like children playing office. I've come to believe they understand bureaucracy perfectly well. After all, most petty power isn't petty a-tall, is it? These tiny people can stick you back on your plane, impound your whisky, cut off your electricity and keep you out of conferences you so *desperately* wish to attend. Bureaucracy is a weapon. And there is no pleasure greater than turning artillery on just the people who taught you to use it.'

'Calvin,' implored the Director, 'do keep your theories quiet this week. I'm off for some wine.'

Leaving the man toothpicking pineapple to his ill-tempered monkey, Spring felt sheepish for having let the rogue inside. He was haunted by childhood fairy-tales in which the aggrieved, uninvited relative arrives at the christening anyway, to curse the child.

It was a mistake to exhort Calvin to keep his mouth shut. Had Spring encouraged enthusiastic participation in the interchange of controversial ideas, Piper might have loitered listlessly in the back, thumbing abstracts. Instead Calvin perched with his pet in the front row of a session on infant mortality, making just the kind of scandal sure to see its way into the Nairobi papers the next day.

'Why are we still trying to reduce infant mortality,' Piper inquired, 'when it is precisely our drastic reduction of the death rate that created uncontrolled population growth in the first place? Why not leave it alone? Why not even let it go up a little?' He did not say 'a lot', but might as well have.

The room stirred. Coughs. Heads in hands.

The moderator interceded. 'It is well established by now, Dr Piper, that reduction of infant mortality must precede a drop in fertility. Families have extra children as an insurance factor, and once they find most of those children surviving they adjust their family size accordingly, etc. This is kindergarten demography, Dr Piper. We can dispense with this level of discussion. Ms Davis – '

'On the contrary,' Calvin pursued. 'All of Africa illustrates that fallacy. Death rates have been plummeting since 1950, and birth rates remain high. So we keep more children alive to suffer and starve. I would propose instead that this conference pass a resolution to retract all immunization programmes in countries with growth rates of higher than 2 per cent – '

The session went into an uproar. 'Moderator!' cried a woman from the Population Reference Bureau. 'Can we please have it on record that this conference does not support the death of babies?'

The next day the headline in Nairobi's *Daily Nation* read, 'Pop Council Conference: Let Children Die'.

Like everyone else, she had heard he was there, caught the flash of defiant black hair, the screech of his sidekick, and had craned across the rows to find that at least at a distance he hadn't changed much. When dinners roiled with the infant mortality affair, she found herself sticking up for him: 'He just likes to be outrageous. It's a sport.'

'At our expense,' the woman from the Population Crisis Committee had snapped, and Eleanor got a whiff of what even passing association with Calvin Piper had come to cost you.

His arrival changed the whole conference for her. She found herself drifting off with an obscure secretive smile as if she were still the girl she had been then. Yet she never sought him out. She conceded as the conference convened for its final address that she was afraid to introduce herself in case he drew a blank, which would irremediably damage a memory she still held dear. There weren't many of those left.

Eleanor knew copious conferees, but not beyond the level of talking shop, so while many parties would take advantage of free air fare to bask for a week in Malindi, Eleanor had not joined up. She was beyond Africa as entertainment. Besides, had she bundled off to the coast, she could picture the evenings all too well: the men getting sozzled at a cheap veranda bar, telling Third World snafu stories; Eleanor increasingly chagrined as they dared one another to be a little bit racist, until they were actually using the word 'wogs'. She would have to decide whether to object and make a scene and tighten everyone up but at least defend her principles, or to slip off to her room to pick the flaking skin from the back of her neck, worrying into the mirror, her nose gone hard.

As the rest scattered officiously with planes to catch, Eleanor wandered down the steps with nothing to do. It was too early for dinner and her own flight back to Dar es Salaam was not until the next day. She could stroll back to her hotel and pack, but she travelled so lightly now that she was fooling herself – it would take five minutes.

So she dandered down to Kaunda, listlessly scanning shops, most of whose proprietors were Asian, and hardly appreciated by Kenyans for their enterprise. The goods for sale – film, antique colonial silver and the endless *taka-taka* of soapstone wart-hogs, banana-leaf elephants, and ebony rhinoceroses – did not cater to residents but to the scattering of travellers down the walk, unselfconsciously trussed in khaki safari gear and dopey little hats. Along with the encrusted, sun-scorched backpackers who lay knackered on curbs, Eleanor wondered how the tourists could bear their own cliché, though there was surely some trite niche into which she herself fitted all too neatly. The well-meaning aid worker on a junket. Eleanor sighed.

Everywhere, animals. With the T-shirts covered in zebra stripes, lions' manes and cheetah spots, you would never imagine that Kenya had a population problem of a human variety. Stifled by the tinny, tacky shame of it all, Eleanor veered from the town centre towards River Road, where the giraffe batiks gave way to *jikos*, *sufurias* and mounds of second-hand clothes, among which she was more at home. Touts beat the sides of *matatus* for still more fares when their passengers were already bulging out of the windows. These privately run minibuses formed the core transport system of Kenya, painted in jubilant zigzags, with names like 'Sombo Rider and Road Missile' or 'Spirit of Jesus Sex Mashine', 'I Luv Retreads' and 'See Me After Job' on the bumpers. Oh, River Road was as tasteless as downtown really, but with a jostling, exuberant trashiness that Eleanor relished. Everyone hustling for a bob, no one in this part of town would fritter their shillings on soapstone wart-hogs in a million years.

Gradually, however, she grew nervous. While the eyes of pedlars and pedestrians just a few blocks away were beseeching or veiled, here they glared, unmistakably hostile. Children pointed at Eleanor, shouting, '*Mzungu!*' Tall, muscular men knocked her shoulders on purpose. *Matatus* side-swiped her path as she tried to cross the street. Much as she marvelled at the energy and ingenuity of the neighbourhood, this was their part of town and she didn't belong here. Everywhere on this continent her complexion blinked like an airstrip light. The one relief of trips to Boston was to walk down the streets and blend in.

She retreated back to Trattoria for tea, tired from her meagre foray, feeling after the feeble excursion that she had been a terribly long way.

Yet when she bent dutifully over papers from the conference, the print blurred, 'The Cultural Context of High Fertility in Sub-Saharan Africa' having no apparent bearing on the dusty villages to which she bounced her Land Rover monthly. This persistent malaise had been wheedling its way into odd moments over tea with increasing frequency. Perhaps she had malaria again.

She kicked herself for not saying hello to Calvin Piper. If he hadn't remembered her she could have reminded him. Surely there was no great risk to her precious hope chest of girlhood adventures. Eleanor realized she'd just turned 37 and she was still shy.

She discovered that she had left a scarf on the back of her chair in the last assembly, and hurried to retrieve it before the building closed. She was relieved by mission, however mundane.

The conference centre was still open, though cleared out. In the main hall pages splayed the aisles like wings of dead white birds. On the way to her chair she picked up papers. Eleanor was like that – she tidied. In hotels, she made her own bed and rinsed her own water glasses and hung her towels so neatly they looked unused. Her insistence on being no trouble often got other people into it, with the suggestion they were not doing their job. Today was no exception. A girl in a green uniform came rushing up and waved at Eleanor's armful. 'No, no.' The girl took the pile firmly from the white woman's hands.

'It seemed such a chore,' Eleanor said in Swahili, flustered and pinkening. She pointed towards her seat, thinking she had to explain (Eleanor always thought she had to explain, when no one wanted to hear really), nodding and smiling too much.

Of course the scarf was gone – what continent did she think she was on? Looking lamely about, Eleanor was about to scuttle out, for the empty hall disturbed her. The party-being-over sensation reminded her too keenly of her recent life lately – so much purpose and opinion suddenly gone slack.

Laughter caught her unawares. In the stripe of chairs, the far rows were rearranged around a familiar gleam of hair, and a monkey.

She drew closer to find Calvin sitting with several other lingerers from the Population Council Conference, none of whom she knew. Their laughter was of a seditious sort, as at something you were not supposed to say.

'Eleanor Merritt.' He did remember.

'I'm sorry to intrude, but – '

'You were forever *sorry.*' He pulled up a chair for her between him and an older woman, who shot her an icy smile. 'Eleanor works for Pathfinder: opulent funding, international profile and well run – ' he paused – 'for a waste of time. But Ms Merritt has risen high. From hard work, no doubt. She cares about humanity. Ms Merritt,' he submitted to the group, 'is a good person.'

'Not always,' she defended. 'Sometimes I'm a shrew.'

Calvin laughed. 'I would love to see it. Promise me.'

He had called her bluff. She could hardly remember being a shrew; not because she was gracious but because she was a coward. Eleanor vented her temper exclusively on objects – pens that wouldn't write, cars that wouldn't start, the telephones-cum-doorstops that littered any Third World posting. The more peaceable her relations with people, the more the inanimate teemed with malevolence.

'The Pathfinder Fund,' Calvin explained, 'belongs to that dogged IUD-in-the-dyke school, flogging the odd condom while the population happily doubles every eighteen years. When the fertility rate plummets from 6.9 to 6.87, they take credit, and Ford slips them a cheque.'

'It is incredibly arrogant,' said Eleanor, 'to march into someone else's culture and tell them how many children to have. Raising the status of women and giving them power over their own reproduction is the best way to reduce the birth rate – '

'There is nothing wrong with arrogance,' said Calvin, 'so long as you are right.'

'Besides,' interjected the upright, withered woman at Eleanor's side, 'improving the status of women is not pursued as an end in itself, but with an eye to a declining birth rate. You do not get your funding from Ford by promising to give women control over their lives, but by claiming you can reduce population growth. It's duplicitous. If they were no guiding hand of population *control*, you wouldn't pull in any money, would you?'

'All that matters,' Calvin dismissed, 'is that family planning does not work. I am reminded of those women in Delhi employed by the city to mow metropolitan lawns. They use *scissors*. I picture those tiny clinics pitched in the middle of oblivious, fecund hordes much like Eleanor sent to mow the whole of Tsavo game park with her Swiss Army knife.'

Eleanor hugged her elbows. Calvin put a hand on her knee. 'You think I'm criticizing you. No, I'm agog you keep snipping away. It's bloody marvellous.'

'Can you suggest what else there is to do?'

'We sorted things out for India not ten minutes ago,' he noted brightly. 'Institute free amniocentesis. As soon as the mother finds out it's a girl, the foetus mysteriously disappears. Produce an *entire generation of sons*. In sixty, seventy years 840 million Asians would die out completely. Neat, don't you agree?'

Eleanor was acutely sensitive to when people were waiting for her to leave. Calvin stopped her. 'Dinner?'

He'd ridiculed her work. He'd abused her in front of his friends. Eleanor said she'd be delighted, and worried what to wear.

Described in guidebooks as 'a restaurant that wouldn't look out of place in Bavaria or rural England', The Horseman was in the heart of Karen, if Karen could be said to have one. Named after Karen Blixen, the suburb was one of the last white enclaves of Kenya, museumed with mummified women who got too much sun when they were young, women who never carried their own groceries. They were the last of the English to say *frightfully*. Yet they still gave their change to little boys outside the *dukas*, and Karen's beggars were flush.

Aware that ladies are advised to arrive at engagements a tad late, Eleanor took a taxi to Karen early.

'Madam! Please, madam!'

In the car-park she was accosted by a hawker carrying some heavy black – *thing*. It took her a moment to discern the object, at which point she was hooked into a dialogue that would cost her. 'Only 150, I work very hard, madam! You see, *msuri sana*. Please, madam! I have six children and they are so hungry . . .'

The kempt and ingenuous young man held before her a carving of an enormous African family. The carving was awful enough to start with, but had been mucked over with tar. Eleanor was reluctant to touch it.

'I don't – ' she fumbled. 'I'm travelling, I can't – '

'Please, madam!'

The *please-madam*s were not going to stop. She could not claim to have no money, she could not simply walk away from a man who was speaking to her, and some forms of freedom must be bought.

Consequently, she met Calvin in the lounge of The Horseman trying to keep the big dark monster from her dress.

'For me? You shouldn't have.'

'I shouldn't have,' she confessed woefully. 'He wouldn't go away.'

'There's the most miraculous word in the English language: *no*. Most children learn it before the age of two.'

'This is just what I need,' she said, as the head waiter led them to their table, glancing at her souvenir with disapproval. 'A carving of the happy twelve-child family for my clinic.'

'You haven't changed,' Calvin lamented.

Eleanor could no more focus on the menu than on conference papers at Trattoria. The prospect of food was mildly revolting: a warning sign. In the company of men she'd no interest in she was voracious.

Calvin decided for them both. 'The game', he announced, 'is delectable.' His smile implied a *double entendre* that went right past her.

'So,' he began. 'You're still so passionate?'

She blushed. 'In what regard?'

'About your work,' he amended. 'The underprivileged and oppressed and that.'

'If you mean have I become jaded – '

'Like me.'

'I didn't say – '

'I said. But it's hard to picture you jaded.'

'I could learn. I see it happen in aid workers every day. You keep working and it doesn't make any difference until eventually you find your efforts comic. But when you start finding all sympathy maudlin and all goodwill suspect, you think you've gotten wise, that you've caught the world on, when really you've just gotten mean.'

'You think I'm mean?'

'You were, a little,' she admitted. 'At the KICC this afternoon. This is Eleanor, Exhibit A: the hopeless family planning worker, beavering away in her little clinics among the – "fecund hordes"?'

He smiled and said as gently as one can say such a thing, 'You still don't have a sense of humour.'

'I don't see why it's always so hilarious to believe in something.'

'Why didn't you tell me to sod off?'

'Because when people are wicked to me, I don't get angry, I get confused. Why should anyone pick on Eleanor? I'm harmless.'

'It's harmless people who always get it in the neck. Why can't you learn to fight back?'

'I hate fighting. I'd rather go away.'

They talked, as expatriates did incessantly, about Africa, though Eleanor suspected this was the definition of being a stranger here. Real Africans, she supposed, never sat around at dinner talking about Africa.

'I should feel lucky,' said Calvin. 'Not everyone gets to witness the destruction of an entire continent in his lifetime. Of course, if I had my way I would kick every sunburnt white boy off this continent. But not without putting mortality back where we found it, so these witless bastards don't reproduce themselves into spontaneous cannibalism. Import a few tsetse fly, sprinkle the Ngongs with tubercle bacillus, unpack the smallpox virus the WHO keeps in cold storage in Geneva. Did you know that we preserve diseases? The eagles are endangered, but the germs are safe.'

'What about development?'

'Develop into *what*, mind you? Pizza Hut? No, what Africa could use is some good old-fashioned regression.'

'It's seen plenty of that.' Her smoked trout starter was exquisite, and only made her ill.

'Not enough. I'd remove every felt-tip, digestive biscuit and gas-guzzling pick-up from Algiers to Cape Town.' Calvin disposed of his boar pâté in a few bites. 'Go back to *Homo sapiens* as pack animals, huddled around fires, cowering in trees and getting shredded by lions to keep the numbers down. No campaigns for multiparty democracy, no crummy tabloids, no Norwegian water projects. Just life, birth and death in the raw, busy enough and awful enough that you never have a chance to think about it before a hyena bites off your leg.'

'Back to the garden,' Eleanor mused.

'You never saw it, Eleanor, but when I first came to Kenya in 1960 this country was paradise.' He gestured to the tarry horror that would not quite fit under her chair. 'No *watu* with their hands out every time you tie your shoe.'

11

'Don't you imagine any twenty-year-old here for the first time is just as knocked out?'

'What knocks them out is it's grotty and crowded and nothing works. And all right, so the Africans should get their Walkmans like everyone else. So Africa isn't special. But when I came here it was. So there's nowhere to go, nowhere special. So it's every man's right to be garish, filthy and completely lacking in foresight. Terrific.'

Eleanor glanced warily at their waiter as he brought her main course; he spoke English. 'You sound like a child who's had his playground closed.'

'Don't imagine I'm reminiscing about how smoothly the country ran under colonial rule. No, when there was no telephone system not to work, no electricity to go off, no water piping to over-extend – now, that is working smoothly.'

'Well,' ventured Eleanor cautiously, 'Africans *do* have a right to telephones, electricity and running water – don't they?'

Calvin withered her with a look of excruciating weariness.

'Then, you should be happy,' Eleanor backed off, relieved the waiter was no longer listening. 'Most Africans have no such amenities, do they? Of which I'm painfully, and constantly, aware. In shops, I put a chocolate bar on the counter, next to a woman with two kilos of *posho* and a little fermented milk with which she has to feed the whole family for a week – I put the candy back. Everywhere I go on this continent I feel ashamed. I'm tired of it, Calvin. I am dying, dying of shame.'

'They like *posho*. Africans do not identify with your life at all. They see white people the way you look at oryx.'

'Hogwash. They want cars and I have one. Try and tell me they don't resent that.'

'Give your flipping car away, then.'

'That won't change anything.'

'That's the first intelligent thing you've said. And at least – ' he pointed to her hartebeest – 'you now eat your dinner.'

In 1972 they had both attended a Population and Environment conference in Nairobi, when the KICC was brand-new and conferences had seemed better than junkets; at least to Eleanor, who was only twenty-one, an intern with the United Nations Fund for Population Activities and fresh from the Peace Corps.

Calvin had just joined USAID himself, and asked her to dine at the Hilton. His fourteen-year seniority had daunted her then, and maybe that's why she'd felt compelled to make a fool of herself: because he was so much older and more important and she had no idea why he would go out with her. She was only aware in later years, once her looks had begun to slip, that she had once been rather pretty.

Half-way through dinner at the luxury hotel, she had been overcome by nausea. Calvin had done most of the talking; she was sure he would pick up the bill and could not see how her company had earned so much as a hard roll. She was gripped by anxiety that she had no personality at all, and concluded that if she had failed to concoct it by twenty-one it was time to make one up.

'I can't eat this,' she announced, fists on the cloth. 'I'm sorry. The idea of our sitting here paying hundreds of shillings for shellfish while people right outside the door starve – it makes me sick.'

Calvin nimbly kept eating. 'If you truly have ambitions to work in the Third World, young lady, you'll have to develop a less delicate stomach.'

'How can you!' she exclaimed, exasperated as he started on another prawn. 'After we've spent all day forecasting world-wide famine by the year 2000!'

'That's just the kind of talk that whets my appetite.'

'Well, it kills mine.'

'If you feel so strongly about it,' he suggested, 'go feed them your dinner.'

Eleanor had picked up her plate and left the restaurant. One of the waiters came running after her, since she'd marched off with their china. Eleanor looked left and right and had to walk a couple of blocks to find a beggar, and was promptly confronted with the logistical problem of delivering her food aid and returning the plate. So she stood dumbly by the cripple with elephantiasis, whose eyes were either uncomprehending or insulted. He rattled his tin, where she could hardly muck shrimp, now could she? It struck her, as saffron sauce dripped from the gilt-edged porcelain, that just because you could not walk did not mean you had no standards of behaviour, which parading about Nairobi with a half-eaten hotel entrée after dark clearly did not meet. She groped in her jeans for the coins she knew were not there; her notes were back in her purse. Shrugging, she turned under the stern, disparaging gaze of the dispossessed and shuffled back to the Hilton, where the waiter stood outside with hands on hips. Eleanor ducked around the corner and scraped the rest of her dinner into the gutter.

Back at the table, she couldn't bring herself to tell him she'd thrown it away, but she didn't regale him with tales of the grateful needy either. Instead she sulked, quieter and less entertaining than ever. At the end of the meal, Calvin inquired, with that delicate ironic smile he had refined even as a young man, whether her friends outside would like dessert. Eleanor glowered and asked for tea.

They had taken a walk and ended up in Calvin's room at the Norfolk, and at three in the morning he had had to ring room service for sandwiches when Eleanor confessed she was famished.

'I'll grant that was histrionic,' she recalled, studying the glistening red game on her fork while the waiter filled her wine glass with an obsequious flourish. 'But I still feel self-conscious, eating in places like this. I may finish my dinner, but I haven't changed my mind that it's unfair.'

'So tell me,' asked Calvin, 'if you had your way, you'd make the world over into one big Scandinavia? Generous dole, long paid maternity leaves and every meal with a compulsory salad. Where every can is recycled and the rivers run clean.'

'What's wrong with that?'

'Justice is a bore. Order is a bore. No one on this planet has any vision.'

'Well, we're hardly in danger of all that perfection.'

'They are in Scandinavia. And look at them: they shoot themselves in the head.'

'So you think it's better, less boring, that we sit carving slices of *kongoni* with good silver while half this city can't find a pawpaw tonight?'

'You're focused on the wrong level, Eleanor,' he said impatiently. 'Prawns to beggars. Your sensation of unfairness doesn't help anyone, does it?'

'I'm still ashamed,' she said staunchly.

'But it is not white, well-off Eleanor who feels ashamed, it is Eleanor. If you were Number Two wife grinding maize, you would feel ashamed – of your shabby clothes, of the woeful prospects for your ten malnourished children, of the fact you could not read. By what, really, are you so mortified?'

She shrugged. 'Being here, I guess. Not Africa, anywhere. In some regards I've chosen perfectly the wrong field, though I doubt by accident. We all talk about over-population, but most of us don't regard the problem as applying to ourselves. We think that means there are too many of *them*. I don't. I think it includes me. I feel unnecessary. I feel a burden. I think that's my biggest fear, too, being a burden. I'm constantly trying to make up for something, to lighten the load of my existence. I never quite do enough. I use non-returnable containers and non-biodegradable plastic and non-renewable petroleum for my car. I cost too much. I'm not worth the price.'

'Is this what they mean by *low self-esteem*?'

Eleanor laughed.

'Why not jump off a bridge?'

'That would hurt my parents. I'm trapped.'

'You can't possibly have persuaded yourself this shame of yours has the least thing to do with environmental degradation and African poverty?'

'Some,' she defended. 'I know that sounds pretentious. At any rate they make it worse.'

'So you have not remained passionate. You realize what you do for a living doesn't make a hair's dent in population growth, which is the only thing that would pull this continent's fate out of the fire. You refuse to become jaded. So what has happened to you? I haven't seen you in sixteen years.'

She smiled wanly. 'I think it's called ordinary depression. And,' she groped, 'I get angry, a little. Instead of helping the oppressed, I seem to have joined them: they oppress me. And after all these years in Africa, I've grown a little resentful. OK, I'm white, but I didn't colonize this place and I was never a slave trader and I didn't fashion a world where some people eat caviare and the rest eat corn. It's not my fault. It's not my personal fault. Anger may be too strong a word, but I am getting annoyed.'

'You are finished, madam?' He had been waiting for her to conclude for five minutes.

'Yes, it was very good. I'm sorry I couldn't eat it all, perhaps you could – '

'Don't even think about it,' Calvin interrupted.

It was true that a doggie bag back at her hotel would only rot. 'Never mind,' she added. 'But thank you. The food was lovely. *Asante sana, bwana.*' The waiter shot her a smile that suggested he was not used to being thanked, though she couldn't tell if he thought she was especially nice or especially barmy.

'If you want my advice,' Calvin continued. 'You're not married, are you?'

He might have asked earlier. 'No.'

'You could use some small, private happiness.'

'Right,' Eleanor muttered, 'mail order.'

'At least buy yourself a new dress.'

'What's wrong with this one?'

'It's too long and dark and the neck is much too high. And at your age, should you still be wearing bangs?'

'I've always worn bangs!'

'Exactly. And do you realize that you do not have to look at the world the way you have been taught? There are perspectives from which starving people in Africa do not matter a toss. Because your dowdy sympathy is not helping them, and it is certainly not helping you.'

They ordered coffee and Calvin cheerfully popped chocolates. 'I am advising that you don't merely have to get married,' he pursued. 'There are intellectual avenues at your disposal. You can allow yourself to think *abominations*. There are a few ineffectual restraints put on what you may do, but so far no one can arrest you for what goes on in your head.'

'I don't see what kind of solution that is, to get nasty.'

'This is a short life, Eleanor – thank God.' He spanked cocoa from his hands. 'And what happens in it is play. Rules are for the breaking. If you knew what I thought about, you'd never speak to me again.'

She ran her thumb along her knife. 'Are you trying to frighten me?'

'I hope so. You're better off avoiding my company. It has even occurred to me – this we share – that I should no longer be here myself.'

'You mean Africa?'

'I do not mean Africa.'

'What are all these atrocities in your head you think would put me off?'

'For starters, I'm no longer persuaded by good and evil.'

'That's impossible. You can't live without morality.'

'It's quite possible, and most people do. They manipulate morality to their advantage, but that is a process distinct from being guided by its principles. Moreover – ' His fingers sprang against each other and his eyes were shining, – 'I don't like human beings.'

'Thanks.'

'Astute of you to take it personally. Most people imagine I mean everyone but them.'

'You're trying awfully hard to ensure I don't dine with you again. Why isn't it working?'

'Because you agree with me on much of what I've said, and especially on what I haven't. All these dangers you skirt, Eleanor – cynicism, apathy, fatigue: the pits in which you fear you'll stumble – they are all yourself. You are an entirely different person than you pretend, Ms Merritt, and I suppose that is frightening. Though my advice would be, of course: jump in the pit.

'Alternatively, you can claim, no Dr Piper, I really am a prim, right-thinking spinster, and I will die of malaria in the bush helping improve maternal health. As well you may.'

The waiter brought the bill, folded in leather and presented on a silver tray like an extra treat. Eleanor asked, 'How do you make a living now?'

'Spite.'

'I don't know that paid.'

'It doesn't pay for one's victims, that's definite.'

She considered fighting over the bill, or suggesting they split it, but somehow, with Calvin, she'd let him pay. For how many bills had she grabbed, how many had she divided painfully to the penny? She felt a rebellion from a funny place, one she did not know very well, but about which she was curious.

'Good,' he commended, signing his name. 'You didn't. *That*,' he announced, 'was from the pit.'

'You said you don't like people. Do you include yourself?'

'First and foremost. I know what I am. I told you, I shouldn't be here. But that kind of mistake, it's been made all through history.' He helped her with her jacket. 'Sometimes, however, I remember what I was. I can get wistful. It's disgusting.'

'You mean you were different before USAID kicked you out?'

'Once I was division head, my friend, I was already an error. No, before that. Perhaps another time.'

'I thought I was supposed to avoid you.'

'You won't. I can rescue you, which you require. But my airlift will cost you, cost you everything you presently are. You can content yourself that means losing little enough.'

'You're being unkind, Calvin.'

'I am being sumptuously kind, Ms Merritt.'

Eleanor considered abandoning the sticky carving under the table, but couldn't saddle the staff with its disposal. Dutifully, she hauled it out, as if the heavy dark lump inside her had become so tangible that it sat by her feet at dinner.

Calvin gave her a ride to town. Eleanor mentioned there was a good chance Pathfinder would transfer her to Nairobi.

'I know,' said Calvin. 'They are going to put you in charge of Anglophone Africa. Otherwise I might not have bothered to see you tonight.'

'What a lovely thought.'

'It was. You don't tend to notice when you're being flattered.'

He dropped her at the Intercontinental. In parting, he was a perfect gentleman – regrettably.

2

Family Planning
from the Tar Pits

It was nearly a year before Eleanor was transferred to Nairobi, and not a very good one. She neglected to visit her clinics with her former regularity, and spent many an afternoon with a wet towel around her neck rather than drive to Morogoro to deliver pills that clients persistently took all at once.

Furthermore, Tanzanian villages, and Dar itself, were beginning to waft with the gaunt, empty-eyed spectre of widespread HIV. Weak, matchstick mothers would arrive at Pathfinder's clinics and there was absolutely nothing to do. The irony of trying to prevent more births in towns where up to half the adult population was dying was not lost on Eleanor, nor was it lost on her patients. Contraception in these circumstances transformed from a perverse Western practice to flagrant insanity. And it shattered Eleanor to watch families bankrupt themselves on bogus witchdoctor therapies, even if she conceded that her own people's medicines were no more effective.

Through the long, white days with little to distract her, she did think of Calvin. She abjured herself to expect little, despite his mystical talk. So many *wazungu*, after a steady newspaper diet of possessed grandmothers, curses of impotence and whole villages running riot from the spirits of the ancestors, began to talk a pidgin witchcraft of their own.

She pondered the contradiction between the icy things he said and the warmth she felt in his presence, as if Calvin's coldness calloused the same helpless sympathy she fell prey to herself. There are people who find it easy to be generous in theory but can't be bothered by the real problems of anyone

19

who smells bad; there are others attracted to being hard in theory but who will involve themselves, impulsively, in finding you a house. That, if she didn't miss her guess, was Calvin.

Eleanor employed a mental exercise – with that car, not always hypothetical – that sorted her friends out in a hurry: it is past midnight, she is driving back to her prefab, she is still miles out. The Land Rover stalls; the battery is old, scummy and shorting out. She has a radio, but you do not call the A A A in Tanzania. Whom does she raise on shortwave? And whom, even if it means curling up in the seat till morning, does she not? Oddly, she knew she could call Calvin, who would arrive jolly as you please with a crate of beer, to make a night of it. She thought he was a nice man. To the very end, she would maintain he was a nice man.

'Duplicitous' as her organization had so recently been described, the idea of family planning as a means of population control in a country where contraceptive prevalence remained below 5 per cent was absurd, so Eleanor didn't think in terms of demographics any more. She regarded herself as providing an everyday service, even if Pathfinder did get its support from agencies with bolder designs. She consoled herself there were times in her own life that she was grateful for the Pill, and to extend this opportunity for pleasure without consequences seemed a reputable calling, if not very glamorous. For she no longer imagined she was preventing worldwide famine or raising the standard of living for the poor. In lowering the sights of her work, she found it duller, but no longer ridiculous. She had helped a few unmarried girls escape the wrath of their families; a handful of already overworked mothers – and in this country women did *everything* – find a contraceptive they could hide from their husbands, whose precious manhood would be insulted if they discovered their wives used birth control.

In Eleanor's case, the pills had worked a bit too well. As she drew into her late thirties, the age at which many of her clients became grandmothers, even her own workers felt sorry for her. Among some tribes of East Africa a childless woman was a contagion, isolated in a separate hut outside the village, not allowed to touch pregnant wives, and sometimes stoned for being hexed. In Eleanor's darker moods the word *barren* would take on an interior complexion as she scanned the hot, dead landscape, unsure why she was here, her face so dry – she was out of moisturizer again. She submitted good-naturedly to nurses' teasing about visiting gentlemen from USAID or Ford, but the men never stayed longer than a few days and were odiously well behaved (or simply odious). It was when the teasing stopped that the situation got under her skin, the downcast shaking heads when one more prospect had fled. These were the times, in private, when she snapped pens that didn't write, threw the phone to the floor and pulled maliciously at condoms, stretching them at her desk and burning holes in the rubber with smoking matches.

It's funny how you just assume you will get married.

No, if you were born when Eleanor was, you don't say *married*; you say, *or something like it*, since the word is sullied from too many wiped hands. But still you have a picture in your mind of a time when everything will be different; when there are no more days you simply haven't a taste for; when something is settled. In a furry, indistinct form Eleanor had always seen a whole other life beginning at about thirty-five; she was now thirty-seven. *Pole-pole*, she was admitting to herself, like cracking open a door, that all women did not get married – or something like it – and though she was an independent, successful Career Girl, the grey shaft of her future that slatted through that crack split down her head like the slice of an axe.

Eleanor looked forward to Nairobi, at least a city where she could buy face cream; all that shops in Dar stocked was curling shelf-paper. And she was ready for the extra remove of a higher position. While Eleanor had been pressuring Pathfinder to integrate contraceptive services with broader health care, in the interim her clinics were barraged with cases of young children with ringworm and TB, and the nurses could only offer depo-provera. Mothers would come in for vitamins and walk out with spermicide, a little dazed, not sure what had happened. It was painful and impolitic. Eleanor didn't want to watch any more; she was ready for one giant step back from suffering, and she was nagged by the insipid mystery of what anyone was suffering *for*.

She even considered declining the post and returning to the States, but while like any astute Westerner she knew she would never belong in Africa, she no longer fitted in the US either. When she returned for meetings in Boston, she found conversation banal. These days all that the women talked about was aerobic dancing, calories consumed per lap while running circles in tiny shorts, while on the other side of the world their counterparts kept in shape by trudging ten miles for water and carting fifty pounds of firewood. Most Americans assumed a blank, tolerant expression as she described the food dependency created by Third World cash crops; they saved their own indignation for passive smoking. She wondered if she would ever be able to return to a country that was sinking millions of dollars into research on fat and sugar substitutes that had no food value at all.

The night before Eleanor left, her staff threw her a party, driving in from clinics all over Tanzania with beans and curried goat. As nurses corked the basin in her prefab and filled it with vodka and passion fruit squash, they traded the latest rumours on side-effects. The usual fear that an IUD could lance a man's penis had become so elaborated that it was now commonly accepted that the device could stick a man and woman together permanently until they were surgically separated in hospital. Eleanor remarked that any contraceptive which would stick a man and woman together permanently might fetch a pretty penny in the States.

For all the jollity and risqué repartee, Eleanor went to bed depressed, feeling she had gone into a line of work for which she was no longer qualified. Staring one more night up at the mosquito netting draping to the sides of her bed, with its taunting resemblance to a bridal canopy, Eleanor felt presumptuous advising any other woman about making love when she herself had forgotten what it was like.

That morning her secretary's tap on her office door was unusually timid. 'Yes?'

'Excuse me, *memsahib*,' said Mary, who would ordinarily call her Eleanor and speak in Swahili. 'I have trouble.' Her boyfriend, she went on to explain, had beaten her because she refused to give him all her Pathfinder salary, and she was sure he would only spend the money on beer. She had to look out for her children. She had been to the police before, and they had arrested him, but he had bribed his way out of custody and returned last week to beat her again. Indeed, Eleanor knew this story, for Mary had shown up for work with a swelling on her temple from a spanner, and the wound had still not healed.

'So you see,' she concluded, touching the bandage, 'if he is to be locked away for good I must pay the police myself.'

'Uh-huh.'

'I am afraid . . . Soon I will be unable to leave my house and go to work for the fear he is waiting . . .'

Eleanor, absorbed in packing the last bits of her office away and checking her watch for how much time there was before the plane, was taking a while to get the message. 'Mary, I have to – '

'My money for this month – ' She looked to her hands. 'It is finished.'

Eleanor was a soft touch anyway, and the party the night before had melted her all the more. Besides, she had been raised on the importance of empowering battered women. She peeled off some notes from her small remaining roll of Tanzanian currency.

Mary had no sooner thanked her and departed than the knocking began again. One of the driver's children needed glasses – without them the boy was falling badly behind in school. The roll got smaller.

By the time the tapping resumed a sixth time, however, Eleanor was at her wits' end. She needed to put finishing touches on the project reports for her successor, the electricity was off *again*, the low-battery light was winking on the computer and in an hour she had to leave for the airport. When she opened the door, Eleanor was sick with disappointment. The little nurse who stood there, Nomsa, had never said much but had been unusually sweet and competent, with a shy, fragile smile, always willing to stay late in the day. She did immaculate work and had never asked for anything before and Eleanor had thought she was special. But there she stood like the rest, hands guiltily clutched behind her back, all dressed up as if she were on her way to church.

'I don't have any more!' Eleanor cried.

Nomsa backed out of the doorway with wide eyes, nimbly stooped at the step and ran away. Only when Eleanor was locking up her office for the last time did she spot the little package in crumpled, resmoothed Christmas wrapping paper and a banana-leaf bow.

Perhaps it was that picture of being rescued in the scrub at midnight that inspired her to ring Calvin to meet her flight, for the dark plain, in her head, was where she found herself, even as the wheels touched down in the unremitting good weather of daytime Kenya.

'Your people took their time. While your promotion was coming through,' he announced as he took her bag, 'eighty-three million bawling babies have bounced on to the planet from nowhere.'

He installed her in a new Land Cruiser. 'Spite must be paying mighty well,' she observed.

'Fantastically,' said Calvin.

Something about Calvin discouraged empty chat, so they sat in silence much of the way, Calvin closed off in dark glasses. She had so looked forward to seeing him, always a mistake, and slumped an extra inch lower in the seat, confessing to herself that he was a stranger. Having heard *about* him for seventeen years had created a sensation of false intimacy. For all the gossip, she would not recall anyone who knew him personally well. Even at their dinner last year, he had used opinion to protect his life. She'd known enough such people, and stared out of the window at the wide, dry fields, not so different from Tanzania, thinking, another African city, the same set of problems from higher up, why was this improvement? What was ever going to change in her life? And what was wrong with it that demanded Calvin's promised salvation? How could she turn to this man she barely knew and assert, I see it's bright out, but I am in the dark; I am broken down in the savannah, and the stars are mean; my battery is full of tar?

As they drew into town, the verges thickened with herds of pedestrians in plastic shoes and polyester plaids. Where were all these people going? From where had they come? As the population density multiplied, the muscles visibly tightened on Calvin's arms.

'Most of the arable land in this country', said Calvin, 'has been subdivided already down to tracts the size of a postage stamp. Farmers grow their mingy patch of maize and still have eight kids. That's real child abuse. What are those children to do? So they all head for the city. Nairobi is growing at 8 per cent a year. No jobs. I don't know how any of these hard-lucks eat. Meanwhile their people back in the village expect them to send money. From where? They should never have come here. They should have stayed home.'

'But I thought you said there was no work for them in the countryside.'

'I mean real home. The big, happy, careless world of non-existence. Where the rent is low and the corn grows high.'

Eleanor never knew what to say when he talked this way.

'Nothing,' Calvin growled on, 'rankles me like these pink-spectacled tulip-tiptoers who claim technological advance is going to sort everything out pretty. You should hear Wallace Threadgill gibber about hybrid crops and the exciting future of intensive agriculture: multiple storeys of artificially lit fields like high-rise car-parks. How likely is that, in a country where just a dial tone is an act of God? I assure you, Africans are not the only ones who believe in magic.'

They were passing Wilson Airport, where several dozen Kenyans gripped the chain-link, transfixed by take-offs. Later she'd discover they could gawk at banking two-seaters all day. She admired their sense of wonder, but how many of those men on the wrong side of the fence would ever board an aeroplane?

At last they arrived at Eleanor's new home, a two-storey terraced-house, what Africans think an American would like. The rooms were square and white, and there was too much furniture, cheap veneer and brand-new. The kitchen was stacked with matching heat-proof dishware and matching enamel cooking pots with nasty little orange daisies.

'Imagine,' sighed Eleanor, 'coming all the way to Africa for this.'

'Early New Jersey,' he conceded.

'I'd rather they'd put me down in a slum.'

'Not these slums. Stroll through Mathare enough afternoons and you will come to love your Corningware coffee cups. You will return home to take deep, delighted lungfuls of the faintly chemical, deodorized air wafting off your plastic curtains. You will never forget, after the first few days, to lock your door, and you will sleep with the particular dreamless peace of a woman without ten other people in the same bed.'

Eleanor collapsed into a vinyl recliner, which stuck to her thighs. 'I'm supposed to be grateful? I'm supposed to run about merrily flushing the toilet and being amazed?'

Calvin turned towards the door, and Eleanor's imagination panicked through her evening. It was now late afternoon. The light would soon be effervescent, although Eleanor would be immune to it, and in the way of the Equator would die like a snapped overhead. Supposing she found a shop, she would return to New Jersey with white bread, an overripe pineapple, a warm bottle of beer. She wouldn't be hungry; she'd nothing to read; and she hadn't seen a phone. So she'd haggle with the pineapple, dig the spines out and leave the detritus to collect fruit flies by morning. Back in the recliner, she would quickly kill the beer with syrupy fingers, staring at her noise-proof ceiling tiles, listening to the hum of neon – she should have bought a second beer but now it was too late; she wasn't sleepy and it was only eight o'clock – the time of tar.

Hand on the doorknob, Calvin laughed. 'Don't worry,' he said, finally raising his sun-glasses, 'I won't abandon you here.' He lifted her lovingly as the chair sucked at her skin with its promise of evenings to come, already imprinted with the sweaty impression of a Good Person and her too-effective family planning, lying in wait for tomorrow night and another tacky expanse of brown vinyl hell.

When he drove her out she didn't ask where they were going since she didn't care, so long as it was away from that chair.

'The driving here,' Calvin ventured mildly, 'now that is population control.'

For some time they were stuck behind a lorry full of granite, with a boy splayed on the rocks, craning over the exhaust pipe to take deep lungfuls of black smoke. Eleanor shuddered.

'It gets them high,' Calvin explained.

'It's carbon monoxide!'

The sun had barely begun to set when Calvin pulled into the Nairobi Game Park, which suited her. She hated safaris, but did enjoy animals, especially tommies and hartebeests, the timid step and frightened eyes with which she identified. The park, so close to the centre of town, was an achievement of preservation in its extent. Yet after an hour of teeming the criss-crossed dirt tracks, they had seen: one bird. Not a very big bird. Not a very colourful bird. A bird.

Calvin parked on a hill, with a view of the plains, and nothing moved. 'Had enough?'

'How strange.'

'The sprawl of Ongata Rongai has cut off migrations. All that granite in the backs of lorries, it's for more squat grey eye-sores up the road. Happy homes for the little nation builders. The animals can't get back in the park.'

However, as the horizon bled, the plain rippled with shadow like the ghosts of vanquished herds galloping towards the car, the air cooling with every wave as their one bird did its orchestral best. The hair rose on Eleanor's arms. 'It's gorgeous, Dr Piper. Sorry.'

Defeated, he reversed out to reach the gate before it closed.

'I've worked in India,' Calvin resumed with a more contemplative voice in the sudden dark. 'There's something attractive about reincarnation – with a basis in physics – that energy is neither created nor destroyed. But when you've a worldwide population that doubles in forty years, the theory has some simple arithmetic problems: where do you get all those extra souls? So I reason the species started out with, say, a hundred whole, possibly even noble spirits. When we exceeded our pool of a hundred, these great souls had to start subdividing. Every time a generation doubles, it halves the interior content of the individual. As we've multiplied, the whole race has become spiritually dilute. Like it? I'm a science fiction fan.'

'Is that how you feel? Like a tiny piece of a person?'

'Perhaps. But from the zombies I've seen walking this town,

there must be a goodly number of folk who didn't get a single sliver of soul at all.'

'You've an egregious reputation, Calvin. But that's the first time I've heard you say something truly dangerous.'

'Stick around.'

He pulled into a drive, and she guessed they were near Karen again.

Calvin's home was modestly sized, and in daylight she would find it a surprisingly sweet brick cottage creepered with bougainvillaea, when she pictured the lair of a famous doomsayer more like the flaming red caves of *Apocalypse Now*. In fact, most of the conservation Jeremiahs with which this neighbourhood was poxed lived in pristine, lush, spacious estates that made you wonder where they got their ideas from. Inside, too, Eleanor was struck by how normal his rooms looked, though he did not go in for the carvings and buffalo bronzes that commonly littered the white African household. Instead she found the room towered with journals and mountainous tatters of clippings. The bookshelves were lined in science fiction, with a smattering of wider interests: *Chaos*, *Eichmann in Jerusalem*, *The Executioner's Song* and a biography of Napoleon. All the records and CDs were classical save a recording of *Sweeney Todd*. There was a touch of the morbid in his Francis Bacon prints, their faces of hung meat, and in the one outsized bone on his coffee table that could only have come from an elephant, but the femur had blanched in the sun until porous like driftwood. It was not deathly, merely sculptural, suggesting that anything killed long enough ago retires from tragedy to knick-knack.

She inspected two framed photos on the wall. The first was of a black diver in a wet suit, her hood down and short hair beaded. The face itself was small, the chin sharp and narrow; but the eyes were enormous and at this angle showing an alarming amount of white. The girl had great buck teeth which were somehow, in their startling, unapologetic dominance of the thin lower lip, attractive. The smile was carnivorous, and she was clutching a diving knife – 'what little good it did her', Calvin would remark later. Though the young woman was beautiful in some inexplicable way, the face was haunting and a little fearsome, all eyeball and grin, and the contours of cheek or chin, the tiny body they guarded, would always seep away in Eleanor's memory however many times she'd study the photo when Calvin wasn't in. It was a face you wouldn't want to come upon in the dark, though that is exactly when it would float before her, gloating with all that underworldly power that Eleanor herself felt cheated of.

The second photo was of Calvin, posed in a cocky stetson and muddy safari gear, one hand akimbo and the other on a blunderbuss, with a rumpled grey mountain range behind him. Calvin, too, was grinning here. He did not have the girl's enormous teeth, but both sinister smiles and sidelong glances alluded to the same unsaid. They seemed to be looking at each other. Eleanor felt excluded.

In the safari photo Calvin could not have been more than twenty-five, and the image challenged her original assessment from across the conference hall that he had not changed. Oh, he'd lost some hair, which lengthened his forehead and made him look more intelligent; and the weather had leathered him, for here he was seamless and by the time she met him he had already slipped into that indeterminate somewhere between thirty-five and sixty that certain men seem able to maintain until they're ninety-two and of which women, who have no such timeless equivalent, are understandably jealous. Yet none of this transformation was interesting. In the picture his stare was searing; now Calvin's eyes had gone cold. They no longer glinted like sapphire but glared like marble.

She did a double take. The mountain range was a stack of dead elephants.

'In the early sixties I culled for the Ugandan game authorities,' Calvin explained. 'They were the first on the continent to realize they had a population problem. Despite a two-year gestation, elephants multiply like fury. And they devastate the land – tear trees up by the roots, trample the undergrowth. By the time we arrived the vegetation was stripped, and other species were dying out. Left to their own devices, elephants eliminate their own food supply. In earlier times, they'd migrate to wreck some other hapless bush, and slowly the fauna they plundered would grow back. Now, of course, there's nowhere for them to go. Once they've ruined their habitat, they starve, by the tens of thousands. In short order the species is in danger of extinction. So we were brought in to crop. We took out seven elephants a day for two years.'

'That sounds horrendous.'

'Those were the best years of my life. And the work was a great cure for sentimentality. In culling, you have to shoot whole families. Orphans get peckish.'

'No wonder you have no feeling for infant mortality.'

'That's right,' he agreed affably. 'And it was a professional operation, with full utilization: we'd cut out the tusks, carve up the carcasses and fly the meat back to Kampala. Not bad, elephant meat. A little tough.'

'I'm confused – I thought the problem with elephants was poaching.' She fingered one of the stacks of clippings: deforestation, ozone holes, global warming – fifteen solid inches of disaster, teetering from constant additions on the edge of his end table, like the world itself on the brink.

'It is now,' he carried on. 'But as soon as you clean up the poaching, over-population sets in again. Why, in Tsavo – Starvo, as it is better known – the Game Department insisted for years their elephants were dying off because of poaching, but that yarn was a front for their own mismanagement. You got game wardens carving out the tusks of emaciated carcasses to make it look as if the animals had been poached; but the real story was the monsters had over-reproduced and torn the place apart until there wasn't a leaf in the park. It was grotesque. I *begged* David Sheldrick to let me in there to cull, but no-no.' It was hard to imagine Calvin Piper imploring anyone. 'He hated me.'

'Lots of people seem to hate you.'

'Flattering, isn't it? As usual in issues of any importance, the conflict degenerated to petty vendetta. I said the problem was population; Sheldrick said it was poaching; and the lousy animals got lost in the shuffle. All that mattered to Sheldrick was being right.'

'What mattered to you?'

'Being right, what do you think?'

'Over-population – I thought elephants were endangered.'

'Oh, they are,' he said lightly. 'Then, so are we.'

'What's happening in Starvo now?'

'A few sad little herds left. Now the problem's poaching, all right. While the *elephant community* spends its time firing furious, bitchy articles at each other, I've retired from the fight. The absurdity of the poaching-population controversy is that they are both problems. If you successfully control poaching but restrict migration, the ungainly pachyderms maraud through the park and then they starve. If you fail to control poaching, they're simply slaughtered. The larger problem is that humans and elephants cannot coexist. The Africans despise them, and if you'd ever let one of those adorable babies loose in your vegetable patch you'd see why. The only answer, as much as there is one, is stiff patrolling and a regular cull – what they do in South Africa.'

'They would.'

Calvin smiled. 'South Africans aren't squeamish. But here culling has become unpopular. The bunny-huggers have decided that it traumatizes the poor dears; that we create whole parks full of holocaust survivors. And you would like this, Eleanor: they're now trying to develop elephant contraceptives.'

'Do they work?'

He laughed. 'Do they work with people? You should know.'

'I suppose the acceptance rate is rather low.'

'It's technologically impractical. All that money towards dead-end research just because young girls who take snaps have weak stomachs. But in East African parks, it won't come to over-population. As human numbers here go over the top, the desperation level rises as steadily as the water table goes down. You know that Kenya has imported the SAS? They use the same shoot-to-kill on poachers as they do on the IRA. Still, as long as a pair of tusks will fetch sterling pound for pound, the poachers will keep trying. And I don't blame the wretches. If I were some scarecrow villager, I'd probably shoot elephants wholesale. The dinosaurs are doomed anyway, so someone should cash in.'

Calvin's green monkey had screamed and run away when Eleanor first walked in, but since had climbed to a balcony overhanging the living room with a basket from the kitchen. For the past five minutes, he had been pitching gooseberries from overhead, and the accuracy with which they landed on

Eleanor suggested the target was not arbitrary. She had tried politely to pick the green berries from her hair, but the squashed ones were staining her dress. 'Um,' she finally objected. 'Calvin?'

'Malthus!' Calvin picked up the handful of gooseberries she had neatly piled on the table and threw them back at the monkey, who scurried down the stairs, to assume a glare through the grille from the patio more unsettling than pitched fruit. 'Sorry. Malthus doesn't like guests. Don't take it personally. Malthus, I suspect, doesn't even like me.'

'This culling work – ' She collected herself, still finding pulp in her cuff. 'Is that what got you into demography?'

'Quite. Ah, but graduate school was deadly dry after Murchison Falls . . . Perhaps demographics was a mistake. Since then my life has been conducted on paper. It's not my nature. I like aeroplanes, projects, a little bang-bang.'

'Was the work dangerous?'

'Not at all. Shooting those massive grey bull's-eyes in open grassland was easy as picking off cardboard boxes. And they're supposed to be so intelligent, but they're hopelessly trusting. That isn't intelligent.'

'You don't talk about elephants with much affection.'

'They make me angry.'

'Why?'

'I don't know.'

'So in your view the elephants have had it?'

It was a little queer. While she had noticed the cold in Calvin's eyes, they had at least remained dark and clear; but as she watched, a film cast over them. Calvin sat down abruptly as if someone had pushed him. 'It doesn't matter.'

Eleanor cocked her head. 'That's odd. I was getting the impression only a moment ago that wildlife meant a great deal to you.'

'A moment ago it did.' Calvin's body gave a short jerk, as if starting at the wheel. 'Curry,' he said.

Trying to be conversational, Eleanor asked while nibbling her chicken, 'What do you think of the AIDS situation in Kenya? Do you expect it will take off?'

'I think far too much is being made of that virus,' he said irritably. 'What's one more deadly disease?'

He didn't seem to want to discuss it, so she let the subject drop.

3

In the Land of Shit-Fish

For all her training in contraceptive counselling, Eleanor's work in family planning had less to do with babies than with vehicles. In every organization she was juggling transport, half its fleet forever broken down. Eleanor hated cars; like telephones, computers and other people, they seemed determined to take advantage. While a Land Rover formally came with her job, she was constantly having to lend it back out. Today a botched backstreet abortion case had turned up in their Mathare North Clinic and hers was the only car available to drive the girl discreetly to Kenyatta Hospital for a D and C. As Director she might have refused, but Eleanor Merritt was not that kind of director. And she hardly wanted to admit to her brand-new staff that she was too frightened to drive to Mathare Valley by herself.

As Eleanor turned into the slum, a billboard at its entrance advertised VACATIONAL TRAINING FOR YOUTH, like a promotion for holidays in the South Seas at the entrance of Dante's Inferno. Far off to the very horizon quilted cardboard and corrugated tin. The road was lined with purveyors, squatting beside piles of plastic shoes, sacks of dried beans, but these were the high-inventory salesmen. Between them, women balanced four potatoes into a pyramid, stacked five small onions, or fussily rearranged three limes that would not pile. Grimmest of the wares were the fish. Brown and curled, dried in the sun, their stacks resembled thin leather sandals more than food, or even, she thought reluctantly, shit on your shoe.

'*Mzungu! Mzungu!*' The Land Rover attracted attention, and

the road had a surface like the moon, so in no time she could barely crawl, surrounded by whooping ragamuffins.

It was curious, though: these kids seemed so good spirited, rolling cigarette-pack trucks on bottle-cap wheels, twirling Mercedes hubcaps on coat-hangers and throwing shrivelled banana skins at starving goats. On whatever cast-off crusts and sandal-fish they had reproduced a few cells, many of the older ones had grown fetching – the girls, superbly tall, who hid behind their hands; the boys, with taut, hairless chests and supple shoulders, who shot her sly, salacious grins she could not help but return. As Calvin would say: they were too dumb to be miserable. Her mind was developing an echo.

Even names of hopeless enterprises were buoyant: 'Jolly Inn'; 'Golden Boy Shoeshine'; 'Joystick Hair Salon'. Mangled English worked a peculiar charm: 'Annie Beauty Saloon for Browdry'; 'Happy Valley Studio: Portrats, Photo Alburms, We also sell rekurds'. Transcribed as the words were heard, the phonetics suggested a larger perspective: that what was received was accepted.

Finally the Land Rover had accumulated so many children that Eleanor ground to a halt. Delicate bips on the horn only drew more urchins to her bumper. She was about to park and proceed on foot when a boy of about sixteen loudly cleared the crowd and motioned her on. He escorted her up the hill.

With the boy's help, she located the Mathare North Family Planning and Maternity Home, painted in bouncing baby blue, and even more cramped, gungy and obscure than she'd imagined. When she climbed out to thank him, he introduced himself as Peter and begged her to visit his house around the corner. She could not say no. Oh, Calvin, she implored silently. How learning that small word might transform me.

She left the car keys at the clinic and apprehensively followed her new friend.

'Don't be afraid,' he kept assuring her, though it was Peter who was shaking. When he led her into his room, he opened the window (a cardboard flap) and left the door (a sheet of tin) propped ajar, observing propriety. Still the room was black, and Peter lit a candle with, requiring dexterity with a glorified toothpick, one Kenyan match.

The walls shone with glossy photos from *Time* and *Newsweek* –

soccer players, motor scooters, skyscrapers – so that if it weren't for the glint between the cutouts of winebox cartons, Eleanor could easily imagine she was in the bedroom of any adolescent in DC. Likewise when he showed her his notebooks from the mission school, the handwriting was the same round, exacting cursive of students anywhere to whom words did not come easily but who were trying hard.

He insisted on tea as Eleanor began her ritual mumbling about having to leave, and led her out through the back to his family compound, where his younger siblings gathered in the corners to stare at the prize Peter had brought home today. They all shook her hand, exerting no pressure so that her own gentle clasp folded their fingers, and then retreated in new awe of their older brother, who could entertain a *mzungu* for tea. The service arrived, jam glasses and a beaten pot, the brew generously thick with milk and sugar. The mother's deferential bearing, a little stooped with too many smiles, made Eleanor feel undeserving, since for the last ten minutes an ugly worry had needled: *what will they want?*

Quickly a bowl of pinto beans and corn kernels were delivered with tea, and Peter's mother asked if she would please stay for a meal, the preparations for which, the daughters scurrying, were already under way. When the eldest scuttled off, Eleanor was terrified the girl had gone to shop.

'No, no,' said Eleanor hurriedly, knowing the word when employed on someone else's behalf. 'I can't.' And certainly she could not. To be polite, Eleanor helped herself to one handful of beans – well cooked, salted and slightly crunchy – but she was mindful of her appetite because of a forthcoming dinner with Calvin. Watching your weight in Mathare Valley was humiliating.

Peter's mother was pregnant, and dutifully Eleanor drew her into a conversation about family planning, explaining she worked for the clinic near by. The mother nodded and said this was definitely her last child, but Eleanor recognized the desire to please. The same graciousness that produced the beans and would have laid out a bankrupting meal would also tell Eleanor what she wanted to hear. How many times had women claimed to her face they wanted no more children and come in the next month for perinatal care?

36

Peter walked her to the clinic. A funny formality had entered the occasion, and she was let off easily with providing her address. She yearned to press him with a hundred shillings, but the ruse of hospitality had become real, and neither could violate courtesy with cash. Even in Mathare, paying for your tea was gross. For the life of her she couldn't fathom why he didn't slit her throat and steal her watch.

Though Calvin had agreed to retrieve her readily enough, when she found him in the waiting room he looked annoyed. Eleanor chattered nervously with the nurses, asking about the tubal ligation programme, hoping they didn't know who he was.

'I hate that language,' said Calvin malignantly once they started down the road. He hadn't dared park a new Land Cruiser in the slum, so they were in for a slog.

'Swahili?'

'*Chumba cha kulala, chakula cha mchana, katikati, majimaji, buibui, pole-pole, nene-titi-baba-mimi* . . . Baby babble. The whole continent has never grown up.'

'Do you hate the language or the people?'

'Both.' The statement didn't seem to cost him much.

'Do you like English?'

'Not particularly. Angular, dry, crowded.'

'Americans?'

'Grabby, fat, empty-headed pond scum.'

She laughed. 'Fair-mindedness of a sort.' She was coming to like Calvin best at his most horrid, and was reminded of a story she was fond of as a child, 'One Ordinary Day, with Peanuts'. A man goes out and feeds peanuts to pigeons, gives coins to beggars and helps old ladies across the street. When he comes home, his wife reports cheerfully how she shortchanged a salesgirl, screamed at a bus driver and had a child's pet impounded for nipping her leg. They were very happy together, and this suggested to her that she and Calvin had the makings of the perfect couple.

Calvin sighed, casting his gaze over the hillsides winking with tin. 'The *Chinese*, now. I had great hopes for them once. I thought, here was one government that knew the stakes. But their last census was disappointingly large. And now they're loosening the screws. They'll be sorry.' He was airy and aloof.

'China has committed a lot of human rights abuse with that one-child programme.'

'I don't give a tinker's damn.'

She touched her forehead. 'There's more to life than demography.'

'Not to me. Population is all I care about.'

She slowed. It was a stark admission if it was true. If he also intended a personal warning, she picked it up. 'That's appalling.'

'Perhaps.' Calvin used mildness as a weapon. 'So,' he proceeded, 'did you give out a birth control pill today? Fob off a condom on a little boy for a balloon?'

'Why are you so snippy?'

'I'm taking the neighbourhood out on you.'

'It is hard to handle.'

'Get used to it. Mathare Valley will spread over all of Africa in fifty years. I'm not such a Pollyanna that I predict worldwide famine. Why, what do these people survive on? But they do survive. No, we will be fruitful and multiply ourselves right into an open sewer. Whether ten people can eke out a few years in eight feet square is not the question. Look around you: it is obviously possible. But – ' He nodded at a mincing radio. 'You don't get much Mozart in a slum.'

'Fine, so one of the values we have to protect for the future is human rights – '

'*Human rights!* No one has the right to produce ten children for whom there is no food, no room, no water, no topsoil, no fuel and no future. No one has a right to bring any child into the world without Mozart.'

She glanced at him sidelong with wary awe. 'Do you ever talk to these people, Calvin? Whose little soul-slivers you're so concerned about?'

'I sometimes think,' he considered, 'that's not in their interests. One gets attached and loses perspective. Culling in Uganda, members of our team would occasionally form an affection for certain elephants. This maudlin naming, cooing and petting – it made them less professional. And the work a great deal more difficult.'

'The parallel eludes me.'

He smiled. 'It was meant to.'

Their accumulation of tittering children on the way back did not seem heartbreaking and inexplicably buoyant as it had on the way in, but plaguesome instead. As they did not realize Eleanor spoke Swahili, she picked up comments about her ugly dress and porridge complexion and funny hair. One of them screamed that he could see her bra strap, and she had to stop herself from adjusting her collar right away. An older boy carped to his friend about *wakaburu* come to tour the slums when they were 'tired of the other animals'. Eleanor allowed herself a tiny nasal whine, jaw clenched.

'Why don't you say something?' asked Calvin.

'Like what?'

Calvin turned on his heel and menaced, *'Nenda zaku!'* The crowd froze. *'Washenzi! Wamgmyao! Futsaki!'*

It was magic. Thirty or forty children seeped back to the trickles of raw sewage from which they'd come.

'Now, that should have been you,' said Calvin.

'I don't use that kind of language.'

'Go home and practise, then. Your Swahili's better than mine. What do you think it's *for*?'

Eleanor was both mortified and grateful. The valley was suddenly so quiet.

She told Calvin about tea with Peter.

'Don't tell me. He wanted you to take him to America.'

She kicked at the road. 'Probably.'

'Haven't you had thousands of these encounters?'

'Sure.'

'They still affect you.' He was impressed.

'In some ways, it's worse than ever. Not prurient. Not interesting, not new. Still painful.'

'They all think you're a magic lantern, don't they? That you own Cadillacs and a pool.'

'In his terms,' she soldiered liberally, 'I am rich – '

'Aren't you tired of saying these things? How many times have you made that exact same statement?'

She sighed. 'Hundreds.' She added, 'I had a feeling the next time I stopped by Mathare I would avoid Peter.'

They had reached the car, from which point they could see the whole valley of shanties bathed in a perverse golden light, under which hundreds of handsome adolescent boys cut out magazine pictures of motor cycles under cardboard with a candle. 'Eleanor,' said Calvin quietly, taking her by the shoulders, 'don't you sometimes just want them to *go away*?'

She squirmed from his hands and huddled into the seat. Though the air was stuffy, she did not unroll a window, but sat breathing the smell of new upholstery: soft leather, freshly minted plastic. She buckled the seat belt, tying herself to the *motakari*, as if the hands of Mathare threatened to drag her out again. She locked the door. 'Yes,' she said at last. 'But there's only one way to manage that. For me to go away.'

'They would follow you. You will always have 661 million black wretches breathing down your neck. By the time you're ninety? *Well over two billion.*'

'I'm sick of these figures.'

'In a little over a hundred years this continent's population will quadruple – '

'Calvin, please!'

'By 2000 Mexico City will have thirty million people. These are not just numbers, Eleanor. We're talking billions of disgruntled, hungry, filthy *Homo sapiens*, starting to turn mean. they will all want a Walkman. They will all want you to take them to America.'

'I have been trying my whole adult life – '

'You would be far more generous to launch into Mathare with a machine-gun.'

'I don't think that kind of joke is very funny.'

'It isn't a joke.'

Eleanor folded her arms. 'You have no business undermining my work just because you've fallen by the sidelines.'

'Women tend to interpret any argument as personal attack. There is such a thing as fact outside whatever petty professional bitterness I might still harbour. I will remind you that I singly have raised more funding for population programmes than any man on earth. *Family planning?* You are riding, Ms Merritt, with the father of family planning, so that if I tell you it is a waste of time, I at least expect you to listen.'

'Yes . . .' she drawled, balled up on the other side of the car. 'I remember stories, all right. Of you walking into Julius Nyrere's office and dumping a bag of multi-coloured condoms

on his desk. "How many children do you have?" you asked.
'Oh, that went the rounds, Mr Diplomat.'

'Fine, that was a stunt, and I pulled a lot of them. Some worked, some didn't. That one backfired.'

'I'll say.'

They were driving down the long hill towards Lang'ata, where trailing through the scrub Kenyans filed six abreast and chest to back from town to outlying estates. With so many marching feet skittling into the distance in unbroken lines, it was hard to resist the image of ants streaming to their holes. Or it was now. Eleanor didn't used to look at Africans and think insects.

'Demographically, the future has already occurred. That by 2100 we will have between eleven and fifteen billion people is now a certainty.'

'So the answer,' said Eleanor stiffly, 'is despair.'

'A large bottle of brandy helps. But no. Not despair. Let's see if they have Martell.' He swung into a *duka*, for Calvin did not suffer the same qualms as Eleanor, shelling out 1,200 shillings for imported liquor when everyone else in the queue was counting out ten for a pint of milk.

After another forty-five minutes behind Volkswagens being push-started, hand-drawn carts dropping melons on to the tarmac and a lorry with a broken axle that had spilled its load of reeking fish over both lanes, they retired to Calvin's cottage. Even at his most insufferable, Calvin's company was preferable to another evening of the brown chair. On the way home Calvin had picked up his mail at his Karen post box, and he opened a fat manila envelope of newspaper articles on to the table.

'My clipping service,' he explained. 'Courtesy of Wallace Threadgill. One of the space travellers. That crew who think if it gets a bit crowded we can book ourselves to Venus and hold our breath. They are quite remarkable. I've never figured out what drugs they're on, but I would love a bottle.'

'Why would he send you clippings?'

'It's hate mail.'

She peered at the pile. 'I thought you weren't interested in AIDS.' For these were the headlines on top: 'Confronting the Cruel Reality of Africa's AIDS: A Continent's Agony'; 'AIDS

Tears Lives of a Ugandan Family'; 'My Daughter Won't Live to Two, Mother Weeps'.

'I'm entirely interested. I just find the alarmist impact projections optimistic. One more virus: we've seen them come and go.'

'You find high infection rates *optimistic*?'

'Threadgill is browned off with me. HIV – he thinks I invented it.'

'That's preposterous!'

'Not really. And I was honoured. The virus is ingenious. But from my provisional projections, AIDS will not stem population growth even in Africa. HIV has proved a great personal disappointment. Why, I rather resent it for getting my hopes up.'

Eleanor stood and picked up her briefcase. '*Disappointment? I refuse to sit here and –* '

He poured her a stout double. 'Young lady, we are still working on your sense of humour.'

She paused, stayed standing, but finally put the briefcase down. 'I think we need to work on yours. It's ghoulish.'

He smiled. 'I was the boy in seventh grade in the back of the class telling dead-baby jokes.'

'You're still telling them.'

'Mmm.'

'That was quite a leg-pull. Touché.'

She ranged the room, taking a good belt of the brandy. It was an ordinary room, wasn't it? But the light glowed with the off-yellow that precedes a cyclone, and she was unnerved by a persistent *scrish-scrash* at the edge of her ear that she couldn't identify. When she looked at the photograph of the diver, the eyes no longer focused on Calvin but followed Eleanor's uneasy pace before the elephant bone instead. Their expression was of the utmost entertainment.

4

Spiritual Pygmies
at the Ski Chalet

Wallace didn't attend social functions often any more, but an occasional descent into the world of the pale *kaffir* was charitable. As he glided over their heads in his airy comprehension of the Fulgent Whole, it was easy to forget that most of his people were still piddling in the dirt with their eyes closed. While Wallace had the loftiest of interior aspirations, he did not believe that individual enlightenment should be placed above your duties to the blind. Revelation came with its responsibilities, if sometimes tedious.

He set up camp on a stool by the fire, scanning the gnoshing, tittering, tinselly crowd as they tried to numb their agony with spirit of the wrong sort. Aside from the Luo domestic staff scurrying with platters, the entire gathering was white. The usual form, in Nairobi. The pallid, both on the continent and on the planet, were being phased out, so they huddled together through the siege in lamentable little wakes like these that they liked to call 'parties'.

He glanced around the house, an A-frame with high varnished rafters, like a ski chalet: Aspen overlooking the Ngong Hills. Dotted around the CD player perched a predictable display of travel trophies – bone pipes and toothy masks – whose ceremonial purposes their looters wouldn't comprehend, or care to.

The herd was mixed tonight. A larger than average colony of aid parasites, each of whom was convinced he and he alone *really* understood the Samburu. The clamour of authority was deafening: 'The problem with schools for the pastoralist is they discourage a nomadic life . . .'

43

'And you have to wonder', a proprietary voice chimed, 'if teaching herders to read about Boston is in their interests. When you expose them to wider options, you educate them, in effect, to be dissatisfied . . .'

'Aldous Huxley,' a woman interrupted. '*Brave New World* argues that the freedom to be unhappy is a fundamental human right . . .'

From an opposite corner came the distinctive whine of the conservation clique, always indignant that their sensitive, sweet and uncannily clever pet elephants had been entrusted to brutish natives who didn't appreciate complex pachyderm kinship structures and had the temerity to worry about their own survival instead. 'It's *much* too early to lift the ivory ban, *much* too early . . .'

'On the contrary, I thought Amboseli was bunged with elephants. Turning to a rubbish tip, a dust bowl – '

Wallace shook his head. These interlopers thought Africa belonged to them.

'I don't see why Kenya should suffer just because South Africa wants to cash in its ivory stockpiles – '

'Why shouldn't good game management be rewarded?'

'I *know* culling makes a lot of sense,' a girl in several kilos of Ethiopian silver was moaning. 'But I simply can't *bear* it – '

Sifting aimlessly between the gaggles, ex-hunters fetched themselves another drink. As masters will come to resemble their dogs, the thick-necked, snouty, lumbering intrepids suggested the animals they'd shot. Hunting had been illegal in Kenya for years now. Grown puffy and cirrhotic with nothing to murder, most of these anachronisms were reduced to trucking pill-rattling geriatrics and shrill, fibre-obsessed Americans around the Mara, or had secured contracts with Zanzibar, where the gruff lion-slayers now picked off over-populated crows.

On its outer edges, the throng was laced with the independently wealthy and the entrepreneurial élite. If they deigned to work, husbands ran light industries and were sure to own at least one aeroplane, a house in Lamu and a camp in the Ngurumans. Not particularly bright, few of these spoiled, soft-handed colonials would have done well in Europe or America, while in Africa they'd little commercial competition. The baby-fat faces beamed with self-satisfaction. Here their dress ran to sports jackets, but out in the wilderness they were given to orange Bermudas and loafers without socks. Their conversation, anywhere, was entirely about cars. 'I had my Daihatsu kitted out with . . . forgot about one of those bloody unmarked speed-bumps and cracked my engine block . . . found a way to get around the duty on . . .' Wallace didn't need to listen very hard.

Their wives, on the other hand, were at least an eyeful. Balanced on legs no thicker than high heels, these emaciated elegants could raise millions on a poster:

SAVE THE ENDANGERED CAUCASIAN FEMALE

Anna has not eaten in three days. She is five foot eight and weighs little over a hundred pounds. Anna requires a full litre of vodka just to survive the cruel leisure of one more back-biting social function. She needs your help. For just a thousand pounds a week, you could adopt a rich white lady in Africa.

As if to torment themselves, Nairobi's physics-defying two-dimensional were all clustered around the buffet, one licking a surreptitious drip of meat-juice off her finger, another fondling a leaf of lettuce. Wallace disapproved of gluttony, but he had no time for greedy asceticism either. Fasting was for mental purification, not miniskirts. And their ensembles, over-accessoried and keenly co-ordinated, betrayed how long they had spent trying on earlier combinations and taking them off. Most of their mumble was inaudible as they confided in one another who was copulating with whom, for in the week since their last party the couplings would have done a complete musical chairs. With the sexual turnover in this town, gossip was a demanding and challenging career. The remarks from the buffet he could hear, however, regarded the timeless servant problem. 'George had his camera disappear, and with nobody coming forward, just looking, like, duh, what's a camera, I was sorry but I had to sack the lot . . .'

'You have to draw the line right away. Little by little, they bring their whole families, until the *shamba* is overrun, mat-

45

tresses and plastic bowls; it's hardly your house any more! Cheeky bastards!'

'And when we took her on she said she had *one child*, can you believe it! Of course she had six, and now she's pregnant, *again* – '

'You really have to employ all the same tribe, sweety, or they're at each other's throats morning and night.'

Add a few pilots, a sprinkling of journalists waiting for some Africans to starve, for another massacre in Somalia or the rise of another colourful dictator whose quaint cannibalism they could send up in the *Daily Mirror*, and that, in one room, was *mzungu* Nairobi – inbred, vain, pampered, presumptive and imminently extinct, thank heavens.

Wallace declined to mingle, and perched on a three-legged stool, rocking on his chaplies with his cane between his legs, rearranging the straggles of his faded *kikoi*. It was times like these, while around him the bewildered got motherless, that he might have missed his pipe, but Wallace had given it up and regarded himself as beyond desire.

He had noted before that the mentally mangled found the proximity of perfect contentment and inner peace an upsetting experience and so they tended to avoid him. Conversations with Wallace had a habit of dwindling. Why? Just try explaining how we-are-all-one when your companion is fidgeting for a refill of whisky and looks so palpably disheartened at the demise of the banana crisps. So he was surprised when one of the paper dolls tore herself away from ogling the buffet table of forbidden fruit and sidled over to the fire. Perhaps, so tiny, she was cold.

'So what's your line?' she asked distractedly, no doubt having just learned her husband was bedding her best friend. 'KQ? WWF? A & K? I'd guess . . .' she assessed, 'UN, but not with those sandals. NGO. Loads of integrity. SIDEA?'

'I did,' he conceded, 'once work in population research.'

'Oh, brilliant! I know this sounds awful, but when I read about a plane crash or an earthquake, I think, well, good. There are too many people already.'

'And what if you were on the plane?'

'I suppose then I shouldn't have to think anything about it whatsoever.' She giggled.

'I've given up population work rather.'

'Well, I don't blame you. It must be so discouraging. Everyone giving food aid to those poor Ethiopians, who just keep having more babies. And frankly . . .' Her voice had dropped.

'Sorry?'

'This AIDS palaver. I've heard it said, you know, that it's Nature's way. Of keeping the balance. Do you think me just too monstrous?'

Wallace was about to say 'Yes' when a cold draught raised the hairs on his neck. Even facing away from the door he could feel the room tingle. The girl who didn't really care if she was a monster clapped delightedly. 'Calvin!' she cried, and scampered off.

Wallace forced himself to turn slowly, by which time Evil Incarnate, Inc. had already set up shop at the big round table on the opposite side of the room. Too insecure to arrive without a protective claque, Piper had gathered his dwarfs around him, commanding the whole table so that no one could get at the food, and annexing most of the available chairs in one swoop. Arms extended languidly on either side, he took an audience as his due. That ghastly simian was always a draw, though gurgling fans got their comeuppance soon enough – already, from the sound of a yelp and covering titter, the hateful beast had managed to bite a hand that fed it. Shortly, standing room behind the circle filled up, while energy bled from other corners. Alternative conversations grew lack-lustre while trickles of prima donna pessimism drizzled to Threadgill's ear: 'You realize there are *actually some people* who believe that human population can expand infinitely?'

Wallace smiled. So Piper had noticed he was here.

Calvin was the prime of a type. They saw only mayhem and degradation, for you can only see what you are, and squalor was what these deformities were made of. Piper would never perceive the canniness of the planet or the ingenuity of his own race, for his vista was smeared with greenhouse gases and acid rain. Would Calvin ever bother to read articles about new high-yield hybrid crops? Or Simon's irrefutable evidence that far from being a drag on a poor country's economy, population growth was its greatest asset?

For as often as nihilists concocted 'solutions', they raised

47

the prospect of any salvation to prove it wouldn't work. All progress was palliative, and their favourite phrase was 'too little, too late'. Some were content with keening, others with debauchery. Clubs of Rome lived high, having already consigned their people to the trash heap. There was money in fear, but you had to move quick – *Famine! 1975* didn't sell well in 1976. How many copies of *The Limits to Growth* and *The Population Bomb* now yellowed in Oxfam outlets? These gremlins had squealed that civilization was finished ever since it had started. They were a waste and an irritant, but they were decorative.

Should they remain in self-important think-tanks competing over who could concoct the most gruesome scenario for the year 2000, Wallace was content to let them hand-wring their lives away. Another sort of dread merchant, however, he could not conscionably ignore.

Because Calvin Piper had never been all talk. To give credit where due, the man was bright, effective and fantastically well connected. He was a seducer. His ideas, in their extremity, had a sensual thrill. He would never be satisfied with predicting disaster – he would help make it happen.

Wallace might have relaxed when Calvin was fired, reduced back to the Bacon spoiling on the walls of his Karen lair, unemployed. Wallace knew better. The very appearance of inactivity over at that cottage gave him chills. Calvin could not bear to be still; he did not have the spiritual sophistication. Released from the constraints of bureaucracy, Calvin was less demoted than unleashed. Why, that scoundrel had had no visible means of support for the last six years. But look at him: his slacks were linen, his shoes kid and outside the A-frame undoubtedly sat his new four-wheel-drive. What, pray, was he living on? Wallace may have dwelt in the realms of the ancestors for most of the day, but he was still aware that it was on the detail level that you found people out.

It was late enough for Wallace, who liked to be in bed by nine o'clock, to make his exit, but he did not want to appear to be fleeing because Calvin had arrived. Wallace might be repelled but he certainly wasn't frightened. And there was one woman creeping over to his side of the house who stood out from the rest, if only because of her outfit. Long hem, high neck: she was hiding. Brown hair sloped either side of her face as she tiptoed towards the veranda, hoping to make it the distance of the living room without being caught. When he looked closely, he thought her rather prettier than much of the Lycra-nippled competition, but she did not have the conviction to match. That was half the game with beauty, keeping your head high, and she stared at her sensible shoes. Beauty was deception, and you had to have the shyster's smooth sleight of hand to pull it off. This one thought of herself as ordinary; consequently, she was. Wallace didn't think about these things any more, though as the theory fell to hand like the drop of an apple there must have been a time when he thought of little else.

He almost left her alone, so apparent was her desperation to be overlooked, but were she allowed to achieve what she thought she wanted – solitude – she would be miserable. More, he couldn't resist a woman whose instinct with Calvin Piper on stage was to sneak in the opposite direction.

'Pardon – ' At his hand on her sleeve, she jumped. 'Have you a clue where I might get a spot of tea?'

She stumbled through something about the kitchen, leaving him in no doubt that contact with another human being was the most fearsome thing that had ever happened to her.

He returned with his cup to find her on the veranda as if they had an assignation. 'Astonishing sky, isn't it?' A moan of assent. About her frantic desire that he should go away he had no illusion. But winning her from a bogus trip to the loo was a snap. 'Sorry,' he introduced, after an unencouraging but obligatory exchange about where she was from and where she lived. 'I'm Wallace Threadgill. And yourself?'

That was all it took. She stopped leaning over the railing and gaping dolefully at the Jasper Johns Equatorial skyscape and faced him with keen reassessment. 'Eleanor Merritt.' Though she needn't, she shook hands, and he was struck by the fact that now, far from wishing he would disappear, she was suddenly worried he might leave.

'And what brings you to this blithe bacchanalia?'

She laughed, dry. 'Awful, aren't they. I always promise myself I won't go. And then the alternative is staying home . . .'

'What's wrong with home?'

'Malicious furniture.' Her eyes kept darting to his face, then back over the rail.

'I'm surprised you're not attending to our charming ersatz host. Funny, you'd never know, would you, that this wasn't his house? And how high are the chances that he and his whole band of cronies weren't even invited?'

'Some people are very – comfortable, socially.' A diplomat. 'I'm not. I like to think I've improved, but I doubt it. Every time I walk into a party I feel thirteen: dressed like a ninny, terrified of dancing and wishing I'd brought a book.'

'How does such a shy creature come to be in Africa?'

'Family planning,' she groaned.

'Ah.' That explained the shift.

'And you – you're the heretic.'

He smiled. 'Quite. And how long have you –?'

'Nearly twenty years. I was with the UNFPA before Pathfinder, and the Peace Corps before that.'

'Peace Corps I could have predicted.'

She stood more upright. 'Everyone finds the Peace Corps so hilarious. That we're a sad little sort. But it's done some fine –'

'Look at you. You're already getting *kali*.'

'I just don't think it's fair –'

'Perhaps you and I are such natural enemies that we should acknowledge irreconcilable differences and skip the fisticuffs.' He made a motion as if to part.

'No, please –' She touched his arm. 'I have always wanted to talk to you. More than ever now.'

'Why? Are you questioning your faith?'

'Let's say my convictions have been challenged. They are not bearing up well.'

'But you have a life's work to defend. No doubt you believe in its merit and conduct it conscientiously. But in my experience, your kind find my message unsettling. They listen only just so long as it takes to invent all the reasons I'm a hairbrain. They march off with their fences built even higher than before, having learned nothing. I'm a little tired of wasting my time. It's more than likely we have little to say to one another.'

'I'm not afraid of information.'

'Then you are a brave young lady. The entire population industry is mortified by information. That's why they make it up. So they can live safely in their fairy-tale future, where we are all balancing tiptoe on one leg in the remaining three square inches apportioned to us, packed on all sides by the seething, copulating ruck, fallen angels on the head of a pin. But look around you.' He waved his hand at the Ngong Hills as a voluptuous breeze ruffled her soft brown hair; indeed, from here there was not a glimmer of human habitation in sight.

'My confidence in what I do has been shaken,' she admitted. 'We've had so little effect.'

'Large families will persist. But you can make people ashamed of their children, just as Jesuits made women ashamed of their breasts. You see, I don't simply believe that population programmes are inadequate; I believe they are evil.'

'That's going a bit far.'

'Let me tell you a story,' Threadgill intoned, leading her to a porch chair and seating himself at an instructive angle.

'I was Kenyan-born,' he began, 'but educated in Britain. It was the late sixties, when horrors were foretold for the land that I still cared for very much. You may remember, in those days it was to be thirty-three billion by the turn of the next century – and isn't it intriguing that twenty years later the same prophets are now saying fourteen? So I enrolled in Oxford's new Population Studies programme, and went from there to work for the Population Reference Bureau in DC. My life was numbers. We ran the profession's first computer simulations, and when the zeros trilled off perforated sheets my blood would pound. Money pumped into the field and I could travel. Reports with their daunting digits stacked my desk. At night my colleagues and I would gather at exclusive clubs and loudly compare the multiple nightmares sponsored by our competing organizations. Everywhere we went, our lapels flashed ZPG.

'My work was going well and I was important. Yet the better it went, the more my soul was sick. I drank heavily. My relations with women were frantic and short-lived, and I was careful not to beget children. I began to develop health problems – I was pre-ulcerous and probably an alcoholic. Inside I was heavy, and though I was free to see the sights of the world the earth was a bleak and hopeless coal to me, and showed itself in dark pieces. Every new country appeared distraught and degraded, perched on a precipice, about to fall apart.

'One day I was walking out of the Kenyatta Centre, during one of those costly conferences we were so fond of. I ran into a young Luhya I did not know, with his small son. He was angry and accosted me. "You are the enemy of the smile on this child's face!" he cried. The boy looked at me, and he had supernatural eyes. I realized the man was right, that my work was all about preventing his son's conception. I was relieved that his parents had prevailed over my reports. I wasn't sure of myself then, as you are not now, and until I was sure again I would cast my ZPG pin in the gutter.

'I entered into a different sort of research, the kind where you are not given the answers before you begin. I was astonished at what I found. Most of all, I was amazed that the facts I uncovered were easily available to everyone, and I became appalled by a conspiracy of despair, a pact of gloom to which I had signed my own name.

'Because the holocaust of the population explosion is a myth. That we are all dropping into a fetid cesspool is a myth. Life on earth, historically, has done nothing but improve. And the profusion of our species is not a horror but a triumph. We are a thriving biological success story. There is no crisis of "carrying capacity" – since the Second World War, the species has only been better fed. Per capita calorie production continues to rise. Incidence of famine over the last few hundred years has plummeted. Arable land is on the increase. Pollution levels are declining. Resources are getting cheaper. The only over-population I uncovered was in organizations like the one I worked for, which were a scandal.

'Yet when I attempted to publish these findings, I was turned away from every journal and publisher I approached. I finally found one feisty university press. But that spelt the end of me. Once word was out I had parted with orthodox demography, I lost my funding. I became a clown for my fellows. There is nothing so absurd to a Western academic as an optimist.

'I lost my livelihood, but I inherited the earth. The illness with which I had been afflicted lifted. I felt no more need for alcohol, tobacco or the flesh of dead animals. When I went abroad, even poor countries appeared lush, whole and at peace. Their people were fruitful. It was my society that had sickened me. My society that hated its own children. And now I have recovered and know boundless joy.

'So I returned to Kenya. Since then I have been working with game parks to encourage their utilization by the Masai, for I believe setting man's persistence against Nature's to be a mistake. It was pointless, you understand, to pursue a position with university population programmes or family planning donors when my purpose would be their destruction. Recently, I have been offered a contract by the World Health Organization, helping with their sero-prevalence research. A dreadful disease stalks the land. These doctors need Swahili speakers who know the people and the country well. I know little of medicine, but I am grateful to be of any assistance I can.'

'Mmm.' Eleanor seemed to nudge herself out of a queasy trance. 'There's a lot of money in AIDS right now.'

'You have lived far too long in the company of those who profit from suffering.'

'I didn't mean that's why you – '

'Please. This issue is grave to me. The money is quite irrelevant.'

Eleanor picked flakes of varnish pensively off the arm of her chair. He could see she disagreed with everything he said. 'If "orthodox demography" is a lie,' she said at last, 'why do most people believe that population growth is a threat, except you and a straggle of your disciples?'

'If I were to use your way of thinking, I would say money. The population conspiracy is based entirely around this "explosion" hypothesis, and without its ranks of whole organizations are unemployed. But the idea preceded its institutions. And "over-population" has taken hold on the common man, who has no apparent vested interest in these unwieldly "charities". *Why?*' He leaned forward and fisted his hand. 'Self-hatred. Copious quantities of people are therefore intrinsically repellent. Have you noticed the metaphors that population biologists enjoy? Oh, the politic will say humans breed "like rabbits", but give them a few drinks and the bunnies turn to rats. The literature is strewn with allusions to flies, maggots, cancers.'

'Why, if Westerners find one another's company grotesque, would they choose to live in New York City?'

'Density is in the interests of the species. It promotes competition, which begets invention. The more of us there are, the cleverer we get. And if crowding does become as desperate as the Cassandras predict, you can bet the solutions will be nothing short of spectacular. We are magnificent creatures. Why, the rise of population and urbanization in Europe made the Industrial Revolution possible. How can you proceed from a history like that to claiming that population growth is economically oppressive?'

She twirled her empty wine glass. 'If the field's reasoning is so illogical, what motivates the US to pour so much money into Third World fertility decline?'

'Because there is only one thing an American hates more than himself and that is anyone else. You remember the early days, when African governments were convinced that family planning programmes were racist?'

'The genocide superstition.'

'That was no superstition. Those programmes are racist. I don't mean to suggest that diligent women like yourself are not well meaning. But there are siroccos in the air by which you have been swept. We've a demographic transition afoot, all right, and the population moguls are trying their pathetic best to forestall the inevitable. In their moribund, corrupt self-loathing, Europe, America and Russia are under-reproducing themselves into extinction.'

'Wattenberg,' provided Eleanor.

'Quite. But Wattenberg mourns the collapse of the world of pallor, where I see the demise of "developed countries" as a blessing. Riddled with homosexuality, over-indulgence and spiritual poverty, the West has lost its love of its own children, and so of humanity itself. The very myth of "over-population" is a symptom of our disease. It is a sign of universal self-correction that a people grown so selfish they will no longer bear children because they want Bermuda vacations will naturally die out. The sallow empire is falling. In its place will rise a new people. A hundred years hence the planet will be lushly poppled by richer colours of skin, the hoary old order long before withered and blown to ash.'

'I'm beginning to understand why every press in DC wasn't leaping to publish you.'

'Africans have an ancient, wise civilization and they will survive us all. For consultants to arrive on this continent to convince its governments that Africans are on the brink of extinction at the very point in history when their tribes are expanding over the earth – well – I find it humorous. What I do not find humorous is when African leaders believe the tall tales they are told. That the Kenyan government now promotes contraception is the product of mind control.'

'Do you have any children?'

'No. I am celibate. I am trying to make up for my former blindness, but very likely I, too, am beyond salvation, and truncating my lineage is part of my destiny. However, I have come to believe that I will be called to a final purpose before I die.'

'AIDS?'

'Perhaps. Or even grander than that. I see before us a great light, but before we break into the new aurora we have a war to fight. Have you ever watched a wounded animal charge? It is dying, but from damnation the more dangerous – desperate and with nothing to lose. That is the West, shot but standing, and its death throes will shake the earth.'

Eleanor stood and gazed listlessly through the glass doors at Calvin's table. 'I don't suppose you listen to a lot of Mozart?'

In the blessed peace between CDs, Wallace extended his hand to the whispering trees, where crickets churned. 'I have no need. The forest is my symphony.'

'Right,' said Eleanor.

He followed her off the porch, but stopped at the door as she drifted towards the black hole at the far end, like everyone else. 'You are in peril,' he cautioned her, 'and allied with misanthropes. Have you ever had a baby?'

'No.'

'Perhaps you should. You might change your profession.'

'According to your vows, you're hardly volunteering to help.'

'That was not a proposition.'

'Well, Dr Threadgill, no one else is volunteering either. Besides, I'd just have one more of those selfish little Americans who demand big plastic tricycles for Christmas and make wheedly noises on aeroplanes with hand-held hockey games.'

'You are terribly unhappy.'

'So everyone seems intent on telling me.'

'Stop by sometime. We'll talk again.'

'The tented camp on Mukoma, right? I might at that.'

The poor woman was then sucked into orbit around the cold dark centre like the rest, another innocent particle lured by the inevitable gravity of super-dense nothingness. Wallace turned back to the healthy fresh air of the veranda because he couldn't bear to watch.

As Eleanor left Wallace to his porch she wondered how a man of such unbounded elation could be so depressing. His eyes were ringed as if he had trouble sleeping. His cheeks sagged and his body was sunken. Worst of all was the smile, which curled up as if someone had to lift strings. It was a marionette smile, mechanical, macabre.

She might dismiss him as a kook, but in his time Threadgill had been widely published. Further, since he'd left the field revisionism had gained a respectable foothold. It was no longer considered laughable to debate the effects of population growth on the poor. As a result, the discipline was divided and disturbed. The hard-liners like Calvin were more rabid than ever, driven to a corner. The born-again optimists, being novelties, got spotlights on MacNeil-Leher. In the middle, the majority of the population profession was increasingly cautious. No one was quite sure whether demographers were brave pioneers who, diaphragms in hand, would change the face of history and shoulder the greatest challenge of our time, taking on the root cause of environmental decay and poverty, or were instead gnome-like recorders, accountants of births and deaths who, when they ventured beyond their role of registrar with bungling programmes of redress, were ridiculed by their own forecasts in ten years' time. The population community was no longer confident of its calling, and the last thing Eleanor Merritt required was to feel less needed or more unsure.

Leaving Wallace Threadgill's morbid euphoria for Calvin Piper's genial despair reminded Eleanor of plane trips, Dar to DC, entering a tiny compartment and promptly changing hemispheres. In thirty feet she got jet lag. Seriously entertaining contrary positions felt dangerous. If she could accept every creed for a kind of truth and call any man a friend, then she could also be anyone; arbitrary, she disappeared. It was possible to be too understanding. Eleanor wondered if it was preferable to keep the same insufferable, obdurate opinions your whole life, piggishly, even if they were wrong, since they are bound to be, because once you opened the emergency exit to the wide white expanse of all it was plausible to believe you broke the seal on your neat pressurized world and got sucked into space. Lurching from Threadgill to Piper made her airsick.

Eleanor had come to the party on her own, having arranged to join Calvin's coterie here once they were through with 'a meeting'. The way he'd announced he was occupied for the early evening reminded Eleanor of the cryptic explanations for why her stepfather would not be home yet one more night. Ray would be at 'a meeting', no of-what or about-what for a twelve-year-old child. At thirty-eight, Eleanor resented don't-worry-your-pretty-head-about-it from a superannuated layabout.

As soon as Calvin had established himself at the table, they closed in around their – leader, she was tempted to say, though what was there to lead? When all the chairs were scrabbled up, Eleanor had shrugged and drifted to the porch, where she had hung on through that interminable recitation on the off-chance she might get up the nerve to ask one truly interesting question. She never did. It was too potty. Why in heaven's name would Wallace think Calvin Piper invented HIV?

She retrieved a straight-back from the kitchen and wedged between Calvin and the ageing shrew in pink. The woman pretended not to notice and refused to move the extra three inches that would have allowed Eleanor in. She was stuck, then, slightly behind the two, not quite in the circle and not quite out, which was destined to be Eleanor's relation to this crowd for the indefinite future.

Malthus gargoyled on Calvin's shoulder, daring Eleanor to tickle his chin. Nothing would make Malthus happier than to take off her middle finger to the second knuckle.

The woman's name, incredibly, was *Bunny*.

'The whole race is lemming off the cliff,' she despaired, 'while demographers fuddle over fertility in Popua in 1762.'

'Lemmings,' Eleanor intruded bravely, 'did you know they throw themselves off a precipice in response to population pressure? They *crowd* off cliffs. When Walt Disney filmed the rodents, the crew trapped hundreds and then had to drive them over the edge, beating sticks.'

'It must be terribly frustrating if subjects won't obligingly commit suicide when your camera is rolling.'

That was Wallace, passing comment on his way for more tea. Only Wallace heard Eleanor at all. It was a perfectly serviceable party anecdote, but when Eleanor told stories that worked for everyone else they dropped, lemming-like, to sea.

Eleanor took being ignored as an opportunity to study the round-table. Bunny showed all the signs of having once been quite an item, and would still qualify as well kept – thin and stylishly coiffed, with unpersuasive blonde hair tightly drawn from a face once striking, now sharp. But she had retained the mannerisms of beauty. Sitting at an angle with her cigarette coiling from an extended arm, she spread a calf on her other knee as if posed perpetually for a shutter she had failed to hear click twenty years ago. Such miracles of taxidermy might have cautioned Eleanor to age with more grace, but she herself had never felt dazzling, and perhaps this was the compensation: that in later years, at least she would not delude herself she had retained powers she never thought she wielded in the first place.

Eleanor conceived few dislikes, being more inclined to give strangers a break, and another after that, as if beginning a set of tennis with first serve in. When company repeatedly made remarks that were out of bounds, she would promptly provide them with incestuous childhoods, crippling racial discrimination or tragic falls down the stairs to explain the viper, the thief, the moron. But Eleanor's distaste for Bunny was instantaneous. British, the woman only turned to Eleanor once, to translate that 'nick' meant steal. Eleanor suggested, 'Be sure to tell Calvin. He's American, too, you know.'

'Only half,' said Bunny coolly.

Bunny was loud and over-animated, but Eleanor was convinced that as soon as Bunny strode out of earshot of Calvin Piper all that environmental indignation would fall by the wayside like paper wrapping.

The rigid man to Calvin's right was the only guest in a suit and tie. Every once in a while his mouth would quirk with annoyance. He gave the impression that he disapproved of their contingent's retirement to some petty Nairobi social fritter; he'd have preferred to continue *meeting*. His surface was metallic. His name was Grant. Tall, grave and grey, he was one of those people, she supposed, who had been told the fate of the world rested on his shoulders and actually believed it. He reminded her of the men you found in Washington shuttle lounges, furrowed over computers, using their oh-so-precious five minutes before take-off to write that crucial report on sales of soap. You would never catch them out with a mere magazine, though Eleanor was always convinced that behind their PCs they were secretly weaving sexual fantasies and the screen was blank.

On the other side of the table, a small, nervous Pakistani and a corpulent Kikuyu were exchanging stories about murderous eight-year-olds in Natal. The Pakistani, Basengi, could not sit back in his chair or keep his hands still. He would pick up his glass and put it down again without taking a sip, and his place was rubbled with a shrapnel of potato crisps. His eyes worried about the room as if, should his glance not pin every object down to its appointed place, all of their host's possessions would run away. He perpetually wiped his palms on his trousers. 'Louis, you hear so often "innocent children",' he said. 'I never meet innocent children. They are like us. They are little barbarians.'

'A woman's view, Eleanor?' asked Louis. 'Do you believe we are all born saints? Do we only learn to slit throats from watching grown-ups butcher each other first or does the idea pop up of its own accord?'

'I suppose it's some of both,' Eleanor stuttered, flattered to be brought in finally. 'Of course I've seen malicious children. Horrid children. But I've also seen children that, yes, were pure. Generous, affectionate and utterly without guile. Some children are innocent. Then, so are some adults.'

The African chuckled. His laugh was splendid, booming and amoral, and from it Eleanor could picture this prankster as a boy – a plotter, a snitcher of sweets. 'Name one.'

'Eleanor Merritt.'

She turned to Calvin, surprised. 'From you,' she considered, 'I wonder if that isn't an insult.'

'Ray Bradbury, Louis,' Calvin commended. 'All the kids in his stories are holy terrors. For Bradbury, the question isn't whether children have the capacity for evil. It's whether they have a special capacity.

'Yet if we concede that kids have roughly the same proportion of treachery, dishonesty and cussedness as the rancorous adults they become, why do the little nippers occupy an exalted moral position? Why in war is it especially appalling to kill *women and children*? Why is it so much more tragic when the roof falls in on a kindergarten than on a shoe factory?'

'Maybe it's all that life unlived,' said Eleanor.

'Well, doesn't that make them *lucky*? And won't there be plenty more drooling, farting, upchucking runts to replace them? No, it's this myth of innocence, which is maudlin tripe. Why, you have to kill ten adults to get the same size headline in the States that you can score with one dead toddler.'

'These days,' said Bunny, 'you'll earn far better coverage with cruelty to rats.'

'Mice!' cried Calvin. 'She's right! There's a lab where I started my density experiments in DC. I had to move operations, because you would not believe the restrictions. The mice eat better than the staff. They have clean little beds made for them every night. They have their own vet, their own surgeon, and if you're caught so much as pricking a paw without due cause, the approval of the Animal Care Committee or adequate anaesthesia, you're out on your ear. Humidity and temperature control, vitamins – those mice are pampered brats. I began to detest them personally. Noses in the air, they swaggered across their gilded cages, pugnacious in their confidence that they couldn't be made to suffer without your funding going to hell. I wasn't a scientist. I was a mouse-sitter.

'However,' he continued, and no one would interrupt, 'some of the Little Lord Fauntleroys have since escaped. I gather there's a huge population of pests in the basement. The janitors kill them mercilessly by the dozen every night. None of the scuttling hoards in the basement is protected by the Animal Care Committee. They're exactly the same species, but slaughtered with impunity and no one cares. No vitamins. No fluffed pillows. Just the usual desperate foraging and sticky traps.'

'Life is cheap in the under class,' said Louis.

Eleanor was struck that while Calvin spoke of people as vermin, he spoke of vermin as people – she had never heard him describe his relationship to any human population as personally as his relationship to those mice.

'These animal rights people,' Basengi was saying excitedly, 'they are crazy. They have started shooting and bombing in London. And yes, you cannot do the simplest experiment in universities any more. This alone is a very good reason to keep our own – '

'Basengi,' said Calvin sharply.

The Asian clapped his mouth shut and mashed another crisp. The others, too, resettled in their chairs and reached for their drinks and laughed, at nothing. It was hard to get conversation going again. Three rose to go. When Calvin himself stood up, half the remaining party began collecting their coats.

'Grant, you will remember to –?' asked Calvin.

'Yes.'

'And Louis, you will call –?'

'Right away.'

'And send me –?'

'Of course.'

Bunny loitered behind after the others had left, conferring with Calvin in a low voice, inclined as far forward as Malthus would allow. Eleanor positioned herself determinedly at Calvin's other side as the threesome drifted towards the door. With an irritated glance at Eleanor as if to say, well, we can't talk about anything with *you* here, she resorted to the monkey.

'Malthus doesn't despise Bunny *quite* as much as everyone

61

else, does he?' she said in that gurgling falsetto people use compulsively with pets. In a show of bravado, she reached to stroke the green monkey's head. Malthus promptly shrieked his claws across the back of her hand.

'Yes,' said Eleanor, as Bunny tried to hide the fact that Malthus had drawn blood. 'I can see you have a special relationship.'

To keep from bleeding on her dress, Bunny was forced to find a napkin. When she returned she assessed Calvin and Eleanor side by side, as she might eye a skirt and blouse in the mirror that, no, from any angle, simply didn't quite *go*.

'You're all right?' asked Calvin.

'A mere love-scratch,' she smiled with a salacious arch of the brow. 'I've drawn worse in my time, believe me.' She was one of those slimy sorts who would get sympathy by refusing to ask for it.

'*So* nice to see you again,' Bunny offered to Eleanor, and then pre-empted to Calvin. 'Shall we?'

Eleanor cursed herself for having her car. Bunny had contrived to ride with Calvin, leaving Eleanor to dribble down the stairs by herself, while Bunny earnestly wittered in Calvin's ear, her bandaged hand slipped around his elbow.

Eleanor said '*Kwa heri! Asante sana!*' to the *askari*, while the rest of the party stumbled around him as if skirting lawn furniture. She joined the line of cars filing from the drive of the great bright A-frame, beamed with security floodlights. In the front another guard raised the heavy metal gate, riveted with warning signs – PROTECTED BY . . . – with crude paintings of little men beside outsized Alsations. Off in the distance, a burglar alarm yowled; a Securi-firm van U-turned and sputtered away. As she drifted down to the corner, the barking of razor-backs marked her progress. Every property, with big recessed houses and plush gardens, came with its sultry, sleepy Masai with a *rungu*, stationed by more gates and more warning placards. At the turning, a uniformed patrol with batons trudged through its midnight round. Funny, most of these *wazungu* had come thousands of miles to this continent, only to spend a great deal of money keeping Africa *out*.

The guards looked so tired. Imagine staying up all night, every night, stationed by some rich white home, with absolutely nothing to do. Though she supposed they were grateful for a job – the work paid an average of seventy-five dollars a month. Driving back across town, Eleanor considered Calvin's proposition that *Africans do not identify with your life at all. They see white people the way you look at oryx.*

Supposing you work at an enormous house for a childless *mzungu* couple and they throw generous parties at least once a week. Afternoons you slog up the stairs with crates of beer and soda whose empties you will cart back down the next day. You lug trunk-loads of meat, vegetables and crinkling packets of crisps to the kitchen, and sometimes you glance at the price tags of the items on top – that 120 shillings for American ketchup would buy *posho* for a week. Later that night, you help direct Mercedes to pack tightly in limited parking space. Music pounds out of the windows for hours while women's laughter pierces from the veranda, where you can sometimes see men put their hands up ladies' shirts. Finally these inexplicably malnourished women weave down the stairs, congratulating each other on avoiding the chocolate cake. They never speak to you. They are always drunk. In the morning, the housegirl is cleaning glasses by eight, so that by the time the inhabitants arise a little before noon the spilled drinks are wiped away. You cart the garbage from the bin and later sift through it for the empty vodka and wine bottles – Africans never throw away containers. If it hasn't been fed to the dogs, the rubbish is full of leftover meat, salad and crunchy bits, but it is spoiled with cigarette butts and you are not, after all, starving. It never occurs to your employers to deliver what they cannot eat to the fire where you keep guard over their CD player. You know your employers treat you better than average, pay you more than many *askaris* on this street, though you have calculated in the copious time on your hands that this household spends more on Team Meat and Hound Meal than it does on your salary. At least next pay day you will be allowed to go back to your village and share the money with your wife, to feed your five children. Perhaps you shouldn't complain. But you watch, week after week, as these tipply, giggly, shamefully underclad girls fall insensible one more night into cars you have never learned to drive because you can only afford *matatus*, keeping awake until sunrise, aware that if you are caught drinking yourself you will lose your job.

Calvin, are you going to tell me that's like looking at oryx?

5

What Some Women Will Put Up With

'Calvin, who *are* those people?'

'Just think of us as butterflies over Tokyo,' he said obscurely.

'And why do you put up with that *Bunny* person? I hate the way she keeps touching your arm.'

'Now, why – ' he brushed her temple – 'would that bother you?' Eleanor blushed and turned away. 'Bunny Morton works for Worldwatch. Keeps me informed. And she has money.'

'So?'

'Basengi,' Calvin proceeded, 'is a jumpy but brilliant economist. So is Grant, if a pompous bore. Louis is a biologist; upper-class Kenyan, schooled in Britain, sharp.'

'They make me uncomfortable.'

'Come, come. Drinking all night and passing comment on the world in which we no longer participate is the common solace of the unemployed.'

'They're so grovellingly attentive to you. And you sit there as if holding court. They're all eager and they laugh too much at your jokes. They goon forward on their elbows and never interrupt. Like a pack of dogs with their tongues out.'

'So – ' He sat beside her on his couch, close but not too, and Eleanor felt the calculation in the distance down to the quarter-inch. 'I surround myself with yes-men and sycophants.'

'They ignore me.' With Calvin right beside her she could no longer look at him when she talked.

'They ignore most people.' He put his arm on the back of the couch, though his fingers did not, quite, touch her shoulder.

'What do they pay attention to, then?'

'The fate of mankind, of course.' His face remained dead-pan. Eleanor could never tell in such moments whether he was being genuinely pretentious or taking the mickey out of his gullible new friend. She suspected that he wasn't sure when he was larking himself; that maybe when the whole world seemed funny you became incapable of making a joke.

Eleanor swilled her remaining wine to rise for a refill. When she returned, she sat an extra inch further away. 'I met Wallace Threadgill last night.'

'Did he regale you with his conversion? *You are the enemy of the smile on this child's face*?'

'Quite a set piece, isn't it?' But Eleanor could not concentrate on anything save the precise proximity of the fingers on his right hand, which had moved to exactly the same pencil-width distance from her shoulder as before. Eleanor was beginning to feel physically sick. She wished he would do something with that hand or take it away. 'He claimed I was in danger.'

'You are.'

Calvin finally touched her sleeve, only to cross the room. He paged his clippings – census inaccuracies, crop failings and the odd small, personal account of sheer meanness.

'I found a choice morsel this morning,' he said, waving fresh newsprint. 'Mexico dumps ten million gallons of raw sewage a day into the Tijuana River – among other things. The river *glows red* at night. If you step in the water with gum boots, the plastic melts. Wetbacks slithering for San Diego wrap themselves in garbage bags, but those dissolve, too. What is the problem? In sixty years, Tijuana's population has gorged from 500 to two million. Get Wallace to explain to you how density is increasing ingenuity and healthy competition in Mexico. Take him to the border and get him to describe how *muy magnifico* the human race is, how the more the better. Ask if he'd like to go for a swim.'

Eleanor rested her head back on the couch, following a large moth as it *smack-smacked* against the ceiling. She had never been a complainer. She never fixed on what she lacked; she'd known since childhood to make do. Consequently, she wouldn't give it a second thought when the Land Rover's clutch cable snapped and she had to walk five miles to the nearest garage, when there was no more beer, or toilet paper, or water in the taps. And just as she would not fantasize about a shower, she would not fantasize about men. She would fall asleep designing a broader-based health care clinic, because much as she might have enjoyed a hand on her cheek, she did not regard tenderness as what she deserved; it was instead one more luxury to prove she could do without. However, unlike beer or toilet paper, arms around her waist, lips to her temple would flash single frame through her day, with all the craftiness of subliminal advertising. Late Tanzanian nights, in the flicker of her paraffin lantern, figures had flitted in the shadows, and she would glimpse a whole couple intersticed behind the mosquito netting over her bed. As with all spectres, if she stared them straight down they would evanesce, but if she ever leaned her head back and closed her eyes as she was doing now, a mouth would spread over her neck.

She opened her eyes again – *smack-smack*. The fingers on her shoulder had been an accident, because look, one brush and he'd dived for a polluted river across the room. She would be well behaved. But in that case it was 8 p.m, she was tired and she did not have too suffer *Tijuana*.

'Calvin. I have heard nothing but demography all day. All week. Sometimes, I think, my whole life. Please. I do not want to talk about the population of anywhere on earth. Nor do I wish to discuss environmental decay, the demise of African wildlife or tiny children with machetes in Natal. Much less wellington-melting sewage in Mexico.'

'Good gracious.'

She had rarely seen him awkward. He shuffled his article back into its pile and shambled to the couch in silence. When he edged into the crook of the sofa he looked trapped.

'You are still quite – pretty, did you know that?' he asked in a defeated voice.

'No, I don't. In Dar es Salaam, I lived for two years without a mirror. It's queer, not seeing your own reflection. You become like anyone else you haven't met for a long time – you forget what you look like. Though there's something right about that. The all-looking-out. I've wondered if you were ever meant to look into your own eyes.'

'But no one ever tells you? That you're pretty?'

'No.'

'I'm telling you.'

'Thank you.'

'Would you stay tonight?'

'All right.'

'Are you hungry?'

'Yes.'

At dinner, Calvin had a hard time adhering to Eleanor's restrictions: he would slide into toxic waste as easy as slipping in a puddle, but then wipe his feet again and apologize, nimbly sidestepping the live slave-trade in Mozambique, necklacing in Soweto. Eleanor could hear the deletions in Calvin's discourse, bleeped like Lenny Bruce on prime-time. The effort was charming, though it was alarming, once you siphoned the scum from Calvin's monologue, how little was left.

She did get him to talk about music. Though she'd have pegged him for Wagner, he preferred Debussy and Elgar. While his recitation of his favourite pieces was a bit tedious, she was relieved to isolate at least one passion – St Matthew – outside population growth. Walton, Barber and Ravel got them through the better part of a roast chicken; Chopin, Copland and Albinoni dispatched a little rice. Yet by coffee Calvin had a constipated expression, and implored, 'You don't mind –?'

'Oh, go ahead,' Eleanor granted.

'Yesterday I read about a uranium mining town in East Germany called Crossen. The incidence of still births and deformed babies is ten times too high; cancer and skin diseases rife – the works, the whole village is poisoned, nobody lives past forty-five, right? You know what the company does about it? They distribute *free wigs*.' Calvin laughed heartily for the first time in an hour. 'Thanks,' he said, wiping his eyes. 'I needed that.'

'Some day I'll teach you to hold forth about gardening.'

'It's far more likely I shall teach you to hold forth about uranium poisoning.' He led her back to the couch.

Though resolved sleeping arrangements should have eased their earlier clumsiness, when Calvin put his arm around her shoulder something was peculiar. His body was still. His hand draped at her upper arm exerted no pressure, and she studied it with disturbed curiosity. The fingers were long and languid, the wrist small boned, and despite its manly slashings of old white scars, the hand seemed feminine. Then, it was girlish less from appearance than from what it was doing: nothing. His body against hers felt uncannily at rest. She could feel his chest expand at her breast, and his breathing was so Zen-slow Wallace Threadgill would tip his hat. Eleanor may not have been seduced in a long time, but she was dead sure this wasn't it.

Without urgency, he lifted the hand and moved her head to his shoulder; his eyes were closed. 'Why don't you tell me about yourself?' he asked quietly. 'You never say anything about yourself.'

'You're one to talk.'

'No, I tell you everything, if you know how to listen. I'm not nearly so secretive as I would like.'

'Me, what's to know?' Though he was not groping into the folds of her dress, their voices, gone low and soft, did mingle and interweave, and Eleanor was reminded that the best sex she'd ever had was in conversation. 'I didn't grow up in East Africa. My father wasn't in the British Army. I didn't shoot elephants in my youth. I was never the eccentric head of the largest population donor agency in the United States. I'm not very interesting, Calvin.'

'Leave that for me to decide. Tell me anything. Tell me about your childhood.'

'I was born in Virginia,' she despaired.

He laughed. 'Is there anything you're not ashamed of?'

'My father. Or not my real father,' she hurried. 'Ray. I'm proud of Ray. Bright, dedicated – '

'To what?'

'Justice, I suppose.'

'What a thorn in the side.'

'He's a US senator!'

Calvin laughed again; Eleanor amused him more often than she'd like. 'That's the first time I've ever heard you display a character flaw. Does he make you feel more important?'

'Well – yes.'

69

'You don't mean Raymond Bass? I've met him.'

'He was one of your supporters. He voted you oodles of money.'

'He was not one of my supporters when I *retired*. Then, no one was.'

'No one could afford to be.'

'We are already back to me. Go on.' He smoothed her hair. 'You were born in Virginia.'

'My mother was a schizophrenic. I lived in a strange world until I was nine, a little like flipping the channel all the time. I never knew what programme I'd wake up in. You learn to be co-operative with a schizophrenic; if she says she's Jacqueline Kennedy, then your mother is Jacqueline Kennedy. What was the phrase in the sixties? "Go with the flow"? You develop sea legs.

'But then she was put away, and for three years I was kicked about from relative to friend. That life, it wasn't so different from being with my mother. With all these foster arrangements, they had their own kids, they were being nice, and I knew they'd only be nice for so long. So I kept being co-operative. I learned to keep my head down. In school I kept my hand down. In fact, I wouldn't even – oh, Christ.' She giggled.

'What?'

'I just remembered an ordeal I haven't thought about for a long time. Fourth grade. Mrs Henderson – funny how you never forget those names – that was my teacher. I was living with my Aunt Liz, who called me into the house one day after school. Mrs Henderson had phoned, it seems. Liz wanted to know if, in class, did I have a problem, uh, did I need to go to the bathroom. And the real story was yes, after lunch I was too embarrassed to raise my hand, so I would hold it in, and eventually it would get, well, bad. You know how little girls will grip themselves? I guess I did that, at my desk. I'm not sure if you stop holding on down there when you're older because you're socialized out of it or because you figure out it doesn't help. Anyway, if I was too embarrassed to raise my hand, I was certainly too embarrassed to admit that to Aunt Liz. So I told her I itched; that my underwear was too tight. Pretty resourceful.

'So the next day, spanking new, were six pairs of panties laid out on my bed. They were *enormous*. Far from being too tight, they waddled down my legs. I always hated that underwear.

'What's funny is I only figured out years later what Mrs Henderson was really on about. She thought I was masturbating. In class. Or no – Mrs Henderson would have said "playing with herself". So the whole débâcle was even more horrific than I thought.'

'When you try too hard to be no trouble, you often cause a great deal of it.'

'I've noticed that. One of the things that used to drive Jane – that's Ray's wife – to distraction was when she'd ask what flavour ice-cream I wanted, I'd say, whatever there's more of. She'd say there's plenty of vanilla *and* chocolate, and I'd shrug, and she would go bananas until I wouldn't get any ice-cream at all – which, I would claim, was fine with me, too. I do recall, I was difficult to punish. I'd get sent to my room, but I was perfectly happy in my room.' Eleanor clasped the hand on her shoulder, but it did not seem to have a life of its own. He had given it over as something to play with, a bauble to a child.

'I was improbably well behaved,' she went on. 'When I was punished it was usually for something one of the other kids did. I'd take the rap and keep my mouth shut, and Jane's kids figured out early that I was a bonanza too sweet to pass up. What always amazed me was that Ray and Jane weren't clued in enough to figure that of course I wouldn't have swiped Ray's stapler without asking; I was terrified of his study. Or it would have been unheard of for me to spill Kool-Aid all over the floor without cleaning it up. That was my only criticism of them – they were bad readers of character.'

He rearranged her with her head on his knee, stroking her forehead with the warm distraction of petting a cat. Perhaps because you couldn't do that with Malthus, who was now glaring at the two of them from the opposite side of the room, gnawing on a kernel of hard corn as if he wished it were Eleanor's head.

'Anyway,' Eleanor continued as Calvin's fingers coaxed the tiny hairs on the edge of her scalp, 'that house was the last place I was going to run amok. Jane was a college friend of my mother's before Mom went completely gonzo. They had no obligation to keep me. But I adored them. I was petrified they would give me up. I was intent on being above reproach. That was the tragedy – we both read each other wrong. In fact, they had no intention of abandoning me. Moreover, they wished I would act like a normal, demanding child. They wanted to be generous, and for me sometimes to ask for something unreasonable so they could be stern and teach me that, no, there were limits; I could not have a Jaguar on my sixteenth birthday. In fact, birthdays – I'm sorry, am I running on?'

'For once, thank heavens. Keep going.'

'My thirteenth birthday Jane wanted to make special – I now realize. She wrapped up several packages with voluptuous ribbons. When I opened them I was so overwhelmed and, I don't know, even upset that I went rigid and shut up. I didn't respond at all, jump up and down – I'd make a deplorable game show guest. I just fingered the presents lamely and stared at the floor. From the outside, I must have looked sullen, because I'll never forget Jane slamming down the box on that slinky dress with matching shoes and shouting. "Well, you wouldn't say what you'd like, if you're not satisfied, it's your fault!" and whisking away to splurt furious sugar roses on the cake I'd not be able to stomach. I incurred her displeasure every time I tried too hard to avoid it. I made such an effort not to be burdensome it was – '

'Burdensome. People who ask for nothing leave you guessing. Because it isn't as if they *want* nothing, is it?'

Eleanor looked at her lap. 'I need very little.'

Calvin raised her chin. 'I wasn't talking about what you *need*.'

He leaned down and kissed her, with that odd stillness, on the lips. She thought that this was the beginning of, you know, but he leaned his head back and asked her to keep talking. She felt a brief panic that she had already run out of stories, since in Eleanor's version of her life nothing had ever happened in it.

Her eyes narrowed. 'Then there were the *hunger meals*. Did those ever backfire.'

He sighed, obscenely content. 'This sounds too perfect. What in God's name is a hunger meal? I detect a contradiction in terms.'

'Ray and Jane were keen to impress their kids how unjustly privileged we were and how the rest of the world was much worse off, though my bids to post my morning oatmeal to the "starving Armenians" went, regrettably, nowhere. You know that Skip Lunch campaign in the UK, and then you send a quid to Save the Children? Ray and Jane were way ahead of that game. For a while, once a week, Ray would begin dinner by reading some titbit about the Third World – yes, I am used to news clippings at supper, why do you think they get on my nerves – one of those heartrending vignettes of deprivation you get out of Oxfam in the *Guardian*. We put up with it. Another friend of mine had to listen to Bible readings, which must have been worse – those gospels were longer. So then Ray would sonorously take ten bucks out of his wallet and put it in a jar in the middle of the table, money that would get sent to CARE or something.'

'What a hopeless ghett,' said Calvin.

'No, there's more. The ten dollars was what we were saving on food. We were supposed to learn how the world's poor had to eat every day, so instead of pork roast and broccoli, at a hunger meal all we had was rice. There was only one little problem.'

'The Burger King next door?'

'Worse. I loved rice.'

'You were supposed to suffer.'

'Exactly. All the other kids groaned, and whined for dessert, and moped about how dumb it was, and probably did pick up a burger at that. They acted the way they were supposed to: deprived. I was delighted. I detested pork roast; I was a picky eater but I adored starch, especially buttered rice, and I looked forward to our hunger meal all week. Jane went – *insane*.' Eleanor started to laugh. 'I'll never forget one week she exploded: "In China you wouldn't get any butter, you know!" Until finally, if I was going to be so damned happy about it, they refused to have any more hunger meals to spite me.' Eleanor was doubled up with the memory, a precious subversion, though she feared that, given opportunity, she herself would turn into just the same sort of parent, with stagy liberal rice bowls on Thursday nights. Why would that be so terrible? But somehow it would be terrible. She couldn't explain.

'I love it when you laugh.' He curled a ringlet at her ear. 'You don't do that often enough. . . . Sleepy?'

'A little.' Her yawn was fake. She rose with an exaggerated stretch, but froze at the picture of two V-shaped indentations in the arms of the opposite chair. Like – elbows. Incredibly sharp elbows. And there was a malicious little snicker on the edge of Eleanor's ear. Eleanor rubbed her eyes, and when she looked back the indentations had disappeared.

Calvin shot her an inquiring look when she took her briefcase into the bedroom, but said nothing.

Eleanor snapped the case open on the bureau gaily, a family planning toy box. 'What'll it be? We have red, black and clear condoms, lubricated or ribbed. Advantages: non-systemic, easily stored, no side effects. Disadvantages: not always effective in use, and may reduce pleasure. Unpopular in most of Africa. Injectables? Long-acting, not related to coitus, and can be provided non-clinically. Disadvantages: minimal side effects, and removal of implants requires clinical back-up – '

'Eleanor – '

'Rhythm has no side effects and is approved by the Catholic Church – '

'Eleanor – '

'But poses difficulties in calculation of safe period in lieu of a thermometer – '

'Eleanor!'

'I thought you'd appreciate my growing sense of humour about my profession.'

Calvin had removed his jacket and tie and hung them up, and was methodically unbuttoning his shirt, undressing, she could tell, in exactly the same way he did every night without her. His shirt open, she stared at his chest, taut and dark, and she could not help but think, in an almost male admiration, that he had the most beautiful breasts she'd ever seen. His face, however, looked pained.

'I owe you an apology,' he explained. 'When I asked you to

stay, I did not mean like that. I would enjoy *sleeping* with you. I like companionship.'

Eleanor coloured. 'You did only ask if I wanted to – stay.'

'It's not you.' He arranged the arms of the hanger into the shoulders of his shirt. 'I don't do that any more, with anyone. Not for years. Please don't take it personally.'

'Of course not!' Eleanor turned aside to practise a trick developed as an easily injured adolescent: if you press a forefinger to the inside corner of each eye before it floods, the overflow will run down your hand rather than your cheek and no one is any the wiser.

'If you'd prefer to go home, I'd understand.'

'No, it – might be nice.' She closed her briefcase and hid it by the bin. She did not know whether to undress or not. She slipped off her shoes.

'I could loan you a T-shirt if you'd feel more comfortable.'

'Yes. Maybe so.' With her back to Calvin, Eleanor scrabbled into the oversized T. Funny, she'd made love to him seventeen years ago; how strange that you returned to being bashful having once been so intimate. Hadn't he seen her breasts before? She supposed they were prettier then.

She slipped under the sheet, thinking that this made two celibates in one weekend. Much as he dismissed the man as a nincompoop, Calvin had a fair bit in common with Wallace Threadgill. They were both fanatics, and they were both, according to their habits, destined to die out. Well, thought Eleanor, pulling her impromptu nightdress down her skinny thighs, *no big loss*.

She felt a little silly about the shirt when Calvin stripped to nothing, and as he strode to turn off the light she noticed, resentfully, that he still had the body of a twenty-five-year-old. Probably he always slept in the buff, and since tonight was like going to bed on any ordinary night, why change habits?

Eleanor turned on her side away from him; he put his arm around her waist and instantly fell asleep. His *companion* was not so lucky, though she did get a chance to employ yet another skill most single women have perfected by the age of thirty-eight: how to cry with a man's arm around you without waking him up.

Eleanor got through half of breakfast with hollow cheer, insisting on making coffee, though that was Solastina's job. Calvin said little, perhaps waiting for her to run out of twitter. Since Eleanor was never very good at twitter, she did so by the second cup.

'Are you disappointed,' he asked, 'because you couldn't have something you wanted or have I merely offended your pride?'

'I just don't understand.'

'You didn't answer my question.'

'You're acting as if it's some kind of abnormal impulse.'

'It has become abnormal for me.'

'Why?'

'If you have ever been happy once, that spoils you. The misery that follows is your only comfort. I have come to love mine. I'm rather protective of it, in fact.'

'You don't seem miserable to me.'

'Quite so. The misery mellows into nothing in particular.'

'So what's the point? Why not?'

'Long after an emotion has passed it is possible to pay tribute to it. The less you can recall the feeling, the more important that tribute becomes. Ask widows who visit graves on Sundays. Their diligence redoubles once the loved one fades. The diligence is all that remains. And I am hardly going to visit the Mombasa morgue. Instead, I practise abstinence. It's easy, though you are an attractive woman. A bit like dropping something on the road, you aren't sure where. That side of me is lost.'

'Impossible. It's never lost.'

'Sex can be surgically removed, like a tumour.'

'More like cutting off your head.'

'Think of me as the victim of an accident, then – with an injury people feel awkward discussing.'

'You look intact to me.'

'I'm not. But being a cripple has its compensations. What do we call the handicapped now? *Differently enabled*? Other capacities gain ground.'

'This woman. She's the one on the wall? Who you said was a missionary?'

'*Mercenary,*' Calvin corrected, and had a good laugh. 'Oh, Panga. I hope you caught that.'

'So what happened?'

'In due course,' said Calvin. 'But you and I need to get this established. Don't imagine I'm restraining myself. I am without sexual desire, and don't feel sorry for me either. Imagine how liberating it must feel. You remember the enthusiasm you once felt for history in high school, when what really made your heart race was the boy in the front row, and impressing him with your politics? I am no longer subject to ulterior fascinations. I'm never distracted by where-is-she-now while polishing off July's *Population Bulletin.* Shouldn't you envy me?'

'I might, a little,' she admitted, 'if I could believe it. Maybe everyone fantasizes about being out from under. But I don't believe it.'

He took her hand. 'You think it's your fault and I'm being polite. Please, my lack of interest is not from lack of interest in you. On the other hand, if you are looking for passionate involvement you will need to go elsewhere. I confess I should be sorry to see less of you.'

Eleanor realized with a thud that she had been seeing Calvin about five times a week. How this had occurred she couldn't fathom, but insidiously he was all her social life in Nairobi; just as insidiously, all her life. And here he was, offering to sacrifice her to the sticky clutches of the brown chair.

She took his hand and sandwiched it between her palms, stroking his forefinger across her forehead. 'Threadgill is right. I'm in trouble.'

'You are only safe when you're dead.'

'I'm beginning to look forward to it.'

'I assure you it's quite pleasant.'

'How do you know?'

'I am pre-dead.'

She sighed. 'Calvin, sometimes you get just too strange.'

'Pre-death is supremely useful. A man without feelings is a merciless sword. The limits dissolve like cotton candy. Did you know there are no rules really? That most of the ones you obey you make up? I could teach you a great deal I'm not sure you want to know.'

'Everyone around me lately talks like J. R. R. Tolkien.'

'No hobbits and fairies,' said Calvin. '*Gormenghast*.'

Eleanor was poorly read in fantasy, but she didn't like the sound of that word.

'My dear,' he advised her, 'the whole of this century has increasingly closed the gap between science fiction and fact. I have a hard time finding any novel sufficiently outlandish . . .'

'Isaac Asimov has been upstaged by history, it is reliably more fantastic to read the newspaper. Old hat.'

'Yes. Clichéd, isn't it?' His mouth stirred in a particularly rich, thick smile, double cream. 'Now, I've some appointments this morning, but my afternoon could be tidied up with a few phone calls. Could you get free?'

'This morning I've got to hand out awards to the CBD agents who have brought in the most new clients, but I should be through by two. Why?'

'Because we are going to buy you a new dress and matching shoes. And you will jump up and down if I have to fill your overly large knickers with fire ants. Now, let me see about those calls.' Though there was a phone in the living room, he rose to ring elsewhere.

She stopped him. 'You never tell me anything but jokes and veiled, mystic warnings from cheap sci-fi.'

'Then I must be highly entertaining.' He jingled down the hall with his keys and spent a good minute or so unlocking a door there; and then she heard him secure the dead-bolt on the other side.

As he'd promised, Calvin swept her from Mathare to the YaYa Centre. Kenya's styles are conservative, but at last he seized upon a short, sleeveless black dress with a scandalous neckline and rhinestones on one shoulder. He located sheer seamed black stockings and precariously high black patent shoes with twinkles on the heels. He brought Eleanor home and made her put her hair up.

'I feel like a total whore,' she complained.

He led her to the mirror. Eleanor had long legs, and now you could see most of them. The new push-up black lace bra made the best of her modest endowment. She had never noticed before, but with her hair raised she seemed to have a long, lean neck to which the little gold pendant drew attention. Walking in these shoes, however, would take practice. She was both pleased and a little frightened. 'You don't think I look ridiculous?'

'You looked ridiculous in that *plaid*.'

In fact, it only took the evening for Eleanor to master her shoes. This time when she strode to the Ladies' in the Horseman, diners turned their heads. Despite Calvin's generous offer to special-order buttered rice, Eleanor had lobster and frozen lemon soufflé. She did not cart the claws out to beggars on the pavement or try to doggie-bag her jacket potato. While Calvin might have had 'no feelings', he was a terrific lot of fun, and Eleanor was rapidly developing sufficient feelings for the both of them.

By Nairobi standards they'd spent a fortune, but Calvin paid for everything and assured her that there was plenty more where that came from. Eleanor had the fleeting impression of what it must feel like to be a Mafia princess. It seemed she had acquired a sugar daddy who was determined to make up for the fact not that he repulsed her but that she found him attractive. She was clearly in training for a new life, one which she could assume much more gracefully than old Eleanor, saver of tinfoil and hoarder of plastic bags, would ever have expected. Perhaps anyone is capable, she posited nervously, of becoming their opposite, since, in its abstract absolute, black was white.

6

Recipes for Romantic Evenings

Wipe your muddy hands on his clean white towel. Don't rinse your glass. Leave the dirty pan in the sink. Advice teased over Eleanor's shoulder as she went about her business in Calvin's house. Sometimes she took it; with Nairobi's red clay, that towel would never be the same. Later, more pressing: *Why do you ask so few questions? What are you afraid of?* The snicker. Eleanor felt continually mocked.

Lord, what was she not afraid of? Tentatively, she did ask questions. 'Calvin . . . Where's this from?'

'That's Panga's *kukri*.'

Eleanor hefted the knife up and down. She had not seen it on the table before; no, it had not been there before. The weapon was daunting. Its short handle wrapped in leather, the blade was broad and curved, weighted forward. Traditionally when a Gurkha lost a wager, he was obliged to lop off his own left hand. This would do the trick – wickedly sharp, with a nick at its base so the blood would drip from the knife and not down your arm.

'How would a Kamba get hold of a *kukri*?'

'Stole it,' he said crisply. 'She worked as household staff, you know, during those rare little lulls in African massacre. Swiped it from some ex-Army pillock who served in Burma, when she was employed to not-clean his kitchen. In my experience, even with the most trustworthy there's one perfect temptation they can't resist. With Panga, it's knives. Like the Masai and cattle, she thinks they all rightfully belong to her. All knives are therefore borrowed. In her book, she doesn't steal; she takes them back.' His present tense was unsettling.

Over the weeks, more bevels carved Eleanor's path: machetes, bowies, bayonets, a samurai scimitar with a sharkskin scabbard. They were neither cast carelessly in a corner nor arched decoratively on the wall. The blades were placed, squarely, where Eleanor would find them, then removed, just as peremptorily as they appeared. When she cajoled, 'Are you trying to tempt me to domestic violence?' Calvin acted perplexed.

There was one more photograph of Panga besides the one in the diving hood. Eleanor found it by accident – if indeed she was finding anything in this apparently innocent cottage by accident – scrabbling for a handkerchief in the drawer beside his bed: crinkled, out of focus, black and white. Leaning on a hijacked Red Cross van, its roof flame–cut off to mount a machine-gun, there was the same lanky black woman in tatty hair, jauntily cradling an A K–47 like its mother. She wore shabby khaki, sleeves and ankles rolled up, and no shoes.

'Do you think she would be jealous?' supposed Eleanor, studying the photo that morning. 'Of me?'

'I don't imagine you bother Panga in the slightest,' he said tersely.

'Why *not*?'

'She is only jealous of women the least bit like her,' he said impatiently. 'There's no question that given half a chance Panga would make quick work of Bunny Morton; any day now I expect to find Bunny's individually wrapped packets stacked in the freezer like steak. But I can't think of two females with less in common than you and that hellcat.'

'I don't see how we're different as all that.'

Calvin laughed. 'Where do you chart the resemblance exactly?'

Eleanor glowered.

'Are you jealous of her?'

'Intensely,' she confessed.

But Eleanor was being less than candid. She was also entranced. She found the story, as she pulled its details from Calvin tooth by tooth, incredibly romantic. In fact, she wondered if she wasn't more taken by the tale than by Calvin himself. And later she would need an explanation, though

Calvin would no longer imagine there was anything to explain.

Panga had first arrived on Calvin's doorstep, delivered by the extended family of his housegirl, who had married off to Machakos. Sinewy arms akimbo, flounced in a floral print, she looked 'for all the world', he said, 'like a Doberman pinscher got up in a dress'.

He spoke to her in his stiff pidgin, the weak, ungrammatical Swahili Eleanor deplored. While in time he would realize Panga's English was better than she let on, she first feigned incomprehension, loitering to eavesdrop, trying to maintain a stupid look on her face, which for such a weasel of a woman must have required cunning concentration. Panga liked the advantage, Eleanor decided, knowing more than you thought. It was good military strategy.

When he showed the new housegirl the detergents, brooms and pots, she would have gazed at the ceiling, insolent. The job was beneath her, and Panga would not easily, like that *askari* the other night, watch spoiled, rich *wazungu* titter through his house without comment.

Eleanor, who compulsively swabbed the ring of her bath and swept up toast crumbs even in a house with servants, admired Panga's atrocious housekeeping more than her employer had. In the heavy red clay that settled daily in the dry season, Calvin would find a few disdainful swipes on his bureau, with nothing moved; on the glass table in the nook he drew pictures all through breakfast, if he was not picking the hard crust of old dinners from his plate. Panga's idea of dish washing was drawn from quick decampments at dawn with the rebels on your trail, a swish in a stream and you legged it. Wonderful, thought Eleanor, rinsing, drying and returning her coffee cup to its cupboard, upside-down to keep out dust.

Barring Panga's one specialty, she was a wretched cook as well. The Kamba had contempt for vegetables, and left them on the stove to melt, run out of water, char. If she served sweets, they were commercial and stale, and she all but threw them at him with coffee; considering the quality of Nairobi cakes, they'd have made formidable weapons. It was only meat she had time for, and even her chicken ran red.

When on the verge of giving her notice, Calvin began to observe that there were a few things she did commendably, albeit not what she was told. She was fast and accurate with an axe, and splintered a cord in two hours. She could slit the throat of a sheep cleanly, skinning, gutting and butchering the animal in minutes. She could wring the neck of a hen with what looked suspiciously like pleasure, and while she might have made a hash of green beans and aubergines, the *thwack* of her cleaver neatly jointed the fowl in a few strokes. And she was a *fundi* with vehicles, clever at cutting a fan belt out of an inner tube or improvising a new accelerator cable from fence wire. SWAPO could not always send off for parts in the middle of the Namibian desert.

'I've tinkered with a few cars myself,' said Eleanor.

'Oh? My fuel pump's packed up in the old Toyota. Want to give it a go?'

'No, thank you,' she said coldly. 'I have a report to finish. I was just mentioning it, that's all.'

Once he decided to keep her on a bit more, Panga approached her employer, stooping to English because this was important. Would it be possible, *bwana*, if she could come to work in something other than this dress. He remembered her air, not pleading but martial, as if requesting to stand at ease. He replied that she could work in a polar bear suit as long as she repaired his carburettor, and she refused to smile.

The next day she appeared, relaxed and cocky, in threadbare fatigues, the sleeves and trousers rolled up, her hard, bony feet bare.

Panga had a distinctive smell which still lingered in the cottage – strong and tangy, just shy of rancid; it was a classically African aroma of beef fat, smoke and dung. As Eleanor once more slavered on her stern morning deodorant, Calvin commented, 'Panga was filthy.'

'Oh, terrific,' said Eleanor, tossing the roll-on in disgust. What a waste of imported perfumery, when what clearly got Calvin going was dirt. Trouncing into the living room, Eleanor could imagine the Kamba slinging out from under his Toyota and sauntering to the house, languishing into that armchair to smooth the grease into her skin like cold cream, relishing the sheen she could raise with the help of a leaky gasket. Blacks, thought Eleanor, really had much nicer skin.

'When she admitted she was a mercenary, I laughed,' Calvin related. 'A mistake. Panga has a vicious sense of humour about everyone but herself.'

'A familiar quality.'

'I find myself quite a cracker,' he defended.

'Only when you're telling the joke. You have to control everything,' she ventured boldly. 'Especially jokes.'

Panga had hit on one line of work in Africa where a woman could excel. Far from suffering discrimination, Panga rarely lacked for employment so long as governments had a shelf-life of unrefrigerated milk. Most troops were terrified of female soldiers, more so of Panga in particular. With one look at her protruding, two-jaw grin, the skin mummified to her skull, her AK–47 nursed at her breast like a suckling *toto*, seasoned rebel soldiers would drop their weapons and shriek down the hillside in the opposite direction. No one had ever run from Eleanor, except from sheer awkwardness.

Panga had no politics. 'She didn't have convictions,' Calvin explained, 'only attitudes.'

'So she would fight for Idi Amin? Charles Taylor, Mengistu, Mobutu? What about South Africa?'

Calvin shrugged. 'If they'd have her. Marxists, capitalists, governments or insurgents – as long as they could get their hands on a can of petrol and a round of ammunition or two.'

'You *admired* that?'

'Enormously.'

'You stagger me.'

'Panga acknowledged only one side of all conflicts: her own. And I respect anyone who can flight, never mind for what. I sometimes think the West is losing its capacity to act, to execute. I can't count the colleagues I've suffered who, after assessing the likely demise of the human race in our lifetime, promptly schedule another *conference*.'

'How did you know?' Eleanor prodded. 'It's possible to be around someone for a long time before you realize you're in love with them. Isn't it? They're just sort of – there. Until one day you realize that if they left town, or fell for someone else, your whole life would cave in.'

'I suppose...' Calvin drummed his fingers. 'When she started poisoning my girlfriends.'

'You had girlfriends?'

He frowned. 'Too many. Whole evenings. Could have been working.'

'And now you get more done,' she said drily. 'With no girlfriends.'

'That's right.'

The early mischief Panga passed off as careless: flies in pasta, fillets all fat. But the pranks got more rancorous, and when Calvin entertained a young lady in the sitting room, Panga clanged so in the kitchen they would have to shout. The night Najma came to dinner, his guest pushed her entrée reluctantly around the plate and only chewed at her salad, whose grit ground audibly like a hand-turned *posho* mill. At last she confessed she hadn't a notion how to go about attacking this creature. Calvin poked at her meat and pried the wings out.

'Bloody hell!' he exclaimed appreciatively. 'It's a fried bat!'

He chortled, and that was the end of Najma.

Panga crossed a line, however, with Elaine Porter, whom Calvin 'truly fancied for a time', albeit in that 'sensible way' – she would have been good-natured, engaging in conversation and interested in current events; in short, made a solid, reasonable choice for a life partner – that Calvin had 'only since recognized as the mark of a relationship destined to go absolutely nowhere'.

The excess of garnishes might have alarmed him, for the chicken breasts arrived with a diagonal of courgette, a daisy of carrot, a flourish of parsley. He recalled, Elaine was on a rift about rangeland degradation, and between decrying the over-grazing of the Masai and the cultivation of marginal farmland by the Kikuyu she actually ate some. Half-way through, her jaw slowed; she stopped talking and turned the breast upside-down, and then she screamed.

Calvin claimed Elaine wasn't a dainty woman, more the sort you could take to the bush who wouldn't whine about having to wash her hair. Like Eleanor, you could bring her to tribal ceremonies and she would taste the blood and milk and manage a smile and claim it was very good. She would not have been given to squealing over ordinary chicken, so Calvin leapt to her plate while Elaine stood trembling on the other side of the room, her hand over her mouth.

He saw her point. The underside of the chicken was writhing with maggots.

Calvin tore into the kitchen, where Panga was innocently trickling water over dirty dishes, though it was only by the fact that some of the bowls were in the drainer that you could tell which stack was washed. Panga had a spatial relationship to hygiene: if the dish was on the right side of the sink, it was clean.

'If I were Kenyan,' growled her employer, 'I'd have you beaten.'

Panga stood erect with her small, sharp chin in the air – even sitting, though you could say she slouched, her body remained straight, her legs extended as if hoping you would trip on them. She was actually shorter than Eleanor, but seemed taller, because Panga didn't bend. She was most certainly didn't apologize. 'Try.'

'What's the idea?' He was angry, which may have been the idea at that.

'You bring these *malayas*, stinking of powder so they make me gag. I serve them alcohol and they giggle. Then the meal. And sweet. So you can take them to your room. In the morning, I wash the *shahawa* from your sheets.'

'That is what you are paid to do.'

'Not enough.'

'Are you telling me you serve my guests food crawling with maggots because you want a raise in salary?'

She turned to the sink, washing her hands, as if of him. 'I will go to Angola soon. Then you may take as many *malayas* as you like.'

He had to admit she was the strangest-looking beautiful woman he'd ever met. Eleanor pointed out that protruding teeth, because they were reminiscent of cows, were a mark of loveliness among Kambas, which would help explain Panga's haughty bearing. They were not, however, ordinarily appealing to Calvin. And she was mercilessly thin, the chest at her collar striated; she hadn't a curve on her, and the boomerang shoulders would be lethal in bed. All tendon and gristle, Panga was inedible. Skinned and roasted you wouldn't get a bite off her, and the strings of her arms would stick in your teeth.

He had backed out of the kitchen to attend to his date, because Elaine was throwing up.

Calvin and Panga had barely spoken to one another for days. Panga sullenly soaked the parts of her AK in kerosene, or put an edge on her *kukri*, the scrape of that ghastly blade on carborundum grating Calvin's nerves. He hid behind newspapers, scanning nervously for renewed hostilities near by. For once Calvin was a peacemonger. If Renamo resumed hostilities in Mozambique, he would lose his new servant and she was irreplaceable. Where would he ever again find such an appalling housekeeper?

He decided that inviting any more women to his cottage would be medically dangerous. That Friday night he went out and came back the next morning expecting to find his mattress slashed with a cavalry sabre – something extravagant. His bed was in perfect trim.

So Calvin announced boldly on the weekend that he was having 'an important, intelligent woman to dine' on Sunday, and she was 'very pretty', so he expected 'an especially good meal'. A gauntlet. Panga coolly dripped oil in her revolver, testing the trigger, *snap-snap*.

It seems that Lisa was a ninny. She was stunning all right, but in the early stages of Euro-gaga over Africa. Not over the people, of course – animals. Eleanor knew the type. She would expect him to spin exhilarating tales of life in the bush without telling a single decent yarn in return. These women never feel, as Eleanor had so disastrously at the Hilton, the need to redeem their company, for Lisa thought if she clapped her hands and hiked her dress, men were more than compensated for their efforts because she had nice legs. Calvin had balked. He valued the collateral of shapely ankles as spare change, and if he were billing Lisa per story she was running a wickedly high tab by the third glass of wine. He was looking forward to dinner and rose, rubbing his hands to suppose out loud, 'I wonder what Panga's cooked up this time!'

At table, Calvin kept eyeing Lisa's trout for the naked mole rat stuffed up its belly but spotted only lump-meat crab. He fidgeted, and over salad – *washed* – began to despair. Calvin slipped into the kitchen and folded his arms.

'This is the sneakiest trick yet,' he accused her.

'There was something wrong with the fish?'

'Not a thing. *Why?*'

'You said, special meal.'

'That was an ordinary meal,' he protested. 'What's wrong? You're not leaving?'

'I go to Angola, I told you. What do you care? You get another girl. It is easy. Look at you. *Bwana* Piper is very good at getting more girls.'

'Don't go. Or go if you have to. But come back.'

She smeared at a plate. 'To this? I am a soldier.'

'No. Forget the dishes. Work on the jeep,' he proposed feebly.

'And wash your sheets?'

'No. Do what you're good at.' He touched the car grille at her collar. 'Get them dirty.'

She eyed him; he had finally offered her a job worthy of a buck-toothed mercenary.

'But tonight,' said Calvin, leaning closer, 'you've got to help me. That pinhead is driving me *mwenye wazimu*. I want special coffee. Got it? I want *extra special coffee.*'

'It is not so easy – just like that – to make special coffee.'

'You have powerful witchcraft,' he said in her ear. That must have been when he first kissed her – without, Eleanor imagined bitterly, that exasperating passivity with which he still kissed Eleanor herself. He did admit to lingering in the kitchen a long time.

'Sorry,' he'd explained to Lisa, the door swinging jauntily behind him. 'Trouble with the staff. Bloody difficult to get your hands on a good servant.'

Panga brought coffee; Lisa might not have been in Kenya long, but she would already have mastered the art of looking straight through black help. The Frenchwoman sipped the better part of the cup without incident, until it looked as if

Calvin was stuck with another two hours of elephant stories over brandy while she waited for him to make a pass. It was going to take a fair bit of yawning and knee-slapping to encourage her departure – 'though I could always resort to my secret weapon,' said Calvin.

'Telling her you're celibate and "don't do that any more" and she's to imagine you like someone who's had a terrible accident?'

'*Demography.* I find the least census compelling, but mortality/fertility ratios turn most women to stone.'

He had been readying a good diatribe on Philippine population policy when Lisa yelped. He had to turn away, because he was smiling.

Calvin tipped her cup. Nice Lisa took it black, providing the fat white slug the proper venue to be appreciated.

'So what happened to Panga? What did you mean about a morgue?'

'Oh, we had an idyllic life for a couple of years. She stopped cleaning altogether, and the house looked exactly the same. Disappeared regularly to Angola or Rwanda for a month or two. It's always healthy when the woman has a career of her own, isn't it?'

'Meanwhile I soldiered for USAID, though with a moderation I now find foreign. These days, I don't think about anything but population. Back then I had hobbies, of all things.'

'Population is all you think about now? All day long?'

'Mm,' he hummed. 'I will entertain the prospect of a cup of tea, and usually discard it. Decide whether a shirt is clean enough to wear a second day. That's about the extent of my diversions, yes.'

'I don't believe you.'

He laughed. 'I haven't begun to stretch your imagination yet, my sweet. You have a way to go.'

Eleanor was getting impatient with his coy warnings. 'Your secrecy is pathetic, Calvin. It just makes me feel sorry for you.'

'Does it?' His eyes glittered. 'The side lined has-been with his delusions of grandeur. You go right ahead and feel sorry for me, then.'

Eleanor seemed incapable of annoying or insulting him in the least. 'Panga,' she commanded.

'She'd return from the bush, caked. Slept for fifteen hours. She didn't explain much. A few stories, but she left out the worst. We were both involved in population control. In hindsight, Panga's methods were the far more effective.

'I always expected that one day she'd never come back. No one would ever tell me what happened. Because the real story is inappropriate. Perhaps if Panga had a proper death – under an acacia with her eyes pecked out, a hole in her head – she wouldn't still loiter about this house.'

'What are you talking about?'

'Come, come,' he tut-tutted. 'Surely you've heard that hackle-raising scrape. Her knives are never sharp enough. At times it's impossible to get any work done.'

It was the same tone he used – come to think of it – with everything he said. Martini-dry, he was either having you on or dead serious; either droll or a lunatic. To cover herself, Eleanor had to strike a returning tone that could pass for both keeping the joke going and humouring him.

'It is nerve-racking,' she concurred. 'But how did Panga die?'

'Some other time,' he yawned. 'My past is of no concern now, least of all to me. Did you see that Harrison book? By 2100, humans will infest four million extra square miles of virgin forest, savannah and everglades. An aggregate area larger than the United States, and twice as much land as all of the earth's national parks and nature reserves combined . . .'

Eleanor suddenly began to feel rather sleepy herself.

7

Dog Days of Millennial Dread

She opened the first letter from Peter with foreboding, but what could be so fearsome from the poor? Tea and beans, and now this harmless, engaging note:

Dear Merritt,

Hallo to you! here is hoping everything is well to you. we have good weather in Nairobi in this season, God willing. much greetings from Mum and members of the family.

Merritt, here is hoping that when you come again to our plot you will say hallo to your old friends. mum says you should be coming to be eating with our family with all God's power.

Our plot is still slum condition, as you did see. mum is facing against the city commision coz of that plot (houses) that they are supposed to pay every month. others have build permanent house the black ones but we still hope one day we shall also with the Lord on our side.

Merritt, here is praying that this does find you in good health. I am eagerly wait that we see you soon.

Yours sincere,
PETER NDUMBA

She did not quite understand about the City Commission, skimming only for what she neither found nor formed in her mind precisely. She wondered if he had confused her Christian and surnames. The 'Merritts' gave the letter a sporty, intimate tone. She penned him a warm reply, on a postcard of the Nairobi Hilton, crass but destined to please. When she told

Calvin she had had a very nice letter from Peter, he said, 'Oh, I'm sure you did', with a cynical edge that made Eleanor feel she had something to prove.

Second letter: just lovely. More about Mum and weather and school and a lot of Jesus. Eleanor felt triumphant, she wasn't sure why.

The third letter, however, came quickly on the first, a bit too. The earlier trepidation visited once more, and Eleanor did not respond to the familiar painstakingly neat print with enthusiasm.

Dear Merritt,

Here is hoping all is going on well for you. we have wait and you are not come to visit your friends every day I look down on the road where I did lead you. are you forget that day when I show you where Mathare Family planning is and did make all the children move for your automobile? Lord be praised I come by you that day coz these children can problems.

Merritt, I will ask you to bring or send me some few things to me first shoe number '9', long trouser 44cm waist 32 and shirt or even jacket long 27cm Mum also had requested you if you can please send her shoe number '8' for Easter celebration. Wish you a nice time in your work in the name of Christ our lord.

Yours sincere,
PETER NDUMBA

This time she put off sending a card. She didn't mention she'd heard from Peter to Calvin.

The fourth letter was only two days later. It was all about basketball shoes. She didn't read it carefully; her eyes wilfully blurred the little block letters – something about sport and a particular brand and more about housing. She put it to the side of her desk and massaged her temples. Through the week she didn't reply. The flimsy brown envelope nagged until she responded just to get it out of her sight, though there was bound to be another flimsy brown envelope to replace it by return post.

Eleanor hadn't meant to tell Calvin, but while trustworthy

with other people's secrets she couldn't keep the slightest of her own. Walking down Kenyatta Avenue, she showed him the petitions, by which time there were three more. He shuffled through them quickly, as if he already knew what they said.

'Why in God-with-all-his-power's name did you give him your address? What did you expect?'

'It seemed the least I could do at the time.'

'The least you can do is nothing, not become a private mail-order business. You're not telling me this surprises you?'

She sighed. 'No. But it's still disappointing.'

They ambled on to Uhuru Highway, passing the corner where some hundred men perched on buckets and old tyres huddled around *jikos* turning maize on grates. Their gaze was milky and many were not attending the cobs with care; the air stung with burning corn. In over-large trousers tied up with string, some laceless brogues but never socks, these same men roasted and conferred with one another in this waste-ground every day. Heading for grilled squid at the Toona Tree, strolling before them in her ironed white blouse, polished heels and neatly combed brown hair, Eleanor felt superimposed, like a cutout from a detergent advertisement pasted on to a news photo. Sometimes it was hard to feel real in this town.

'You didn't imagine that urchin was writing to you because he *liked* you?'

'No,' she squirmed. 'But I wish someone on this continent would do something once – because they liked me.'

'Impossible. You're white. You will never stop being white. White equals rich. Rich equals gimme. Go back to DC if you want someone to like you.'

'I sometimes think the nicest thing about a just world is it wouldn't mangle relationships like this. I know his asking for presents is inevitable, but his growing shopping list is depressing.'

'What are you going to do? Tell him to bugger off or just wait for the entreaties to dwindle? You'll find his persistence impressive. Just don't come across with so much as a sweetie or you've a pen pal for life. From the sound of the last one, he's working up to a Mercedes.'

Eleanor stared off interestedly at Chester House.

'Eleanor?' He turned her chin back to face him. 'You didn't.'

She scuffed at condoms and corn cobs, admitting with a groan, 'I sent the shoes.'

It had been when buying Peter's basketball shoes that Eleanor reached for her VISA card and found it missing from her wallet. After combing her office and New Jersey in vain, she'd reported it lost. She thought the absence odd, for she was neurotically responsible about finances. Credit cards made her feel both flattered and unworthy, being trusted like that, and she always paid the bill in full.

When the bill arrived the next month – along with one more letter from Peter, including measurements for a suit – she opened it with a cursory glance, unable to recall any charges on her account.

The bill was for $1,208.31.

As she unfolded an impressive list of Nairobi restaurants and boutiques, a little memory that at first had tickled now began to itch. About six weeks earlier Eleanor had left for lunch without her wallet. She'd returned and walked in on her messenger, who had no call to be in Eleanor's inner office having already picked up the mail. Florence peered in the empty Outgoing basket, smiled and hurried away. There was a funny gnarling in the air Eleanor chose to ignore. Later at lunch, when she thought she had nearly 2,000 shillings she found only 500.

Eleanor had gone out of her way to hire Florence in the first place, for most Kenyan messengers were men, though the job entailed only the nominal responsibilities of running post, fetching sandwiches and scanning local papers.

Naturally Florence was not merely a messenger, for no one survived as a faceless lackey in Eleanor's orbit for long. They had long talks. Florence's daughter was HIV-positive and Eleanor was keen to discourage her from spending her meagre resources on witchdoctors. Her employer had insisted that the first-name basis work in both directions, not the form, to dispel any impression of being a superior. More than once Eleanor had 'lent' the woman several hundred shillings to finance her latest misfortune. And now Eleanor was sponsoring a 220-dollar spree at Wild Orchid and a binge at the Tamarind . . .

Eleanor was seething. At ten, Florence delivered a cup of coffee, chatting about how Jennifer was gaining some weight. Eleanor was cryptic. Florence didn't notice, flashing the bright flowers of a new silk shift.

'What a pretty dress,' Eleanor hissed in English.

'*Asante sana!*' Florence chirped. It was a tribute from her eldest son, for a few young people still gave their mothers respect . . .

Eleanor couldn't say anything. Couldn't. Her eyes hurt. Her breath whinnied through her nose. '*Kwa heri.*' She dismissed the woman abruptly, her clipped quality wasted on Florence, who would only fully comprehend, 'You stinking thief' or still better, 'You're fired.'

Florence left early to take her daughter to a clinic, leaving Eleanor to collect a package at the post office herself. A full afternoon's work, customs. Eleanor presented her yellow slip to one desk, where the man painstakingly took down its number in a ledger, stamped it, sent her to a second desk to pay a fee, where they sent her to a third . . . At the seventh station she chafed, 'And what is *this* fee for?'

The gentleman responded with a smile. 'To pay my salary.'

By the time she got her hands on the parcel, however, it had been opened and hastily taped together again. She scanned down an enclosed note. Most of the treats Jane mentioned that Eleanor must miss in Africa – American peanut butter, pesto, not to mention Jane's belated birthday cheque – had mysteriously disappeared. Consequently Eleanor spent two hours of her time and hundreds of shillings in duty on one can of lychees, a tube of olive paste and a jar of satay sauce.

After work as she marched to her car, Eleanor's regular parking boy ran in the opposite direction. The door had been jimmied. Of the five in the glove compartment, three cassettes were missing: Phil Collins, Neil Young and Peter, Paul and Mary. One of those days.

'Well,' Calvin drawled as she slammed her portable computer on his dining-room table, 'how much did she rack up before you reported the card missing?'

'Maybe 500.' The software took ages to load.

'You were lucky, then. You must have a credit limit of at least 3,000. The rest VISA swallows. I'll give you the five if you're short.'

'That's not necessary,' she said icily, beginning to tap an irate disclaimer that she had ever been to Wild Orchid in her life. 'I pay for my own guillibility, thank you.'

'Why so angry?' he purred, and she could not work out why the incident pleased him so. 'Is it the money?'

Eleanor kept typing, but made so many mistakes that she finally slammed the computer shut. 'I've been nice to her! Treated her like a human being! Professional counselling! A Christmas bonus *and* a box of home-made shortbread! An endless string of *loans*, not that I'll ever see two bob of that again. Still – OK, I bargained for that, fine! But now at the first opportunity – '

'She's supposed to be *grateful*? That you treat her like a human being?'

'I didn't mean it like that and you know it. But, yes, grateful, damn it! Very grateful!' Eleanor raged about the room, unable to sit down.

'What are you going to do?'

'What I'd *like* to do is turn her over to the police. I want her arrested.'

'Uh-huh.'

'Oh, don't say it! I know the police are a joke, I know that with 200 bob she'd be out again, and besides which I don't have any evidence. At least, if I have anything to say about it she'll lose her job.'

'Eleanor!' he exclaimed. 'With her ailing daughter?'

'Damn straight with her ailing daughter, I don't care. And don't look at me like that. Panga would take off her hand, if not her head.'

He tsked. 'So vindictive. It's not like you.'

'What's like me is to treat people decently and expect to be treated decently in return.'

'It's not in the least like you to expect decency in return. What's like you is to go out and charge up 1,200 dollars to buy your messenger dresses and dinners yourself.'

'Exactly. That would be different. I don't mind generosity, but I revile stealing.'

'How much does she make a month?'

'About 4,000 shillings,' said Eleanor grumpily. 'but that's *more* than the going rate by far, and you can't fight the local economy, we can't pay her like the United States – '

'Say, 160 bucks, then. What do you make?'

'3,000.'

'Dollars?'

'But that's before taxes – '

Calvin laughed.

'Stop it!'

'Isn't your salary, in international terms, a kind of theft? Who deserves 36,000 dollars a year? How can you blame her?'

Eleanor stamped her foot. 'I can blame her and I will! I give a huge proportion of my income away. Isn't that enough without involuntary contributions? It's one thing to say that distribution of wealth is unjust, but it's another to condone pickpocketing and fraud!'

Calvin's mouth kept twitching with a suppressed smile. Malthus, in collusion, displayed a rare and exasperating equanimity, neatly tapping a raw egg, first a little hole in one end, then one at the other, finally sucking it dextrously from the top.

'What is wrong with you?' she exploded. 'I thought you of all people would say, yes, Eleanor, it's pretty depressing when people you trust betray you at the drop of a hat; yes, Eleanor, you don't owe Africa *everything*; and yes, giving money away is a very different experience from being ripped off.'

He pulled her to the sofa with both hands. 'Young lady,' he began, 'what do you think we talk about all day? Do you think it's all on paper? Yes, they steal from you at their first and every chance, and they will keep stealing. Moreover, they deserve everything they manage to swindle and a great deal that they don't, and the only thing that will deter them is not stern moral instruction that you don't touch what isn't yours but a high electric fence and a very large dog. As the years go by, the fences will make the Great Wall of China look like a tennis net and the dogs will be crossed with *Tyrannosaurus rex*, but some of the rabble will still claw their way over and they will abscond with not only your credit cards but the wires from your walls and the pump from your garden, the shoes from your feet and the clip from your hair, and leave you nothing but your life if you're lucky and you still care to keep it. You think I'm being racist, but if I were on the other side of the fence I'd do the same and should. There are too many of them, pet. And plenty are enchanting and only want ordinary comfort, and work, if there were such a thing. It's not their fault. And it's going to get worse.'

She could not believe that, coming to him for a little sympathy over fleecing and treachery, she only got more *population*. 'You're saying that Florence has every right to run up charges on my credit card. That theft is the solution to social inequality.'

'It's not the solution because there is none – ' He paused. 'Yet. But it's fair, anyway, in your own terms.'

'I thought – ' She rubbed her eyes. 'That you were always trying to get me to splurge on prawns and not issue excuses for every abominable behaviour like fabric-softener coupons in *Woman's Day*.'

'I am trying to keep 500 dollars in perspective. I still find it amazing you can walk down the street in Nairobi with ten shillings in your pocket and not have your throat slit ear to ear. Credit card fiddle is civilized; it still obeys the rules, going into a shop and signing slips instead of smashing the window and bundling off with as much as she can carry. Kenyans are uncannily biddable, but when the desperation level tops up they won't stay so compliant. And you're alarmed that your parking boy takes three of five cassettes?'

'Next time he'll take all five.'

'Don't be ridiculous. Next time he'll take the car.'

Eleanor was coming to realize that a great deal could be fearsome from the poor.

Early that evening, Solastina entered the living room with a particular inability to meet Calvin's gaze which Eleanor recognized at once. 'My daughter, *bwana*. She is very sick.' She explained that her eyes were infected, and that without costly antibiotics she might go blind. Health care was subsidized in Kenya, but it was not free.

Calvin asked questions about symptoms and treatment with

uncharacteristic patience. Solastina knew the name of the drug; the story sounded legitimate. To Eleanor's astonishment, Calvin produced 2,000 shillings without hesitation, warning Solastina, 'Whatever you do, don't go to Kenyatta. That should be enough for Nairobi Hospital, and if it's not, come back for more. Understand?'

When the servant had thanked Calvin and left, Eleanor studied this man who was becoming only more of a puzzle.

'Two months ago,' he explained, 'my gardener's youngest son had a bad case of malaria and might have died. I wouldn't give him five bob.'

'This – capriciousness is meant to teach your wards something about arbitrary Western charity?'

'I don't fund terminal illnesses. But I think being blind must be bloody awful. Live people torture me; I do not feel sorry for the dead. Rather envy them, in fact.'

'You regard this as a logical position.'

'I am regretful about auto accidents where a good Rugby player loses his legs. If instead the chap is decapitated, I don't bat an eye. Surely you've attended to those stories of recovered flat-liners, floating above their bodies feeling peaceful, no doubt for the first time in their lives. Why I should pity such people is beyond me.'

'What if *you* were the one with malaria?'

'I don't bother with chloroquine, even on the coast. I don't dread my own death more than anyone else's, and take no steps to avoid it. I neglect inoculations, ignore cholesterol and only decline cigarettes because I don't enjoy them. I like nothing more than to take aeroplanes during a bout of Iranian terrorism. I don't look both ways before crossing the street and the only reason I drive carefully is to avoid a collision I might survive. The irony of this sang-froid is that, as a consequence, nothing ever happens to me. I have reasoned that nothing happens because everything bad has already occurred. In that I regard most of life as a stringing together of calamities, mine is already over.'

He said all this cheerfully, and was now feeding pieces of banana to Malthus, as if he had not just been talking about death but the funny thing that happened at the store today.

The malaria tale was harsh, but he'd been generous with Solastina, more so than Eleanor all week.

Later that night, calmed, Eleanor deleted the paragraph that named the thief from her letter to VISA. It was true she was only operating on a hunch – a good hunch – but Florence would have to be caught red-handed or let be.

Back in the office, she continued to be curt with Florence, who didn't noticeably miss Eleanor's earlier mateyness. *She would rather have the dresses*, Eleanor fumed. Meanwhile the petty cash accounting at Pathfinder was looking dicey. Peter wanted a bicycle. One of the Pathfinders's vehicles was hijacked in Kisumu, though God knows what the thugs would do with an entire van-load of foaming contraceptive tablets. When her Land Rover's window was smashed one night while she and Calvin were at the Japanese Club, the vandals only got a jacket; she no longer listened to cassettes in the car. Rather than stockpile all the more tolerance and compassion for those less fortunate than herself, Eleanor's shame was beginning to ferment, and what began as perpetual embarrassment burbled into suppressed, impotent rage.

Wallace was a consultant with the National AIDS Control Programme and had helped design a bus campaign, a series of ads in the *Standard* and a leaflet for the airport that, while sufficiently stern, did not frighten tourists into turning heel to book for home. With such a paucity of medical strategies, the job felt akin to selling insurance. When he heard the car drive up, he was hard at work, coloured pencils everywhere, on an AIDS postage stamp.

At first Wallace didn't recognize the woman who marched towards him as the same shy, awkward lady at that party six months ago who wished she'd brought a book. She was stylishly dressed for one thing. When she stepped on his dog Oracle's tail and he yelped, she did not bend down, ruffle its ears and apologize, but barely glanced with a look that life was rough and it could lick its wounds on its own time. Perhaps he'd misread her.

She took a seat around his campfire, refusing to small-talk about the elegance of his platform tent. She would not sit for parables. She was harder work.

'I'm sorry, but this idea you have that everything is only getting hunkier and dorier simply flies in the face of my daily life.' She had already begun before the water had boiled for tea.

'Your own life,' Wallace explored, 'is growing both less hunky and less dory at the same time?'

'Wallace, Nairobi is collapsing! Not in the future, now!' She sounded hysterical. 'Graft is rife, theft incessant. There hasn't been any water downtown for three weeks. They have to douse all the toilets in Nyayo House with Jik to keep them from stinking. The fire trucks sell their water for domestic use, and then when there's an alarm the trucks are dry. In Karen – '

'Karen?' He looked up from his contented doodling with coloured pencils. 'I recall you live in Parklands.'

She blushed. 'A friend of mine has no water, then. Don't evade the point. It's population, Wallace.'

'Why do you *want* to regard Africa as falling apart?'

Wallace's resident wart-hogs had arrived for their early evening feed and snuffled contentedly in *posho* a few feet away. One female had piglets, and they leaped and squealed around their mother, tails high like splayed paintbrushes – ruined, but with which some child has had a wonderful time. Overhead, the jacaranda's pale lavender tinged to violet as the light ripened to mango. It was all Wallace could do not to burst out laughing. *They lived in paradise* and this poor woman had shut herself in a mean little outhouse with a lot of books, pulling the door to with all her might, and then complained that it smelled in here and it was crowded.

Eleanor allowed herself to be captivated by the piglets for a moment or two, but with resolute perversity resumed. 'I look around me – ' refusing to do exactly that – 'I can't help what I see.'

'How do you manage from day to day with such perpetual anxiety?'

'With difficulty.' She was growing out her bangs, which had reached that awkward length, not yet long enough to tuck behind her ears, so they kept drooping forward and trailing dismally over her eyes.

His camp was within the fencing of Giraffe Manor. As if to torture her, one of the exquisite creatures wafted near the fire, nibbling at the tender leaves of the jacaranda. That sublime subaqueous ripple: he half expected the vision to turn her to salt.

'Haven't you noticed, even when cities "collapse", that people manage?'

'That's what –' She stopped. 'I mean, yes. But in what condition? What happens to the libraries? Did you know that the Kenya Museum is infested with rats?'

Wallace smiled; with the wart-hogs, the giraffe, the sunset – at a certain point you positively had to admire the woman. 'Rats, is it?'

He flicked the flies amiably from his face with his cow-tail wisk, as Eleanor swatted with annoyance.

'The danger is not only extinction –' swat! – 'but another Dark Ages.'

'I believe we are in the Dark Ages.'

'I've also heard it proposed that we are living in the golden years of humanity.'

'You don't sound like a woman who is seeing a great deal of gold lately.' He poured her a solicitous cup of tea. 'You said you've been in the population field for so many years. Why did you choose it?'

'Well, I'd give you a different answer now from what I would have done a short while ago.'

'That's not surprising. Everything you've said in the last hour has been different from what you said a short while ago.'

'I could admit I was trying to please my stepfather, but there's more to it. I grew up being told there were too many people. I've always felt unnecessary. Now I've come full circle: I *resent* feeling unnecessary. Does that make any sense?'

'You are turning malignant.'

'I didn't say that. It just seems – I know you don't believe this – that everything is getting worse. That things are going to get worse still. I do feel, Wallace, as if something awful is about to happen.'

The giraffe, as if acknowledging that this latrine-dweller was beyond his illumination, shimmered back to the forest again. Wallace noted that at least Eleanor looked after the apparition's departure with regret.

'Perhaps for you the awful has already occurred.'

'How do you mean?'

He bent towards her with concern. 'Where do you get all these terrible pictures, Eleanor? What is tormenting you?' Though he might have asked, *Who?*

'The terrible pictures are in Mathare, Wallace. I'm not making them up.'

'So what do you propose to do about them?'

Eleanor sighed. 'The family planning side is discouraging. I know this sounds cold, but I wonder if something like AIDS coming along isn't fortuitous. Maybe it's lucky we can't cure it yet. Maybe we should let it run its course.'

Wallace was convinced that the woman he had met six months ago would have been incapable of this statement. 'You have let him go too far.'

'Who?'

'You know who. I'm sorry. You should have come here earlier. It may already be too late.'

'I haven't a notion what you're on about.'

'Have you slept with him?'

Her face went hot. 'That's none of your business.'

Wallace tapped his cane, victorious. 'You see. You do know who I'm on about.'

Eleanor folded her arms in stolid silence.

'I will give you this much credit,' said Wallace. 'I do not believe you have any idea who, or what, you are contending with. If you did, you would run a mile. By now it is much harder to get out. Soon it may be impossible. You're a woman. Any woman wants to love one man more than all humanity, and she will sell her entire race down river for his sake. You have to know this about yourself and be watchful. In mountain climbing, there is a move any climber knows well: the kind you can make in one direction but cannot take back. You can get quite stuck this way, out on ledges from which there is no return. If you think several moves ahead, however, you predict the danger and avoid it. You can step somewhere else.'

'That's just what I've been saying about population.'

'You see, your illness is already advanced. I am talking about your soul, and you are talking population growth. So tell me: how bad is it?'

'Nothing is bad.'

'You just told me everything is bad. I believe you. My dear lady, why did you come here today?'

Eleanor rubbed her face. 'Things have been happening lately. I'm changing – I think it's necessary, but I'm nervous. I'm not as *nice*. For some obscure reason, I thought you'd understand.'

Wallace nodded. He was used to seekers making pilgrimages to his camp for spiritual advice. 'How deep in are you, Eleanor? Have you made the fateful move yet? Or can you still get back?'

'I don't want to get back.'

'I know you don't. I realize he is, on the face of it, handsome and even charming. But inside that head is a fetid, cankerous sore. He had already infected you, and if you let him he will destroy you. Calvin Piper is an evil man.'

'You throw around *evil* a bit too casually for my tastes.'

'I use the word rarely,' said Wallace, taking a moment to reflect that this wasn't exactly true, though he didn't use it nearly as often as he wanted to. 'You would at least concede that Piper is a racist?'

'Calvin's not a racist. He hates everybody. Besides, he even had an African lover, didn't he?'

'If you regard seducing the servants as a sure sign of racial open-mindedness, most of the slave owners of the American South would qualify as founding members of the United Negro College Fund. Furthermore, your friend Calvin is a sadist.'

'Rot!'

'I've known him longer than you. We first met in Kenya, when Piper was involved in that Ugandan culling scheme. I'll tell you this much: he enjoyed it.'

'I'm sure he liked the bush, the planes, the camaraderie. He has said you couldn't remain heartbroken and get the job done. That's a far cry from finding it fun.'

'Hunters enjoy killing. That's what the sport is about.'

'Not Murchison Falls. Without culling, all the elephants would have starved. However paradoxically, cropping was an act of love.'

'You poor duped little lamb! I would submit to you that Calvin reviles elephants.'

'Wallace! I'm sorry, but we seem to be talking about two different people. It's true he has a warped sense of humour, and some of his opinions are extreme, but they're for effect. He likes to offend to make people think, and rhetoric doesn't hurt anybody – '

'Don't be so sure.'

'He is also, despite what sounds like vitriol, very warm. I came here knowing hardly anybody, and he's been wonderful to me – '

'I'm sure he has.'

'I didn't mean in some sleazy, filchy way.'

'No, that's not what Piper wants – or all he wants. You have minion-potential.'

'What a lovely thought.'

'Piper loves followers. He has plenty, more than you realize. But they curl up over time, into distorted, boggy little gnomes. I've watched them grow physically shorter.'

'Hold on, Calvin is a friend of mine – '

'You're aware Piper and I were once good friends as well?'

'No, I wasn't. I admit he doesn't talk about you as a long-lost brother either.'

'So if I were you I would assume something happened. Something did. To Piper. He once had a markedly different personality. On the outside, he maintains a magnetism, though I myself am repelled. Young, he was full of life: Africa was his garden. There was always, however, a little spoiled spot in him. He was never able to accept defeat, injury, disappointment. He still can't, and that makes him vengeful. The spoiled spot has spread over the field of his mind like potato blight. If you could reach behind his eyes, you would find nothing but noxious brown ooze.'

'I think he's sad.'

'And you're going to make him happy?' asked Wallace sardonically.

'It's true he's sad about women. But he's also profoundly disturbed by what's happening to this continent and this planet. He and I share a deep concern over the growth of population and the fate of our ecosystem – '

'If you believe that, you are not only under Piper's spell, you are an imbecile.'

'Well, thank you very much!' She stood up.

'You cannot imagine for a minute Calvin Piper is a philanthropist. And sit down. The fact is, "over-population" is a chimera, and without it Piper is a nonentity. As the man himself begins to have doubts, the more drastic he'll become. Piper's about to fly out of orbit, mark my words.'

'What in God's name can be so dangerous about a *demographer*?'

'Darkness does not distinguish between professions.'

'The most untoward thing Calvin ever did was ship contraceptives and vacuum aspirators to countries where they were illegal. So he disguised copper-sevens as Christmas ornaments. As a result he lost his job. But he was still supporting something I believe in.'

'All right. Why don't you find out something for me, then? I've been digging in data bases. Mind, his name was not on the top – minions – but Piper was definitely behind it. Why don't you discover for me why Piper has a grant from the WHO, quite a large one, and what it is actually for.'

'Population research, I assume.'

'No, no. This grant is from the AIDS programme.'

She faltered. 'That's odd.'

'I thought so as well. Isn't Piper the mad magus of mortality? So why would he do AIDS research?'

'He did say,' she remembered, 'it wasn't the right disease.'

'The right disease?'

'But he was joking.'

'Or so you assumed.'

'Then he is a philanthropist.' She recovered. 'You just don't like the idea of his working on AIDS. It doesn't fit your portrait. And it's your adoptive hobby, isn't it? He's butting in.'

'I hope the explanation is benign as that.'

'You are one melodramatic mawk, Wallace.'

'I have come to believe that in the twentieth century it is now impossible to be melodramatic.'

'That's Calvin's line: no one can write science fiction any more. It gets surpassed by history.'

'Maybe because Piper has taken up writing it himself.'

'Science fiction?'

'History.'

He saw her to her car. 'You will try to find out about that grant?' he reminded her. 'Though asking directly will probably get you nowhere. He'll lie. But a little nosing about might turn up some surprises.'

'I can't see why Calvin would have anything to hide.'

'On a personal note . . .' He paused decorously. 'I could suggest that semen is a powerful fluid and can accomplish the most insidious septicaemia, and you would dismiss me as mystical. In our current medical climate, however, the concept is no longer absurd. I don't know what habits he keeps lately, but there was a time Piper was quite a lady's man. These are hazardous times.'

'I believe his habits are quite conservative,' she said icily. 'Thank you for your concern.'

'All the same, we don't know what work he's about, do we? I guarantee you that man is toying with viruses. You're aware he keeps a lab?'

'I know nothing about it.'

'For such a close friend, we're not too clued in, are we? But no one knows where it is, you see. That would be interesting to discover as well. Find the lab.'

'Why do you keep thinking I'm working for you?'

'In your heart, you are still on my side.'

'There are no sides that I'm aware of.'

'That you're aware of.' He placed two fingers on her arm. 'It may be hindsight advice, but I would ask Piper to get tested.'

'Thanks.' She didn't sound very grateful.

'I would like to say you are always welcome. But there may come a point where I cannot retrieve you to the light. Then, while I find you an ingenuous, provocative guest, I will have no choice but to smite you with the worst of them.'

Eleanor looked at him dully. She couldn't engage on this level, of course. He was soothing his own conscience; in future he could tell himself he tried.

'As for Piper's deep affection for humanity,' Wallace added as an afterthought, 'why don't you ask him what happened to his African girlfriend. It was his fault. You ask him what happened to Panga.'

In the dust of her accelerating anger, he coughed and considered the truth of the matter: she wasn't as nice.

8

Bitter Pills
in the Love-Stone Inn

'That man is certifiable,' Eleanor railed, once more in Calvin's clipping den. While she spent single nights in her cubicle of wall-to-wall Formica to prove her independence, most of the week she slept at Calvin's. The evenings she endured New Jersey proved nothing to Calvin, who didn't seem to notice, and to Eleanor those long neon vigils proved only that she couldn't live without him. 'Why is Wallace so obsessed with you?'

'Maybe he's homosexual, though that's a bit of a bore. He used to doggie after me in the sixties. Plagued my regular Nairobi bars. Where do you think he got the idea to go into demography in the first place?'

'Is that why he's so consumed by your *minions*? That he used to be one?'

'Minions, is it?' Calvin laughed. 'Maybe. But there are two sorts of minions, aren't there? The kind that truly want to trot after you and wish only to be tolerated; and the other kind that really wish to *be* you and haven't the flair. If Wallace was a minion he was the latter variety, and they always turn on you in time. In Washington, he was competent, but undistinguished. Meanwhile, to his consternation, I got the USAID post. Then he hit on this inspired gambit of rampant cheerfulness. For all his whinging about having his grants withdrawn, Threadgill made quite a splash – guest appearance on *Firing Line*. These days you can't achieve any notoriety at all by pointing out the world is in the toilet. Everyone knows we're in the toilet. It's optimism that's become outrageous. Addled rays of sunshine have co-opted the avant-garde.'

'He unnerves me. There's something ghoulish about the man. Those cadaverous bags under his eyes.'

Calvin eyed her as she kept rearranging the new clothes she was still not used to. 'What did he say that's got you so rattled?'

'I dislike hearing anyone tear into you like that.'

'You have got to stop leaping to other people's defence. Leap to your own.

'All right. He wasn't very sweet to me either.'

'Into which soft spot has he sunk his shaft?'

'He's got this weird – he thinks you're programming me or something.'

'That would only upset you if you thought it was true. You have changed, haven't you?'

'I suppose,' she said glumly.

'Do you want me to fetch your plaid dresses that button to the chin? Return to regaling me about the CIA in Nicaragua?'

'Just – that's not what you think of me, is it?' she burst out. 'That I "trot along after you" and "only want to be tolerated"?' She all but asked, *you don't think I'm growing shorter?*

'Don't be touchy. It's unbecoming.'

'Calvin – ' She stopped.

'Mm?'

'Could I have a whisky, please?'

Eleanor got up and fidgeted, and while she scanned the titles of his pulp sci-fi, her attention was more on the adjacent armchair. Panga was watching. She smirked at this smart, sleek dress, at the increasingly abrupt and impatient way the new girlfriend moved, and seemed satisfied by the peculiarly callous remarks that were beginning to lash from the mouse's throat. Eleanor herself had noticed a growing capacity to demand, where not a few months before she would have sat in a man's living room all evening and never asked for a drink if it wasn't on offer. The *sing-swish, sing-swish* edged the air again.

Calvin was bringing her a drink, and she'd have to ask him. It explained too much – the absorption with *mortality*. But one thing most of all.

'Calvin – ' She took a swig. 'The reason we don't make love. You're not – trying to protect me, are you?'

110

'Certainly not. I'm protecting myself.'

'From what?'

'I thought we'd discussed this,' he said irritably. 'If you're not prepared – '

'Calvin, you don't have something, do you?'

'Have what?'

'You're not – infected with anything, are you?'

'Anything *like what*?'

'Anything – sexual, anything – contagious.'

Finally Calvin raised his head, light-bulb. 'Threadgill!'

'This has nothing to do with Wallace.'

'It has everything to do with Wallace! First I invented it and now I carry it! Obsessed? There's only one thing he's more obsessed with than me and that's his pet virus! And now he's convinced you I'm sero-positive!'

'You mean,' she pressed shyly, 'you're not?'

Calvin picked her up by the waist and swirled her a full turn. With those strong slim hands on her rib-cage Eleanor experienced a surge of desire like nausea. 'My darling,' he confessed gleefully, 'I am infected with death itself. I do not have disease. I am disease.'

She kissed him. 'Tell me no, though. Say no.'

'No, what?'

'Say, no I do not have – I am not positive.'

'I'm a nihilist. I've never been positive in my life.'

'No! Say it and I'll believe you. Say, *No, I am not HIV positive.*'

He hesitated a moment that gave her a stab, but Calvin Piper rarely did anything he was told. 'No-I-am-not-HIV-positive,' he recited, and kissed her forehead. 'Regrettably for my contemporaries, I am not about to die. Tell Wallace I'm sorry not to be more obliging. And some day, far, far away, this mangy species will be grateful.'

Normal couples, at this carthartic juncture, would have gone to bed. *Calvin* suggested they read population journals. She couldn't concentrate. Malthus, who had recently deigned to share the same couch with her, groomed himself blithely on the opposite end as if Eleanor weren't there – the monkey's idea of a compliment. Panga, in the simian's view, was there; he threw a stray corn kernel at the elbow-dented chair in that blend of hostility and affection which suggested that in their most extreme one was always a version of the other.

Calvin's ostensible good health both relieved and deflated her, for now she was stuck back with the old explanation that she simply left him physically nonplussed. Moreover, Wallace had planted three further questions, and they plagued her like unattended homework assignments as the evening dragged on. Several times she looked up from her book, and Calvin would glance from his fray of torn and paper-clipped articles inquiringly through his glasses. The horn-rims gave him a husbandly air, as if their ascetic arrangements were waxed passion. She would shoot him a timid smile and bury herself in her novel again. She tried to form the questions beginning with a casual, 'By the way', or 'I meant to mention, you wouldn't *believe* what Threadgill claims', but then she could hear his, 'Yes?' just waiting to get back to his beloved *Population Bulletins*.

No, it was impossible. She *could not* ask him why he had a grant from the WHO. Most impossibly of all, she couldn't form the question about – Why not? Why was this the one inquiry that was not on? Fine, she was a coward. But what was so intrusive about asking if he ran a lab?

At last she couldn't pretend to read and set the book down. Just now she was no longer pestered by the accumulation of mismatched details that surrounded Calvin Piper – the appointments, the meetings that queered as soon as she walked in, the office door down the hall, the obscure infusion of inexhaustible cash, the envelopes of AIDS horror stories that continued to arrive in the mail with no return address, even the grant, this crazy business about a hidden laboratory: all stray parts that would never fit together if she hadn't a clue beforehand whether she was assembling a printing press or a toaster. *What was wrong with Calvin Piper?* This was, so late in the evening, the only thing she wished to know.

'I believe you,' she bravely interrupted his scissoring of cataclysm, 'that you're not sero-positive. And I'm willing to allow that, though the nature of your work right now doesn't make a lot of sense to me, it's none of my business. But I think it's time you told me what happened to that girl.'

Calvin took off his glasses and looked at his watch and then admitted it wasn't a very long story, and did not, on the face of it, have anything to do with population, since single disappearances from the planet did not show up as dips on a graph.

Calvin failed to notice, when he first proposed teaching Panga to scuba-dive, the mist of presentiment that clouded those clear-skied eyes, for he considered Panga fearless. Eleanor could have told him there was no such quality. Everyone was afraid of something: blame, thirteen, intimacy; *water*.

To Calvin, Panga belonged undersea. He evaded unseemly details, but when Eleanor pictured them making love, in the watery soft-focus that characterizes visions of parents coupling or lovers with someone else, the mattress spread into an ocean bed, branches listing out of the window like kelp. For her own sake, Eleanor did want him to remember his original surprise: that just like diving, below his life the wide, sumptuous quiet of a deeper world thrived. He skimmed the top of what could be penetrated to its floor, wasting years splashing the surface and learning to swim when he should be learning to sink instead. When pressed, he confessed that all the other women Panga had poisoned had been clumsy drill, like the first few dives in a swimming pool, and all there is to explore is the drain.

He resisted describing himself as happy, a word used too often by drabs who meant their bills were paid. Even at the time, he had never spoken of Panga to his colleagues, not wishing to expose his secret, boundless suspension to their bobbling inflatable prattle about *relationships*. No one around him noticed he had become a completely different person. Most people lived, he claimed, in a dinghy. His office mates crowded into their little rubber boats cracking beers, and if Calvin went diving they were privy only to the surfacing of bubbles; otherwise he disappeared.

Even when Panga was out with uprisings, slashing her *kukri* through bamboo, she left him in a buoyant emersion, and should he drift to a party in her absence he did not so much tread the rooms as fin. He had never been so graceful, physically or socially, and it was those two years, when every look in his eyes was a documentary by Jacques Cousteau, that must

113

have turned his tide in USAID, churned the currents that would eddy him shortly to the top of his field. It was a time when no statistic was insignificant, no country irrelevant, no official too lowly to be won. He retained his rancid humour, for in becoming 'a completely different person' he had not turned into a stranger, but into himself. He impressed everyone with his commitment, and while they imagined this was purely to population control, he might have effused just as eagerly over orchid raising or polo.

Panga did well enough in their exercises in the Banda swimming pool, but he had plenty of confirmation that diving was not her sport, though could dangerously be her destiny, the very first time he took her to the Malindi Marine Park. Calvin had always been at home with scuba, released from the dry drone of demography into the quiet under-populated deeps of the earth's amniotic fluid, so he could not conceive that the woman he loved might feel otherwise. Yet most Kenyans weren't much for water, as Eleanor could have told him, and this one didn't even like the bath. He had forgotten, too, that the sea and a blue square of cement had about as much in common as a wounded buffalo and a pet cat.

As he revved from shore in the inflatable, Panga went quiet; he assumed she had nothing to say. When he dropped anchor, the weather was iffy, reason to be quick about kitting up. Instead Panga took longer than usual, mis-snapping her stab, fumbling her fins, and for God's sake she forgot to turn on her air. By the time she was ready, the waves were high and the horizon dark, and Panga kept testing her regulator until he had to shout at her not to empty her bottle while still in the boat. Eleanor had faced that same barking irritation when they were on their way out and she stopped to comb her hair, or when she interrupted a soliloquy with questions he thought niggling or irrelevant. Calvin may have been in love, but so newly 'himself', that didn't mean he was patient.

He instructed the Kamba to meet him at the anchor line, but after they flipped off opposite sides he had surfaced to a manic churn. Working round on the ropes, he found Panga writhing and pawing at the boat, letting the swell surge over her snorkel, which was not even in her mouth. He found the demand valve and shoved it in her face, but it was difficult to get near her, with those limbs thrashing like a ceiling fan. He ferried her towards the anchor line and gave her the signal to descend, but Panga was less trying to submerge than to fly. Meanwhile her voice was of a ten-year-old child. *'Hapana!'* she said, high and breathless, the water frothing around her, outboard. 'Calvin!'

After five minutes this cut-throat mercenary, who could hike with seventy pounds of military hardware all night in thick bush, was utterly exhausted. Her breathing shrieked over the smack of the waves, and in those rare moments she had remembered to keep the reg in her mouth she had killed a quarter of the tank. He slew himself back into the boat and dragged her over the side with him. 'Forget it!'

Panga immediately went limp. As he pulled up anchor, she collapsed into the bottom, making no effort to pull off her gear. Calvin ripped the starter and admitted he'd not been very delicate about banging the inflatable against the swells. Usually so angular, Panga drooped boneless and rubbery, and bounced with every wave. Calvin didn't like, or, Eleanor sometimes thought, even comprehend weakness; it had taken him a little too long to feel sorry for the girl.

When they docked Panga wouldn't talk, but neither would she leave the boat. As it began to pelt, Calvin waited out the downpour in the car. Eleanor framed her through his drizzling window, her head draped between her knees with the snorkel poking out.

The squall passed. Calvin got out of the car. Panga raised her head.

'Shall we go?' he proposed.

'Down,' she growled.

'You want to try again?'

She had nodded resolutely. Eleanor posited that perhaps there was only one thing which mortified Panga more than this contrary white man's fondness for breathing under the sea, and that was disgrace. Bravery, Eleanor was sure, is not lack of fear but one more – the horrors of humiliation loom consumingly above the rest. 'No doubt,' Calvin concurred. 'And a little reputable cowardice at the outset would have saved her life.'

So he took her out once more. She was docile and mechanical and did everything he told her and went down just as in the swimming pool, though Eleanor suspected that if he could have seen those eyes behind the mask they would have been wide and blank. On the bottom, he held Panga's hand. It was flaccid. She had absented herself. Calvin might have reasoned that if she was not really there they were going to an awful lot of bother for nothing.

He had dived with Panga several more weekends. The panic never recurred. If Eleanor didn't miss her guess, Panga never suggested a trip to the coast, but she never rejected a proposal either, and doggedly hauled bottles and wet suits to the car. She never once would have intimated that she didn't enjoy it. Then, Eleanor noted, the woman had something to prove, and when you are trying to prove a lie you can never set about your demonstrations enough times.

There was a Second World War wreck near Diani, so he hired a boatman who knew the site. The weather was splendid. At the time, Calvin had been in that fulgent humour that he could now only recount like a statistic: I-was-exuberant – it was technical information about the past, the number on a cheque-stub, an old address.

For the second dive of the day, Calvin estimated they'd enough air left for a quick twenty-five-minute foray, though Panga's bottle, since she still breathed too fast, was lower than his own. He wanted Panga to get used to carrying the surface marker buoy, a balloon attached to a reel of line that kept the boatman apprised of their location. The quick-release clip with which the reel fastened to her stab jacket jammed, however, and, not thinking, he knotted it to a loop as a substitute. ('Stupid.') And he could swear he told her to tie off to the wreck once they found it, but maybe he hadn't. Probably the knot on the jacket was too tight. ('Easy to say now.')

All went according to plan until they found the hulk, and in a wink the current washed Panga from view. Calvin toured around the silenced rotors, blades poking from the heap like the ribs of rotting elephants. In death, he remarked, machines achieve an increasingly animate aspect, just as animals become objects; they meet in the middle. He had bonged the sides of the carcass, trying to attract Panga's attention, casting about overhead, unable to find the yellow line of the buoy. Calvin sighed into his regulator, the bubbles disgruntling overhead. He'd looked forward to this dive, all month inundated by the smelly crawl of unwanted babies across his desk, stuck in the traffic jams of spewing lorries full of rocks for more dumpy houses in this low-rent Eden, bustled by the *siafu* of pedestrians in town, hustled by legless beggars and shrill homeless scruff – he didn't want his brief respite from the multitudes cut short. Panga had been drilled, however, that if they ever got separated she should surface. Reluctantly he drifted back to the loud, jabbering, overrun world up top.

When he emerged, however, several hundred feet away there was the buoy, diddling in the poppled calm, and opposite the boat and its lone attendant: no Panga. Calvin checked his own air, and he hadn't more than ten minutes left himself. For the first time in water Calvin discovered what panic felt like. He lashed on to self-possession like tying his body to a post, and finned like the blazes on snorkel to the buoy. Calvin descended the line more quickly than was advisable, neglecting to clear his ears because he could not distinguish the pressure of the water from the pressure of imminent disaster.

The line led to the wreck itself; she had not tied off. He followed the nylon hand over hand and switched on his torch, remembering that Panga didn't have one and the dark of the corrupted corridors must have crowded her; he explained that it is almost as frightening underwater to run out of light as to run out of air. Still the cord proceeded in and out of portholes and through doorways. Air supply *very* low, but finally the rope led outside the wreck. At that moment the sun broke from behind a cloud, filtering through the sea and cruelly improving visibility.

For overhead, dangling at the end of the line like a hooked fish, was Panga. She listed to and fro in the current, relaxed underwater at last. As he rose, the bright yellow strap that bound her diving knife to her thigh caught the sun. The story was laid out for him: in trailing the rope through the wreck and out the other side, she had exhausted the reel and run out of line. It was knotted, he remembered, to her jacket. She had struggled towards the surface and been tied down. But he wanted Eleanor to taste the irony: here was a woman so adroit with knives that she was nicknamed after one, but that was in deserts. It had never occurred to her these edges applied to the undersea. Calvin slipped out his own dagger and cut her free, as she might have done for herself. He tried to inflate her jacket, but there was nothing in her tank but a sigh. The artificial respiration in the boat was merely a schoolroom exercise.

If you can scissor your own life into unrelated pieces of paper, that was where Calvin snipped his in half. For he despised his mother, 300 rancorous pounds of gin, and his father was going senile; he was an only child. None of his colleagues had ever been invited that step closer that would make them friends. According to Calvin, Panga was his lifeline to every attachment he had ever knotted to his own kind, though what he described as a cord Eleanor saw as a thread.

The slice through sentiment took effect right away. He left Panga's body carelessly in the bottom of the boat, curled as it had once been in shame, now in common abandonment. That was where it started, his merciless lack of sympathy for the dead. What did a little frenzy cost her? Did she feel bad? For Calvin that sprinkling of terror on a pretty day cost all he had.

To the boatman he must have seemed hard. They had dredged up his diving partner drowned and Calvin merely acted terse, out of sorts, jerking the anchor as if the accident were an inconvenience. The boatman asked if they should ring a hospital at the dock. 'What in God's name for?' asked Calvin incredulously, and that was their only discussion all the way to shore.

He drove her to the Mombasa morgue; Eleanor could see him sloping the Kamba over his shoulder with her fins batting at his thighs. Kenyan morgues were hellholes; thieves were always running off with the refrigeration. Here, too, he was surely curt and unceremonious and dropped her with the rest, willy-nilly on the floor, trying not to retch. Calvin planned to notify the family, he informed the attendant, who would have eyed him with slatternly savvy – did the *bwana* want to take the wet suit back? Of course the *mzungu* did not feel anything, because the corpse was black. And there would be no investigation; this was Africa.

Gunning off from the morgue, Calvin found he'd been in such a clench of fury that his jaw ached. He was afraid the anger wouldn't last, and did not feel prepared for what came next. The Nairobi – Mombasa road was death in the dark, and he had had enough of that, so when he passed a calamine-pink square signposted 'The Love-Stone Inn', Calvin pulled in.

Ensconced in the stark hotel room, with its squeaky camp-bed, one blanket and rickety wooden chair, Calvin stood under the swaying bare bulb convinced that the next few decisions he made, however trivial, could have profound consequences. He might go to sleep, but sleep was like diving, and he was not about to be lured into depths. With robotic determination, Calvin went to his briefcase and pulled out the latest addition to his library, *Bitter Pills: Population Policies and Their Implementation in Eight Developing Countries*. He put on his spectacles with all the grim resolution of a pilot donning his goggles for a bombing mission. He had never read any book with such intensity. He claimed that it did not matter which work it was, so long as the word *population* was somewhere in the title. This was his field. This was the issue he had given his life to.

Gradually the sun rose outside the window and he switched off the light. He turned his last few pages. Calvin could remember every point he contended, every anecdote of potential utility; he later employed some of them with Eleanor's stepfather. He slid the volume victoriously back into his briefcase. Calvin willingly admitted to no longer loving anyone, yet could not be accused of not loving any*thing*. He had salvaged a passion with *Bitter Pills* in a Gethsemene of a night after which he was resurrected as the demon of demography.

Unlike the tale of the poisoned girlfriends, Eleanor did not find this story romantic. She didn't care for that book at the end, not one bit.

'You say you "saved something". Saved *what*?'

He must have sensed she wasn't bowled over, but wouldn't go to lengths. 'My work.'

'Don't you think a more competent response to that event would have been a good long cry?'

'A little therapy, is it? I'd forgotten, the latest fashion in the States is grief. Perhaps Americans can afford to be keen, since in comparison to the rest of the world they've come to so little of it.'

'Did you think her drowning was your fault?'

'I made some misjudgements. But I believe you're missing the point.'

'I'm asking if you feel guilty.'

He rankled. 'It doesn't matter if I feel guilty. That is not the moral of our story. There isn't even a moral, but a fact, which does not lend itself to interpretation of any kind. Anything you might say about it, who is to blame, dwarfs before the big, stupid, immutable truth.'

'Which is?'

'*Panga is dead.*'

Eleanor was getting cross herself. 'That's your excuse?'

'I didn't ask to be excused.'

'You regard lying next to a – ' She finished with effort – 'an attractive woman night after night like an inert vanilla pudding as perfectly normal?'

'I have never aspired to norms.'

'Oh, right. We wouldn't want any passing relationship to intrude on your preoccupation with the fact that there are far too many of us to relate to.'

'I'm aware you find me insensitive. On the contrary, I am stifled by crowds because they asphyxiate me with suffering. Indeed, that is my shorthand definition of *over-population*: when you can no longer contain the whole of your race's anguish in your head without going insane. If I were as hard as you seem to think, I might easily share this planet with 5.3 billion failed romances, degenerative rheumatisms and disfiguring scars. As it is, I can't bear it.'

'Then there's no room for any of us, is there? You can't even hold your own anguish in your head.' She added as an afterthought, 'Let alone mine.'

As a display of his stupendous sensitivity, he let the remark slide.

'So you're trying to tell me that the reason you're so pathologically obsessed with population that you can't have sex and never, never think about anything else at all aside from the odd cup of cold coffee is that your girlfriend had an accident?'

Calvin rose and picked up *Stand on Zanzibar*, shoving it angrily on to a shelf. 'For some reason, while capable of following the quixotic emotional logic of their own history, most people still expect others' lives to read with the undemanding linearity of *Babar Goes to the Circus*. Yes, that is the "answer", as much as I have one: *Panga is dead*. If that doesn't make tidy story-book sense, I am terribly sorry.'

'It fascinates me,' she said to his back, 'that nowhere in exploring your problems does the information feature that you lost your job and your career is in the sewer. That's too *linear*, I suppose.'

He scooped up Malthus, who clambered to the usual shoulder and leered. Pointedly, Calvin chose a chair further from this harpy with no sympathy for his terrible experiences, and stationed himself with the monkey as if posing for a portrait. What a team.

'Pardon,' he said stiffly, recomposed. 'Which problems are these?'

Eleanor guffawed. 'You have almost nothing but!'

'Nonsense. The fact is, USAID did me a favour.'

'Like fun they did.'

'They stopped wasting my time. I no longer fritter my evenings popping finger sausages with congressmen to fund a sprinkling of unattended clinics. I am back,' he announced, 'to elephants.'

'It's always gratifying when you see fit to entrust me with the intimate details of your research.'

If anything, these carps of hers only drove him to be more secretive still. He smiled, curling the monkey's tail around his finger. 'Furthermore, I have found personal catastrophe professionally enlightening. Disaster on a small scale makes disaster on a global one easier to grasp. If my own life can fall apart, the earth I walk is not, therefore, a reliable place. Employed family men have no business in the sciences of dread, for no matter what our dedicated professional studies, his stable universe is a faithful dog. My universe has bitten me on the leg. Big bad things do happen, because they have happened to me.'

'You do feel terribly sorry for yourself.'

He considered, looking in Malthus's eyes. 'I do often feel *sorry* for myself, but I am oblivious to my future. An attitude I fear extends rapidly to the rest of the species.'

'Why do you bother prophesying disaster all day if our future doesn't matter to you?'

'I don't bother, always,' he said lightly. 'Have I ever told you about *neutrality*?'

Eleanor felt a queasy foreboding. 'No.'

'It's a term I've coined for a little affliction of mine that doesn't seem to be curable and lately is getting worse. The condition kicks in at the most arbitrary times. Everything goes horribly equal. I feel intensely *interested* in people, but I don't care what happens to them. I experience curiosity but never revulsion. I am not upset by the torture of political prisoners in Somalia, but I might be intrigued by the techniques. Barbarisms from Caligula to Pol Pot fail to excite my distress or even regret. If anything I'm rather grateful for a monster or two just for the variety, like a few bombastic chords in a quiet quartet. That's it – the world goes to music. Now, there's trivial music or loud or dull, but there's no such thing as wicked music. Do you understand? I become an impartial voyeur who isn't fussed what occurs as long as something does and I get to watch. I do recall that once this intellectual weightlessness descended on me while I listened to some medical chap depict the consequences of all-out nuclear war. The details made Nevil Shute sound like *Bartholomew and the Oobleck*. Of course, neutral, I found the prospect of no more life on earth perfectly *interesting*. All I could say afterwards was, "Well. What is wrong with rock?" I remember feeling very peaceful myself, but the conversation came to a complete halt and in two minutes flat the whole dinner party of guests came up with reasons why they had to leave early.'

She stood up. 'I might have called it an early night myself.'

'You haven't understood a word I've said.'

'I've understood perfectly well. I think you're depressed. I think you're incredibly cut off and withdrawn and terrified to have feelings because then you might get hurt. And I'm quite tired of listening to men describe how they've turned into emotional fence posts as if it's some kind of achievement. It's flagrant cowardice. Now let's go to sleep. I know I'm not an exotic black mercenary, but you could at least put an arm around me. I seem to have caught a chill.'

9

The Enigma Variations

Eleanor woke the next morning curt, and plumped the impression of her head from the pillow as if trying to irradicate any trace of her presence from the bed.

Calvin had risen irritable as well. 'After all my effort describing a severe and congenital case of the existentials,' he said at breakfast, 'you make the momentous pronouncement that I am *depressed*. It is so like a woman to reduce philosophy to petty distress. I sometimes worry if your sex is capable of pure thought. Nothing seems real to women besides *feelings*.'

'And nothing is real to men but facts. Do you think we'd have names for emotions if they didn't exist?'

'By that logic, witches and dwarfs and goblins are all leaping about the room because we have words for them.'

'In your house?' Eleanor drawled. 'Maybe they are.'

'Perhaps in future,' he announced, while scanning his latest issue of *Omni*, 'I should keep my confidences to myself. They don't seem to bring us closer, do they?'

'It's a little unreasonable to expect me to get weepy over one of your old lovers. Especially if she explains why I spend most nights curled around a doorstop.'

'No one is forcing you to sleep with me.'

'No one is forcing you to be celibate. Do you think she's watching or something?'

'Yes,' he said coolly. 'Panga has been in Eritrea, but she got back last week.'

'Weirdo,' Eleanor muttered.

'I'm afraid you disappointed me last night,' he continued, in glasses, still reading. 'I'm sometimes convinced you have no interest in what I've been through, least of all in anything I think. You seem solely concerned with how I care for you.'

'In which case I'm not concerned with very much.'

'You cheat yourself, Eleanor. You are in the presence of major historical forces. They are far more fascinating than whether I hold your hand.'

'Well, maybe I'm just a dizzy, air-headed nit who only cares about boys. That's why I'm thirty-eight, single, childless and have spent my whole life working in Third World population assistance. I set myself up in Dar es Salaam to find a man, and I chose to look for one in a hot, smelly, barren garbage heap because I'm an idiot.'

'I was trying to give you some advice. If you're insistent on conducting your mental life on the trifling level of *relationships*, I can't stop you . . . now, hold on!' He interrupted her indignant departure with a hand on her arm. 'When are you coming back?'

'Tomorrow,' she said reluctantly. 'Maybe.'

'Tonight.'

'Why should I?'

'I've grown accustomed to your face,' he sang merrily, Rex Harrison. 'Come here straight from work. I won't be back till eight; take the key. Put your feet up with this month's *Demography*; then we'll step out. Now you may go. You're late.' He went back to his magazine.

Eleanor might have taken heart that she was getting a reaction, and any was more important than what kind; and that if it behooved Calvin to deride *relationships* this implied that they actually had one.

The trouble was, she was desperately jealous of a dead person. Panga was so perfectly designed to make Eleanor feel inadequate that Calvin might have made her up. Worst of all, she was black. How delicious it must feel to be a victim for once instead of one more unwilling perpetrator.

Eleanor returned after work as she was told, fighting the impulse to apologize. As ever she felt watched; if anything, the sensation was the more violent in Calvin's absence. She paused before the study, with its gleaming row of brass locks.

'Panga?' she asked out loud. 'Did he ever let you in here?'

Was it whim or did someone over her shoulder suggest she

125

try the knob? To her astonishment, it gave. Perhaps he now trusted her enough to leave it open, so she nervously accepted the compliment.

The room was larger than she had expected, its lighting bright and clinical. Its absence of windows created the atmosphere of an underground bunker. The desk was arrayed with a row of screens, and the computer was a massive high-capacity model that must have cost – she couldn't say. But that was no home-office laptop.

When she turned to the walls, she felt intensely she shouldn't be here. On the one side was a montage of photographs – severed heads in Salvador, hacked children in Mozambique, careless rumples of discarded bodies in Chatila, bloated Ugandan torture victims by crocodiles.

The opposite wall was papered with graphs, the lines swooping and peaking and plummeting, their design Miro, Klee, portraiture. So this is what it looked like inside Calvin Piper's head. When she inspected more closely, all the high points before the ski slope down were labelled 'Crop Failure', 'Malaria', 'Plague'. One aspirant worm wriggled ever upwards: 'AIDS'. The borders of this composition was framed by all the careening streaks of Third World population Eleanor had grown so tired of.

She scanned the bookshelves behind her: years of *Morbidity and Mortality Reports; Plagues and Peoples; Population and Disaster*. Along with the usual journals, she found a peculiar preponderance of highly technical epidemiology texts.

She could not put her finger on what was wrong, but her uneasiness went beyond having ventured into his study without permission. Germanically organized, this was not the messy crumple of clippings she'd have expected, the notes and motley stacks of a man trying haphazardly to keep up with a field in which he no longer played an active part. The room was concentrated and clean. When she noticed there was text on one computer screen, and print-out on the desk, Eleanor stepped away. She remembered an earlier temptation, and once in a great while you learn from your mistakes.

She had been seriously involved with a man in DC, Edward, and Edward had left a letter out, opened and in its envelope, addressed in a willowy hand. She knew he saw other women, but only as friends. It was easy to rationalize that if Edward left it so carelessly available he subconsciously wanted her to read it, just as Calvin had lured her with an unlocked door. Freud is handy for the prying. Well, in DC she'd burnt her fingers, and her bridges. When she confronted Edward, he could never forgive her for invading his privacy; she could never forgive him for lying. The point was, having invited them, she could never get those phrases out of her head: *the most exotic sex I have ever known ... I can't understand how you put up with that Eleanor doormat.* Once you have allowed information into your life, you cannot get it out. She reasoned that innocence, naïvety, even gormlessness were often preferable to feeling completely sick. Why, the affair might have blown over, and she could still have married him, deluded and happier for it. Studying the aqua pulse of text a few feet away, still mercifully undecipherable, she was reminded of Threadgill's advice, that there are moves you can make forward that you cannot take back, and Calvin's computer screen was like that: if she read it, she could never unread it. Eleanor treasured her ignorance so would protect its bliss. She backed all the way out of the study and pulled the door to, clinging to the world in which it is still possible to shut Pandora's box even if you have peeped inside for an instant.

Eleanor retreated to the living room and stared at the bone. She wouldn't roam the house, refusing any more discoveries. Lately her posture had improved, but now she slumped like a teenager. She picked up pulp sci-fi for something to hold. Eleanor had always defended herself with books; she wore hardbacks like sun-glasses. It was the house itself tonight that she held at bay, and she guarded her place like a sulky *askari* with a *rungu* in his lap who spoke only Swahili and would do his job, but who had no idea what the *mzungu* who hired him was up to and didn't care either and was only waiting for his shift to be over so he could go home.

Calvin returned springy but inattentive. Claiming to have a quick phone call to make, as usual he ignored the phone beside her and strode to his office as Eleanor bulwarked behind trashy fiction. She heard him fit a key, lock, unlock – so he had left the office open by accident. The door slammed. While he was gone, Eleanor created the sound of turning pages with fraudulent absorption. Calvin was in his office a long time.

The man who emerged was a man she had never met. His progress down the hall was grave, where Calvin's common pace was brisk; and his face had lost the asymmetry of sarcasm. Why, she must never have seen Calvin completely serious. His whole body was ominously at rest; the relaxation was somehow frightening. Having arrived in the living room, he did not aim directly for her chair, but stepped sideways towards the front door. Eleanor had the irrational impression he was blocking her exit.

'Why don't we start with why you stayed.' His voice, too, had changed, lower and even softer, and she only now noticed that he would ordinarily talk from the side of his mouth, because he finally talked from its centre. In other circumstances, she might have felt overjoyed: at long last the real Calvin Piper had spoken. Just now, however, she would have gratefully taken the entertainingly embittered fake, as she also preferred the contented delusion of his locked office door.

'I don't know what you mean,' Eleanor peeped from over the book, her own voice gone squeaky. 'You said wait for you till eight. So I did.'

'You're a terrible liar, Eleanor.' He sounded tired. 'I simply don't understand why you didn't clear out. I might easily have had you stopped, even at the airport. But I'm surprised you didn't give it a go.'

Eleanor maintained her stolid incomprehension. Calvin sighed. 'You put me in an awkward position. Now I don't know what to do with you.'

'Dinner would be nice.' She tried a smile, but her crumpled grin might have just collided with an oncoming *matatu*.

'Panga would shoot you. Wouldn't even say a word, just walk straight in and shoot you, and rout the disks from your dress. But I'm afraid she wasn't alive here long enough to teach me much. Dead, she can only make suggestions; otherwise, I'm on my own. She always found me a little wet. At the moment, I'm inclined to agree. After all, I do have a revolver in the bedroom. I could have fetched it before I came in. I thought about it. But I didn't. Perhaps I'm not quite up to playing my part. I'm a bit disappointed in myself.'

'Calvin, have you lost your mind?'

'I have kept up appearances. I dab the corners of my mouth after dining. I do not drive my Land Cruiser through the middle of the Karen Provision Store. When you say, "Good morning", I do not return, "Stink-suck-ga-ga", but, "Lovely day." That is all the sanity the world requires. They really don't care what you're thinking.' Again, what he would ordinarily deliver with a smirk hadn't a trace of humour. Eleanor thought, my God, this man has been pretending to be a nay-saying buffoon, and if that is only a performance, a distraction, *who is he really and what has he been distracting me from*?

Calvin nodded to the chair opposite. 'You realize she finds this hilarious. And me pathetic. Then, it's all a game to her, everything always was. She never cared who died or who killed her. And she doesn't care either what happens to my project, whether you spanner it. I care about it, however; it is all I care about. So you see my quandary. If she finds it funny, I don't.'

'*Who* are you talking about?'

'Can't you see her? Panga told me that sometimes you did. She's given you more credit than I have from the start. She said you would surprise me. I've been waiting. Now you have, once: you're still here. I'm not sure how to interpret it. Were you hoping to confront me? Did you have some sad, woman's idea of talking me out of it? Or – ' She saw a flicker of anxiety. 'Do you have a plan?' He took a step forward. 'Did you make any phone calls?'

She flinched. 'No.'

'You're not meant to keep me here? Nattering away as I always do? Don't you think that was abusive of them? To put you in this position? Don't you think they knew I was dangerous?'

'Calvin, I didn't make any phone calls. I haven't told anyone anything.'

He grunted, and was moved to sit down. He clasped his hands conversationally. 'No, I suppose you didn't. As I said, I can tell when you're lying; you're an improbably transparent woman. Besides, Panga says she was watching. You haven't finked. Yet.'

It was a slow dance, and she had accepted. It's tricky, as

the second in command, to negotiate the floor, to anticipate feints to the left or right, to execute moves the partner determines as if of perfect like minds. It was critical for grace to keep the delay between signal and submission as short as possible.

'I might lock you in the bedroom,' he speculated. 'Feed you along with Malthus. But I would have to keep you for years. You'd get depressed, and I would feel guilty.'

'Why do you assume,' stepped Eleanor (*left, right*), 'that I will tell anyone? About – ' She paused. 'Your project?' That was it: the move from which there was no retreat. The ledge was waiting.

'Haven't you spent your life trying to help people? Aren't you still a compliant girl trying to impress Stepdaddy with how upstanding you are? Aren't you revolted? I didn't think we had managed to broaden your horizons as far as all that. You are still, though you dress better, an earnest, liberal Democrat. Why not try to stop me, then? Wouldn't that make Raymond's day?'

'Because,' she calculated, 'I love you.'

It was the only answer he could conceivably accept. He might never know if it was true or merely ingenious. Eleanor wasn't sure herself.

'That's just an idea you've got,' Calvin fumbled. 'You want to love someone. I'm nearby, and a bloody queer choice. But there is nothing to love. You'll find that out soon enough and become a liability. Vengeful, if I fail you, which I'm bound to.'

'Panga's right,' countered Eleanor. 'You underestimate me.'

'I cannot imagine you think it's a fabulous idea.' He seemed offended at the prospect. Much as he might entice her to dinners without doggie bags, she was meant to give him a proper contest. He wanted a fight. That would be hard to organize, since Eleanor hadn't the foggiest what the argument was over.

'No,' she said, 'I don't. I think you are afflicted. I think you've – dismantled.' Eleanor said anything that came into her head. 'This *neutrality*. Isn't it merely a haven from agony?'

'Is it inconceivable to you I should have a conviction, just one, that doesn't have to do with a frivolous psychological maladjustment? Does the rest of the world exist to you at all?

Does everything you see reduce down to you, your lovers and your friends?'

'Most of the time,' she conceded, 'yes.'

'So you have to drag me down to your level.'

'Or up.'

'But don't you have anything to say? Don't you find my intentions frightful?'

'Quite,' said Eleanor.

'So will you not regale me? Where's the we-shall-overcome rhetoric now that you need it? Aren't Ray and Jane let down? Did you ever where-have-all-the-flowers-gone with any feeling, or did you just want a bunch of adolescent long-hairs to like you?'

'What good would consternation do? Have I ever convinced you of anything? And why give you the satisfaction?'

'The satisfaction would be entirely yours. Boldly defending your values, what sorry tatters are left of them. Most liberals spend their lives at piety, indulging the same selfish, destructive habits as everyone else but decrying them the while and therefore feeling superior. Everyone is bad, but liberals *know* they're bad, which, in the convoluted hypocrisy of their creed, somehow makes them good. They talk a lot. They also drink a lot, understandably. This is your big chance. Grandstand. Please.'

Eleanor reached for one of Calvin's own phrases, 'In due course,' and added, 'I don't harangue on command. And I'm willing to hear your side of this. After all, hasn't this – project – been in the works for a while?'

'Six years.'

'So you must have built quite a case by now.'

'I have. I don't expect you to be susceptible. You don't take nearly enough trips to outer space. Intellectually, you're provincial.'

'This isn't the hard sell, Calvin. Now you're disappointing me.'

Calvin rubbed his chin. 'I can't get over it. I expected you'd be hysterical.'

'I get hysterical when for the third week in a row there is no water and I can't bathe. I get hysterical over trivia – like most people. On issues of import I am level-headed. I spent my childhood in books, my adulthood in offices. I can even sleep placidly by you night after night and be *reconciled*. I imagine that makes me an abomination of what a real woman was meant to be, but my culture has done its dastardly work and this is the result. So if you were hoping for tearful entreaty, sorry. You're not the only monster in this house. I'm still waiting for you to defend yourself. Besides, am I right, that you have yet to do anything dire?'

He grunted. 'We're still drafting.'

'So you're hot air, too. Like the rest.'

'I have never at any point in my career been hot air.'

'Oh, man of action,' she jeered. 'Great White Hunter of the population game.'

'We have to get our parameters straight. They are nearly complete. If *who* is not solved before *how*, the whole scheme could end up a hash.'

' "Parameters – ?" '

'You didn't get to read much in there, did you?'

She answered honestly, 'No.'

'The issues are stupendously complex,' he began, no longer able to remain seated and beginning to pace. 'How much of the reproductive age to target, how much to trim off the bottom and the top so we're left with a viable society and not just a crop of kids and their grandmothers. That's one of the problems of AIDS, you see: too centre-cut. Or economics: maintaining enough of an adult labour pool, keeping agricultural and industrial capacities viable. In all these calculations, there has to be a wide acceptable margin of error. And there will be sacrifices, even cock-ups – we're resigned to that. Sectors of some economies, or possibly whole countries, may fall out. Yet they will, based on research of earlier cataclysms – wars, natural plagues and famines – recover with astonishing rapidity.'

Eleanor was beginning to feel physically strange – carbonated and lifted above the sofa. She felt obscenely calm. The room had scooped and upended, as if reflected in a spoon. Calvin, worked up now, wanting to explain the *complexities*, sounded like a small boy piping about his go-cart. Eleanor was trapped humouring this *enfant terrible* when she would prefer to slip over and gossip with Panga. She wanted to tittle-

132

tattle about boyfriends. Did he tell you about his work, Panga? Could you make head or tail of it? Eleanor had been a precocious child, an articulate woman, but just now she would like to be a pea-brain. She defended herself with all the feeble-mindedness she could marshall, but intelligence, like information, cannot be defeated; it is simply there. So she knew. She had not said it to herself in so many words, but she knew. She wondered when she would have a reaction.

'The stickiest wicket is politics,' Calvin was exhorting. 'It would have been more ideologically convenient to move twenty years ago, when growth rates in the First and Third World weren't quite so disparate. But now the First World barely has a growth rate. Yet if we strike only in undeveloped countries, we create a politically destabilizing situation of astounding proportions. Therefore, we must take a token shave off the US, Europe, Russia. And more than a shave off China, that goes without saying. They're already backing us heavily, and they've more than a clue what we're up to.'

'Calvin,' she asked nicely, 'how many?'

'Good question. Ehrlich thinks a steady-state of three is ideal. But we think that's a bit low, and besides, probably overly optimistic on the technical side. We could see ending up at five, about where we are now – crowded, but a damned sight preferable to fourteen. We may even be stuck with six, at the end of the day. But to finish up at six, you've absolutely got to cut back to four by the turn of the century. So that means taking two, minimum, off the top. We're setting our sights on 1999. We thought Nostradamus would be pleased.'

'Have you noticed,' she inquired, 'that when you quote these figures you leave off the *billion* part?'

'Even great white demographers have their shy side.'

'There's another word you're not using. It's ordinarily such a favourite.'

'Which is?'

'Death. Or,' she corrected, '*mortality*. Since death gets on your hands, doesn't it? *Mortality* happens only on paper.'

'What are you getting at?'

'I want you to do me a favour. I want you to say out loud – ' She took a breath. 'Out loud to my face: *in 1999 I plan to murder two billion people.*'

133

'Mmm,' he hummed noncommittally. 'I am devising a strategic, first-strike cull of the human race. In the interests of preventing extinction; or worse, the devolution of the species to head lice.'

'No. Say it. The way I said it. I don't ask for much.'

He shrugged. 'Very well. In 1999 I plan to murder two billion people. Happy?'

She looked at him in dull disbelief. She felt – well, she felt absolutely nothing, if she was to be honest. The concept was too big and bizarre to get her head around. It remained a sentence. She had no response besides, *What?*, an insipid compulsion to ask him to say it again when she had heard him the first time. In fact, her strongest impulse was to laugh. Curiously, had Calvin confessed plans to kill a single rival – say, Wallace Threadgill – she would be up in arms, telling him to be sensible, that there were limits. If he proposed killing two billion instead she couldn't come up with a reaction of any description. Who could take this seriously? But look at him. She had never seen him more serious in his life. Is this *neutrality*, Calvin? Have you sucked me to Andromeda as well?

Abruptly a great deal of what had always seemed unfathomable to Eleanor now made sense. How many autocrats had supposed about earlier nuisances, 'Don't you sometimes want them to *go away*?' It was easier to eliminate six million than 6,000, or six – somehow, the more zeros the better. Calvin had added nine of them.

Numbly, she asked the logical next question. 'How?'

'QUIETUS – '

'What's that?'

He looked at her sharply.

'I mean,' said Eleanor hastily, 'what does it stand for?'

'Quorum of United International Efforts at Triage for Ultimate Sustainability. QUIETUS has code-named the apparatus Pachyderm. We're exploring viruses, fast-acting poisons, microbes. But the technical parameters – '

'More *parameters*,' Eleanor moaned.

'Are staggering. Pachyderm has to be quick, single application, taking no more, say, than a week, ideally overnight. Can't allow time for some beneficent to cook up a cure. And we are opposed to suffering. Most deaths are painful, that can't be helped, but prolonged moribundity is unacceptable. The most difficult engineering feat, however, is to target the proper percentage of the population. We need an ailment to which 30 to 35 per cent are susceptible and the rest immune. And Pachyderm has to slice the proper age groups. Still, you'd be amazed, with a grasp of DNA, what's possible. How tailored a virus can be.'

'But you're no epidemiologist.'

'I *know* epidemiologists. Just as I know economists, biologists and more sophisticated demographic modellers than I. Believe me, I know the best of them all.'

'Surely no scientist of integrity – '

'You'd be surprised.'

She was not surprised, or only at herself, at her capacity to pursue like a thorough journalist with a micro-cassette, 'You're not getting involved in eugenics, are you?' How could she even think of such questions? *What had Calvin done to her?*

'We toyed with eugenics at first. But the demographics alone are formidable. We had to stick to our purpose – quantity, not quality. It was not out of the question, I suppose, to design an organism that only attacked stupid people. But I have a soft spot for stupid people; some of the most endearing sorts I've met have been pig thick. It's the clever ones cause all the trouble.'

'Like you.'

'Like me.'

'I don't understand your angle on this whole thing.'

'I have lots of them. I find it likely, for example, that I am a ghastly mutation that must be stopped. In which case, someone must stop me. But that's not my job. I don't have to do everything, do I? Perhaps it's yours, Eleanor.'

'I haven't applied.'

'Anyway, eugenics?' he resumed gamily, tossing one of Malthus's chewed-bald tennis balls up and down. 'I suppose if we're to dwell in the realm of fantasy – '

'Which we have been doing all night – '

'It would be attractive to target the chromosome of sadistic deviance – to concoct a little nostrum that eradicated all the horrible people.'

'Everyone's horrible some of the time.'

'Most of the time. There'd be no one left. But if I could be selective? I would save the contented. Ordinary, pleasant people, not very thoughtful and with no ambition and hopelessly in love with someone who loved them back. Only a handful would remain, but that might be a planet I could stand.'

'You would never qualify.'

'The very attraction of the vision is as a world where I wouldn't belong. Groucho Marx.'

He bounced the ball medatively on the wooden floor, *pong, pong.* 'We shelved the eugenics angle early on. It was a biological can of worms and a moral hornet's nest.' *Pong.* 'Instead, we will design Pachyderm to imitate nature: gross, random unfairness, with no regard for excellence or good behaviour. The trouble is – ' *Pong, pong.* 'Nature hasn't been doing a good enough job, though she will eventually move in if we don't, and – ' *pong* – 'without *parameters*. Nature doesn't care about suffering. Smallpox, leprosy, plague? Only humans have invented injections and overdoses of sleeping pills. Mind, I don't especially want to kill anyone.' *Pong.* 'I just don't want them to be there any more.'

Thwap. The tennis ball hit the carpet. To Eleanor's relief, he left it there; its relentless punctuation had been driving her mad. Maybe it was true, then, that only the little things got under her skin.

'You don't want a virus,' she said, nudging the ball out of his reach with her toe. 'You want an eraser.'

'With what's feasible now, an eraser's not far-fetched.' His eyes ranged the table for another object to torment. His hands clawed at each other's already clean, pearly nails, until they discovered the glasses in his shirt pocket, and set about furiously de-smearing their lenses with the tail. It would take one thorough burnishing, Eleanor reflected, to get Calvin Piper to see straight.

'Though we have faced logistical limits,' he admitted, the shirt-tail circles becoming obsessively tinier. 'At the outset, we investigated substances which merely created a percentage persistence of infertility. We came up against a technological brick wall. It is our command of death that has advanced in this century, well beyond research in contraception. I don't need to tell you that this species has designed a hydrogen bomb, but not a birth control pill without side effects.' He tried on the spectacles and didn't seem to like what he saw; he took them off and sat down.

'We also pursued libido suppressants,' he proceeded, holding his frames up to the light and squinting. He seemed to be talking to himself; no doubt he did talk to himself like this all the time. No wonder his coffee got cold. 'Benperidol, ethinyl oestradiol and cyproterone acetate – drugs that were originally developed to administer to convicted perverts. But they had almost no effect at all on the sexual enthusiasm of test populations. Did you realize,' he raised brightly, with the amiable informativeness of a cocktail party anecdote, 'that the main reason people copulate is not to orgasm?'

Eleanor was all too aware she was not at a party. 'You said eugenics was a "moral hornet's nest". Do you mean QUIE-TUS is considering the ethics of Pachyderm at all?'

'Almost nothing but. Find it ironic as you like, but QUIE-TUS is my very purchase on morality. Its sole purpose is the perpetuation of the human race in some form any of us can tolerate. This is not *neutrality*, my dear. This is Calvin Piper with his feet on the ground.'

Calvin's feet were propped high on his elephant bone.

'Now, I concede we run into ends-means problems.' Calvin rose and began to pace again, professorial. All he lacked was a pointer and a blackboard, and he glanced over at his student's increasingly lassitudinous sag on the sofa as if annoyed she was not taking notes. 'But that has always been a bugbear for ethicists, hasn't it? Thou shalt not kill, and then you let the Japanese help themselves to Hawaii? If someone doesn't do something about population, we are headed for a brutal, cramped, cultureless, cut-throat *sty*. I believe that, Eleanor, it is all I believe. I'm willing to prevent it, even if the cure is cruel. Ends have justified means from the year dot. Doctors routinely amputate a gangrenous limb to save the whole body from a lingering, terminal rot.'

'You're staking so much on being right.' Eleanor refused to follow his back and forth, and picked up the mauled, sickly chartreuse tennis ball, cupping it protectively in her hands.

Tossing it up and down, bouncing it around his rarified cloister – that was what Calvin did with an entire *planet*. 'What if Wallace has the ticket after all?' she pursued, smoothing the remaining tufts of the tattered toy. 'What if population is a bogyman? A fashionable fable of our times, like blood-letting?'

'Everyone always thinks they're right.'

'That's what I mean.'

'Follow that thinking and you never do anything, ever, your whole life. You're recommending self-doubt so deep that it amounts to permanent paralysis. It is always possible that you are wrong. But you can only proceed with a life on the assumption that you are right. Otherwise you sit eighty-five years in a chair.'

It was still only the middle of the evening, yet Eleanor found it impossible to rouse the liberal indignation that Calvin required from her – positively craved, since he could no longer rouse it from himself; what is more, she felt narcotically tired. Her lids were heavy. Her chin kept dropping to her chest. The tennis ball rolled from her hands and dribbled towards the monkey, and even Malthus could not be bothered to play with it. 'Calvin.' Her tongue was thick. 'This target population of yours. Of whom is it largely comprised?'

'Well . . .' For the first time he showed visible signs of embarrassment and met her eyes with effort. 'It's been impossible to get around, you know. Especially in the Third World. Age structure. There's not much choice. And we've thought about it – morally – there's no difference. It sounds bad. But there are no special classes of humanity that it is particularly villainous to kill.'

'Who?' she asked dully, only wanting to sleep.

'Children.' His eyebrows took a brief, apologetic shrug. 'Not only. But well over half, according to the computer, should be under the age of fifteen. In principle I don't think it matters a jot. But it's bad PR.'

Finally she allowed herself to laugh. 'You're going to rub out two billion people and you're worried about your *image*?'

'Of course. I'm not qualified in microbiology, so while QUIETUS is my brainchild my major role is fund-raising. You remember the hoo-ha at my suggestion that we eliminate infant mortality and child survival programmes in Africa.

Even among the ruthless, you find these maudlin areas. So we've kept this parameter quiet.'

'I'd think you'd keep the whole proposition quiet.'

'Only a small central core know the full scope of our campaign. So welcome to the inner circle – whether you like it or not.'

'Forgive me if I feel less than honoured.'

'I never meant to drag you in. This enterprise is a bit of a millstone.'

'I'll say.' She allowed herself, for a good thirty seconds, to shut her eyes.

'There's one other matter – ' again, a tinge of chagrin – 'which we don't often raise. It has played a role in our mathematics, though the effect is difficult to gauge.'

'What?' She really didn't want to hear any more.

'Um. Bodies.' He coughed. 'There will be scads. Disposal will be problematic. A subsequent outbreak of opportunistic infections is inevitable.'

'Put the fat people on top,' she slurred. 'The grease drizzles down and makes the whole pile burn better.'

'We're not concerning ourselves with this,' he hurried. 'Dust to dust and that. Over time, the problem solves itself. Yet including the physical remains in our calculations is understandably unpleasant.'

'Why not can the meat? Isn't that what you did with elephants?'

'I can see you're going to be a great help.'

'You imagine you could live with yourself afterwards?'

'Living with myself is already rather tedious. Of course it will be tempting to leap from a Nyayo House window. But that would be selfish.'

'How so?'

'A scapegoat is a sociological necessity.'

'Do you ever suspect yourself of a Christ complex?'

'A mass murderer makes an unlikely Messiah. And my martyrdom will be no great sacrifice. I shall find my trial terrifically *interesting*.'

'Neutrality.'

'About my own death I have no feelings whatsoever.'

'I do.'

'Save your concern for the more deserving. I'm just a binman. I take out the rubbish so the rest of the world can get on with symphonies. It has to be done, Eleanor. And I don't care how they damn me later. You may imagine my designs as egotistical. On the contrary, if the death of two billion don't matter, I can at least follow the logic that mine doesn't amount to much either. And if QUIETUS succeeds, I will be only too happily boiled in oil. If I fail, we should both find bare bodkins. Because I have seen into the future if no one hacks back on our profusion while there's time. You will not want to be alive then, Eleanor, though the worst will occur in your lifetime. Especially in Africa. If population is allowed to take its natural course, a hundred years from now *the death of two billion will be nothing.*'

Calvin truly believed what he was saying, and this kept her from despising him. Then, she was not so inclined. Instead, she felt more sorry for him than ever, motherly. She drew him over to the couch. 'I know you don't want me to care for you. But I do. And now, more than ever, it looks as if you and I are stuck with each other.'

Calvin put his head in her lap, and she stroked his thick black hair. 'There's only one thing you must tell me,' she said. 'And I want you to be honest.'

'What's that?'

'Is this a joke?' It was her last chance.

He sighed. 'I am not pulling your leg, but all these parameters: they are difficult to satisfy. There is only a small percentage chance we will solve Pachyderm. If we do not, we sit tight. In the meantime, there are mattressfuls of money about. We may accomplish nothing, my darling, but we will live nicely.'

'So if you don't find this perfect, painless, overnight, statistically precise organism to do your "rubbish collection", you just theorize.'

'Right. Have meetings and lunches and clip newspapers. It's far less likely that I finish on a gallows than by choking on prawn pili-pili at the Rickshaw.'

He had finally said something to help her. Of course the proposition was lunatic. Would he ever do anything besides con mean-spirited donors into paying his exorbitant dinner tabs?

'Put some music on,' he requested.

She slipped up for Elgar. Though weary, she stayed awake, smoothing his forehead. They said nothing. The music was beautiful.

At the pitch of an oboe cadenza, the CD cut clean off, along with the lights. The electricity died all the time now. In the subsequent silence, hyenas ka-rooed from the park; hyraxes screeched on the roof; moonlight hit the elephant femur, which glowed an eerie blue-white. Panga grinned from the opposite chair and slid her *kukri* from its sheaf. Eleanor felt a sickly thrill, imagining what real social collapse might be like. It was clearly a life without Elgar. In Nairobi there was already a scarcity of electricity, water, natural gas and wheat. Further north, another famine was projected for Ethiopia, Somalia, the Sudan . . . The only complaint she could make about his predictions of approaching degradation was that so much of Calvin's future had arrived.

'Have you read *Fahrenheit 451*?' Calvin asked in the dark, after what seemed eons. Odd, how long time lasted without electricity, as if a stopped clock held you in its eternity.

'No.'

'It's another post-awfulness novel. A fascist government has burned all the books. There's a resistance underground, each member of which has memorized a work of literature cover to cover – *Alice in Wonderland*. They've retrieved civilization by becoming walking libraries.'

'So?'

'I've wondered if you could save music the same way – with no more recording, or violin repairmen, scores long ago up in flames. Maybe I should start memorizing Mozart's Requiem. Learn to whistle the bassoon part or something.' He attempted a few bars, but couldn't overcome the animals outside and gave up.

10

A Drive to Bob's Save-Life Bar

Eleanor slept so deeply that waking was like crawling up a shaft. Half-way up, she could discern a dawning over its rim, the light an altered colour: something had happened last night. There was something she hadn't remembered yet and she sank back, hoping she could fail to remember a little longer.

It was a familiar morning sensation. How many times had she cracked open puffy eyelids to shut them again, face tight, head pounding, mouth dry, trying to go back to sleep but unable to fight memory: right, X and I broke up last night, or Y is having an affair, and has been, it turns out, all year – and that is why my face is a mess and that is why my head hurts and that is why the pillow next to me is empty.

But underneath her fingers was chest. There were arms around her. Why, she was intertwined with a handsome man, who was holding her closer than he had ever done, so that when she did recall he wanted to obliterate two billion people she was relieved.

Calvin kissed her. 'Aren't you afraid of me now?'

'I've always been afraid of you, Calvin.' She moved her knee between his thighs.

Breakfast, however, was both warm and wary. Neither had an appetite. They sat on opposite sides of the table. Calvin didn't say much, drumming his fingers.

'I want the disks back,' he said at last.

'Disks?'

'What can you possibly do with those files? Send them to the WHO and demand they rescind my funding for having drawn it on false pretenses? They can't be authenticated. I could always claim I was writing a science fiction novel.'

'I don't have any disks.'

'You might try the Kenyan government,' he recommended. 'Moi would credit any Western skulduggery. Put the story in the *Nation*, it wouldn't even stand out. "American Population Expert Apprehended in Genocidal Subterfuge".' He flipped the paper on the table. 'Look here, we could fit it side by side with "USA, Shop-Window of the Earth's Evils".'

'I did walk into your office yesterday, I admit. You left it open. I read a few book titles and looked at your disgusting photographs. The room gave me the creeps. I left. I took nothing. I read no papers, no screens. Everything I learned about your unhinged confederacy you told me last night.'

'You mean, you didn't – '

'You wanted to tell me, Calvin. Keeping it to yourself was making you lonely. And now we can discuss it, and it's all you want to talk about.'

'When you came here yesterday, was the front door locked?'

'Come to think of it – no.'

'I thought I locked my office. I was sure I had.'

'What's the problem?'

'A box of floppies has been lifted.'

'You didn't lose them?'

'You've seen my office. Does it look like the kind of room where important files would get mislaid?'

She remembered the methodical stacking of every print-out, each pen in its place. 'Well, no. But who on earth – '

'Threadgill.'

'But why – ?'

Calvin was inaccessible for a minute or two.

'You said I couldn't do anything with those files; QUIETUS is too preposterous. Threadgill would confront the same incredulity.'

'I am not concerned with Mr Jolly-hockey-sticks turning to an authority. But he could be a force to be reckoned with in his own right.'

'I got the impression he was an eccentric, hermetic guru in a tent. A bit of a fruit – like you. I don't see why he'd worry you.'

'Wallace is a tit, but he keeps a hand in. These fluffernutters, they club together and agree how everything is pink and how very, very much pinker the whole world is going to be next year. And they have a hit list; they have it in for Garret Hardin, Paul Ehrlich and Calvin Piper. Threadgill's convinced it's his job to save the race from the anti-Christ. Don't let the *kikoi* and the campfire fool you. He's certainly an idiot. But he could be a problem.'

'What do you think he'll do?'

'Get underfoot. I was worried he'd more or less twigged. But it doesn't help he has the *parameters* in print . . . Where are you going?'

'It's Thursday. I'm going to work.'

'Maybe you shouldn't.'

'Maybe I should.' Eleanor stood up. Calvin stood up. 'Calvin Piper. If I went around the office gibbering about what you told me last night, I'd be laced in a strait-jacket by lunchtime. And you're not going to strap me here, like Malthus, on a leash for ten years. I'm going to the office.'

Calvin looked helpless. He was actually a mild-mannered man who could decimate throngs with his *delete* key, but couldn't lay a hand on a single underfed young lady. 'Oh, go on,' he said feebly. 'Only, come back here, would you? We may pay a call on His Ebullience tonight.'

'What good would that do? Even if he did swipe the disks, he's scanned them by now and he's unlikely to bow his head and say he's sorry, he knows it's wrong to play with other children's toys without permission. And look at you: you can't even strong-arm a family planning worker. What are you going to do to Wallace? Magic Marker his teddy bear?'

'A skip down the yellow brick road would give me a little exercise. I feel like a spar, and you won't put your mits up. And he's browned me off frankly. Burglary is hardly above board.'

Eleanor choked. 'Above board! You're playing video games with life and death and then you get peevish when your opponent *cheats*? Is this a conspiracy or checkers?'

'The game,' said Calvin coldly, 'is the highest form of civilization. Life is sport.'

Eleanor rolled her eyes. 'Pardon me, but the normal person

has to go to work. I hope the two of you have a delightful day wreaking international havoc on paper. Goodbye, my darling psychopath.' She kissed him and shouted behind her, 'So long, Panga!'

Once Eleanor left, Calvin felt petulant. Panga ignored him, endlessly sharpening her *kukri* the way some women filed their nails. He told himself to be grateful. Eleanor's arch relation to QUIETUS was convenient. If she dismissed his enterprise as a fanciful, fatuous delusion, she was less likely to squeal. Calvin was offended all the same. He felt obliged to prove to Eleanor he was not a crackpot. She should have been aghast. 'But she laughed!' he smarted out loud.

'I tell you before,' said Panga, *scrish-scrash*. 'This girl is not how you see. Eleanor and Panga, I think we get to be *msuri rafiki.*'

'Just what I need,' said Calvin. 'Both you birds ganging up on me.'

'We think you are funny,' she announced, inspecting the blade in the morning light, and pressing the feather-edge on Calvin's coffee table – damn it, she would leave marks.

Reaching for one ally in this household, Calvin retrieved Malthus, who clung to his neck and hissed at the poltergeist. Malthus was none too keen on Panga. Malthus was none too keen on anyone, discernment Calvin could only applaud.

'You'll see,' he grumbled at the ghost. 'You think it's a lark, a jest; you think I'm all micro-floppy – ' He realized he sounded childish.

'Calvin is like *ugali* with too much water,' she goaded, testing the steel by running the calloused whorls of her thumb over the edge so the knife sang. 'He cannot stand upon his plate. Calvin, you have to eat with a spoon.'

'What makes you think I won't go through with this?'

'Easy.' She tossed the *kukri* on the table so the femur rattled. 'You make all these – palavermers – '

'Parameters.'

'Rules,' she shrugged. 'You have to be so candy. Why does Calvin's poison have to taste pretty?'

'Clean shot,' said Calvin.

'Clean shot: that is only professional.'

'I, too, am trying to be professional.'

'A real warrior would borrow my *kukri* and take off their heads.'

'Do you have any idea how many two billion is?' Calvin had a feeling he didn't have any idea himself. 'Be practical.' He reached for his calculator and stabbed at it – all his aggression seemed destined to be vented on keys. 'If you filleted one unwanted ragamuffin *per second* with that *kukri* of yours, it would take you 66.59 years to dispatch two billion. In the meantime three-quarters would live to reproduce, so you'd have to chop closer to three or four ... Mathematically, you'd never finish.'

'So we would never be out of a job.'

'I'm telling you, we need Pachyderm.'

'As always, you hide behind your machines, your numbers. Your pictures on the wall with the lines that go up and down. How much does Calvin know about killing?'

'A fair lot, by now.'

Panga snorted. 'Potions. Books. Admit it, has Calvin ever killed one person? *Moja toto kidogo?*'

'Elephants.'

Panga shook her head. 'You see why Eleanor is not frighten. You see why she laughs.'

'I dare say a good number of defence contractors, presidents, even generals have never killed anyone hand to hand. There are other methods. You may not find them admirable, but they work.'

'These generals, then, they are women. Do you not see? That you make so many perambulators – '

'Parameters!'

'*So you do not succeed?* It is like saying, I will only do what I say and say I will do when the moon falls out of the sky and I can bounce it like a ball. Like saying, I will be a terrifying warrior when my trees grow hair and bark like dogs.'

Calvin slumped. 'It has to be the right organism, Panga. Otherwise the whole operation could dribble into a few more rows of stinking pits. Say we only manage to nix a few million and the virus peters out. What good would that do? We'd have no long-term demographic impact. No, Pachyderm has to be a clean shot. I know you think I'm a coward. OK, I'll suffer that. I don't think, sometimes, you understand me at all.'

'I understand. There is a Kikuyu word, *karamindo*. A man of much wealth, from rich parents, who has lost it and tries to get it back. This *karamindo*, he is angry and will do anything.'

'It doesn't matter what my motives are, so long as my research is sound. If I'm secretly getting even with short-sighted USAID quislings, or even with my fat, sotted mother, so what? I'm no purist. I dispensed with the right-things-wrong-reasons hair-tear ages ago. So long as you do the right things, I don't care if your mind is as warped as a ten-cent violin. Why I'm doing this is my business. And the fact is, things have gone badly for me for years. You're dead, which irks me no end – I have to listen to your knives rasp all day, when we used to go to bed, remember?'

'Tsss,' she hissed. 'Calvin. *You* do not remember. Not any more.'

'And they kicked me out of Washington. Now I've finally got something to live for. It's in the long-term interests of the race – '

Panga yawned.

'It is theoretically possible,' he levelled, in that voice which had taken Eleanor aback but which Panga adored, 'to revenge yourself on an entire universe.'

'Do you,' she studied, 'think your life is so special sad? More than the others?'

'Not at all. It's been cushy, I dare say, by comparison. But I take offence. Everyone else slings and arrows their way through eighty years, *shauri ya Mungu*. I personally get hacked off.'

'You are spoil.'

'I am spoil. The idea of fifteen billion grubby, thieving degenerates on this planet curdles my stomach. I can't bear five.'

Panga sighed and holstered her knife. 'Calvin does not know Calvin so well. And you remember: if you say you do nothing and you do nothing, *sawa-sawa*. If you say you do something and you do nothing, you make me shame. You understand, *bwana*? You stay in that room and go tap, tap, tap for years until you die, I go haunt somewhere else. I think it

147

start to look *mzuri sana* in Liberia.' She sauntered through the back wall.

Calvin was in a mood, so he gunned his Land Cruiser down Magadi Road, where most *wazungu* would aim to Euro-gaga over the escarpment to the daunting sweep of the Rift Valley and take snaps. Calvin sought the Rift to annoy himself. Oh, at a distance the land *looked* deserted, but that was like standing a mile from a house and observing it didn't *look* infested with termites. Because up close the whole valley was shambling with degraded Masai, no longer draped in their dignified russet blankets but flapping in strawberry polyester blends, wrists flashing digital watches. They poked ratty herds of starved cattle, ribs like rumble strips, to DANIDA water projects that invited over-grazing for miles around, cows stubbling the grass to five o'clock shadow.

He slowed the car and studied the herdsmen, the wizened women parked with garish bead-work in wait for tourists when it wasn't the season. *Why was everything getting uglier?* Had we always been so vulgar? He tried to recall cathedrals, the Taj Mahal, while grinding past Bob's Save-Life Bar, girls wrapped in clashing paisley and polka-dot, scuffing in vinyl loafers under flaking adverts for Vermoflas Fluke and Worm Drench. Why did modern man jangle against the landscape so? All the other animals mutated for eons to fade against mottled trees – zebra, giraffe; why did people wear Day-glo pink Bermuda shorts? Even the contemporary poor had lost their dusty camouflage, but slapped in electric-blue plastic sandals, failing to obey the ordinary biological edict that as potential prey you lurked in the shade and didn't call attention to yourself. His species had grown so alienated from the planet that they were determined to *look* as if they didn't belong here.

Now, possibly they didn't wear Day-glo pink Bermuda shorts in the Middle Ages because no one could make the dye. Maybe his people had never been constrained by good taste but by the inability to accomplish bad taste, a technical problem we have overcome. Maybe we have always yearned for ugliness, our streets hoarded with our own image, and at last we have found the means to display our jarring, trashy interior on an international scale.

Calvin did not think of himself as nostalgic, but he did wonder if he'd been born in the wrong time. He tried to imagine the Rift only a hundred years ago, when crossing the valley with thirsty donkeys would have been an achievement – no DANIDA water projects. A time, not so long ago, when you didn't have to hunt down the odd gazelle in parks to gawk from the car you were not allowed to leave, but had to duck behind bluffs to keep from getting trampled by thousands of them. Or even earlier, when humans, too, were an endangered species – not from their own suffocating fecundity, their smutty use of the earth as a giant commode, but from wolves, lions, buffalo. Calvin seemed like a man so hostile to children, but in an earlier era he might have been fiercely protective of them. He dreamt of the days when every child successfully reared against the unlikely odds of tsetse fly and leopard was a prize of survival, a strange, upright, sparsely haired creature with exotic long fingers and dextrous opposable thumbs – quick, laughing, with too many questions. How he would have relished being prehistoric. How many twee dinners at the Horseman he would have sacrificed for one rabbit, roasted on an open fire, that he'd stabbed with a stick because he was quick and the clan was hungry. He craved a country where a glimpse of your own kind was a shaft of light, serendipity, instead of one more prat to keep from running into on the footpath. For as much as he thrived on *overpopulation* he resented it. Calvin himself would like to be rare. Instead he was stuck in a world that replicated him at every turn, trapping him in a fun-house of the slightly fatter or shorter. He was not incapable, he supposed, of joy or even gratitude in the face of company so long as there was not so much of it.

To waylay depression, Calvin entertained notions of a far less populated vista, not of the past but of the future, thanks to the dire designs of the dastardly Dr Piper. Since he would never be allowed to see the day, it was up to Calvin to imagine the forthcoming paperback exposés: *Cropped!*; sensationalist biographies: *The Baby Slayer*; or maybe someone in the future would have a sense of humour: *The Population Bum*. Photographic inserts: Calvin in his stetson before the heaped grey carcasses; a few winsome black and whites of Eleanor Merritt, a name every schoolchild would know, in some histories an unwitting dupe, blinded by love, in others a conniving, sex-crazed accomplice to worldwide pogrom. Documentaries: *Show-on*, nine solid hours of survival footage everyone in New York would have to watch in one sitting and pretend to like. Perhaps a comic book: *Dr Demo*. Children's rhymes! *Calvin Piper pricked a pack of knackered peckers* . . .

Calvin arrived at Lake Magadi, a bizarre natural soda deposit where he must have felt comfortable because it looked so entirely extraterrestrial. For miles the lake was covered in a pinkish scab. Insects fled before his bumper in ashen waves. The alkaline water was toxic; if you waded the shore it would slough your skin. Calvin idled on a spit. Below the chalky crust, from an algae that thrived in so perverse a liquid, the stagnant water was scarlet, as if the nearby plant was not a soda factory but an abattoir. He had to resist the temptation to dip his hand in the red sea and taste it: salty and thick, the pool of Lake Magadi was murderous.

Magadi lapping sluggishly at his tyres, Calvin careered its bloody shore picturing the post-Pachyderm century – when in yearly ceremonies all over the world (pleasantly diminished) crowds would pass the peace and close their eyes in minutes of memorial silence. Dark marble monuments would wall Washington, the big stone commissions splayed across two-page spreads in Sunday magazine sections. Scholars would paw through his flawless primary school reports and uneventful childhood diaries for confirmation of obscure developmental theories; university libraries would battle for original files. Despite his public execution, tabloids would headline that Calvin Piper was still alive, toil and troubling in Argentina and dining with Elvis Presley. Meanwhile Interpol would be following the faint beige make-up trail of the bedraggled Bunny Morton, who, still grieving over the only man she ever loved, would betray herself to undercover agents because she craved celebrity and couldn't keep her mouth shut.

In his own field, even the most brown-nosing Ehrlich-ers would be falling all over themselves to disown him, and anything that smacked of population control or even family planning would get its budget nuked. Yet every once in a great while a brave biologist would suggest that, really, the race had been awfully fortunate to suffer a cutback right before the species would have burgeoned to destabilizing size, hinting that maybe QUIETUS was not so barmy after all. The poor sod would get shot down as a fascist. So no one would observe that economies were booming, jobs plentiful, hunger and disease rare; that by the time the population returned to six billion its growth rate had safely levelled off; that after the disappearance of a third of their citizens overnight most countries had had enough war for the time being. Matters really much improved would prove politically awkward, and presidents and PMs would rush to take credit for the new world order. No one would thank him, you could count on that.

Except a small, perverse cult of votaries after his death, reviled by the majority but still legal in a democracy after all, would keep his portrait on their walls and trade among themselves in a black-market of Piper paraphernalia: old population articles, conference abstracts, crusty condom packets that their owners would claim really landed on Nyrere's desk.

Driving back, Calvin contented himself that even if this little diet he planned to put the population on turned into a complete and utter horlicks, he would still have done mankind a favour: something (anything) would have happened. How destitute the world would be without tyrants! For wasn't any event salvation from the simpering daily maw of cups of coffee and go-slow bumps? Weren't people hungrier for meaning than for virtue? Weren't world wars, in their very badness, really rather a good thing? So the benevolent Calvin Piper would martyr himself for incident, for a turn of the page.

For truth be told he did feel a bit peculiar about sprinkling Pachyderm over sparsely settled Iowa and the one-child families of France. Calvin consoled himself that Western civilization required regular cathartic upheavals. Wasn't the First World always stirring up trouble, without which life became one big plumped pillow?

Because give the West a catastrophe and it was Christmas. Anything but lie in the neatly turned bed it had made. Calvin was amused at *wazungu* ranting at how nothing in Africa worked. Why did they imagine they stayed? To wallow in the pleasant obstruction of a country where sending a single parcel took half a day. Suffer any inconvenience to avoid the horrors of efficiency, the grim success of Scandinavia: the racially balanced curricula, the dogged recycling, the healthy salads, the loom of a tall athletic population with white-gold hair, as if fresh from terror. No, give them a little plague, a baptism of disaster and the too-white world would thrive. It needed setbacks to reprieve itself from the organized nightmare of perfectly separated garbage.

As for the Third World, they'd barely notice. Thirty-five per cent of their people dropping dead overnight would seem perfectly normal. They were used to rotten luck.

11

The Battle of the
Bunnies and the Rats

It was not a good day at Pathfinder. The Family Planning International Association had been caught funding abortion; its USAID funding was therefore withdrawn overnight. The newly impoverished FPIA was frantically off-loading projects it could no longer afford on to foster organizations like Eleanor's. Suddenly her desk was piled high with reports on incompleted role-playing workshops on AIDS and sexuality for Nairobi grammar schools, as if amateur theatrics changed what those kids did in the bushes after class. Meanwhile the UN had just released a new study suggesting that world population was likely to reach ten billion as early as 2050. She tucked the booklet in her briefcase to bring home her offering of despair the way other women might arrive with aftershave; Calvin would find the numbers bracing.

Eleanor was oppressed by the report, for Calvin's visions of a few bedraggled remnants humming through gaunt crowds trying to remember the fourth movement of the Requiem had started to undermine her. Even as she defended it, she found her work increasingly absurd. The statistics were stifling, and in private moments she confessed that Calvin was right in his way, that the answer would be death, and she wondered why he bothered to arrange it when attrition was bound to arrive of its own accord. While she found her ersatz lover's solution deranged, she did not, today, find her own any less so. Trying to avert the world's population from doubling in sixty years by supervising seminars of twenty-five on 'Adolescent Empowerment', Eleanor felt much as any scientist might if, concerned about the rising sea level from polar melting, he

153

spent his days at the shore spooning the ocean into a paper cup.

At the bottom of her mail was another one of those horrible brown envelopes. Last time he had wanted a computer; that meant America was next. She refused to open the letter at all and instead penned a note, which she immediately sealed, addressed and threw in Outgoing to ensure she didn't change her mind:

Dear Peter,

I hope this finds you in good health, and give my greetings to your family. It was my pleasure to post you the basketball shoes, and I am assuming they fit. The shoes are all I intend to send, however, and I do not wish to receive any more requests for articles of clothing or foreign education. In my country, this behavior would be considered very rude. I have to warn you that should any more demands for favors reach my desk, I shall be forced to return your letters unopened. I try to be generous, but I am a very busy woman, and I am not paid as much as you must think. I'm sorry you have problems, but so do I. Much as the unfairness of the world saddens me, I cannot personally make everything right. If you will take my advice, you will at least encourage your mother to have no more children. That way when you need them she will be able to buy you shoes herself.

Your friend in Jesus,
ELEANOR MERRITT

She lunched with a colleague from Population Health Services who was leaving the profession to administer food aid with Oxfam. That's all there was left, he said. That's what was going to be required here, wasn't it? Family planning was too late. Commonly Eleanor could be relied on for chin-up-manship. Today she played with her soup and concurred: family planning was a farce. There was a funny silence. It was the second time in two days that Eleanor had refused to play her traditional part.

On her way back to International House from lunch, a parking boy extended the usual hand for her spare shillings –

'Please, madam! I am so ho-ongry! Please, madam!' but in a tone less a plea than a taunt, or a threat even, that he would nag behind her for blocks until she bribed him to be off. Routinely, she emptied her pockets on these streets, and the urchins had tagged her as a mark. Other children were already running from the other side of Kenyatta Avenue. This time, however, she said, '*Hapana!*' and so sharply he stepped back. For good measure she added, 'It's *my* money! I earned it, didn't I? What did you ever do to earn my money?' The boy fled, as if from the possessed.

As Eleanor prepared for a staff meeting that afternoon the rebellion persisted, for she resented being branded a Pollyanna, all trussed up in lace and bows, conveniently ridiculous. She was tired of providing ready target practice for cynics. In earlier meetings she mediated staff conflict and claimed there was always a solution to please everyone (there wasn't), inviting co-workers with a problem to come to her – which they did, in droves, not just about whether Pathfinder's clinics should offer tubal ligations without the husband's consent but about their cramped apartments, their wayward boyfriends . . . And Eleanor would listen and comfort and stay in the office until nine at night.

Well, she was sick of it. Often as she had been in trouble with her superiors for 'loaning' her own salary to hard-pressed clients, for once Eleanor was sure that if one more sob story walked into her office she would scream.

Eleanor opened the meeting to announce a change in personnel. 'Would you ask Florence to come in for a moment, please?'

When the messenger was duly brought before the oval table, looking frightened and unquestionably innocent, Eleanor hesitated, but only a fraction of a second.

'I gather it is common for employees in your position to take modest advantage – to return with insufficient change from the post office, or to take a *matatu* when we give you money for a taxi and pocket the difference. Do you think we are stupid or don't care? No, I have noticed, but let small things go. Perhaps my error. You imagined stealing would be overlooked. However, you took my credit card out of my wallet and have been using it to run up very high charges on my account.' Florence's eyes bulged, but Eleanor kept talking. 'I have chosen not to have you arrested, but I warn you that if you ever appear in this office again or charge so much as a Crunchie bar on that VISA card I will have the police on your step before you've wiped the chocolate from your mouth.'

'No, *memsahib*, I never, you are mistaken – '

'You misunderstand. I am not *asking* if you have been stealing, I am *telling* you. Now clear out of this office immediately.'

Florence raised her head high and walked out of the room, indignant. Staff shifted nervously in their seats.

The rest of the meeting was fractious. The orphaned FPIA schemes had to be adopted by various departments, and a few programmes everyone wanted, and most no one wanted. She let them fight. For a full hour, arms folded, not saying a thing. Finally they turned to her, for it was no fun scrapping if no one was trying to stop them.

'I don't care,' said Eleanor.

'Come, now,' said the Publications Officer. 'Someone has to take responsibility for Male Involvement.'

'Do they?' Eleanor arched her eyebrows. 'And what's going to happen if they don't?'

'Then the programme – ' he scratched his nose – 'would fall between the cracks.'

'So?'

'I'm afraid we're not communicating here.'

'You're afraid we are. For once.' She pulled the UN report from her briefcase. 'Have you seen this?'

'I glanced at it. Just another tale of grief, isn't it? Everything that office puts out is the same, give or take five billion people. Why?'

'But you do believe it, some of it. If you didn't you wouldn't work here, isn't that right? The pay is lousy. You think we have a population problem. You want to help.'

'Of course.'

'But how much of a dent do you think all these programmes together will make in the growth of African population in the next century? Go on, off the record?'

'Some,' he declared. 'We have plenty of evidence from our surveys that contraceptive demand is not being met – '

156

'We have plenty of evidence that even if we meet that demand growth rates remain sky high.'

'Eleanor,' he said, with the coaxing used to lure suicides from a ledge, 'maybe you have had a hard day.'

'Hell yes, I have,' said Eleanor, who rarely cursed. 'I've had years of bad days. That's my point.'

'It hardly seems the time, when we're inundated with newly unfunded projects, to start questioning the viability of our whole enterprise.'

'When is the time? When do we ever admit it, that we're a gesture, nothing more? Because I for one would be content to feed the FPIA's abandoned children to the hyenas in Nairobi National Park.'

'What else can we do about population growth,' he asked hotly, 'besides provide contraceptives?'

Hadn't Eleanor asked that not long ago herself. She understood Calvin better now. How delectable to have a secret, even if it was absurd, a malevolent paper pastime of the unemployed. With every phone call from one more hysterical FPIA administrator who wanted to kvetch about USAID, she had fondled QUIETUS in the back of her mind like a skin-hot shilling in her pocket.

'We should obviously resume when you are not so tired,' the man proceeded, leaving his question rhetorical.

'I'm not tired,' said Eleanor.

All the same, the staff dispersed, with tentative pats on Eleanor's arm. The next morning cups of coffee would arrive every fifteen minutes and someone would have baked her biscuits. They would bribe her with whatever it took to get Eleanor Merritt – sweet, self-sacrificing Eleanor Merritt – back to the same old sucker.

Eleanor sped to Karen. The UN report was a prize and she was pleased with her outrage in the staff meeting, though she'd best not keep it up or she'd be carpeted. And she was grateful, if by accident, to be included in Calvin's work. In the most important sense she had at last been invited to his bed, for Calvin was in love with his project.

'Where's Panga?' asked Eleanor, glancing around after a kiss.

'Slouched off in a huff. We fought. She thinks I'm a nancy boy.'

'Is she coming with us to Wallace's?'

'Threadgill makes Panga puke. We're on our lonesome.'

When they pulled up at dusk, Wallace seemed to be expecting them. Perched on his three-legged stool, he leaned both hands on his walking stick, staunchly planted between his knees as if warding off demons. His grey locks shaggy, his *kikoi* bedraggled, his baggy, sleepless eyes harrowing towards the drive, the vision was Old Testament.

'*Habari yako?*' asked Threadgill gravely.

'Swell,' said Calvin.

'Tea?'

'I detest tea,' he declared, which Eleanor knew to be a lie; he had no feelings about tea whatsoever, along with most comestibles. He liked to spend money on meals, for example, for the sheer profanity of the bill; the food was chaff. He meant he detested *Wallace*'s tea: quaffs of the pale, the watery, the gutless.

Prepared, Calvin pulled out a bottle of White Horse. His relation to alcohol, too, was casual. She'd never seen him go out of his way to procure it, nor had it much effect; he'd mentioned once that it 'didn't help', whatever needed helping. But he enjoyed its social employ. With heavy drinkers, he ordered Diet Coke; at Wallace's camp he arrived with spirits. The same perversity applied to accent: Calvin's pronunciation travelled from straight DC, with As like wide, flat, lettered avenues, to Oxford, where they condescended downhill and cornered on consonants neatly trimmed as hedgerows. Yet while most inflections migrate towards company kept, Calvin's paddled reliably to the opposite shore, American with British expats and English with Washington bureaucrats. Consequently, wherever he went his accent annoyed people enormously.

Wallace witnessed Calvin's gallop on his White Horse with a disdain that far better resembled envy. Eleanor was sure Wallace would have relished a shot; Calvin didn't care. All three lived, it seemed, in a perpetual state of punishment. Wallace denied himself any desire that might scatter his ashen happiness; Calvin allowed himself to think or do anything until he was a prisoner of his own freedom; Eleanor not only wallowed in other people's pain but took responsibility for it, making sure to address herself to problems large enough that she was guaranteed to make no difference. Not one of them around that campfire seemed to be getting what they wanted: Wallace wanted the whisky; Calvin would settle for Wallace's even bogus joy; Eleanor wanted Calvin.

'This fire is niggardly,' Calvin complained. It was a cool evening, and the little fog wisping from the skinny sticks had the same emasculated ambience as Threadgill's tea.

'You of all people should be aware there is a timber shortage in this country.'

'Which only inspires me,' said Calvin, throwing logs on the smoulder. 'But aren't you the prince of abundance? How could there not be enough of anything? I thought resources are limitless.'

'With proper reforestation, the timber in this country could be logged and restored indefinitely. The government has yet to instigate an effective programme; until then we conserve.'

'Ah, yes.' Calvin rubbed his hands. 'The old shortfall between fantasy and fact. For example, people like you are always pointing out that, rationed like kindergarten cookies, the food we produce would feed everyone handily?'

'You know that's the case.'

'Ever observe that this one-kernel-for-you and one-kernel-for-me is not actually happening?'

'You lost me,' said Wallace coldly.

'What Calvin means', Eleanor intruded, recognizing straight away that getting a word in edgewise was going to be a fight, 'is it's all very well to suppose if we distributed food equally we would each have enough to eat. But in the whole of human history, maldistribution has been a given. Food production must accommodate that reality. To put forward if-we-all-shared-alike is to posit the one social arrangement which will not occur. If our survival as a species is dependent on the evolution of perfect justice, we are doomed.'

'We are certainly doomed,' said Wallace, turning to Eleanor with an expression of parental disappointment, 'if everyone thinks like you.'

Meanwhile Calvin's overkill of wood was smothering the

fire. Fussing with the logs, he nearly managed to put it out altogether. Wallace quipped, 'You are a genius of destruction.'

Though Calvin had guessed she'd stay home, Panga drawled from the shadows, shaking her head in disgust. With a single nudge from her calloused foot, the whole stack burst into flame. She strolled off, eye-rolling. Wallace stared after her.

Calvin knocked back a tot of whisky. 'Eleanor's right, but it doesn't matter. In twenty years, even if we're equally issued with maize meal chits, none of us will make it through the day without feeling light-headed.'

'On the contrary, we have tripled world food production in the last forty years – '

'And *only* doubled the population – '

' – Proving once and for all the folly of Malthus's unfounded assumption that agriculture could only grow arithmetically whereas population grows geometrically.'

'Of course that theory was drivel. Malthus was a reasonable economist but sorry biologist. I'm impatient with the assumption that if you discredit Malthus you undermine modern demography. He was right about one thing: that unchecked population growth is deadly, and that sooner or later population will outstrip resources.'

'It hasn't yet.'

'The Green Revolution can't loaves and fishes for ever. You're spot on, Wallace, food production isn't arithmetic. It increases in fits and starts, and *sometimes it goes down*.'

Eleanor rubbed her arms and huddled on her stool. Her head swivelled as the rally rapidly degenerated into a volley of mathematics. There was no point now in trying to intervene; she felt irrelevant, the Girlfriend, without the common compensations of the role when they went home. She was torn between malicious, aggressive boredom and admiration. For Calvin was a seamster with data, and could weave the loops of zeros in and out until he knit a dazzling tapestry of dread, so densely sewn it would take a sharp eye to find the holes. This was a particularly meticulous performance, and Wallace couldn't quite keep up. Though Calvin's position came down to the view that the world was a terrible place and only getting more hideous still, she compulsively hoped that he would win. That was what Girlfriends did.

As a visual aid when Calvin began to get the upper hand, first one, then another Kenyan trudged through Wallace's camp, swinging bags of groceries, slinging infants on their backs, toddlers in tow. The parade – the invasion, even Wallace must admit – grew steadily more insistent as the sun set. Since Wallace's love for people was as abstract as Calvin's commensurate disdain for them, Threadgill's eyes darted to the singing, murmuring string of locals through his land with noticeable irritation.

Getting desperate, Wallace attacked. 'Are you not embarrassed by being a type? One more over-excited Chicken Little that every generation spawns, indulges and deserts? Why, there's one of your sort on every corner. Have you ever been in New York City on New Years? Crowds in Harlem walk-ups stay up holding vigil for the end of the world, all waiting for Jesus to foreclose. I've sometimes liked to imagine the sleepy gatherings the next morning: bleary-eyed at the light, annoyed to find no one arranged for breakfast because there was never supposed to be breakfast again. You encourage irresponsibility, Piper. You advise your flock that the sky is falling so fast there is nothing to do but sigh. But humanity will be propelled by those who continue to plan for breakfast. Only the optimists will still have corn flakes.'

'*Type?*' asked Calvin. 'Better Jeremiah than one more lying whitewasher. Ibsen's baths are not poisoned; there is no cholera in Venice. The sky is not falling; it just looks brown because it's so full of pie. Now, I'll grant you I encourage paralysis. I believe environmentalism is too late, and I'm not getting the neighbours to put bricks in their toilet tanks. But to advise the rabble instead, never fear, you'll be all right dears, is just as irresponsible. In either case, the lot do nothing.'

'The forces of unity and joy are anything but paralysed, Piper. Have you stopped reading the paper because miracles depress you? All over the world, countries are throwing off weary and oppressive ideologies. It's uncomfortable to remember, isn't it, how recently your crew were gorging on fantasies of nuclear inferno? That's a loss for you gloom grubbers, the close of the cold war. Perestroika must be breaking your heart.'

'Hardly.' Calvin clasped his hands, for he had worked this daunting spree of dancing in the streets until it represented – that's right – more calamity. Eleanor had watched him scowl over the front page as East Germans made confetti of Stasi files and playwrights rose to presidencies. He was crushed at the fall of the Berlin Wall – he liked that wall, he said; it was *interesting*. 'Eastern Europe is already shattering into petty ethnic dispute – that's improvement? Nuclear war is more likely than ever. Bi-polarity was at least stable; now we just have polarity, and any rinky-dink Qadaffi can pick up an H-bomb at his local souk. You're not seeing the rise of *unity and joy*, Threadgill. More mayhem in sheep's clothing.'

Following their ritual dismissal of one another, Eleanor tentatively wished to propose that maybe some things had got better and some things worse, without pattern; and so human affairs had always proceeded, lumbering through regardless of the labels its commentators laid on arbitrary eras of their own creation. She wanted to explore if maybe mankind was less streaking towards the firmament or hurtling to purgatory than toodling in an unremarkable limbo, with the occasional improvement and occasional lapse. However, this point of view was not sexy, and she could not think of a way of expressing it that was moving or eloquent. So she kept quiet, though with an inkling that there were multitudes out there who thought exactly this way and who couldn't get published or appear on TV because such a frumpy perspective was both dull and frightening. Eleanor's shabby vision of humanity infinitely shambling on had its own hopeless horror as well as hometown appeal.

As the fire towered and Eleanor had to move her stool back from the heat, the circle of light increased to include a stump, on top of which, fanned defiantly in the open, were ten microfloppy disks.

'Why, Wallace,' said Calvin, 'you don't have electricity. What do you do with micro-floppies? Are you so spiritually advanced that you can Ouija board them on your knees and scan the files with your fingertips?'

'Laptop batteries. Computers only get lighter, cheaper and

more efficient every year. One of those many upswings of which you must despair.'

'Enjoy the toy while you can. After the Collapse, there won't be power in Nairobi, and you'll have exactly eight hours of light, cheap, efficient amusement to last through your old age.'

'Dr Piper, such humility. I thought that is a collapse you personally intend to avert. I thought we might all rest easy now.' Wallace paused. 'Or two-thirds of us.'

'The other third will rest easiest of all.'

Wallace leaned on to his walking stick so it sunk in the dirt. 'I weary of this banter. I need to know: *are you serious?*'

Calvin sighed. 'I'm tired of that question.'

'Why did you come here? And drag this poor, enslaved dwarf with you?'

'I misplaced some of my work. I thought you might have come across it.'

'You knew I had. That's not why you came by.'

'I'm not interested in discussing my designs with you, Threadgill. I'm interested in what you're going to do about them.'

'Were I to move against you, I should hardly warn you how. No, you came here to explain yourself. That's pathetic, but go ahead.'

'I'm aware you find me despicable. But I was concerned that you may also consider me insane.'

'I don't think you're insane,' said Threadgill unexpectedly. 'I rather wish you were. But for some inscrutable reason you still want to tell me something. I wish you'd get it off your chest.'

12

Maggots in the Breezes of Opah Sanders's Fan

Calvin clipped newspapers, labelling and filing away just those snippets that most people were happiest to see twined safely away for recycling. Recycled they would be, the same vicious page-eleven stories returning on resurrected manila, as if not only the paper but the news itself were wetted down, mashed and rolled out again for tomorrow's edition.

'In the Bronx this summer,' Calvin began, bedtime story, 'there lived a couple, 32 and 34, happily if frugally on social security. They had been released from a program called The Bridge only a year before, which helped young adults like themselves adapt to living on their own. You see, Opah Sanders and her boyfriend Freddie were both mentally retarded. Opah had a younger sister, who had lived off and on in their apartment. One day Opah's sister knocked on the door. No sooner was the sister let in than she had visitors – two boys and a girl, her friends, all teenagers. Children,' Calvin smiled, 'really.

'Well, one of the boys had a gun, with which he hit Freddie over the head. Between them, they taped Freddie's nose and mouth over with duct tape, and bound his hands with telephone wire. They put him in the closet. In the next room, the second boy hit Opah over the head, tied her up, and put her in a second closet.

'Then the foursome took Freddie's TV, stereo and VCR outside and sold them on the street. With the proceeds, they bought beer, potato chips, and a padlock for Freddie's closet. Sometimes the kiddies got too loud and the neighbours complained. The only trouble was, Freddie's mouth and nose had been taped pretty tight, and after two days he'd begun to smell. So they wrapped him in a shower curtain, twist-tied him in a garbage bag, moved him into the bedroom, and turned on the fan.

'After six days, I guess the fun began to pall. They untied Opah, whom they'd been feeding a bit of orange juice and even a cigarette from time to time, and said their goodbyes.

'Oh, and let's not forget. "None of the suspects showed any remorse for the crime, investigators said," ' he recited. 'The usual.'

Their own small party suffered a prolonged and inept silence. Calvin poured another shot. Eleanor measured the bottle's demise sidelong, reconsidering his capacity for handling his liquor. Wallace, in so far as he allowed any emotion to pass his face besides that stolid, funereal cheerfulness, looked annoyed.

'I could tell you more,' Calvin assured them, as if they were nervous he might run out of dismal clippings while the evening was yet young. 'Last week Renamo in Mozambique gang-raped a woman in front of her husband and then forced her at gunpoint to cut him to pieces.'

'Calvin, I really don't see – ' said Eleanor.

' – Or how about Richard Ramirez in LA? More of the same, really; these fables get repetitive, I'm afraid. Richard raped a Thai woman in bed as she lay next to the husband he'd just shot, then sodomized her eight-year-old son. Ramirez was convicted, you know – '

'Enough.' The angle at which Eleanor's hand protected her face from the heat also sheltered her from their narrator.

'What,' said Threadgill, unfazed, 'what is the point?'

Calvin stretched. 'Ramirez has become a folk hero. He has women writing into him on death row, star-struck. *Maybe I'll have to shoot the President to prove I love you.* I understand these serial killers have a competition going, whose life story sells the most paperbacks. To Americans, they're sex symbols. Think I've got it in me, Eleanor?'

'No.'

'Or I could tell you about little girls settling over farmers' fields from hijacked aeroplanes. But I, personally, am fondest of our mentally challenged couple in the Bronx. I'm a detail man . . . I liked the fan.'

Oh, yes, he loved the fan. For the first time Eleanor coloured with a tinge of the repulsion she had tried to rouse from herself for twenty-four hours. *He loved the fan.* When Calvin found that article, he wasn't upset, he was delighted. He had saved it and folded it and dated it and memorized the part about the orange juice and no doubt Opah Sanders was her correct name. That he remembered the story so well was almost as repugnant as the story itself.

'Presumably,' said Wallace, tolerantly tapping his cane, 'this viscous wade through the cesspool of your brain you regard as connected with *population*.'

'None of these party anecdotes occurred in my *brain*. Still you are correct. The earth is over-populated, all right. *But with what?*'

'The only over-population self-evident to me is that there is one too many of you.'

Calvin's eyes glowed, foot in the door. It was not easy to tempt Threadgill the all-merciful into vitriol. 'Come now, are we not, each of us, perfect marvels? Me, Ramirez and Opah Sanders's loving sister? Every one of those Renamo insurgents holds a whole spangling universe in his spattered hands.'

'You see your own reflection. You find what you seek.'

'I find what's *there*.'

'But your response to "what's there" is to imitate it. You choose to become what you claim to revile.'

'I choose nothing.' Calvin knocked back the rest of his glass. He leaned towards Wallace, who recoiled from the reek of his breath. 'I am what I am, and what I am is like everyone else. And what we are isn't even reprehensible, Threadgill. We're animals. We're not important. Look at me, Wallace. You don't like me very much, do you?'

'I pity you,' said Threadgill.

'You hate my guts, Wallace. So I rest my case. There's a lot more where I came from. At least I've stopped pretending to be any different from the rest of this over-active fungal rot. We are blight, Wallace. We leave nothing in our wake but stench and destruction. So all right, I am blight. I have no redeeming qualities. Don't imagine insults upset me. Decry me as vile, Wallace, and we only agree. The trouble with all you Jesus people is you trap yourselves with your own throat-slitting inclusion. If we are all so God-chosen, if humanity is so bunnies and chickies according to you, then you're stuck with *me*, aren't you? I am one of your little lost lambs. I, on the other hand, regard myself as a maggot and reserve the right to act like one. I've given up fighting. I've joined with open arms.'

'Oh, tripe, Calvin, I'm sorry, but I've listened to this long enough. You don't think you're a maggot, you think you're a hero.' It was Calvin's own fault if, after months of re-education, Eleanor interrupted from time to time.

'She's right,' said Threadgill. 'I've read your *parameters*. You think you're a saviour. You believe you'll do your victims a favour.'

'I will. The dead are a contented lot. They don't complain, they don't suffer, and they don't get up to bad business either.'

'What if I decided *you* were better off dead, Piper?'

'I'd take you up on your kind offer, sport, but I've some work to do before I indulge myself a vacation.'

'I'm warning you, *bwana* – ' Threadgill picked up Calvin's White Horse and threw his remaining whisky on the fire. 'Virtue as well as vice can be violent.' The flames shot three feet high.

'People who think they're virtuous are almost always violent,' Calvin purred. 'How the concept gets turned on its ear.'

'Listen to you!' Eleanor exploded. 'Talk about turning virtue on its ear!'

'I have never claimed to be virtuous, my dear.'

'Nonsense. You're the most self-righteous jingo I've met in my life.'

'All that matters,' he turned from her coolly, 'is my research is accurate. Humanity is headed for extinction without a little help from its friends.'

'You're a music lover,' said Wallace. 'Do you ever wonder how many Bachs and Bucherini's you will exterminate? Or Frank Lloyd Wrights, Rembrandts, Einsteins?'

'How many Mussolinis and Caligulas? How many petty, tiny-eyed coke addicts with a knife in your back? How many Hindu mothers who cut off their children's feet to make them better beggars? How many fat nurses who leave geriatrics dozing in their own faeces and have another cigarette? More, Threadgill. A lot more. Einstein, at his most exacting, regretted himself. For that matter, once Mathare Valley spreads the globe like ringworm, what are the chances that if Mozart were born in a fetid slum with two potatoes a day some aid agency would float down from the sky and give the kid a piano? What would Dickens be worth growing to premature old age with a whore mother, never learning to spell his name? What would Frank Lloyd Wright build with mud and corrugated iron?'

'Does he build,' Wallace corrected. 'Frank Lloyd Wright knocks up shacks out of cooking-oil tins. Mozart hums kwasa-kwasa in Mathare. Dickens cannot write his name.'

'Right. And Christ is selling badly carved elephants on Kenyatta Avenue. So what good is he? No one will bother to crucify the bastard.'

'I'm disconcerted. If we are all "maggots", and you truly believe we are over-populating ourselves into oblivion, high growth rates should drive you to the violin. Why fiddle with viruses? Have dozens of children instead, to hurry us toward the Armageddon that will put us all out of our misery. Why, Dr Piper, try to save a race you hate?'

Calvin shrugged. 'I'm sentimental.'

'I hope so.'

Calvin stood up. It seemed time to go. Collecting to depart, they shuffled. Presenting his case did not seem to have refreshed Calvin as much as he might have hoped.

Before his guests ducked in the car, Threadgill placed a ministerial hand on Piper's shoulder. 'I don't know why it is,' he began, 'but for some reason everything we have and everything we make is gradually taken away from us. Your life is a leaky vessel; no matter how much you pour, your cup will never overflow, because there is a hole in it. The universe has a hole in it. Your lovers die or betray you; your professional successes are diluted by failure or by simply being past; the summer homes where you spent the idyllic holidays of your childhood are bought by strangers and painted a garish green. So you can never stop making; maybe that's the reason for the hole. I don't know where these things go; I don't believe they vanish. I wonder if there isn't a magnificent junk heap in the next dimension of favourite train sets before they were broken and golden afternoons before the last terrible thing was said that parted two friends for ever. Whyever, the hole is there. It will suck from you everything you love. You have stopped pouring, Piper, and your cup is bone dry. No wonder you're dying.'

'I have my work,' said Calvin.

'You'd have done better to start a pottery.' He turned to Eleanor. 'You can still save him. Though you might do better to save yourself.'

Eleanor held Calvin's hand defiantly. 'I'm very happy.'

'That's what I was afraid of. Piper,' he charged, 'it isn't too late. Forswear demography. Study a whole new field. Go back to university and read archaeology. Marry her. Make something.'

'Not on your life. Population is all I know and all I care about.'

'Then take the consequences. You think you're so ruthless. You haven't seen ruthless. Now, get off my property.'

'Why didn't you take the disks back?' asked Eleanor in the car.

'He made copies. I have copies. What's the point?'

Even were they one of a kind, she couldn't imagine Calvin physically retrieving them, having to hit Wallace on the head. She couldn't penetrate this man – so rancorous over newspapers, while with Eleanor he was considerate: he met her for dinner on time, tendered wine or flowers in bursts of uncalculated affection, and always noticed when she was tired or sad. It grieved him to see her cry. She couldn't picture Calvin lifting up one of those logs and clumping Wallace on the temple if the fate of six years' work or, as he saw it, the survival of civilization depended on it.

'I didn't like that story,' said Eleanor. 'About the retarded people.'

'Nor did I. That's why I told it.'

'But you enjoyed telling it.'

'It illustrates something. After all, we've both seen and read worse.'

'I wonder.'

'You find a story like that and you think, *it should't be possible*. Why, ask Basengi some day what happened to his parents. So if you think it shouldn't be possible, there is clearly something wrong with the way you think. It's attractive to imagine there's a separate class of human being that's depraved, so we need only identify them and put them away. But that version is too transparently self-serving. So you have to look in the mirror and confess, I, too, could tie up my retarded sister in a closet and suffocate her boyfriend and throw a party until he begins to smell.'

'You would never do any such thing.'

'Eleanor. Look at what I am planning to do. Isn't QUIETUS far more nefarious?'

Eleanor twisted in her seat. 'You sit at your computer and play with numbers. It's not the same. I've never seen you step on a spider.'

Calvin laughed. 'Women are miraculous. I can't imagine any greater test of devotion than I put you through yesterday. Why, I was dead sure you'd rung the police. And still you can cling to this myth of Calvin the Nice Person. I'm impressed.'

'To be willing to trade two billion people for one man; it's not very admirable, is it?'

'It is, in a way. Panga would trade, of course – with pleasure. But Panga is merciless. You're not.'

Eleanor stared out at the dark game park, oppressed with the helplessness that characterized her life. Now it was just the two of them, the intimacy of a common foe fell way, and she was left with the drone of that fan unsuccessfully wafting the smell of putrefying flesh out the window. She felt soiled. Eleanor searched for redemption. Whom did Calvin care about? One drowned Kamba. What did Calvin love that people made or people did? Music, cheap science fiction and population studies. What a surprisingly narrow man.

Eleanor combed through her own life for antidotes to the fan. The lamest tale would do so long as it illustrated qualities of bravery, honesty and affection that her race must conceal in at least small quantities. But was it a spell Calvin cast? The harder she tried to remember acts of kindness and sacrifice, the more memories of malice and avarice came back to her, clippings from her own private B-section: Edward in DC; the lies; the letter: ... *that Eleanor doormat*. Andrew, who after living with her for eight months in Addis Ababa, had left her with a hug at the airport, off to the States for a three-week vacation that turned into the rest of his life. He didn't write. Or that whirlwind with Mwema in Arusha, when it transpired she was merely a ticket to America ...

And in the Third World aid biz, you might allow that your motives weren't as sterling as you first pretended; you might project yourself into the victims of your generosity and see through their eyes the resentment of being given some microscopic portion of what you have, or even their casual acceptance of what they never asked for in the first place, none of which prevents you from expecting they'll feel appreciative – which they do not. Didn't Eleanor travel with that single carry-on because anything she owned of value had been stolen? Florence, Peter, her parking boy shuffled her mind, a tatty, dirty deck. Eleanor was not, like Calvin, repelled by other people; yet she had found them thoroughly disappointing.

What did people do or make that Eleanor loved? She didn't mind music, but she could live without it, whereas Calvin claimed when the stereo was down it was like spending too long in the dark. Literature? It was more for filling time. Should she ever consider suicide, she could not imagine any novel tipping the scales towards staying alive. Art? Museums had never lost the atmosphere of a grade school field trip. She did, she recalled, love light: the hour between six and seven on the Equator when the colours went insane, what those poor painters could never seem to imitate quite. But people didn't make light. And she adored a comfortable chair. It embraced you without expecting anything back; it couldn't make you feel bad. People designed chairs ... This was precious little salvation from someone who considered herself a humanist.

One memory rose, however. She'd been twelve years old. Her mother was in hospital again. Eleanor was staying with Ray and Jane, and they took her for a walk. One held each hand. They stooped towards her in the park. 'Would you like it very much,' asked Jane, 'if you stayed with us? Not just for a little while, like before, but always?'

The child had exhaled. 'Yes,' said Eleanor. It was the sweetest moment of her life.

They needn't have done that, she realized over and over, with an incredulity that almost destroyed the generosity in the end. She was just their loony friend's daughter, a strange child and an added burden to a large family. A maggot wouldn't do such a thing, would it? A maggot didn't adopt lonely little girls.

Yet the last time she'd seen Ray and Jane they were busy, if kind; they were always so kind she couldn't trust them, and Eleanor had been away too long. All the people she mentioned they'd never heard of. Andrew had left her, and he was just a name. She could only tell floating, disassociated stories that drifted separately off, helium balloons. More, her mother, an outpatient once again, had been a witch the week before, screaming outside their house that Jane had stolen her daughter. Eleanor had kept apologizing, perfectly aware that when she apologized she was at her most irksome.

Here she was, childless and thirty-eight, on this brutal continent with a job that seemed increasingly futile and nothing much to return to in the States. What did she have left, what or whom did she care for herself?

Eleanor sighed. The dark car was cosy, their silence comfortable. Admit it: Calvin. Calvin the Psychopath.

She turned to stare at him as he swerved around an oncoming *matatu* as it swayed over the centre line with one working headlight. His face was arguing: she wondered who was winning. She tried to hold QUIETUS in her mind and could not. The premise was so extreme and abstract that she still could not be taken aback. The project was so like him she was charmed. But what kind of *poor enslaved dwarf* could find mass murder adorable?

Then, something did not line up. Tone of voice. When Calvin talked of death, he sounded festive. How he spoke belied what he said, and when you sing, do the words matter? Isn't the spirit of a song almost always in the tune? How then could she interpret the tousled, boyish abandon of his hatred?

Cynics are spoiled romantics. They are always the ones who

had the highest expectations at the start. They were once so naïve themselves that they despise naïvety more than any other quality. Alchemists, they turn grief to gold. They take quinine in their tonic, Campari with their soda – bitterness is an acquired taste. Cynics have learned to drink poison and like it. They are resourceful people, though the sad thing is, they know what's happened to them. They remember what they wanted to be when they grew up, and not a single one of them dreamt of becoming a cynic.

But studying Calvin's over-active face, recalling the jubilance with which he foretold apocalypse, Eleanor could see his complement, the past. She remembered that look in his eyes in the photograph from Murchison Falls, the cocky hat. For Calvin to be so disgusted with humanity, there had necessarily to have been a time he had the highest hopes for it. Eleanor felt a little less demented. Because that was attractive, old girl. That was attractive as could be.

Wallace had said she could save the man. Must you persist in being a cynic if your aspirations, however belatedly, come to pass?

'Isn't there anyone,' she asked when they were almost home, 'whose death you would regret?'

Calvin didn't answer at first, and seemed to entertain the notion of one name, but then to think better of it. 'No.'

Eleanor slumped against the car door.

She couldn't sleep.

'Calvin,' said Eleanor at last, for he was wide awake – Opah Sanders must have mewled for more orange juice in his head. 'If Panga were still alive, would you expose her to Pachyderm, too? Just to get population down to size?'

'It is only her absence that makes Pachyderm possible. With Panga, I'd plant forsythia.'

Injured silence. He seemed mystified.

'What is the problem?'

'Well . . .' She didn't want to cry. 'What about me?'

'What about you?'

'Am I included, too?'

'Of course. We both are.'

Her chest shuddered. 'I'm not enough for you to plant forsythia.'

'Eleanor.' He was trying to be patient. 'I am not the same man. I couldn't garden for the Queen of Sheba. Please stop taking everything so personally. Try to get some sleep.' He put his hand on hers, with effort.

'I simply don't understand – how you feel about me.'

'I'm quite fond of you.'

'It's just – ' Even in that nasal, quivering voice she herself despised, she had to get this out. 'If you believe all human beings are slimy crawly things, well, it's your privilege to regard yourself that way, but don't expect me to see you as a worm, and sometimes I wonder if you say you're a swine or a slug for someone to complain it's not true, you're lovely . . . I object as often as I'm allowed, which isn't often. If I say I love you, I'm undermining you somehow, because you don't, or no longer, believe in it, and I join the enemy, the soppy, sappy enemy, and you'll push me to the other side of your bed. You seemed positively crushed when I didn't call you a reprobate last night . . . I mean, if we're maggots, Calvin, am I one? To you?'

He squeezed her hand. 'We're both maggots.'

It was his idea of romance. 'No,' she insisted. 'The way you claim to feel about the human race, you can include yourself and you enjoy that. But you have to include me, too. That makes me sad.'

'I cannot – ' His voice was hesitant, and Calvin was rarely inarticulate. 'I cannot feel beyond a certain point for you or I betray something.'

'Panga?'

'At one time, but no longer. Myself, I suppose.'

'You claim to have a distaste for yourself.'

'I have no love for myself. But something lasts beyond self-love. A feeling of obligation. Of having started something and having to finish. Thoroughness.'

'Is thoroughness an emotion?'

'It can be. In my case it is overriding.'

'*Your work*,' she said mournfully, for to get on the other side of Calvin's work was to join the fifth column for good. He could say his persistence had nothing to do with love, but it was love; QUIETUS was all he loved, and in this way his plan to wipe two billion people off the face of the earth was the healthiest thing in his life.

'If I fall head over heels for you, my darling, I cannot finish what I started.'

Eleanor was startled to find herself thinking, for once, in bed, about population – she felt like Calvin. There was a cold, hard logic to his proposal that we throw our excess over the keel to save the boat. It struck her, however, that the forces of hardness and coldness already had the upper hand; that the very arrangement whereby species success could about-face to species failure was heartless and unfair; that Nature herself was sufficiently abusive to speak for heedlessness, disdain, the impassive. Misanthropy was programmed into the character of the universe, and what was there left in a place which they did not control and which would ultimately defeat them but to hold one another on a cool Nairobi night? She tried to say what she was thinking, but it came out small and trite.

'But I, too,' said Calvin, 'am a force of Nature.'

13

The Diet of Worms

'That was a good point you made at Threadgill's. About inequity, that it's a given.' Solastina poured Calvin's coffee and rushed off for toast.

Eleanor was uncomfortable with servants. Pathfinder had hired a housegirl for the laminate palace, from whom Eleanor hid her laundry in order to wash it herself. She rinsed her own glasses and swept up her own crumbs until there was patently nothing for Beatrice to do. Eleanor knew the old argument that they needed the work; you did no one any favours here scrubbing your own tub. Very well, but she couldn't stand it. And now on rare visits home she found Beatrice smoking and laughing with friends, and crept about the bedroom trying not to interrupt, stuffing some extra underwear in her bag, to skulk out again, leaving Beatrice with her overly generous salary and cash to take care of 'expenses' (more cigarettes). She had allowed what most white Kenyans abhorred: the staff had become uppity and taken over, and those were the ones you sacked. Eleanor was grateful, however, to pay those stray shillings every week to escape the role of foreign master in a country where she was only a guest. She was aware that Beatrice did not consider Eleanor a noble, fair-minded benefactor of the Third World, but a fool. Go ahead, take advantage of me, the American thought. I have taken advantage of more than you will ever. Eleanor was stuck with a crude good fortune she couldn't shed – luck can be a curse, for it prevented her from feeling sorry for herself much as she would sometimes appreciate the pity.

'Solastina, this butter is hard, and the toast is cold,' Calvin carped. 'Bring fresh toast, *upesi*.' Calvin felt natural in the role of master. 'I thought we made a good team back there. I was wondering if you'd consider working with me.'

'You mean for you.'

'Mmm.'

'That would be strategic, of course. If I'm involved, I'm less likely to be a problem.'

'That's right.'

'And the complicity. If I refuse to play my part, indignation. Complicity's the next best thing.'

'Quite.'

'You tend to forget I have a job.'

'What I have in mind sorts right into your job. Though why you insist on keeping that position with Pathfinder when it's obvious it has no impact on population is beyond me.'

'*Your* work is more important.'

'It will make more difference.'

'That's what I'm afraid of.'

'Have you decided what you think of it yet?'

'No. It's not real to me.'

'It's real to Threadgill.'

'He's as looped as you are.'

'More. But would you? Work for me?'

Though the fresh toast had now arrived, Eleanor took a piece of the old, cold batch (not wanting to waste it) and balanced squares of icy butter on top, trailing blackcurrant jam in little streets between the butter houses with childlike concentration. The jam was from one of the tiny airline jars Eleanor compulsively saved. Calvin scowled, took the hot toast and disdained her silly salvage for the bit pot of marmalade.

'What have you in mind?' asked Eleanor. 'I'm no *fundi* of fatality, you know. I wouldn't have a clue how to go about giving the over-populated a bad case of psoriasis.'

'I could use some help fund-raising, for one. QUIETUS is expensive.'

'Would it involve much of my time?'

'Weekends. We've targeted some wealthy right-wing Brits right here in Kenya as likely donors. Flights to the highlands? Drinks on verandas? As long as you could tolerate the company, you might enjoy it. Since I'll warn you, the marks I've identified you won't like.'

'What does that say about us? About QUIETUS?'

'Nothing.'

Eleanor stared into the garden with a crooked smile. 'All this talk of death. And it's so beautiful here.'

They were breakfasting out at the back, and it was one more of those flawless Equatorial mornings that became a plague, one after the other, pretty and sunny, until you prayed it would rain. For the purpose of this discussion, Eleanor could use a downpour, since the shining pinks and peaches of this garden made QUIETUS the more surreal. After so much talk of having *exceeded the carrying capacity of the land*, the foliage was thriving, and she wondered if both she and Calvin were deranged, fund-raising for viruses while wrapped in papery bougainvillaea, its leaves the translucent pastels of Monet's, while jasmine laughed down trellises behind their backs. Ten-foot trees of poinsettia spangled the walkway and mocked the failing potted blooms Jane nursed for the centrepiece at Christmas. Elephantine mother-in-law's tongue lashed on either side, sturdy and intimidating. Amid these, birds flickered everywhere, bright, quick and clever. The only mournful note in the whole yard was struck by the weeping gums, whose leafy tears dripped from the upper branches, crying for the *wazungu* who, nested in the blowsy, blushing flora of East Africa, could only contemplate holocaust. *What are we doing?* she wanted to ask. *What are you talking about?*

'It won't stay beautiful,' Calvin was opining. 'Even this property will be bought up and tik-tak-toed.'

'Maybe it should be.'

'Some day I would like you to admit, for once, that social justice is one value of several. Not that it has no value. Just that it doesn't supersede every other. And you can't have an infinite number of people with their fair ration of space and food and *motokaris* and still have flowers. Africans, you know, don't give a frig for callililies; you can't eat them.'

'All right. I like flowers.'

'Thank you.'

'Doesn't it bother you, a colleague who can't take QUIETUS seriously?'

'As our chances of designing Pachyderm to the proper specifications are slim, a measure of scepticism will serve us both better than an extra dose of angst.'

'But why is your work in my interests?'

'Because – ' He leaned and kissed her. 'It would be a riot.'

She laughed, an unfamiliar laugh, loose and full like her hair today, washed and unbound. 'All right,' she said. 'You're on.'

They drove to town together, Calvin as ever grumbling about the incessant rumple of speed bumps; weren't there enough sleeping policemen in this country?

'There's some research we need done,' he suggested, 'preferably by someone who might have reason to do the work anyway and wouldn't attract attention as being about anything odd. You'd be perfect.'

'For?'

'This AIDS business. We need to know what the demographic impact looks like. Not only to build AIDS mortality into the parameters, but to table Pachyderm entirely if this pre-existent virus looks capable of doing the job for us.'

'AIDS isn't really my area.'

'I don't expect you to do sero-positivity studies, computer modelling; umpteen well-funded epidemiologists are already doing the work for you. We've gotten a file together, but the results are conflicting and incomplete. There are several computer models that we haven't gotten our hands on. Solicit them. Compile and compare. How much will that disease cut into population growth? We don't think much, but we need to be sure. Just in case we're superfluous. Maybe Nature's ahead of us. You might find the research intriguing in its own right.'

'I'll consider it.'

'Do. And you are free this afternoon?'

'Could be.'

'There's a meeting of the Peace Corpse at three.'

'Sorry?'

'A little nickname of mine they don't much like. QUIETUS rents an office suite at Nyayo House.'

'That's ironic.' Nyayo House, home of the Kenyan

government, was rumoured to keep detainees naked up to their waists in cold water; they would often plunge inexplicably to the car-park from the fourteenth floor.

'I'd like to introduce you as a new member. Though they won't be keen at first. Ordinarily application is quite a process. We do a lot of checking background, references, interviews, and it has to be a unanimous decision. You're coming in through the back door. My back door. They won't like it.'

'This all sounds so juvenile. Masonic.'

'Our caution is not clubhouse blood-brothering. If Moi ever got wind of us, we'd be on the next plane, if not out the window. We hear a lot of screams coming up through the carpet; they keep us on our toes. And if QUIETUS gets any publicity at all, its ambitions are thwarted. That's why this business with Threadgill is no joke. But as for you and the Corpse, consensus is a formality. QUIETUS is my baby. They do what I say.'

They met outside Nyayo House, a sulphur-coloured skyscraper with the rounded contours preferred by architects in the mid-sixties with a penchant for designing office buildings to resemble giant toiletries. This one looked like a twenty-storey tampon holder, the plastic kind that holds two. It was the suspicious ochre of a yolk you have too sniff to check if it's gone off.

She didn't recognize him at first as Calvin strode up the steps. His languour was arrogant – the others could wait. In his bearing, newly smooth and self-possessed, she discerned an earlier incarnation: Calvin Piper, who had all of Congress quaking at massive migrant families as near by as Mexico; who commanded his own jet and the best hotel suites; who could stroll into any US government office without an appointment. The Director was back.

Though the colour of poisonous puffball spoor, Nyayo House was a persuasive Western skyscraper from the outside, yet its lobby was Kenyan: directions to offices were handwritten, the floor gritted, two of the elevators didn't work. In every hallway identical glassed photographs of President Moi glowered down at *wananchi*, giving the intended impression they were being watched.

The QUIETUS office was on an upper floor, and the door,

unmarked, resembled Calvin's office with its several locks. She wondered if the cards and codes were necessary, or 007 self-importance.

Calvin pushed the heavy sound-proof door on to a different world. Though the afternoon was sweltering, the suite was arctically air-conditioned, and raised the hair on Eleanor's arms. The room suffered none of the scrawled signs and peeling linoleum of Nyayo proper, its sweeping conference table Tanzanian teak, the thick salmon carpet slashed with recent vacuuming. Sealed by wide double-glazing from the shanty patchwork of distant hills, the suite was muffled with self-congratulatory creams. Calvin was aware that you could not convincingly debate global annihilation with a handwritten sign on your door or weigh the fate of billions in folding chairs.

A bank of computer screens covered one wall: 3-D continents revolving in full colour, vectors of increase streaking in alarming diagonals, spread sheets trilling margin to margin. As the displays flickered manically through their paces, the earth revolved with patches of green and grey and then bright red until Eleanor feared for it. On screen the planet seemed small and at their mercy.

The Corpse was gathered: Bunny, Basengi, Louis, Grant and a handful of others Eleanor couldn't take in from nerves. They turned to her with stony astonishment. Eleanor perched by Calvin, arranging her skirt, trying to keep her teeth from chattering and wishing she'd brought a sweater. Bunny shot her a curdled smile. Eleanor wanted to go home.

Calvin assumed the head of the table and took out a device like a traffic radar detector. No one spoke as the black box gave off a restless static. After a full minute of white noise, the company relaxed and muttered as if some silent prayer had been offered and answered.

'Bug free,' he said. 'So far. Most of you know Eleanor Merritt,' he introduced. 'Pathfinder. She has agreed to join QUIE-TUS. I have hopes she will give us a hand on the fund-raising side and take over our AIDS research. Basengi has enough on his plate and cannot handle the work as a sideline; it's too full-time. Any objections?'

'I'll say,' said Bunny. 'Haven't you flagrantly circumvented due process?'

'Yes,' said Calvin happily.

'You're going to explain why?'

'No I'm not.'

'How much,' inquired Basengi, 'you have told Ms Merritt, please?'

'Eleanor has been fully briefed.'

'So,' said Bunny, 'a *fait accompli*, then?'

'That's right.'

'You wouldn't mind if we asked her a few questions? Even if they're rather too late?'

'Be my guest.'

When Bunny swivelled to the new member, Eleanor made herself sit up straight and look Bunny in the eye, though inside she was shrivelling like pawpaw peel in the Sahel. To think Calvin had roped her into this on the premise it would be fun.

'You realize, Eleanor, that this is not one of those clubs you can join and then quit because it doesn't have a sauna?'

'I'm not partial to saunas,' said Eleanor. 'What are you getting at?'

'We can't afford to have disenchanted dilettantes gossiping at parties. That is why we like to do these interviews beforehand. To route out qualms. Do you have qualms?'

Eleanor asked incredulously, 'Don't *you*?'

'My commitment to QUIETUS is not in question here. Of course none of us has entered into this alliance lightly. I'm wondering if you have.'

'I'm willing to do research,' said Eleanor. 'I can't see how gathering accurate estimates of the demographic impact of HIV can do anyone any harm. But if you expect me to assure you that I have unflagging, blind faith that the objective of this operation is in the interests of the human race, I can't. I'm willing to listen. I have seen in the field that sometimes quick, cruel solutions are kinder than keeping doomed populations lingering through one more day.'

'Cruel solutions. You mean death.'

'Yes.' Eleanor raised her chin. 'I've worked in Ethiopia. I hated to see those people suffer. They lead fearful, tormented lives, for if they're not starving they're worrying about starving. I know all the arguments about food aid, how all it feeds is hunger. But I do not feel easy sitting in judgement, branding them better off dead. That is an assessment people may best make for themselves.'

'Yes, but what is the price?' Basengi jittered. 'If the only question was these people starving, we could let them decide to live or die. But the land, it is destroyed – turned to desert, thousands of years of topsoil gone in ten. The politics, they go haywire. The animals, they are slaughtered. It is to the earth itself we owe a sacrifice – '

'Time,' called Calvin. 'We're not here to debate the whole hoop-la into the ground again. We arrived at concensus years ago. Please, Basengi, cut it short.'

'But I am most interested in Eleanor's point of view,' said Bunny. 'I wanted to see if she had qualms. Now it seems she has nothing but. How did you persuade her to join our merry men, then? I'm confused.'

'Eleanor has a mind of her own,' said Calvin. 'That seems an asset to me.'

'I would be only too delighted,' Bunny snapped, 'that Ms Merritt has a quick, inquiring spirit with her own opinions of the world under ordinary circumstances. It is quite a different matter, however, to invite someone into our company who is not convinced of our purpose. At this stage, we hardly need a devil's advocate.'

'Considering the nature of your purpose,' Eleanor returned, 'the question is whether you're all devil's advocates.'

'See?' Bunny seethed. 'You said yourself, Calvin, you don't want us going round and round in circles we squared years ago. It took us relentless agonizing to finally transform from one more garrulous think-tank to effective sting operation. I do not relish wasting my time coddling a squeamish neophyte out of her naïve moral hand-wringing into the merciless realities of biological crisis. This is not a sorority. We aren't budgeted for initiation rites.'

'Eleanor's candidacy is not up for a vote,' said Calvin abruptly. 'As you noted, Bunny, QUIETUS is for life. Eleanor's in; she can't get out.'

Eleanor turned to Calvin. 'But what if I did want out? What would you do?'

'Oh, I don't know,' said Calvin, offhand. 'I suppose we'd have to kill you.'

Once again she had the inappropriate impulse to laugh. 'It would almost be worth it,' she said softly. 'To walk out that door and see if you'd put a bullet in my back. Single pieces of information may be worth risking your life for.'

'I shouldn't try it,' said Calvin.

'I'm chuffed,' said Eleanor, the Britishism for Bunny's benefit. 'You always kill the thing you love? I suppose two billion others should be chuffed as well.'

'A good many elephants have suffered the same affection. Even in 1963 my threats weren't empty, Eleanor. Don't push me.' His voice was friendly, intimate.

'I assume, if our new member is so well informed, she is aware that none of us participates in QUIETUS on a purely research basis?'

'We have discussed it, more or less,' said Calvin.

'What?' said Eleanor.

'Should Pachyderm come to fruition, we have all agreed not to simply administer the organism but to subject ourselves to it,' Bunny explained. 'If the agent meets specifications, two-thirds of us should survive, possibly more, since the parameters demand a high mortality among juveniles. Membership is no guarantee of exemption; quite the opposite. This stipulation is a moral imperative, which I'm sure, so scrupulous, you can appreciate.'

'Everyone except me,' said Calvin jovially. 'The scapegoat gets drawn and quartered.'

'It's outrageous,' said Eleanor, 'to regard participation in your own cataclysm as brave resolve. Your vows are ignoble. If you're forcing Russian roulette on the rest of the world, of course you play.'

'This moral posturing is a waste of time,' Calvin interjected. 'Can we get to work? Grant has been modelling labour-force projections. I'd like a report.'

Grant sat at the keyboard and a screen flashed a 3-D graph that resembled a quarter-volcano made of stair steps. 'The situation in thirty-five years looks volatile,' the dreary man began in a monotone. 'Because African economies cannot keep pace with population growth, up to 50 per cent of the work force will be unemployed. By 2025, 60 per cent of Africans will have migrated to urban centres . . .'

Numbers of any kind were coming to have a hypnotic effect on Eleanor; a mere post code could put her to sleep.

'Aquifer depletion, agricultural subdivision – a huge, unsatisfied, young, hungry population with no work – '

Eleanor's head took a speculative tilt. She hoped she appeared intent; in truth, she was remembering that Solastina was completely out of pasta.

'We predict total anarchy,' Grant declared with a grim smile. 'Nairobi in 2025 will make Nairobi in 1990 look like Gothenburg.'

The screen changed; the peak of the volcano shifted, with a shelf on its right side. 'Here we have the Pachyderm Effect. With approximately 20 per cent cropping of current reproductive ages, concentrating on younger parents so that progeny are not readily replaced, and 40 per cent cropping of juveniles, especially the under-fives, we see a very different picture for 2025: a population gently larger than today's, with plenty of time for economies to catch up with employment.' The screen changed. 'This is a labour force of a size that could conceivably sustain its own population. Environmental strategies have some chance of success, crop yields are likely to increase. With Pachyderm, Africa could easily become the dominant economic power of the next century. Ready for South America?'

She had to give QUIETUS credit: their attention span was astounding. Continent by continent they suffered Grant's statistics, and no one around the table ever looked less than rapt. Eleanor had a hard time keeping her eyes open. When he arrived at North America, she woke up.

'We have discussed designing an alternative pathogen for industrialized nations, with their below-replacement fertility rates. The North is threatened by an ageing population. Shrinking labour pools will force it to accept immigration, transforming the cultural complexion of these countries. The old are economically unproductive and burdensome to social systems.

We recommend an agent that hits geriatric targets and leaves the juvenile cohort largely intact.'

Eleanor squirmed. She liked her grandmother.

The meeting went on to 8 p.m. In the main of it, Eleanor, too, got caught up in the exercise: the optimum labour force, country by country, for 2025. By then Eleanor would be out of work herself. What would she do, with family planning deprived of support after Calvin's purge?

Flower-arranging. Towards the end she could no longer attend to the digits flashing across Nyayo's computer screens and imagined a little shop she could keep through retirement, shifting jonquils, snipping stems. Plants you could always get on with. Better than pets: if you abused them they didn't complain, but withered humbly to the soil from which they came. Eleanor and plants understood each other.

When the session broke up, Bunny put her hand on Calvin's arm. That woman was always touching him, with her little excuses.

'I would like to speak with you,' said Bunny severely.

Calvin glanced to Eleanor.

'It's OK. I just want to go to sleep.'

'The car – ?'

'I'll take a *matatu*.'

Bunny raised her eyebrows, disapproving. *Wazungu* took taxis.

On the way to catch her bus, Eleanor passed the hawkers on Moi who were just wrapping up their remaining flowers. She bought the remnants off several, and swayed down the avenue with an abundant array of glads, sweet peas, baby's breath. When she boarded the 'The Shining Way', TOLERANCE OF LADIES on the bumper, commuters stared; she was the only white on the bus. Eleanor didn't get a seat, and drew her shoulders around her blooms, glads poking other passengers, baby's breath exhaling against her cheek. The *matatu*'s loud disco suggested the many parties Eleanor had attended tongue-tied, wallflower; she and her bundle made one big wilting bouquet.

By the time she reached Karen and trembled down the steps, in the dark press of Kenya's population the glads were dejected, the sweet peas had soured and the baby's breath had the croup. She tossed the defeated blossoms in a ditch and fled to Calvin's bed.

'Calvin Piper, you astonish me.'

The screens were dark; a single spot lit the conference table. Calvin poured two neat shots from the well-stocked QUIE-TUS bar. Dealing death all day required a healthy allowance in the budget for whisky.

'I thought I was beyond astonishing you, Bunny. How encouraging.'

'You of all people dragging your latest skirt along to QUIE-TUS! Did you hope to impress her?'

'Not nearly as much as anticipated. She's taken the proposition in her stride.'

'But after all our precautions! How many years have we kept the operation tight? For God's sake, Calvin! Have you gone off your head?'

'*Inshe Allah.*'

'Don't *que sera sera* me. *Shauri ya Mungu* is for passive pastoralists with goats, not for a man with a brain. And just how many more forty-year-olds will be trotted to our multi-media show on afternoons you're too cheap to take them to a matinée?'

'Eleanor's thirty-eight,' said Calvin.

'Don't be cute. Eleanor Merritt constitutes a heinous security lapse. You were entirely out of order! Couldn't you tell that the whole committee was outraged?'

'Imagine my concern.'

'I'm awaiting an explanation.'

'Then you'll wait a long time.'

Bunny drummed her fingers. 'You don't really fancy her, do you?'

He considered, 'I do, a bit.'

'She doesn't seem your type,' Bunny ventured.

'What's my type?'

'Someone your intellectual equal. You're brilliant, CP. You need a woman who can challenge you.'

'Eleanor does challenge me. She cries. It's mysterious. I couldn't cry with a gun to my head.'

'If QUIETUS is exposed in the morning papers, popsy, you will bawl. Behind bars, with no hankie.'

'I'm looking forward to prison.' Calvin clasped his hands behind his head. 'I'll keep my feet on the ground with leg-irons.'

'You've time for reflective incarceration in 1999. Meanwhile you have a job to do. The future of this planet depends on it, and part of that job is keeping your trap shut. Do let's make this Eleanor creature your first and last indiscretion. Besides the risk, she's terribly wet. Oh, I'm sure she cries. I can see her bursting into tears in the middle of one of Norman's presentations, overcome by how we can murder innocent babies. You need the constitution for this work. Mark my words, she doesn't have it.'

'Which may be to her credit.'

'Don't go schmaltzy on me, CP. A woman like that is best off dabbing sticking plasters on little boys' boo-boos and squeezing fresh lemonade. Calling the kiddies in for din-din. Making pies.'

'You're making me hungry.'

'*Not*,' she continued, 'meddling in designer viruses. Just you wait. If you hand her the HIV research, she'll come back with one or two computer models and her heart breaking. All these weak TB-riddled skeletons covered in herpes, we have to do something.'

'She'd be right. We do. We will.'

'Give her a project that's less important.'

'Coffee, you mean. Tidying up.'

'Just not HIV, it's too crucial.' At last the older woman couldn't contain herself. 'Honestly, CP. I don't understand what you see in that girl!'

'She's warm.'

'So is a kitty cat.'

'Or a bunny?'

She flustered, 'You and I are beyond that.'

'Eleanor says no one is beyond that.'

'You've claimed to be.' She bristled. 'Or have you changed your tune?'

'Oh, no,' he assured her. 'Eleanor and I are chums. Full stop.'

Bunny visibly relaxed. 'Well, you had better stay chums. I hope you like her, because now you're stuck. And she'd better not get too sweet on you, because *some* women finally weary of a peck on the cheek. You've given her quite a weapon. She can ruin us. I should simply upchuck if we were undone by a scorned female.'

Calvin sighed. 'Madame Mort, can we clarify something here? I did not tell her. She found out.'

'Whose fault was that?'

'Mine,' he admitted. 'It's true I could have shot her then and there. But leaving aside my weak stomach, the police might actually investigate the disappearance of a *mzungu*. Instead, luring a nigger-loving DC Democrat into a holocaust conspiracy is quite a coup, don't you think?'

'An an intellectual exercise it's commendable, but you cheated. You didn't convince her; she's smitten.'

'QUIETUS concluded long ago that it doesn't matter how you do it so long as it works. And I'm afraid we have a much graver leak than our friend Ms Merritt.' He told her about Threadgill.

'How can you be so sure flavour of the month wasn't in on the burglary? She had a key.'

'She says she wasn't.'

Bunny snorted. 'She says.'

'That's right. So I believe her.'

'You can be such a pushover, CP.'

'I'm a good judge of character, and Eleanor still has some. I vetted everyone in the Corpse, including you, my duckie. Has any one of them finked? And I have it on good authority that Eleanor Merritt is made of harder stuff than she appears.'

'On whose authority?'

'My dead housekeeper's.'

It wasn't easy to do, but that shut Bunny Morton right up.

14

Paying the Piper

'After all this hugger-mugger, you go out with an organ grinder and Malthus on a string with a tin cup? Or do you hold 5,000-dollars-a-plate fund-raising dinners for the promotion of disease?'

They were curling out of Wilson Airport. As the twin-prop gained altitude Calvin relaxed, all signs of human infestation reduced to scabby rash. In flying, even rivets on wings decrease velocity; he imagined that soon the nuts down on the planet would be sufficiently numerous to slow the earth's orbit by several miles a second, an aeronautical inefficiency termed *parasite drag*.

'We don't tip our hand, if that's what you're asking. Follow my lead; shy away from direct questions. And Eleanor, you're going to have to control yourself. Remember that we don't have to fall in love; we just want his money. Save the ACLU rhetoric for after hours.'

'In other words, we're about to pay a call on a bigoted old coot. I'm supposed to cross my legs and sugar my tea while he trashes Africans as subhuman breeding machines.'

'Precisely.'

'I don't think I'm qualified for this work.'

'It's good for your education. Spend too much time in aid cliques concocting synonyms for *blackmail* because *extortion* is less racist and you get a distorted picture of the rest of the world, which is still carping contentedly about coons, nignogs, steelies and baboons.'

'Are you?'

'I think every race on earth is chock-a-block with ham-headed degenerates, you know that. We're all wogs.'

'Right. The new broad-mindedness.' She sounded sour.

'Set yourself an assignment,' he proposed. 'Try not to find Bradley-Cox deplorable; try to find him *interesting*.'

Calvin cut a sumi arc through the sky like a brush across paper, one more suggestion of a goodness that bore no relation to justice. Eleanor's religion would have to transform. Grace; light; colour: they were beyond fairness.

'Do you mention QUIETUS by name? It's a give-away.'

'In public we refer to our enterprise as the NAADP: New Angles on Active Demographic Prophylaxis. But that's not what it really stands for.'

'Which is?'

Calvin grinned. 'The National Association for the Advancement of Dead People.'

Despite herself, Eleanor laughed.

Once landed in the Aberdares, Calvin briefed her on their quarry as Wendell Bradley-Cox's driver chauffeured them from the airstrip. 'BC is seventy. Resigning his commission in the Gurkhas, he made a bundle coffee-farming, and got most of the money out before Independence. Lost the *shamba* to Kenyatta, but kept the house. In the meantime he's invested in an international credit investigation company, making oodles off other people's bankruptcies when everyone else is losing his shirt. I'll give him this, he made his own fortune, which is more than you can say for your average Kenya cowboy. One ungrateful daughter, gaga with a guru in CA: dead loss. Wife of twenty-five years left him last year for another woman. Life has gone a bit fast for BC. He's old-fashioned. Cannot fathom what's happened to the world, Kenya, his life. You won't have to push him hard to admit that things are getting worse generally, since they have certainly gotten worse personally, and these perceptions have a way of travelling in tandem. Wealthy, maybe, but a chap of modest needs: vodka and a new pair of slippers. No family, no farm – our man needs a purpose. We aim to oblige.'

Bradley-Cox's manor was constructed on a generous colonial scale when Kenya was still frontier: all the wood and land in the world, the architecture was an attitude. The veranda skirted three-quarters of the house with a possessive view of the Aberdares. In the yard, a gardener desultorily nubbled a hedge clipped the week before: one of those large staffs with nothing to do, but who had to keep up the appearance of industry. A young girl swept stray eucalyptus leaves from the drive. Madam had fled; the young mistress was in America; no doubt BC's decadent dinners were a thing of the past, the silver polished every Sunday and then tucked in a drawer. Their arrival drew a sidelong glance from the yard workers. BC didn't have many visitors these days. In Happy Valley, the whites were no longer up to much mischief.

There were dogs, everywhere, and when Eleanor got out of the car they pawed her dress with mud prints. She pushed them off with pretence of affection, until a haggard but gentle-faced man whistled them from the porch. He was dressed, but the striped cotton shirt with its tail out and the rumpled beige trousers suggested pyjamas. Calvin was right about the slippers, with crushed heels. Bradley-Cox shuffled towards them, *shsh-shsh*.

Calvin introduced himself. 'We met in – '

'I know,' BC interrupted. 'Well, don't just stand there. Come in.' For an old man with little to attend to, he was curiously impatient.

Though it was only two in the afternoon, he met them vodka in hand. Eleanor accepted one herself because people like Wendell were suspicious of tee-totallers. She assessed him as one of those IV drinkers: drip, drip, drip, all day long.

Despite the spectacular weather, Wendell led them to his sitting room, drapes drawn. Eleanor pined for the veranda, the wicker rocker with its mountain view, for the interior oppressed her. The mahogany and oriental carpeting were funereal; the brown glass eyes of koodoo heads looked bereaved. She couldn't figure why such a well-kept room felt shabby, unless mental stagnation could settle on furniture like dust.

While a houseboy padded in with a tray of tomato sandwiches – BC would no more introduce him than he would his spatula – Wendell presented his dogs by name, all eight of them.

'You a hunter?' asked Calvin.

'Oh, I must have bagged my last trophy twenty years ago,' said Wendell. 'I dropped that eland, and when I approached her she was still alive. Animals are so expressive when they're in pain. They know they're dying. She looked at me as if to say, *Why did you do this to me?* That was the last time I killed an animal. I wouldn't do it again.'

Yet the expression he described was his own: confused, wrung, innocent. Much as she had braced herself to bite her tongue and swallow her anger at racist claptrap, Wendell inspired nothing of the kind. His face had the misty, lost look of wounded game – chest heaving, ear twitching, flies beginning to settle on a beast already too far gone to flick them away. Maybe having your wife leave you for a lesbian after twenty-five years was something like being shot.

'Now, people,' Wendell went on, 'I could see hunting them. People are vicious. An animal never comes at you. As long as you leave it be, it passes you by.'

'Have you ever,' Eleanor ventured, 'looked a man in the eye? When he was dying?'

'Only the Japanese,' he dismissed. 'I don't think they count. From what I saw in the war, that race is simply not human. We would come upon their POWs when they retreated. With a lady present, I hesitate to describe . . . Oh, it was dreadful.' Wendell shuddered. 'Men are the only animals that kill for fun.'

'Cats,' said Eleanor.

'You know, you're right,' said Wendell, looking at Eleanor as if for the first time. 'I don't care for cats. Don't keep them. No loyalty. All very lovey-lovey so long as you feed them. But happy as you please, they'll patter off to anyone else with a tin.'

'Did you know,' intervened Calvin, 'that a female cat has an average of 2.8 surviving kittens, two litters a year? So say you start with two cats, and you don't run any of the pussies over with a truck, by the end of ten years, you're stocking Nine Lives Liver and Bacon for *eighty million kitties*.'

'Crikey!' Wendell exclaimed. 'They're as bad as the Kikuyu!'

That was the idea.

'You hunt yourself, Piper?'

'I cropped elephants in Uganda for the game department.'

'Don't know how you could bear it. You biltong the cow, and then you have to take out the babies, don't you?'

'Yes, or they'd starve. But it's for the elephants' own good. You've seen what they do to their own habitat if they're allowed to run riot – '

'Oh, yes. Oh, it's terrible. Still – ' He stroked the Lab in his lap. 'I couldn't shoot the babies. I couldn't look them in the eyes.'

Eleanor thought, *this man loves animals and hates Africans*, then tried Calvin's exercise: Wendell wasn't warped; he was *interesting*.

'You know, when they outlawed hunting in Kenya,' Wendell volunteered, 'they also banned skeet and trap?'

'Why was that?'

'My neighbour Tempest-Stewart asked a minister himself. The MP replied, "Well, they have a right to live, too." ' Wendell laughed until his pupils glistened. 'They thought skeet and trap were animals! Can you imagine, it took two years to get the law repealed.'

'How's the land managed here?' Calvin inquired. 'Still good-sized holdings?'

'What do you think? Most Europeans have been bought out by Moi and his flunkies, for spare change. Who do you suppose oversees Moi's *shambas*, the only farms around here that still get a bean or two out of the country?'

'I can guess,' said Calvin.

'*Mzungus!* As for the rest, the plots get carved up every generation. I don't see where it will stop. So help me God, it's a disgrace what they've done to this country. They say this was the birthplace of civilization. It's hard to believe. Something awful must have happened.'

'What's the water situation?'

'Frightful. We've our own bore hole, and the time was you couldn't sink a bore hole within half a mile of another, and even then with government permission. But now with a little *baksheesh* – ' He rubbed his fingers. 'They're drilled like pins in a cushion. The table has sunk so low that our hole, which used to pump 10,000 gallons a month, now only pumps two.'

Wendell refreshed their drinks, with a disparaging glance at Eleanor's full glass.

'I was warned you chaps wanted money,' Wendell returned. 'So get on with it. What for?'

'The exponential rise in human population in this century,' Calvin began, 'is the most massive biological transformation this planet has undergone since the last ice age. Every year erosion, overgrazing and salinity are destroying three million acres of productive farmland worldwide. People, Wendell, are worse than elephants.'

'I've heard all this before. So?'

'Ninety per cent of population growth in the next hundred years is expected to occur in the Third World. Africa alone will have multiplied itself *four times* in the second half of this century. Nigeria, for example, will rise from a population of thirty million in 1950 to three hundred million in 2025; a tenfold increase in a single lifetime. At that point it will displace the United States as the fourth most populous country in the world – *Nigeria*, Wendell. You know what it's like here – can it afford to get worse?'

Wendell was fidgeting with the dog.

'Meanwhile,' Calvin continued, though even the Labrador was beginning to whine, 'fertility has plummeted in developed countries to *below the replacement rate* of 2.2. Only because of age structure and immigration have populations from our own part of the world not yet begun to shrink. The fertility rate in Germany is 1.4. Italy? A Catholic country? *1.2.*'

He finally got BC's attention. 'I'm gobsmacked.'

It was one of Calvin's favourite figures. 'Small wonder that if you go to New York City now, it's virtually impossible to find a conolli in Little Italy; but you can buy plenty of eggrolls. Have you been to London lately?'

'Two years back.'

'A lot of Pakistanis on the street? Running all the shops? Iraqis? West Indians?'

'Not an Englishman in twenty.'

'It's a dying race, Wendell. And that's just the start. Population growth where economies are drowning will encourage massive migration to countries that still have their heads above water. Are you getting the picture? Wendell: *we are being overrun*. Third World countries may not have nuclear bombs, but they have much more powerful weapons: they have babies.'

Wendell made a gesture of casual despair such as only a man of seventy can afford. This talk of 2025 might have been of the Pleistocene or Mars. He would never submit to such a year, and of that reprieve Eleanor could only be envious. Like most of her generation, she was afraid of the future. How remarkable it must have been to live in the nineteenth century, with its myth of progress.

However, the money Wendell kept in Britain must have grown as abstract as 2025 – with his vodka and slippers? Calvin was offering him a last chance to spend it, and the very old and the very young share a devil-may-care. Since the future is real to neither, they are both rash.

'What are you suggesting?' asked BC.

'I can't tell you.'

Wendell rubbed his chin in baffled amusement. 'You expect me to hand you a blank cheque. To do whatever you please?'

'That's right.'

'Cheeky chap.'

'I dare say.'

'You're with . . . one of those aid capers? Because you people have been pouring money into this family planning palaver for years, and from the sound of your own song and dance it hasn't done a speck of good.'

'I couldn't agree more. I was the head of the Population Division at USAID. I was fired.'

'Goodness.'

'I broke the rules. I don't know your views on abortion, but I shipped off vacuum aspirators like Hoovers to Hiltons.'

'I wouldn't want my daughter to have one,' Wallace admitted. 'But if it meant a few less *watu* – '

'I wouldn't want *your* daughter to have one either.'

'Calvin!' Eleanor exclaimed, unable to control herself.

'My most controversial position', Calvin continued, his glance slicing *shut up*, 'was to advocate the withdrawal of all child survival and infant mortality programmes in Africa.'

'In English?'

'The whole reason there are so many people here, Wendell,

is the missionaries trekked in vaccines for smallpox, eradicated tsetse flies, cured yellow fever and improved nutrition. Not so long ago, women had crops of children and most of them died. It was a hard life, but it worked: populations were relatively stable. I advocate going back to traditional death rates. Stop re-hydrating the five-year-old with diarrhoea. I know it sounds callous, but the alternative is he will starve or, should he live to fourteen, knife either of us in the back for a chicken sandwich. The West created a disease with a cure. Only the West can take its nostrums away.'

'So that's what you're about, getting the nurses out?'

'I can't tell you more than I have. I'm the head of a private organization whose intentions are drastic; even fantastic. These issues are politically sensitive. It's not in your interests to know too much. Your cheque will not be traceable to us. Your name will not appear in our files. Only our visit here today could implicate you, and you may claim it was social. I'm not trying to be coy, Wendell, but to protect you and my operation both.'

'How do I know you're not a charlatan?'

'I am a former department head of USAID, not a ruffian with a crumpled typewritten pledge for radio-television school. I have nothing on paper; printed material could get me arrested. My credentials are easy to check, but if you go looking for my organization you won't find it. I know it sounds outlandish, and I'm asking you to take a great deal on faith. Then, look at it this way: even if this is a flim-flam, what's going to happen to population growth? Nothing. But what will happen if you don't give me support? Nothing. If you fund me, something might improve; if not, everything definitely gets worse.'

BC chuckled. 'By that reasoning, I should bankroll every confidence artist I meet.' To Eleanor's amazement, he took out his cheque book. 'To whom do I make this out?'

'The IMF will do nicely.' When Calvin took the cheque decorously, he didn't glance at the amount but slipped it blindly into his wallet.

'I shall expect a report.'

'How much we report,' said Calvin affably, 'will depend on

our report of you.' He had successfully switched it around, who trusted whom.

'How drastic?' asked Wendell with a mischievous smile, as if he knew very well.

'Drastic,' Calvin assured him, and shook hands.

'You won't hurt any animals will you?' BC called as they departed.

'Not on four legs,' Calvin shouted back.

As they tucked into the jeep, Calvin waved as Wendell stroked his hunt terrier on the porch. Eleanor waved, too, until they were around the bend. The man looked so forlorn. Calvin was already peeping in his wallet. 'Two hundred thousand pounds. Not bad for a day's work.'

'It stretches my credulity,' said Eleanor, 'that the IMF is behind QUIETUS.'

'Use your head,' Calvin chided. 'We just received a donation to the International Mortality Fund.'

Though their mission had been successful, on the flight back Eleanor was acidly silent.

'You're pouting,' said Calvin.

'You forewarned me about bigoted balderdash, but not that I'd have to hear it from you.'

'More complicity,' he assured her. 'But the joke is on BC. He thinks the world is only over-populated with bongos. The truth is it is also over-populated with racist colonialists. After all, what are the chances that a seventy-year-old alcoholic will survive Pachyderm?'

He could not understand why his rogue sense of justice was of such limited consolation. The poor sweet old man. And what would happen to all those dogs?

Their next target, however, was an American who worked for Lonrho, a calm, well-kept and widely read gentleman of modest appetite who early in the encounter moderated Calvin's extreme forecasts with more complex figures of his own; something felt wrong.

The house itself had all the right markings, an opulent spread overlooking the game park, steeped in that funny emptiness that can invade interiors when they are too well done – too spare, too tasteful, with a pillow just here and that print with simply the ideal frame and something in you is dying to toss toys in the corner and invite a homeless person to throw up on the sofa. It was one of those dream houses too clever for its own good, since when Eleanor imagined coming home to such a vision she saw long evenings with no company, walking bereft from one wide-windowed, ethnic-carpeted diorama to the next, the phone not ringing. No one would stop by, since the dream house was, as dream houses always are, out in the middle of nowhere, and consequently was steeped in the air of all dressed up and no place to go. After enough ambling from the game-viewing nook to the bathroom – brass fittings, plush towels so terrifyingly white you end up drying your hands on the toilet paper – she would slit her wrists in the tub, not only to make a mess but to force all this calculated architecture to experience an emotion. Something about perfection is hostile.

Thomas Eggerts shared some of the qualities of his house: he surely took regular exercise, kept his cholesterol low and ate bran cereal. His correspondence would be up to date, and he would never run out of paper-clips. His expression was terminally pleasant, his face unimportantly handsome, and it was so impossible to imagine Thomas doing anything unruly or indulging in substances we have all read are not good for us that Eleanor wondered if discipline itself could become a vice.

Her foreboding intensified when their host sipped passion fruit squash, which drove Calvin as ever into the arms of the whisky Eggerts clearly kept only for guests. Likewise the presence of American inflection drew Calvin's nattiest British accent.

'In famine relief camps,' Calvin introduced after their polite statistical fencing, 'aid workers have found that families themselves will select a child to die. The child is not only banned from his own parents' larder, but will get shunted from the pot of porridge even if it's provided by UNICEF. Brothers and sisters will take *posho* out of his hands. Eventually he becomes lack-lustre and won't even try for food. It makes sense, of course. If the parents die, the whole family is lost. The parents come first.'

'I was running a health clinic in Addis,' Eleanor added. 'A

family in a nearby village had a ten-year-old girl they kept in the back room. She was terribly under-nourished, and ill, but not beyond hope. She needed a blood transfusion, and both her parents were compatible. I begged them – one transfusion would save the girl's life. They both refused. They'd already decided she should die. I know it's a small story, but somehow that experience did something to me. I found it harder to run my clinic after that, and applied for a transfer.'

'The little girl,' said Thomas. 'You were fond of her?'

'Maybe that was it. Yes, very. She was tiny but unusually beautiful and bright. I found myself thinking, if her own parents won't save her, what am I doing here?'

'Africans don't have the same relationship to death as we do,' said Calvin.

'They can't afford to,' said Thomas.

'In the States,' said Calvin, 'have you noticed how bereaved relatives act indignant? Especially in the upper classes. You get the feeling that over $100,000-a-year Americans believe they've earned themselves out of disease.'

'I dread the day,' said Thomas, 'that the rich can pay the poor to die for them,'

'They do already,' said Eleanor.

'You're quite right,' said Thomas. 'We eat off the curved backs of men with a life expectancy of forty-five. Our breakfast porridge is taken from the hands of those little boys shut out from the UNICEF pot.'

'It's not that simple,' Calvin scoffed. 'And I've never seen the point of sophomoric, mawkish self-flagellation. As you've said yourself, Eleanor, maldistribution is a fact of life. My point was otherwise: Africans grasp that letting some sections of the population go can be in the interests of the larger community. They are mature about death. The West, in my view, could use a bit more calamity. I watch my own culture growing bathetic and senile. When I read about millions of dollars spent to mend a single hole in some white baby's heart, I want to gag.'

'All the same,' said Thomas, 'you're not suggesting African parents have no feelings for their children?'

'No,' said Calvin noncommittally.

'And you would admit that, even if this triage you describe

is necessary, parents forced to select their own child for starvation are tragic?'

'I wouldn't call it tragic; I'd call it realistic.'

'Can you imagine,' he pressed, 'in your own family, how you would feel if your mother instructed you that your baby sister, with whom you played every day, was no longer to be fed?'

'With difficulty,' said Calvin. 'I was an only child.'

Thomas sat back. 'Somehow I could have predicted that.' He invited them to his dinner table, though his graciousness was formal for an American; chilly.

'On the one hand,' Thomas resumed, 'I can see your point that up against the wall circumstances arise where some must be sacrificed for the good of all, but you will not win me from my grief should such a choice be foisted on my own family, or on anyone else's. Without that grief I cease to be a human being as I understand the term. I'll grant you the obscenity of spending millions of dollars to save the life of a single American infant when in the meantime hundreds of thousands of children in Mali are dying of diarrhoea that could be cured for two or three dollars apiece. Yet were our resources sufficiently plentiful, I would spend a million dollars to save the life of any child; as they are not, we have to make painful assessments of how much that life is worth. The wealthy can afford to be precious, and the poor cannot – it's not even a question of values, but economics. However, the opposite extreme of your "sentimental" relation to death in the industrialized world I personally find more frightening: where human life no longer means anything at all. Admire African "maturity" with corpses as you will, when things go wrong on this continent that is how they corrupt: people become firewood. In fact, that is what happens by and large when things go wrong anywhere. Historically, I can't think of a society that has collapsed or degraded itself because its people cared for one another to excess.'

'On the contrary,' said Calvin, knife and fork upright on the table, though no one was eating, 'historically, that is what's happening right now. We think more and more people is better and better, we save this lot and that lot from starving, and we can't afford it! The whole planet can't afford it!'

'What no society can afford,' Thomas returned through his teeth, 'is blithely condemning whole populations of its own kind to death because their existence is inconvenient.'

'We are not talking inconvenience, Eggerts, we are talking extinction!'

'So you say. I am not fully persuaded. But I believe there are different kinds of extinction. It is hypothetically possible for us to persist as a species but to lose what makes us remarkable. In my mind, our distinction has everything to do with a capacity for altruism, empathy and, if you don't mind the word in a conversation where it obviously has little place, *love*.'

Calvin leaned forward. 'All right, we agree. Have you ever been to villages where there's nothing to eat? You're so concerned with our sinking to mindless, unfeeling animals, well, that's what happens, Eggerts. They *sit*, all day, with flies in their eyes, and after a certain point nobody bothers to dig graves. They don't sing, they don't read, they don't even bloody talk most of the time, much less pass on quaint anthropological tales of the ancestors. If you starve people enough they don't care about each other any longer, *all* they care about is food. And that's what all of Africa is looking at unless someone or something moves fast.'

'So what do you propose?'

'To begin with – ' Calvin hesitated, though it had been such a breeze with BC. 'I would withdraw child survival programmes.'

'You mean, pack up the vaccines? Tell the Red Cross to close shop?'

'That's right.'

'That would be tantamount to murder.'

'At this point,' said Calvin defiantly, 'I am not entirely opposed to murder.'

Thomas Eggerts stood up. 'Then we have nothing more to say to one another. Perhaps we will skip dessert.'

Eleanor fumbled from her place, her face bright red. 'Calvin – '

Calvin rose. 'You're a wet, fatuous tit, Eggerts. It's people like you who cause a lot of suffering in the end, keeping everyone in sight alive one more hateful day.'

'It's your day that's hateful, from the sound of it,' said Thomas at the door. 'But you wanted money, didn't you? So here, Tin Man – ' He handed out a ten-shilling note. 'Go buy yourself a heart.'

Back in the Land Cruiser, Calvin exploded. '*Who* put that prat on my list? Every single name was supposed to be exhaustively vetted! Somebody's going to get it in the neck! Thomas Eggerts is a pious, maudlin dish-rag! Lucky for us all I kept my cards close to my chest, or we would be up one seriously brown creek! I am not making another appointment until that list is double-checked. And what is wrong with you, anyway? I'm not angry at you. It's not your lousy homework.'

Eleanor put her hand to her cheek so he couldn't see her face and announced quietly, 'I have never been so embarrassed in my life.' From a woman who had spent thirty-eight years in a state of near-permanent shame, it was an extreme statement.

15

More Parameters

When he first proposed taking her to the Pachyderm lab, Eleanor said, 'Where?' She went vague. When pressed, she supposed she couldn't see the harm, but then she hadn't seen the harm in his whole fantasy, and that's why she didn't want to go. Before they left the house, she thought of phone calls to make, postcards to send, until he lifted her from the dining-room table by the nape of her neck, the way you drag cats cowering under the bed when they can hear their bath running.

Eleanor climbed heavily into Calvin's cockpit and entertained various preconceptions. She pictured one of those grotty, fly-away Kenyan concerns, like Nyayo's lobby: a back room in need of paint, counters scattered with half a dozen chipped test tubes, shelves of dusty jars with coloured powders like an array of ceramic glazes, a few spoons, an old hunchback with a manic gleam in his eye stirring a bowl of something brown and noxious all under the omniscient, rheumy eyes of another photograph of President Moi. Or maybe a zany palace full of scientists who would all on cue tear off their white coats to expose garters, corsets and stilettos, to high-kick down the corridors, Rocky Horror. More likely still, there was no lab. Calvin would fly to a pretty, deserted spot in Samburu, lift her from the plane and laugh. They would picnic: salmon and champagne. He had planned it in advance, on ice. Toasting, Eleanor would confess that for a little while she was taken in, that the Corpse meeting and fund-raising alike had been brilliant theatre, and QUIETUS would go down as his wittiest practical joke.

The trip took just over an hour, and Eleanor asked no questions. As they entered the Northern Frontier District, she objected that the flight was making her woozy; maybe they should visit another day. But Calvin had already decreased his altitude, looping around a neat grid of long white buildings with red crosses on top. 'Am Ref?' she inquired faintly.

'Camouflage. And why not? We're flying doctors of a kind, diligently concocting a cure-all for the thousand natural shocks that flesh is heir to.'

Pachyderm had its own landing strip, and Calvin explained that as air traffic control in East Africa was Wild West, it had proved easy to fly equipment and crates of rats and monkeys into the compound undetected. From overhead, he identified research prefabs, residential quarters and supply huts with mayoral pride. Pachyderm was effectively a small town, one of those self-sufficient settlements formed round a single industry, even if most of these townspeople hadn't a clue what they manufactured.

'Oh, they're aware the operation is hush-hush,' Calvin extolled. 'The higher-ups imagine we're on a US defence contract. The peons think we're trying to beat Burroughs-Wellcome to a cure for AIDS. This fuels them with the fires of righteousness when cleaning cages and helps explain why our experimental populations keep dying out.'

'Calvin, this place is huge!'

'We've over 300 employees all told. No one leaves. No one is allowed to. We keep them fed, housed and entertained. We have a PX, bar. And Bunny was kidding about not having a sauna.'

'How could you convince anyone to work out here?'

'Salaries are high. Grants have so dried up in the US and UK that our foremost scientists are paying to publish their own papers. Besides, I not only supply them with state of the art equipment but here their experiments aren't hogtied by nerdy restrictions from the animal rights cuddly-toy brigade. And the way you lure any good microbiologist is with interesting work. Pachyderm is the most fascinating research on the face of the earth. We are on the cutting edge of mortality. Set on stage with the elegant belladonnas you'll see dancing down below, the atomic bomb is a cow in a ballet.'

Landing, Eleanor's stomach flipped. The dust cleared to reveal their welcome wagon of one, who wailed over the dying engine, 'Don't tell me! More *parameters*!'

Calvin laughed. 'Eleanor? Norman.'

Much as she might have pictured the mastermind at Pachyderm as a pewter-eyed Mengele, Norman Shagg was more an ageing Merry Prankster, shirtless with drawstring trousers the colour of Eleanor's complexion: queasy purple. He rocked on rubber-tyre sandals and fingered a Masai snuff box thonged around his neck. His uncombed locks shocked out from his head in various lengths of dread. Instead of the thin-lipped, sinister grimace of her imagination, Norman's slapdash smile appeared to have been papered haphazardly on to his face at slightly the wrong angle. With his nose longish and pointed, his eyes keen and closely set, she wondered if he'd spent too long around his laboratory pets – he looked like a rat. But a friendly rat. Glancing from her psychotic boyfriend to this hyperactive hippie Frankenstein, Eleanor thought, I am surrounded by friendly rats.

'Don't be fooled,' Calvin whispered as they packed into Norman's Suzuki, 'he's a genius.'

'We've shipped in this load of immune-deficient mice, see,' Norman was babbling. 'So we can implant human foetal tissues and they're not rejected. It's dynamite! We're growing intestines, lymph nodes, thymuses, you name it!'

'What for?' asked Eleanor warily.

'Your friend here expects me to design a virus that only works on humans with green monkeys. Well, we've cracked it. We've cracked a lot while you've been gone, boyo. And these mice, with tiny human lungs, t-cells in the bloodstream, b-cells in the liver, you have got to see to believe. What we can't quite figure is why the human cells don't attack the meeses.'

'Human cells are obviously at home in rodents,' said Calvin.

'I knew you'd have a scientific explanation.'

Calvin turned around to Eleanor in the back seat to explain that the facility had originally been established, innocently, for the conduct of his density studies: what happens when you crammed eighty rats in a pen meant for ten?

'Uh-huh,' she grunted, 'and what did happen?'

'It was fantastic!' Norman exploded, gunning up an embankment until Eleanor could feel the Suzuki's centre of gravity tilt backwards. 'We got whole colonies out of their tiny tree. Half the boys were gay, and you don't ordinarily see a lot of buggery in rats. And the girls became lousy mothers; turned their hairless toddlers into latch-key kids.'

'The females under normal density conditions build cup-shaped nests for their young,' said Calvin. 'In our high-density model, mothers would lay their young on a few stray strips and then desert. We developed rat shanty towns.'

'You got whole gangs of sexual deviants that would mate anything from newborns to drinking troughs,' Norman shouted over the engine. 'Males mounted females in the middle of giving birth. Courtship rituals disappeared. The males usually do this little jig outside the female's nest, trying to get her to come out and play – it's cute. With over-population, no more two-step.'

'Though the biggest problem was cannibalism.'

'Wonderful,' Eleanor muttered, gazing out of the window through the billows of the car trying to take in the view. The landscape had that stark, desolate beauty of a place where people didn't belong. Why such a deserted vista would inspire research in depopulation was beyond her.

'They started eating their own young,' said Calvin, as if she wanted to know. 'A mother would consume her litter as it was born. In the third month of this experiment, infant mortality was 96 per cent. In the fourth month, my poppet, the entire colony was dead.'

'Swiftian, isn't it?' remarked Norman to his boss. 'Maybe we should hang on a few more years here. In Africa I can see it: one big feeding frenzy. Kurtz, boy.'

She was clutching the car door to stay upright, as Norman swerved the Suzuki around brush and bounced over ruts, sending her head to the roof. Dust clouded the car, white dirt gathering on the fine hairs of her arms, paling her skin to ash. The grit in her teeth warned of a visit that would be hard to digest.

'You should tell Eleanor about our happy-hour series,' Norman commended sociably.

'Mm?'

'Under normal density conditions,' said Calvin, 'if you give Norwegian rats access to alcohol, a few characters will take to it, town drunks if you will, but most don't have a taste for meth. As we increased crowding, however, the number of tipplers rapidly increased.'

'It was gorgeous!' Norman delighted on a hand-brake 180. 'Huge pens weaving with these totally legless rats. Past a critical density, every one of them tap-tap-tapped at those methanol levers, like those colonial geezers at the Muthaiga Club on Sunday afternoons. They like skipped the water levers altogether. Gave up on sex, food, just hit the booze, all day. That crew died out, too.'

'I liked the behavioural sink,' Calvin reminisced.

'I can hardly wait,' said Eleanor, as Norman screeched to a halt inches short of a wall.

'This wasn't repugnant, just peculiar,' Calvin explained. 'The more crowded the pen got, the more the animals congregated in a single quarter of the compound.'

'Nairobi,' said Norman.

'New York,' said Calvin. 'Rat-Tokyo.'

'Don't you think,' supposed Eleanor, as they strode towards a banal white building that shimmered in the heat (a *mirage*, surely), 'that parallels between rats and people are a bit tenuous?'

'Nope,' said Calvin.

Norman led them down the hall, though the building didn't have that gleaming, twenty-first-century sterility she might have expected. Billboards fluttered with notices for keg parties, reggae nights and weekend discos. She glanced in doorways where, between infra-red photos of the earth, topographic maps of Africa and tables of the elements, the cubicles were taped as well with *New Yorker* cartoons, misprints from the *Standard* and Far Side birthday cards. The desks were littered with granola bar wrappers and toilet-roll Father's Day pencil holders; in the distance a coffee machine gurgled from its build-up of alkaline. A researcher in an Einstein T-shirt looked up from his computer, caught her eye and smiled. His soft hair in a boyish mop, he looked sweet. She caught up with her escorts, who were chuckling together, at jokes she was rather glad to miss. Yet the compound hardly felt clandestine, mephistophelean. She passed two glistening men in shorts slashing the air with racquets, discussing serve and volley.

Turning into the next corridor, however, Norman led them to a massive open room cluttered with equipment; she thought at first they'd entered a gymnasium. No Nautilus presented itself. Eleanor lagged behind to stare: everywhere, big whirling, humming machines she didn't understand. Blue sine waves oscillated on screens, centrifuges whipped the air like propellers, lasers traced keen pure lines from one contraption to another. As Calvin entered the lab, first one and then another technician in sweaty Tusker Ts looked up eagerly from his station. Women in shorts and tank-tops strode with brusque professionalism between the aisles, waving to Dr Piper with scalpels. Calvin clapped his researchers on the shoulder as they peered in microscopes, sometimes stopping to cajole, inquire about an experiment, or bring greetings from family. Eleanor was still waiting for her picnic. 'To fraudulence,' her glass would clink. 'To Andromeda. To dream.'

Cacophony preceded the next chamber: screeing, chittering and scrambling, over the whir of exercise wheels. The three filed past cages of chimps, pigeons, hamsters and, naturally, rats. She looked for signs of abuse, but aside from a few mice looking peaked, most of the animals appeared healthy, leaping and poking through the mesh as she walked by. Only the last cage gave Calvin noticeable pause: one of the green monkeys was dead. It looked like Malthus.

In Norman's office, Ensor's 'Masque of the Red Death' grinned over his potted plants. Norman closed the door and locked it. He fixed them coffee and biscuits; while, prepared for salmon and champagne, Eleanor had lost her appetite.

'Progress report?' Calvin required, reclining in an armchair.

'These mice have sped up a number of experiments.' Norman propped his sandals on his desk. 'Fitting the juvenile bill is a cinch; any number of organisms look promising, since a kid's immune system isn't fully in gear until at least five. It's this discrete shaving of the labour force that's the tall order. We're looking for weaknesses in gene pools that are represented in the proportion of the adult population you want to crop. But chromosomes aren't constant across populations, and that information is hard to come by. We got your Western geriatric requisition, and even that's not as simple as you'd think. Run the gauntlet of seventy years, you're a survivor.

'For the reproductive ages,' he went on, though it was hard to take anyone seriously who discussed the future of humanity with a mouth covered in biscuit crumbs, 'it's a bitch to beat what's on the market already. I've come to have a hell of a respect for HIV – 30 to 60 per cent vertical transmission; and the sexual connection is poetic. In Africa it's spreading like Christmas. Asia may follow suit. How could you ask for more?'

'Takes too long,' said Calvin. 'And all these bloodhounds snuffling for a cure, they're bound to dig up something eventually. There's money in it.'

'Sure. But you know what's going to happen? They'll come up with a therapy, all right. It will cost a bundle. We'll save a handful of well-heeled gays in America. But governments spend an average of two dollars a year on health care here! What are the chances anyone's going to front 6,000 dollars apiece for an updated AZT? Africa will still be a write-off, so will the subcontinent. And the Chinese government will be dancing in the streets to have that disease. I bet they're already inviting Haitian gays, Manhattan mainliners and Nairobi prostitutes as guests of the nation.'

'Pachyderm will outclass HIV. AIDS is a pretty tortuous way to go.'

'That's the other thing,' Norman said. 'This stipulation that Pachyderm's to be like Bactine. We can come up with something quick. But every potion stings, Pipe. Dying isn't usually a lot of fun.'

'Pachyderm doesn't have to be pain-free so long as it's fast. There's only so much punishment people can experience overnight.'

'Pi-prrr,' Norman purred. 'You haven't suffered much, have you? It is astonishing the agony a man can pack into ten seconds. Multiply overnight by two billion and you have an impressive aggregate of hell.'

'We have an impressive aggregate of hell already. Do what

you can. As for HIV, I've put Eleanor on to it. If HIV's up to the job, splendid, we close shop.'

'Eleanor, we'll have to be in touch, then.' He sprinkled in his hand from the snuff box around his neck and proceeded to roll a joint. 'AIDS demography is crucial. Because this country is *hot*. My squash game is off-form. The disco's OK, but we never have live jazz. I don't want to sweat it out in this second-rate Club Med if I don't have to. Which reminds me, my man, we badly need some new films. *The Killing Fields* has shown three times. All things being equal, I would really prefer *The Blues Brothers*.'

'How about,' Calvin suggested, '*The Elephant Man*?'

Norman took a few deep drags and passed the joint to Eleanor. She accepted; Calvin looked over, eyebrows raised. In adolescence she'd avoided dope, for it made her more awkward and tongue-tied than she was already. Right now, however, getting stoned seemed just the ticket. She had a hunch that Norman smoked this stuff all the time.

'No use offering any to Mr Straight here,' said Norman, taking the reefer back. 'He disapproves of drugs that don't kill you. Which reminds me, just in case you think we're flat on our bums here, Pipe, you should know we've come up with half a dozen concentrated virtually instantaneous toxins that will dissolve in water or disperse through the air.'

'So what's the problem?'

'They nix everybody.'

Calvin smiled. 'Has an appeal, doesn't it?'

'And how. If we really cared about this planet, we'd all cheer one last sunset with bright pink Guyana Kool-Aid, in tiny biodegradable paper cups.

'You know,' he went on, exhaling, 'QUIETUS has to make up its mind about a test run.'

'We're uncomfortable, Norman.'

'Even if we make a hash of it and our fatality rates go too high, you're talking a few hundred max.'

'The problem is detection. If we wipe out a third of a village and it becomes an international incident, we run the risk of being traced. No one in QUIETUS is keen to get done for tossing a mere ditchful of unfortunates.'

'Why assume you'd get fingered? Target a village in an

AIDS pocket. A bit of a confound, but whole towns are already dropping off the map in Tanzania and nobody gives a toss . . . Can you imagine,' he supposed, studying the curling smoke, 'the havoc, the hysteria, if towns were dissolving one after another in North Carolina, in Yorkshire? But in East Africa, who would notice one more? Renamo shot up 1,000 Mozambicans last week and the news report was one column long.'

'Things go wrong,' warned Calvin.

'Hell yes, that's why we need a test. Throwing Pachyderm to the winds without a small-scale trial would be like catering a banquet and serving your new recipe for mango chowder without cooking a bowl of it first. You're talking about inflicting a brand-new microbe on the entire human race. The stakes are pretty high if we're a bit off. Especially if we decide on a virus; the bastards mutate on you in no time.'

'The biggest danger is we fail. You keep worrying about fatality going too high; I'm more concerned it won't go high enough.'

'You're not cooking in my kitchen – it's lucky we wash our hands. With the boil and bubble in this lab, it's a miracle the whole operation hasn't melted like the Wicked Witch of the West into the plains of the NFD. Don't you worry about fatality. This lab is a snake farm. I'm not opening the cages until I know what the animal's going to do.'

Calvin grunted. 'I suppose there's time to sort this out. You're not likely to resolve Pachyderm any time in the immediate future.'

Norman leered. 'I beg to differ.'

Calvin's forehead rippled into an expression Norman might read as hopeful, but Eleanor saw as *nervous*.

'We expect to have your elephant on a platter quite shortly,' Norman assured him, relighting his joint.

'How shortly?'

'*Shortly*,' Norman repeated, in the same voice Calvin had reiterated *drastic* to BC. 'And if we get ahead of schedule, why wait for 1999? Sure you're not that superstitious about Nostradamus. The sooner we strike, the fewer futureless five-year-olds we have to put to sleep.'

'True,' said Calvin, without enthusiasm.

'So you'll have to address dissemination more seriously. If we go for air delivery, you'll need to mobilize a fair force of planes, and there's the obstacle of airspace. Just anyone doesn't fly over China. Start collecting data on weather patterns. Seeding could be arranged so if an ill-wind were on its way, you wouldn't have to crop dust directly over countries where getting permission to fly private craft could be dodgy.'

Norman led the visiting director and his research assistant on a tour of the facility, pointing out promising strategies, introducing their authors, updating his employer on the status of each experiment. Eleanor, packed in the protective cotton of powerful Kenyan *bhang*, was beginning to find it all very intriguing. Calvin, rather than shoulder-clap his way through his staff with that fatherly swagger to Norman's office, had curled into himself. He mumbled to technicians, and even with the most advanced projects seemed distracted, uninvolved – or especially with these.

'Just how hard,' Eleanor inquired of Norman as the two walked ahead of Calvin, 'did you work on inducing infertility instead of fatality?'

'Pretty hard.' Norman shrugged. 'Same problem as with our contagions: we could only design drugs that were 100 per cent effective. Throw total infertility at a population and it dies out. So we gave up.'

'But you haven't given up on a pathogen, even when your first solutions failed.'

Norman squinted. 'What are you implying?'

'I simply wonder,' said Eleanor carefully, her words far away and difficult to pronounce, 'whether you gave a non-mortality route your all. Knowing Calvin, I mean. I might find even inducing involuntary infertility extreme, but Calvin wouldn't. It wouldn't appeal to him.'

'And death does?'

Eleanor stopped staring at the floor and looked Norman in the eye. 'You know it does.' She kept her voice down. 'Poison is more attractive than progesterone. To Calvin? It's sexier.' Her brittle laugh was meant only for herself.

'I thought you were into this,' said Norman suspiciously. 'Inner circle. Gung-ho. Or Piper wouldn't bring you here.'

'I found out about QUIETUS by accident,' Eleanor

admitted. 'Calvin hadn't any choice but to involve me. But how I feel about it – I don't know.'

Norman clammed up.

'Doesn't it bother you,' she asked softly as they strolled the hall, 'what you do here? Aren't you a little disturbed, or frightened, or disgusted?'

'Not really. It's a great game.'

'Is it a game?'

'Ask your boyfriend.'

Eleanor's fingertips grazed the wall, checking it was solid. If Pachyderm was a game, it seemed to have got rather out of hand.

'Pipe.' Norman noted at their plane. 'One last thing. I'm afraid we haven't got anywhere on Semitic immunity.'

Calvin looked crestfallen. 'Maybe we can skip Israel, then. Fly over Egypt instead.'

'You soft-headed chump,' said Norman affectionately. 'Israel is smaller than Connecticut. With an airborne toxin, drift alone – '

'I'll warn them ahead, then,' Calvin grumbled, 'to paint ZPG in lamb's blood over their doorways.'

Norman shook his head. 'Remember, the flagellants claimed the plague was all the Jews' fault. Leave them out, they'll get blamed for it.'

'What was that about?' asked Eleanor on the plane.

'I don't want to cull the Jews,' said Calvin. 'They've done their part.'

Eleanor stared. He was, for once, serious. Holocaust II was a pogrom on everyone *but* the Jews – Calvin's gonzo idea of justice. Then, they were sufficiently ensconced in the realm of the ridiculous by now that to find any aspect of Calvin's agenda more cuckoo than another was more or less arbitrary.

When they'd returned to his cottage, Calvin was still somewhere in Andromeda, though from the comet tails creasing his forehead and the meteor craters in the muscles around his mouth, she sensed there was trouble in outer space. Rather than suffer invasions from Mars, Calvin's planet was occasionally attacked by Earthlings, which must have been traumatic on a land otherwise populated exclusively by rats, cockroaches, maggots and cancers.

Solastina lit a fire. Calvin went through the mail. Eleanor fed Malthus, a ritual Calvin observed over the top of his glasses with irritation.

For as Eleanor and the miscreant had shared the same space – and the same master – the animal gradually let down his guard. Early on the monkey didn't glare as blackly as he used to, but shot Eleanor furtive glances. Little by little he executed these circumspections from a slightly more proximate position. The first time Malthus extended his arm to her thigh, Calvin had leapt to her rescue in alarm. But instead of clawing into her leg Malthus clutched a fold of her clothing, looking in the other direction with an expression of bored innocence.

Lately, however, Calvin's arch fiend had taken to resting his head against her knee, until not long ago Eleanor had turned to the animal with calm curiosity as he played with a copper-seven from her briefcase and touched the top of his head. Malthus acted coolly and bent the IUD with only more rapt fascination. Shortly thereafter she had volunteered to feed him and Calvin jeered, good luck, but Malthus accepted the corn as blithely from her hands as from Calvin's, which left his owner stupefied, if not put out. You would never describe the relationship between Eleanor and Malthus as warm, but certainly it was tolerant, and Malthus no more than tolerated Calvin himself. Now Eleanor fed the monkey so often that Calvin, betrayed, told her to take over the job. Ever since Malthus had agreed to ride on Eleanor's back, Calvin had refused to take the turncoat anywhere, as punishment. Indeed, Malthus and his master were no longer on speaking terms.

The whole household now colluded against him. Panga mocked him as a mountebank, and would loll in corners with Eleanor exchanging paramilitary girl's-talk. Solastina had joined their crowd as well, taking his orders from Eleanor, because she was always so beastly decent to him. She made puns in Swahili Calvin didn't get while loitering with the servant in the kitchen. Why, sometimes the daft woman would chop vegetables.

But it was Malthus who had most broken faith, violated Calvin's unshakeable confidence that the monkey was impervious to tenderness.

'I've thought we should stop feeding him altogether,' Calvin growled over his new *Lancet*, after observing the one-time holy terror literally eating out of her hand for as long as he could stand. 'I don't believe in food aid. Creates dependency. Turns its victims soft.'

Calvin smote the evil eye on Eleanor that Malthus had so scurrilously abandoned. It was all her fault. Calvin had originally intended, damn it, that he would temper Eleanor from the floppy mesh of loosely thought-out idealism into a solid ramrod of realism. Didn't she stand gun-barrel straight, no longer ashamed of being tall? Hadn't he cured her of excusing African plug-uglies who threw their own people to crocodiles with that culturally relativist pi-jaw once and for all? Hadn't he trained her to let Solastina make her morning coffee instead of rushing to the kitchen at 7.30 because that's what the man was paid for? Didn't she enjoy a little black humour now and again instead of taking Calvin to task for it, liberal-killjoy, and didn't she slip in the odd crack herself? Why, 'Enry 'Iggins hadn't a patch on Calvin Piper, he should burst into song! So how was it possible that Eleanor Merritt was corrupting *him?* For when Eleanor finished with Malthus and put a hand on Calvin's shoulder while he scrumpled through his post the palm felt so good on his collar bone that he was outraged, and when she took it away again he felt so bereft and wanted it returned to his neck so badly that he could have kicked the lady in the shin.

'Anything interesting?' asked Eleanor of his mail.

'A valentine from Threadgill.' Calvin tossed the envelope on the table with the concern he would expend on the Win KS1,000 Coca-Cola lotto.

'I thought your clipping service went out of business.'

'It did, which I rather regret. Threadgill sent me some bloody good articles. I miss them.'

'So what's he say?'

'I haven't gotten many, so I'm not sure,' said Calvin nonchalantly, 'but I think it's a death threat.'

'*What?*' Eleanor grabbed the letter and read it through. 'Is this bluster?'

'I doubt it. I can easily picture Threadgill advancing on this house with a machete gleaming with the light of the Lord.

Wallace is on a *jihad*. He's capable of anything. So am I. We're both murderous bounders.'

'Nonsense,' said Eleanor with a chary dismissal she could only have picked up from Panga. 'You're a sweet, abstracted, overly detached man, and you're a little depressed. Murderous? Don't make me laugh.'

'I had hoped,' said Calvin through his teeth, 'the NFD to make more of an impression.'

'It made an impression,' said Eleanor lightly. 'A lot of little boys playing scientist.'

'So was Los Alamos.'

'Should you do anything about this?' She waved the letter. 'Take precautions?'

'Like what?'

'Just – ' The hand returned to his neck, for which Calvin was despicably grateful. 'Take care.'

As they prepared for bed, Calvin noted with an aggravation that characterized the evening that she really was quite fetching, more so than she struck you at first. And was it his imagination or had she in the past few months grown prettier still? He couldn't pin the change on her new wardrobe, his banishing of schoolgirl plaids and the morose droop of sale-rack jumpers, because it was naked she seemed to have transformed into a creature more lithe, winsome, graceful. As she lay in bed reading, her long body in a half-twist, her hip arced in a line that traced a continuous S around the opposite breast, and he couldn't take his eyes off that letter: S for sleep, surcease, for sneaky shameful slipping – *S for sentimentality*.

'It rankles me,' said Calvin, 'how much time I waste sleeping. Buckminster Fuller got his down to two hours a day. Think how much more work I'd get done. Twenty years of useless slumber at the end of the average seventy-five.'

Eleanor smiled and pulled him to the sheets. 'You poor dear. Those are probably the best years of your life.'

Calvin lay beside her, reluctant. During the day he droned over this landscape thousands of feet high, great gum trees shrivelled to tufts of weed, city centres squashed to children's blocks, people apparent only as dark shifting roach nests, but sleep was, whether he liked it or not, underwater, and he'd given up scuba for good. Calvin didn't like dreams. They were not logical. He didn't like it when his old office at USAID in DC suddenly turned into Tsavo East without warning, and he really didn't like it when mid-vision Panga would switch to Eleanor and back again. He found it an invasion of privacy when his frog-like, gin-pickled mother barged in on his late nights when she had not been invited. As a man who savoured the relaxing misty pallor of farmland under his plane, Calvin was uncomfortable with the luridly vivid colours of elephant carcasses that stacked the back of his brain. He was impatient with the too personal clutter of school mates he'd finished with, secretaries he'd fired, wrestling matches with Panga on afternoons whose memory he had ejected in favour of tables and statistics and computer screens that were after all so much more important. He resented that while mornings he could smooth into the carpeted posh of the QUIETUS office in Nyayo House as the respected leader of a daring international conspiracy, once his head hit the pillow he would linger outside the door of the Population Council Conference at the KICC and this time the guard would not let him in. His dreams reduced a brilliant, controversial intellect in the flutter of an eyelid to a boy wandering public school corridors in his undershorts.

When Calvin shifted towards Eleanor as she put aside her book, his fingers touched her waist with a little shock, his first impulse to withdraw them again. Merely sleeping with this woman may have been toe in the water, but it was water all the same, and not the thin aeronautic air at an altitude to which his lungs had grown accustomed. As he slid his arm around her until he cupped one of her breasts so small it could not fill his hand, he felt himself slip more deeply into the bath of her skin, that soft maternal temperature of the Indian Ocean which he had not so much as splashed on his face since Panga dandered there longer than was wise. Hadn't the Kamba taught him the dangers of drowning? As he pulled Eleanor's back to his chest Calvin kept his chin above the surface while his arms breast-stroked.

In the early days he'd been scrupulous not to excite her. He never touched between her legs except with his thigh (and it fitted so nicely there). He didn't want to give the impression that if she were simply more seductive she would drag him all the way under. He was loathe to re-enact rejection after rejection, for under such an assault he would have no choice but to send her home. However, Eleanor was easily rebuffed, and after his first refusal had made one or two deft inquiries with her fingertips and quit. She, too, never made sorties into regions that were no-go, and when her hand grazed his penis by accident she quickly pulled away as if she had touched a hot panhandle on the stove. It was sad, really; she would accept so little.

Parameters: by now these were well established, so that within set limits the two could clutch one another without misunderstandings. Their congress was sufficiently routine that neither seemed conscious of anything they were not doing, save an uncanny inability to get close enough, as if there were always some thin but tough diaphragm between their two bodies that would stretch but not tear. There were evenings, with his thigh between her legs, he suspected Eleanor came, but even orgasm didn't penetrate the prophylactic shield. A contraceptive slicked between them and whatever squirmed in him towards her met the barrier and died. He supposed that for Eleanor their union constituted a disheartening professional success.

Some evenings Panga would perch on the edge of their mattress in her fatigues and at first Calvin had pulled guiltily away. But Panga would watch, coolly paring her nails with her *kukri*, and sometimes, bored, would drawl to the window and eye the moon. He was a little hurt she didn't seem to care, though as a result less self-conscious, consoling himself with a loyalty that had grown increasingly legalistic.

Tonight, however, after Calvin and Eleanor had settled down Panga must have imagined him asleep. Through the slits of his eyes he watched the mercenary creep up on the bed with the stealth of guerrilla warfare. Glancing from side to side, checking for witnesses, as if even ghosts had ghosts, she smoothed his hair.

'Do that again,' begged Eleanor in a whisper, awake as well.

But Panga, who of the three was the most terrified of deep sea, took back her hand and rubbed it as if stung by coral; eyes wide, she waded away backwards and vanished to her shore.

16

The IMF Is OBE'ed

After the startlingly solid wrap of her knuckles against the walls of Pachyderm, Eleanor seized on her assignment to research the demographic implications of the AIDS epidemic. If the scenario of unchecked natural contagion was sufficiently dire, Calvin might be convinced to bury QUIETUS – the smug suite in Nyayo House, the Frankenstein play-acting of Pachyderm – back into the muddy black cotton soil of his brain from which it emerged.

From the very start of her assignment, they fought. Eleanor would fling at him the most hysterical figures she could find – 30.3 per cent sero-positivity in Kigali! Calvin would counter that Rwanda had the highest total fertility rate in Africa at 8.3, that only 6 per cent of the population lived in Kigali, and the rural sero-positivity was only 1.7 per cent – *work that out*. Rwandans were hardly about to sink without a trace, now were they? Eleanor had never tried lancing with Calvin number for number, and the duel was sweaty. He was too good at it. Maddeningly, rural sero-positivity in Rwanda was 1.7 per cent exactly.

Though they may have fronted for tuberculosis, Karposi's Sarcoma and pneumonia, Eleanor enjoyed hunting her statistics. The numbers themselves were arranged in neat columns, the studies clean and white. Data did not smell. Data did not ask for water. Data did not have dysentery on your desk. Like her comfortable chair, none of these numbers tugged plaintively at her sleeve, but would wait patiently for her attention. In school she'd loved maths, for even as a girl she was terminally sympathetic, befriending class rejects because she felt sorry for them, and maths was one subject with no emotional content whatsoever. Calculus was a resting place, where right and wrong were certifiable, in contrast to the word problems of politics, where an answer was right or wrong depending on how you looked at it, or perhaps there was no answer at all.

However, Eleanor's original exhilaration at concrete questions with concrete answers soon evaporated. Output is only as reliable as input, and the input was putty: hodge-podge testing of pregnant women in this and that city. On a continent where most of the population scattered in tiny villages with few paved roads, it dawned on Eleanor that no one really knew how many unlucky Africans had HIV. The towering edifice of results made from soft figures had a bedtime sag, and if she poked its walls they gave – '1.7 per cent sero-positivity for rural Rwanda' was Oldenburg.

Eleanor's first intimate experience with the deceptive precision of information grain-of-salted all the other nicely produced booklets peppering her office. She looked askance at the PRB's 'World Population Data Sheet', and finally questioned, How did they know that Cameroon contained 11.1 million people, since African censuses were infamously shoddy? Over her morning *Guardian*, she acknowledged that the authoritative report on the civil war in Liberia was written by a single beleaguered journalist buying unreliable sources drinks at the bar but otherwise too frightened to leave his hotel.

It was so much more relaxing to believe everything.

Basengi collaborated with Eleanor on this fax and phone fest. Even more than Calvin he took refuge in paper, housing himself in print-out and hard disks the way squatters in Mathare assembled shacks from magazines and bits of tin. He was ill at ease in her company or anyone else's. After their third nervous conference, Eleanor suggested a beer at the New Stanley after work.

'Calvin mentioned,' she ventured, while Basengi ripped the label off his White Cap and tore it into obsessively smaller shreds, 'you had some story or – past. I – don't mean to pry.'

'Oh, that, it is not a story at all really.' He rolled the scraps into tiny tubes and laid them out evenly in a row like cigarettes for mice. 'It is only a sound.'

'Of what?'

'It wakes me up. I recognize it in kitchens. A surprisingly dull sound.'

'I'm sure if Calvin finds it interesting, I would.'

'No, not tedious. Blunt. It is the sound of my mother and father being hacked to pieces.'

Eleanor paled. Calvin had set her up for this.

'It was the time of partition,' he continued, though the way Basengi said the word, he seemed to mean less the partition between tracts of land – India and Pakistan – than periods of time: before and after. Before, when he was a child with a child's life, with a sweetness of which no child is aware until it is gone; and after, when he was a midget adult, in only a night advanced to that state where there is no one to turn to and the back yard is not the garden you once thought. 'In Peshawar. The Indian Army was being dismantled, so they could not protect us. It was not their fault.'

'Protect you from whom?' asked Eleanor, frantically scanning her college history courses and turning up nothing on Pakistan.

'My family were Hindu,' he said, as if that explained everything. 'The Pathans went on a frenzy of revenge. They were Muslim and it was at last their country. But this I only understood later. I was a small boy. There had been shooting and I was told to stay inside. I stayed inside. I wonder,' he supposed, 'if I have stayed inside ever since.

'So my parents left me to save their shop from looters. But they did not get further than our gate. The sound I remember was of *kirpans*.'

'Which are?'

'Swords, like *pangas*. I was on the other side of the door. I saw nothing. But the sound was like meat – *chunk, chunk* – and sometimes a crack. The Pathans did this to many Hindus that day. I stayed in the house. I wouldn't look out. And inside the house was untouched – my mother's mending on the chair; a goat's head in a pot in the kitchen, and the second day it began to smell. On the third day, some relatives came to get me out. By then I had heard soldiers take some objects from the lawn, and they landed hollow, I expect on the bed of a truck. To this day – you may think this odd – I am sorry I did not open that door and look into the yard. I have seen dead bodies since, and they are not so terrible as you might think. It is the idea of them that is worse. Your mind is a much more frightening place than the world. That sound – I would have preferred one real picture to the dozens of fancies in my head.'

'Wouldn't such an experience leave you with a horror of killing?'

'No, more like immunity, a fear I am over. I learned at the age of seven: people are animals. Calvin is right. It is no more tragic – ' he kept his voice down – 'to cull our own herd than elephants. Once your own parents are goat in a pot, the rest are spice.'

It was the same old Piper line, but Basengi lacked Calvin's ebullience; his delivery was inert and therefore more convincing.

'Does it at least bother you that if Pachyderm goes ahead you yourself are in danger?'

'Have you read *Miss Lonelyhearts*? There is a last scene where the main character knows that someone has arrived at the house to murder him. He runs downstairs to answer the door with his arms open.'

'Is your life so dreadful?'

'Calvin, you must know, is a maharishi. If I die and help Calvin I am honoured.'

It amazed her how anyone with such a broad suspicion of the entire human race could at the same time place blind faith in a single member. 'Don't you sometimes wonder if Calvin isn't a little bit crazy?'

'Calvin Piper is the sanest man I have ever met. He could save the whole world.'

'Nuts,' Eleanor muttered. 'I'm living in a comic book.'

'You should be grateful. If he has picked you, you must be special.'

It's curious, but somehow the more you care for a man the more you have a perverse desire to tear him apart in public. 'He hasn't the faintest idea what he's doing.'

'Calvin has a mind you or I cannot penetrate. In comparison, we are children. He is perfectly logical.'

'Logic,' said Eleanor bitterly, 'can be an affliction.' There is nothing more irritating than blanket adoration when you are working up a good savaging of your boyfriend. Still, the more she unravelled Calvin, the more he entangled her; the more she whittled at him, the higher the shavings mounted over her head.

'If logic is an affliction,' countered the Asian, 'it is a rare disease.'

'Pure reasoning without emotion is dangerous,' she insisted. 'Look at QUIETUS: that's where it gets you.'

Basengi tightened, just as Norman had in the corridor. 'Our agenda is motivated by many feelings: fear of our own extinction; and sympathy, especially for whole generations not yet born who will live in hell because their grandfathers were too lazy or stupid or cowardly to take action while there was time. Even sympathy for crowded countries now. Did you know that in India the unemployment is so terrible that the government hires women to cut city lawns with – ?'

'Yes,' she cut him off. What little she'd had to do with these people, Eleanor had already noticed their tendency to circulate the same informational titbits, as in small incestuous communities where neighbours copy one another's recipe for chicken balls. For example: that if we had dropped a bomb the size of the one that destroyed Hiroshima every day since 6 August 1945, we would still not have stabilized human population: she had heard that three times now. The repetition felt clubby, claustrophobic and it was boring.

'I know it must be hard for you,' Basengi consoled. 'So new with us. Of course you are turning many questions in your head. Perhaps you think we haven't looked inside ourselves, examined our plans. It is not like that. You are at an earlier stage. There was a time we, too, talked and worried late into the night. But you cannot stay in this place and still take action. You cannot keep questioning; that is like waking up every morning and deciding afresh whether to get out of bed and why. We have made our peace with the painful sacrifice we must make for the future. In time you, too, will stop torturing yourself. You will understand what has to be done and get on with it. This resolution is much more restful.'

'Sounds like brainwashing to me.'

'I thought you liked our research. And you are capable, efficient. Calvin chose well. I am sorry it sounds as if you are not enjoying our work after all.'

'I do like the research. But I don't enjoy being told to stop thinking, and that I'll get over it. Besides, Basengi, I'm a professional woman. I have my own work. I'm not used to entering into any organization on the coat-tails of a man. As far as the Corpse is concerned, I'm just a girlfriend, aren't I? So I have to keep my own ideas. That's awkward, because – because they don't like me!'

'No,' he conceded nimbly.

Though she was the one who said it and she knew it was so, Eleanor was crushed.

Basengi reached impulsively to put a hand on her arm. 'But I like you!'

As she worked with him the next few weeks, Eleanor drew a few more details from the Pakistani. His uncle adopted him and sent him to the London School of Economics. The family moved to Uganda, where he arrived only to be cast out when Idi Amin expelled the whole Asian community in 1972. Basengi left for Kenya, where he worked in developmental economics for USAID and met his destiny down the hall. The rest of his people dispersed to the UK and Brazil. Like every other conspirator in QUIETUS, he had no children. Basengi was a private, ingrown, lonely and disturbed little man, with one remaining alliance with the living: Calvin Piper. She gave up finding fault with their fearless leader, for the least niggle only inspired Basengi to vaults of devotion that Eleanor found a little sickening.

There is a drama to any research, for libraries occasion all the heartaching setbacks, long stalls in the trenches and God-sent ground-gaining that you find in battle. This theatre is considerably heightened when your results determine whether your boyfriend goes on a historically unprecedented homicidal rampage at the millennium.

Eleanor was on a roll. Working from Pathfinder, she stayed far later than her staff. With the time difference, she could ring the Harvard AIDS Institute until midnight, dialling the same number over and over with that exaggerated patience which borders on insanity. In the morning, she was the first to go through the post, flipping for the Anderson article in *Nature* the way the debt-ridden might comb their mail for cheques.

When envelopes arrived from Peter, she threw them hastily in the bin.

Eleanor's diligence vexed her employer. After a vigorous statistical shoot-out at one in the morning, Eleanor accused him, 'You're just afraid you've been OBE'ed.'

'Sorry?'

'It's a diplomatic term.' She undressed, militarily, taking items of clothing off one by one, the way a soldier would put them on. 'Like when you arrive in Ghana the morning after a military coup and the man with whom you'd scheduled break-fast is dangling in the cellar: you are *Overtaken By Events*. You have coffee in your hotel room, dithering nervously with the TV, all of whose stations have mysteriously gone off the air.'

'And how does this apply to me?' He executed the usual fastidious looping of his tie and lining up of trouser creases that Eleanor had come to find repugnant.

'If AIDS takes enough of a chunk out of population growth, Pachyderm will turn into a white elephant. You'd have to convert the lab to a camp for disadvantaged parking boys.'

'Why shouldn't that suit me down to the ground? Think of the trouble AIDS could save me.'

'I think you want trouble. Without QUIETUS, you lose your *raison d'être*.' She faced him naked, hands on hips, with a shamelessness that amounted to assault.

'It is classic that you should approach this matter in terms of what I do and do not want.' He fiddled with his shirt buttons with more concentration than they required, gratifying Eleanor that he could not quite stare her down when she'd nothing on. 'The question is mathematical, and has nothing whatsoever to do with my feelings. The fact is, you continually quote me minor inflammatory sero-positivities in particular pockets of Uganda. You have yet to present me with wider projections that daunt population growth across the board, especially in Asia, where they're a bit less sexually fraught. What have you dug up on the big picture?'

'I haven't finished,' she closed up, curling into the bed with the sheet bunched to her chin.

'So secretive,' he clucked. 'Have you a surprise?'

'Are you worried?'

'I am nothing.'

She tossed a pillow at his taut, hairless behind. 'I wish you would stop pretending to be a machine.'

'I wish you would stop theorizing about my character and turn your full attention to the material.' He picked up the pillow and smoothed it back on the bed. 'I am irrelevant.'

'You are highly relevant.' She raised herself on her elbows. 'The models I've located don't agree. How, then, do you decide which to believe? You do, Calvin, want AIDS to be "just another deadly disease". Otherwise, seven years' work is out the window.'

' "You find what you seek." You sound like Threadgill.'

'All right. These studies fall into two groups.' She dimpled the mattress in two places where he would lie. 'Those by demographers and those by epidemiologists. Which projections are the most extreme?'

Calvin considered on the edge of the bed and smiled. 'The epidemiologists', of course.'

'Precisely. Because the demographers want there still to be a population problem, or they're out of a job. The epidemiologists want AIDS to be as dreadful as can be, for maximum funding. Greed colours their results. Cynical enough? I don't think that sounds like Wallace. It's vintage Calvin Piper.'

The day Eleanor was to present her first report on AIDS demography to the sceptics of QUIETUS, she got up early, dressed, changed her mind, dressed again, dressed a third time. As the sun rose, she fussed with three-colour graphs on her laptop, deciding the right order, crossing out her notes. She was as prepared as she could get, which wasn't very. Eleanor was trying something precarious, but with two billion people at stake it was worth a go.

She couldn't eat breakfast. She and Calvin had nothing to say.

The Corpse converged on Nyayo at nine. For the first time Eleanor took her seat before the keyboard, facing her recalcitrant audience. She felt like a new teacher with an uncooperative class. These boys and girls would not heckle, chew gum, throw spit-wads or write obscenities on the board when her back was turned, but there are worse forms of unruliness: silence, the rolled eye, the stolid square glare of students who have decided before you open your mouth you are wasting their time. When she inserted her disk in the drive, her hand was shaking.

'As most of you are aware, I have been asked to track down the potential impact of HIV on population growth.' Eleanor's voice was an octave too high. 'Most of these projections have focused on Africa, where the epidemic is most advanced, and their application to other areas of the world with high growth rates is not yet clear. Furthermore, all these models rely on the same, often weak data. My presentation is preliminary, then, and open to debate.' *Here you are at one of the most important moments of your life*, she thought, *and you are still apologizing*.

'I have chosen to present three computer models of HIV demography, which embrace the range of opinion and are regarded as the most mathematically sound.' Eleanor loaded a graph on the screen.

'The US Census Bureau predicts the impact of the unchecked epidemic on sub-Saharan Africa over a twenty-five-year period. Without AIDS, population is expected to expand from 540 million to 950. With HIV, however, population is expected to reach only 900 million – '

'*What* a reduction,' Calvin intruded.

Eleanor shot him a black look. 'In lieu of the epidemic, the Census Bureau would expect annual growth rates to have declined to 2.2 per cent; an infected population would still experience a growth rate of 1.8 per cent.'

The company whistled lightly through their teeth and visibly relaxed.

'Obviously according to this model,' Eleanor continued, beginning to relax herself (wasn't this what they hoped to hear), AIDS has the moderate impact on population growth of .4 per cent. This model is, however, the most conservative.

If we proceed to the Population Council simulation – ' She entered her keystrokes firmly, her hands steady.

'Here we see another twenty-five-year projection, only Bongaarts expects sero-positivity to reach 21 per cent. Total population growth rate over this period falls from 3 per cent, without the epidemic, to 2 per cent, with the epidemic. Clearly, however, if the continent is left with even a 2 per cent growth rate, it continues to double its population every thirty-four years.'

Her audience was leaning back, lighting cigarettes. Victoriously, she loaded her last graph, hitting chords of keys like the finale of a Mozart piano concerto. In this picture, the trajectories drooped, dying off on the right side and sagging into oblivion, nothing like the healthy, soaring, barely daunted arcs of the first two graphs.

'Roy Anderson at the Imperial College, London, has run the only model available with long-term prognosis, projecting the course of the epidemic over the next 200 years. In this model, population either levels off or plummets. Whether or not the peoples of Africa are virtually wiped out depends on the variable employed for "vertical transmission": the likelihood of pregnant carriers passing the disease on to their children. At this time, the chances of an infected infant being born to an infected mother are estimated anywhere from 22 to 70 per cent. In the instance of only 30 per cent vertical transmission, population doubles and more or less stabilizes after forty years. With higher values – which appear more medically likely – population declines *below* present levels in between 100 and 200 years. With 70 per cent vertical transmission, in two centuries this continent may be threatened with extinction.'

Bunny, Grant and Louis all put out their cigarettes simultaneously.

'In conclusion, models which give the epidemic only two and a half decades to take off do not produce a sizeable projected decrease in population growth. Only over time does the impact of the disease make itself felt. I would assert, however, that as the purpose of this committee is to design a pathogen with so many of the characteristics HIV already exhibits, we have been upstaged. On the basis of these findings

I could only recommend disbandment. After several generations and a regrettable amount of suffering, biology will reduce human numbers of its own accord. Given the untried and potentially destabilizing nature of Pachyderm, AIDS seems a less dangerous, established pathogen to allow to run its course.'

The committee sat in stunned silence. Only Calvin smiled, more on one side than the other. While she wasn't sure, he seemed to be admiring her. Eleanor took a deep breath and prayed that now she had said her piece she would be allowed to go home.

No such luck. With dim horror, she watched Bunny Morton pull out of her briefcase the same US Census Report with its orange cover, the same brown and white Population Council working paper, the same Roy Anderson photocopy from *Nature*. Bunny smoothed open the first, and it was black with underlining. Eleanor's heart sank. She had done her work well enough to know where the holes were.

'Ms Merritt,' Grant began. 'Are you familiar with the history of epidemiology?'

'I'm no expert.'

'You're no expert, but you're still telling us what to do. To abandon seven years of work on the basis of your "findings".'

'It was my assignment to collect available research. These are not my findings; they are the findings of experts.'

'Can you cite us another example of a disease that has raged through a population unabated for 200 years?'

'AIDS is an unprecedented contagion.'

'Of course it is precedented,' Grant countered. 'We all like to think of our own age and our own problems as special. But the human race has been afflicted by incurable ailments from its beginning. In spite of them our numbers are sky-rocketing. I would submit that this pandemic requires so long to stem the tide that it will subside before it gets the opportunity. You are familiar with viruses?'

'I've had the flu.'

They snickered.

'You're aware that they mutate? That historically viral virulence will peak and weaken? Syphilis – the Great Pox, after which the lesser malady is named – was once a vicious killer, in comparison to which its current incarnation is an inconvenience. And you've read that HIV has already shown signs of change; that HIV–2 is demonstrably less lethal than its predecessor?'

'I haven't found any basis for the assumption that HIV will transform overnight into hives in the foreseeable future.' It occurred to Eleanor that even a year ago under this degree of fire she would already have burst into tears. She looked at Calvin with a funny gratitude.

'You set so much store by the Anderson study,' intruded Bunny. 'How can you defend a model with an assumption of crude sexual homogeneity? Which makes no provision for the fact that not every Kenyan man sleeps with Nairobi prostitutes? A model that makes no distinction between urban and rural infection rates, which are so demonstrably disparate?'

'Yes.' Eleanor's face tingled. 'That is a weakness of the Anderson equations.'

'And you neglected to mention,' Bunny pressed on, 'that the Population Council does not cut off its projection at twenty-five years; rather, Bongaarts established a high likelihood that the epidemic will hit an equilibrium once it reaches an outside sero-positivity of 30 per cent, still resulting, however incredibly, in a sustained 2 per cent population growth rate?'

'That simulator,' she admitted, 'did turn up a levelling off, yes.'

'I am most concerned,' Grant band-wagoned, 'with this business of acting on a simulation of the next 200 *years* based on data you said yourself was unreliable.'

Bunny chimed in, 'Why, Anderson himself asserts, "There is no *a priori* reason to assume that extrapolation is valid beyond a short time span".'

'It seems ludicrous to me,' Grant objected, 'to project the progress of an epidemic about which we know so little and which has *already* defeated, fantastically, the alarmist predictions of AIDS ghoulies for the developing world made only three or four years ago.'

'It seems no more ludicrous,' Eleanor snapped, 'than planning mass murder on the basis of equally conjectural demographic projections. Just twenty years ago, Ehrlich was predicting 33 billion people in 2100, and now we're down to 14.'

'So we're supposed to throw up our hands because we can't trust anyone's projections of anything?'

'Maybe,' she said hotly.

'What distresses me,' Louis raised, 'is the expectation in your models that sexual behaviour remains constant. Do you believe Africans are so foolish? Hasn't the gay community successfully disciplined its behaviour in the US? Why assume Africans can't get the message?'

'In fact, you omitted,' Bunny accused, 'the bulk of this report.' She waved the orange folder in Eleanor's face. 'Intervention strategies. Even with no cure or vaccine, should a mere 10 per cent of this continent begin using condoms, you bring down sero-prevalence in 2015 by over a third. With 25 per cent condom use, sero-prevalence *declines* to less than 2 per cent. With a 25 per cent reduction in casual sex – for the average African man, one less encounter per month – sero-prevalence declines in twenty-five years to nearly zero.'

'To presuppose Africans cannot change their habits as Americans have seems a highly racist assumption,' Louis charged. 'Are Africans not rational? Can they not learn?'

Grant added, 'HIV is an inadequate pathogen precisely for that reason. Even without medical breakthroughs, its spread can be controlled with a little common sense. We need an agent that hits a third of the world up side of the head. It may be taking a long time for people to wise up, but they can, and they will, and then we're up to our eyeballs in as many starving children as before.'

The meeting degenerated into pandemonium, everyone bellowing at once. Calvin allowed them to caterwaul, Bunny jabbing at graphs, members tearing the Bongaarts or the Anderson out of each other's hands, while three-colour graphs glowed munificently over their heads. As his comrades clamoured across the table, Calvin stretched. Eleanor toyed with the computer, playing intervention strategies, age structures, dependency ratios whimsically above their gyrations like videos in a disco. She looked up to find Calvin watching her with that bemused smile, which was, if she wasn't mistaken, unusually warm. After five minutes of Babel, Calvin reached for a pencil, its end sharpened to a pinprick, and bounced it on teak, *t-t-t-t*. They shut up.

'My dear Corpse,' he intoned. 'Eleanor was just doing her job. She warned you her results were speculative.'

'I would like to pursue this research further,' said Eleanor. 'The Sixth Annual AIDS Conference meets next month in San Francisco. I would request funds to make the trip.'

There was no complaint; at least California would get her out of their hair.

The rest of QUIETUS cleared out, irate, arguing, demanding photocopies of the reports. Eleanor and Calvin remained seated until they were gone. He kept looking at her with that appreciative smirk until, flustered, she asked, '*What?*'

He stood up, put on his coat, came round to pull out her chair. 'Nice try.'

'At what?'

He put an arm around her as they walked out of the door. 'You don't really believe AIDS will lead to negative population growth, do you?'

She sighed. 'No.'

He kissed her forehead. 'You're brilliant.'

'I thought you'd be angry.'

'I am,' he corrected, 'entirely charmed.'

17

Back in the Behavioural Sink

There was no need for Calvin to accompany Eleanor and Basengi to the San Francisco AIDS conference, but he had no desire to be left behind, his house bereft of 'Blowin' in the Wind' and 'You're So Vain' – her musical tastes were lamentable. So he would fly to California because the alternative was to admit he missed her, and how could he possibly miss those drippy pieties thrown in the face of the stark, immutable horrors of the hard-hearted real world? What was it about those insipid miniature jam jars she saved from airlines that could make him ache when she was gone?

So he cleared away the detritus of Threadgill's daily death threats to route out a hefty stack of eco-doom for the trip – *The Sea and Summer, The Last Gasp* – and arranged to meet a range of demography denizens in the States just to have his own appointments. He reminded himself that Eleanor was working for him, so he wasn't really tagging along, even if her research was intended to undermine the most important project of his life.

In her own preparations Eleanor fussed over dresses, bought new shoes. 'We're not going on honeymoon,' he quipped as she folded low-cut silk with tissue paper. 'We're going to an AIDS conference.'

'These are highly social events,' said Eleanor. 'Lots of chawing after hours.' She layered linen slacks with micro-cassettes. 'There's one issue,' she raised casually. 'Are we bringing Panga?'

'No one brings Panga. Especially dead. I suppose she'll go if she likes.'

'No, Calvin. You bring Panga. You bring her everywhere. I'm suggesting you ask her to stay at home.'

'In some respects I haven't any choice. It's called history.'

'Panga might be history, but thanks to your regular updates she's current events.'

'She's *your* best friend.'

'She's not my best friend, she's my predecessor.'

'You imply she's been supplanted. She has not.'

Eleanor went stony. 'Can we at least skip buying her a ticket? She can walk the aisles or sit in the loo, can't she? It's 3,000 dollars.'

Calvin smiled. 'Panga prefers to ride on the wing.' He watched Eleanor whisk back and forth from the dresser she'd commandeered to her suitcase. She paused with her back turned, not quite concealing a small blue plastic case. With Calvin in the room she couldn't sneak the thing in gracefully, so she threw the diaphragm on to her peach suit.

'What's that for?' he asked casually.

'AIDS conferences are big pick-up scenes. I might get lucky.'

He was about to remark that considering the nature of the occasion condoms were *de rigueur*, but he was suddenly stricken by an unwelcome image: of it getting later and later in a hotel room and still Eleanor has not returned. He reads badly and tries to sleep and cannot and reads again until sunrise, at which time he finds her at breakfast nibbling toast with some pompous CDC poof. Calvin takes a different table and she nods with a little smile and then goes on ogling this oh-so-fascinating glorified hygienist who is maundering about t-cells, but with a sordid glimmer in his eye and a smutty understanding between them . . . The picture came at him in a rush, in a rage, and this was called: jealousy. Which should not be possible, so he proposed instead, 'Well, then. Perhaps we should take separate rooms.'

'Don't be retarded.'

He was not comforted, for though she would never do such a thing, it didn't alter this new and offensive information that if she did he would be hurt. You could not injure the pre-dead; that's what mobile mortality was all about.

On the plane, she had a regressive attack of Eleanoritus, and saved her peanuts; she saved the chocolate, the towlette, *she saved the salt and pepper*. She tucked the uneaten triangles of Gouda from all three trays into her bag, where they would be found in a week, squished and rancid and leaving a greasy spot on her carry-on. When the stewardess collected their neighbours' discarded rubber chicken, Eleanor craned her neck with all the morbid fascination of passing a gory road accident. Calvin got the impression that if Eleanor had her way she'd amass the leftovers and shove them out the emergency exit, overseeing the first airlift of pineapple fool to the Ogaden. Most peculiar of all was that Calvin wouldn't have her any other way; that should she let her jam jar slip nonchalantly into the bin at breakfast he would feel mournful.

While poor services and limited imports might accustom one to the primitive joys of a simple life, instead prolonged spates in the Third World turn the most high-minded Westerners into raving materialists. In the San Francisco airport, Eleanor and Calvin gaped agog at electronics, delicatessens and the mind-boggling proximity of decent ice-cream. Eleanor was beset by longings for pizza and pastrami as if she were pregnant. In the taxi rank, she had to resist the urge to lie with her cheek to the smooth tarmac, and as they drove past pay phones her impulse was to reach for stray receivers through the window, just to hear the dial tone purr.

In their room at the Marriott, Eleanor took off her shoes and danced on the thick carpet, switching across the 120 cable networks, flicking over the tightly packed radio dial and, best of all, phoning Ray and Jane and getting through the *first time*, and she could *hear them* and they could hear her as well and the call didn't cut off in the middle or anything – it was all too wonderful to bear.

Crossing the two blocks to register for the conference, however, was to run a gauntlet of guilt, for panhandlers had flocked from all over the city to line the corridor from the hotel to the Mascone Center, each with his cardboard concession:

COULD YOU HELP A WOMEN WITH A DONATION FOR SOME FOOD. PLEASE DON'T BE AFRAID – BECAUSE I HAVE AIDS. BUT I AM 'HOMELESS' AS WELL.

Or the more Christian:

GOD GIVES EASE TO THOSE WHO ARE DYING WITH AIDS.
YOU MAY NOT LOVE ME, BUT I LOVE YOU.

When Eleanor started shelling out her quarters, Calvin scowled. 'What are the chances that a single one of these moochers has anything worse than scabies? Next week stage a conference on malaria and the same crowd will arrive Mercurochromed with tropical mosquito bites.'

Of the file of scientists milling from the Marriott under the stern eyes of both each other and the roving TV cameras, Calvin was the only incorrigible who failed to contribute something, until hats on the walk packed with dollars and overflowed. Even Eleanor stopped groping her pockets by the end of the line, remarking, 'This is more of a goldmine than the Karen Provision Store.'

Assembling 12,000 delegates and 3,000 journalists was tantamount to founding and breaking down a small town in four days, so the circus had the latest technology at its disposal – vast photocopying resources and computerized message boards, with which Eleanor promptly left callbacks for Roy Anderson, John Bongaarts and Peter Way. The impromptu city may have convened for the discussion of immuno-deficiency, but its atmosphere was celebrative, like an airless, upscale Woodstock in the windowless underground of the massive Mascone Conference Center. At every level were booths for croissants and freshly baked biscuits, sales counters for AIDS T-shirts, with the silk-screened viruses in a selection of colours. Lobbies criss-crossed with physicians nervous about being late to the workshop on 'Varying Rates of Decline in CD4 Cells in Male and Female PWAs' the way an earlier generation had feared missing Earth, Wind and Fire. On ground level, rows of leaflets advertised forthcoming AIDS conferences, epidemiological travel brochures:

> We'll have you! We'll have fun!
> We'll have season in the sun!
> Come to AIDS Congress India!

festooned with photos of the Taj Mahal.

Eleanor and Basengi plunged into the event with rolled-up sleeves, huddling over the schedule, debating which sessions to attend like children agonizing over a menu of puddings, and regularly queuing at the message centre to leave more and more urgent appeals to their computer modellers, until they were plotting to waylay their victims as adolescents might plan an ambush of the New Kids on the Block. 'You're probably the only woman in America,' Calvin quipped, 'who wants Roy Anderson's autograph.'

Ever the Good Student, Eleanor attended seminars nine to six every day, and Calvin was irascible: 'Not one of these prolix panels has anything to do with *demography*. You're losing your bearings, Merritt. We don't care about needle exchange programmes, condom distribution in Zaire, or sero-conversion among health care professionals – *all* we're concerned with is how many scurfy undesirables this disease sweeps from under foot. You're not an AIDS flunky, you're a population spy, remember? We're at cross-purposes. They want to save the varmints and we want to exterminate. This is the camp of the enemy, and you should be keeping your head low.'

'You're envious,' said Eleanor. 'AIDS is a catastrophe and it's not yours.'

'Hardly. I think AIDS is the best thing since sliced bread. It's inadequate, that's all. I've scanned these papers. The statistics they're quoting are pitiful. Up to ten million sero-positive worldwide? A drop in the bucket! The race coughs up that many extra babies in six weeks! We do better than this sad little virus with malnutrition and the runs.'

'*And*,' Eleanor continued, 'you can't stand attending any international conference you don't chair.'

There was some truth to this. Calvin remained aloof, disdaining their hand-wringing about vertical transmission when the real problem was it wasn't high enough. Once he'd exhausted his appointments with all the reputable demographers in California, he spent the last two afternoons in a Mascone coffee shop reading *The Last Gasp*, a little put out that no one had recognized him. He was used to being scorned, but never ignored.

So he wiled away his hours imagining the Sixth Annual *Pachyderm* Conference – since after 1999, no one would give AIDS the time of day. He hadn't considered the T-shirt market . . . or swanky sportswear, with a little elephant carcass on the breast instead of a croc? Why, the commercial opportunities would be rife! Pachyderm coffee mugs and lunch boxes; Pachyderm loo roll and undershorts; Pach-man video games! Take your turn for a quarter, eliminate a third of humanity and win an extra game! A Pachyderm Conference, that's one he'd attend. Too bad he'd be dead.

It was fantasizing at this table that Calvin spotted through the crowd the familiar flap of ratty yellow *kikoi*: son of a bitch. And still carrying that naff stick, in San Francisco. Of course it made sense he would be here, since the trendy bastard hadn't been able to resist latching on to the latest in global peril, with all its opportunities for implausible optimism. Despite the predictability of his attendance, however, the presence of Wallace Threadgill at this conference alarmed Calvin in instinctive areas of his head that the 'perfectly logical' Dr Piper refused to recognize he possessed.

Through the event, Calvin rarely saw Eleanor, who swished in and out of their hotel room and never seemed to stop talking. She'd managed to get appointments with both Bongaarts and Anderson. Typically female, she found the Bongaarts model increasingly persuasive because John was nicer to her at lunch. Nights she was out schmoozing with AIDS celebs, overall a slicker collection than the frumpy family planning bunch, whose cause was *déclassé*. These viral dandies were finger-on-the-pulse types, into fashionable cataclysm, and paraded their material like the latest in viscose.

The last night, however, which was bound to be one big epidemiological booze-up, Eleanor insisted she and Calvin dine alone. She agitated through the meal, unusually inane. Once they arrived back at the Marriott, it was still early. Calvin reached for *The Last Gasp*, but Eleanor kept him talking. She was working herself up to something – about *feelings*, no doubt, an issue she had promised herself once and for all she would raise before they left San Francisco, and finally they'd reached now or never. Calvin put his book aside with a groan.

He determined this much: he wasn't going to help. If she had some kind of problem, she would have to bring it up herself.

When she launched into Pachyderm, pacing the carpet in stockinged feet, it occurred to Calvin they had never once had a knock-down drag-out over his conspiracy. She might be working for him, but she didn't endorse QUIETUS, not really. She'd dismissed him as a fraud but never argued outright. Tonight, since there was some other subject she wished to avoid even more, she would risk the fight.

'Isn't murder,' she proposed, 'a slippery slope? Even starting with abortion and euthanasia, don't you erode the whole foundation of ethical systems? If you don't respect the sanctity of human life, what's left? Don't you arrive in short order at Opah Sanders?'

'Ethical systems are pious props of social systems,' droned Calvin, bored. 'They merely preserve order, and unless someone does something about population growth we are headed for worldwide *Lord of the Flies*. Moreover, I don't believe in the sanctity of human life. I'm a great fan of algae. Algae, for example, do not bayonet pregnant women and leave them pinned to a wall.'

'There, that's evil. You recognize it when you see it.'

'I see so much of it that I don't see the point of a concept that is merely descriptive of what most people do most of the time.' He lay on the bed, clasping one hand on his chest with the other, in order to keep them from straying to his paperback. He was dying to get back to his book.

'But isn't Wallace right – aren't you yourself on your high horse, trying to save humanity? Isn't that the most pious conceit imaginable?'

'On the contrary, I'm a demagogue,' he said blandly. 'If I were less well educated, I'd end up on top of a shopping mall with a machine-gun.'

'You're being glib.'

'I'm not.' He sat up, resigned to a fracas she obviously required. 'I spent my professional life cocktail-clinking and prawn-peeling, first-classed around the world all under the aegis of aiding the underprivileged. Having lost my cushy job and my sexy housekeeper, I've become a bitter middle-aged megalomaniac: raising money from pampered colonials to slaughter a third of the world's population, using altruism as a cover for revenge. What's more, in my personal life I co-opt my lover into my own back-breaking employ, and give her not an ounce of affection in return. Doesn't that sound like evil to you?' He walked to the bathroom to brush his teeth.

'You called me your lover.' She trailed after him.

'My mistake.'

'If *most* people are evil, who's in the minority?'

'You are,' he mumbled through fluoride. 'You're compassionate. I may never have encountered this quality before. Then, you're unlikely to have children, and there goes the mutation – an intriguing Darwinian experiment, if failed.'

'I wonder why your compliments always make me pale.'

'But, Eleanor,' he continued, spitting and wiping his mouth, '*I do not like people*. If you still don't believe that, you've seen nothing of me at all.'

They squared in the awful neon of the tiny loo. 'You did like Panga.'

'I loved Panga. That's different.'

'Do you – like me?' Such a mild question, it seemed so brave.

Calvin ambled back by the dresser, considering that hotel rooms were pretty wretched places at 9.30 when you didn't indulge in the only real entertainment they could afford. 'You – please me, sometimes, you do not often get on my nerves, I – do not dislike you, Eleanor, and this is – extreme, from me. I feel – gently towards you. And you press me,' he added vigorously. 'I like very much to be pressed.'

Eleanor shook her head in incredulity, as if suddenly seeing this scene from afar: I cannot believe this is my life. Perhaps she was imagining the sweet Virginia duplex with a man who kissed her on the cheek when he came home, and sometimes they went to the movies, or any other of the multitude of credible, pleasant, if unimportant futures she might have drafted for herself that would have precluded conversations like this one. 'So you're evil, and everyone else is evil, except me. Is this what's known as being put on a pedestal? It's overrated.'

'I said you were compassionate, not beyond rebuke.' He turned his back to the mirror, so she would have to face every

241

side of him. 'Why is Eleanor Merritt not evil? Perhaps you've missed the opportunity – one I may provide you. More likely, you merely lack the nerve. You're childlike in a manner not entirely to your credit. Isn't much of goodness cowardice? You won't steal biscuits because Jane would send you back to your loopy mother. You're only good because you're scared, and you treat people well because you want them to like you. You have a sycophantic streak. After all, don't you ever imagine you're being tested? Here a man you rather fancy turns out to be a psychopathic killer. What do you do?'

'Humour him. You haven't so much as flayed a frog.'

'But I shall. Come on. Do you think you're so righteous? Here's Charles Manson II, and you're actually doing his research for him because you think if you're ever so helpful you'll persuade him at long last to have intercourse. Is that a pedestal? You tell me.'

Eleanor's face turned white, and he could tell by the check-mated look in her eye that he had just waylaid her main agenda for the evening: sex.

Her voice was low. 'I can see why you find compassion such an extraordinary discovery, since you glimpse it so rarely in your shaving mirror. I have listened until it's coming out of my ears about humanity having *exceeded the carrying capacity of the land*. Carrying capacity? Well, what about yours?'

'Please keep your voice down, these walls are thin. You may be weary of my work, but I am exhausted by these petulant scenes of yours, demanding that I come clean and confess my undying ardour for you. I am sorry, but I warned you long ago that my *only* ardour is for over-population – '

'*Over-population!*' she shouted. 'There is no one on your planet but you! I cannot understand how you could possibly feel crowded!'

'I've had visitors from time to time.'

'Panga, I suppose? Because I'm sick to death of hearing about Panga – '

'On the contrary, you bring her up all the time. I hardly ever mention the woman.'

'You don't have to. She sleeps with us – or you. She's the only one who sleeps with you.'

'Watch what you say. I think she's in the loo.'

'Come on, neither of us could hurt that Kamba with a meat axe.' She pursued him around the bed, until he was cornered up against the coffee machine. 'How about worrying over the feelings of people in this room who are still alive? There are times that that romance seems a handy contrivance. She proves you're not a racist and keeps me at arms' length, and meanwhile you can act obnoxious and congratulate yourself on being *evil* and still feel sorry for yourself. The whole picaresque is too convenient. I wonder if you ever loved her at all – '

'You have no right – '

'I have every right to think of your sorry excuses as I please.'

'Behind my back you may tinkertoy your tawdry American psychotheories, but you will hold your tongue with me.' He had grabbed her arm; the gesture was out of character.

'I will say what I wish to you. You're my lover, you said so yourself; whether we copulate or not is a technicality. And your celibacy is insulting, it's bitter, manipulative and cruel. You keep yourself back on purpose – you're hurting me!'

'You have noticed I sleep on my stomach to hide my throbbing desire for you?' He didn't let go.

'Go ahead, why not slap me around a bit? You want to murder two billion people, what's one tired family planning worker with a black eye?'

He released her and walked to the window.

'Isn't anything possible now?' she said to his back. 'Couldn't you take shots at strays, torch the homeless, lock your retarded sister in a closet – you say there's no good and evil, why not put it to the test? You abuse me enough, that's a start.'

'I have never meant to abuse you.' His voice had quieted. 'I'm sorry I grabbed your arm. And I take back that remark about – I mean you are a lovely woman. I have never wished to make you feel unattractive. I would say the problem is mine, but I do not consider it a problem. I prefer chastity. Sex has become foreign to me. I would even have to say repugnant. I suggest if intercourse remains so important to you that you find another liaison.'

'Is that what you want?'

He sighed. 'Want? I want nothing but to reduce the population of human beings on this planet. That is the only reason

I keep living. I would enlist your support. You are supremely effective, a good researcher, and to my knowledge you have been discreet. I value both your assistance and your companionship.' His tenderness was leaden and drained his cheeks. 'I admire you. I am impressed with you. You are useful to me. I even enjoy you.'

'My.' The word he refused filled the room. 'But you don't – '

'I no longer know how. Which is the only reason I can execute this project. No one else is sufficiently inhuman. I am perfect. I have no more feelings.'

'That's a damn lie.'

'Either I am lying or you are lying to yourself. Choose the more likely. Beware the convenient on your own account, Eleanor.'

He could see it in her face: she had exhausted herself for months now maintaining that Calvin was entirely other than he appeared, that he was 'repressed', that his callousness capped a well of secret passion, that really he adored life and women and most of all her, but suddenly she was spent and for a moment, no longer able to generate her nutritious myth, could briefly permit: this was Calvin. He was not necessarily any other than as he claimed. Maybe Calvin was a cold, terrifying man.

They slept that night separately. Calvin laid his metacarpus against her wrist, but could not even bring himself to hold her hand. Eleanor sank into a deep, angry sleep. Panga took the chair by the bed table, her long legs extended. No matter how foreign the locale, she laid herself out widely, a possessor.

'Am I being quite horrible?' whispered Calvin at last.

'You say you do not know what horrible means.'

He sighed. 'I must. So this is wickedness.'

'Why do you not make love with her?'

'I refrained for you, at first; and eleven years ago I met little temptation. But now the whole idea's gone strange. Do you realize I can't even do it by myself now? I don't see pictures, women; all I see is me over the toilet and I can't finish, I don't bother. I read articles about how sex explains every little thing you do and I don't know what they're talking about.'

'What are you afraid of?'

'Nothing. I talk to the dead, don't I?'

'The dead are easy company. A cheat ... You think she has this small animal inside her?'

'I expect she has an enormous animal inside her.'

'No. The witchcraft you say is not strong.'

'HIV? Not a chance. She's a regular contraceptive dispensary, isn't she? Why, she might be more appealing to me if she were rash.'

'Are you afraid it would be not same? As with Panga?'

He laughed. 'Maybe I'm afraid it might be.'

Funny, he thought. Calvin commonly felt victorious in his restraint, but just now he recalled being thirteen years old, when his cow mother would note the bathroom had been occupied an awfully long time. Presumptive, she would try the knob, find it locked, and *rap-rap-rap*. 'Cal-vin,' she would drawl, American.

'What?' he'd squeak.

Rap-rap-rap. 'Cal-vin!' No rebuke, just his name, as if that said everything.

Now that he'd all the privacy in the world and the door to his loo was never locked for twenty suspicious minutes, he couldn't help but wonder if in the end not he but his mother had won.

Panga played listlessly with Calvin's Swiss Army knife, for which she had contempt; it was too small. At length she said, 'You say you are part dead; this could be why we can talk. But in our time you were a man. Maybe we killed the wrong half.' Calvin was asleep. He had drifted off in time to escape the notion that the dead, rather hurtfully, were never jealous; and that he too often had these conversations with Panga that might better have been conducted with Eleanor instead.

Their morning was stiff, but Calvin had previously agreed to accompany Eleanor and Basengi to the closing address that afternoon. Outside the Mascone Center, placards – GREED = DEATH; STOP AIDS PROFITEERING – jabbed over the heads of police lines, while gaunt homosexuals in pink-triangled T-shirts accosted delegates to be allowed inside.

The population espionage team burrowed into the audience and took its place near the back. Eleanor sat pointedly with Basengi between herself and Calvin. From the beginning it was difficult to hear as demonstrators cat-called from the gallery. Once the Secretary of Health rose to the dais, the din was overpowering:

PEOPLE ARE DYING, UNDER ATTACK!
WHAT DO WE DO? ACT UP! FIGHT BACK!

Basengi turned around once to look at the hecklers behind him.

The first to detect anything amiss was the woman sitting in front of him, who reached behind her to find a wet, sticky substance on her dress. She may have imagined the protesters had reduced themselves to throwing tomatoes, for she turned to the gallery with the black look of someone already determined to sue for dry-cleaning bills.

Because he'd twisted backwards, Basengi's arm was thrown in Calvin's lap. The hand extended in a weak gesture of supplication – *baksheesh*. He might have been asking for money, but in that half-hearted, habitual beseeching of a beggar resigned to a bad day. Calvin turned to his economist to discover a circle in the middle of his forehead, Hindu. The adornment was neat and dark, with a trim black halo, and its centre seemed to tunnel on for ever. At the least it did proceed to the back of Basengi's head, which had gone curiously indefinite. Calvin kept trying to focus properly. Why, the back of the Pakistani's head wasn't malformed; it was missing. Calvin was actually staring at the floor.

He had to look away. The eyes were still open, and directed unquestionably at Calvin, fixed in the conventional devotion that while Basengi was alive Calvin has basked in blithely enough, but now made him queasy.

Finally the surrounding audience began to scream. The demonstrators – THEIR SYSTEM! THEIR PROFITS! OUR LIVES! – overrode the hysteria until a neighbouring delegate shouted, 'Bring the police! Someone's been shot!' Panic curdled in a circular wake from Basengi's seat. Someone called for a doctor, a little ridiculous under the circumstances, since the hall was packed with nearly nothing but. And shouting for one doctor or several thousand with half of someone's head missing was a cinematic formality.

As word spread, the audience rushed towards the doors. The Secretary of Health implored for calm, while security dragged him from the microphone. Delegates in their row ducked off with hands over their heads in a cringing that never saved anyone from an automatic but does slow you down.

Before they were swept along with the rest, Calvin met Eleanor's wide eyes over the body, and shook his head in a tight, stern motion he hoped would not be too subtle to escape her.

'Did you know him?' asked an adjacent conferee as they crushed the exit.

'No,' said Eleanor. She'd got the message.

As they made their way from Mascone to the Marriott with the short, sharp steps that substituted for a headlong run, Eleanor only noticed Calvin had been clutching her hand because it was beginning to hurt. As murder disinclines one to be long-winded, they also used short, sharp words, and subsequently got a great deal accomplished in two blocks.

'Why Basengi? Could it have been anyone?'

'No.'

'Did it have to do with the conference, or – '

'It has to do with us.'

'So they were aiming for – ?'

'They got their man.'

'Who did?'

'You know who.'

'Why not you?'

'He wants to frighten me first. I don't think a cadaver would satisfy. He wants a convert.'

'It could have been me, then.'

'You could easily be next.'

'It must be a relief not to care,' she noted. 'Whether anyone dies, I mean.' She might have sounded acerbic, but she felt simple envy. 'Can they trace – ?'

'No.'

'What do you want to do now?'

'I want to go into my room and shut the door.'

'Will the police – ?'

'We are two of 12,000 delegates. We know nothing.'

'Calvin, have you ever seen – in your life – ?'

'No.'

'You're shaking.'

'I know.'

When they were asking for their key, Calvin told the desk clerk, 'I would like to take an extra room.'

'We've had a few check-outs already, sir. I'll see what I can do.' The receptionist looked alarmed.

'Thank you.'

Eleanor was so numb, she was surprised to feel her heart fall as he filled out the forms. Of course he had every right and reason to want to be alone. And it was logical, Calvin being Calvin, that his reaction would be isolation. But Eleanor didn't want to be alone for a milli-second and she chastised herself for one more time choosing the wrong man. This is where it got you: a friend of yours is shot before your very eyes and you spend the night in a big double bed by yourself.

'Are you thinking you'll go to sleep?' Her voice was controlled.

'I don't know that I can.'

'I was wondering if you wanted me to wake you.'

Calvin finished signing the VISA form with his right hand, but still had Eleanor's squeezed in his left. He couldn't tear off the card-member's copy with only one hand, so left the receipt behind. What would he do with her hand at the door of his new room? Ask to borrow it?

'Do you wish me to call a doctor, sir?'

'Certainly not.'

She realized the lobby's excited guests were staring at Calvin's chest. He was covered in blood. For the first time he looked down and noticed. 'Demonstrators,' he explained to the receptionist.

The clerk took a full step backwards and moved the VISA coupon off the counter with a pen. Eleanor twigged: he was afraid the blood was sero-positive.

'Do you want to stay the night?' asked Eleanor.

'Yes.'

'So should I meet you in the morning?' She was trying to seem stalwart.

They stepped into the elevator. 'What are you talking about?'

Eleanor was confused, and they rode up in silence. They arrived at the door of the new room, and Calvin unlocked it. He had still not let her go. He pushed the door wide open and stepped aside.

'Would you like me to take this one?' asked Eleanor. 'Because I want my toothbrush. And a book. I don't think I can read, but I could use the prop.'

'Don't talk bollocks,' said Calvin. 'You don't want to be by yourself, do you?'

'No,' she admitted. 'Then why – ?'

'It's for Panga, you nit. Who did you think?'

Just then who should come sauntering down the hall but Herself. Panga leaned on the doorframe and those great buck teeth shone in the side-lighting. She touched Calvin's shirt, not yet dried, then licked her finger. 'So,' she said. 'At last.'

'Satisfied?' he asked. 'Impressed?'

She laughed. 'You didn't even do it yourself.'

'Should I have? Basengi was on my side.'

'You could use some practice. Even Norman says so. But you seem cross.'

'I am cross. He was a nice little man. He didn't deserve it.'

Panga laughed again, and the peal was clear – too clear; metallic. 'Listen to you! According to Calvin, they all deserve it! Besides, *bwana*. Are you not pleased? *Population*,' she whispered in his ear. 'One less is not many. But it is a start.'

'He was a brilliant economist. Feeling a little tired?' He gestured towards the room.

'No,' sulked Panga. 'We go to your room. Buy some *chang'aa*. Play Bongo Man.' She moved her hips in a circle.

'If you don't mind, Eleanor and I would prefer to be alone.'

'Look at this!' she sneered. 'The happy couple.' She slouched unwillingly through the door.

'I liked him!' cried Calvin after her, and there was a tenor to his voice that Eleanor had never heard before.

'*Sentimental*,' she hissed from the dark.

He locked the door.

'But she can walk through walls,' Eleanor objected.

'Not mine.'

Calvin took a moment before drawing the curtains to gaze out on to San Francisco, now deep in a fog that suggested how the sharp lines of his world had blurred in an afternoon. With his inability to see to the next building went an inability to see to tomorrow night, back on a flight to Nairobi with one empty seat and the rest of QUIETUS awaiting his pursuit of a resolve that had suddenly clouded. For once the planet did not seem crowded but forsaken.

Calvin went about the room shutting windows, tugging curtains, and hitching blinds so they met the very sill, as if he were planning not simply to lie down but to develop film. Despite him, cracks shone under the door, through broken slats, in whose glint Eleanor could watch him fumble with slippery buttons. The shirt was sticky and thick, and clung to his chest as he peeled it off.

When he showered, steam billowed from the bath and filled the room – the fog had crept in. Mirrors condensed; his reflection went ghost-like.

'I'm cold,' he said, and buried into the blankets, all balled up with his hands between his legs.

Eleanor sat on the edge of the bed. 'I'm frightened, Calvin. It's not funny any more. Dissolve QUIETUS, disband the lab. Tell Wallace you quit.'

'I'm cold,' he repeated. 'Come under the covers. I'm cold.'

She stripped quickly and crawled into bed, regretful that her body was so slight and likely to provide only a sliver of the warmth Calvin required.

When he pressed her against him it was the same as ever only worse. They were simply not close enough. Skin on skin, each could feel the cells not meeting. Forms that seem to touch, ask any physicist, do so imperfectly, and they could both sense the innumerable pinprick retractions of pores. The tough wet suit that separated their bodies on every occasion was stretched tauter than ever.

Eleanor knew she was not supposed to do this, but there was only way to help Calvin Piper this afternoon, so she reached down for the only part of him that could perforate the noxious rubber shield. As he broke through, his body relaxed and lost its desperation. His breathing slowed and deepened like sleep – he took long, regular draughts of air like water.

You can breathe water. There was a time many years ago that Calvin dreamt of diving all the time, and in a recurring episode he went down without his regulator. After a moment of fear that he would drown, he always discovered that though he had been under for minutes he was right as rain. He could breathe fluid; in fact, it was richer by far than air, and in comparison to the sea the atmosphere was thin, like skim to cream.

Once again he remembered that moment in diving that is the most remarkable experience of the sport and which justifies all the expense and bother of equipment it entails. There you are, bobbling on the surface, lapped left and right, slapped by waves, entangled in tubes and gauges. The surface is loud and here the body is cumbersome. It was at this unwieldy interface that Calvin had remained with Eleanor for months now, half in, half out, buffeted by the cold air of his life without her, swayed below the waist by currents he could not see. It is the surface that tires you, wrenches you between two worlds, and the only justification for suffering it at all is the blessed release when you give your partner the signal to submerge, dump air from the stab and watch the edge of the sky rise over your mask. Suddenly your vista is green and infinite. Your body is light, your limbs graceful, and the only sound is bubbles popping from your mouth. To this liquid quietus Calvin finally returned again, swimming with Eleanor under the spread, with the cool rippling leak of water streaming into his wet suit and warming against his skin.

18

An Elephant for Breakfast

While celibacy over short periods is frustrating or shameful, over long enough it becomes a source of superiority. Calvin had not made love to a woman for eleven years, and had been counting on twelve. As he woke drenched in sweat, piled with blankets, Calvin kicked himself for having ruined an impeccable record in a single night.

His immediate impulse was to flee. Calvin hauled himself out of bed, no kisses, to step over the hard crumple of his blood-soaked clothes. He yearned to retreat to his study and steep in the blue-green of his computer screen instead of the unframed depths of Eleanor's deep sea, but the machine was on the other side of the world. Anyway, the work which routinely saved him from the sordid grope and squabble of human relationships had yesterday gone horribly wrong, spattered with the hot, unseemly stains of exactly what he used it to escape from. For the first time Calvin glimpsed how untidy his own designs could become, even if they were drafted in the abstract vacuum of outer space. Why couldn't demography be revised on paper? Wasn't it true that he did not wish to be a murderer but a mad mathematician with an eraser?

Eleanor rose while he was shaving, and though he feared she would be clingy she was instead withdrawn, making no mention of their indiscretion. She packed efficiently. Instead of looking triumphant after nearly a year of lying chastely by his side, she seemed, if anything, forlorn.

The morning papers were full of the shooting at the AIDS conference. Many Act Up activists were held for questioning, but the assassination had been professional, and the police had found no gun. Editorials decried how in the name of saving lives they could be taken, for the gays got the blame evidence or not. No one had a clue who Basengi was or by whom he was employed.

The clerk downstairs had spoken to the police about the state of Calvin's suit. They were waiting for him at breakfast. Calvin claimed never to have met the Pakistani, and described the incident as an isolated trauma he would like to forget, which was accurate enough. They took his testimony and let him go.

The plane trip home was interminable. Desultory, Eleanor and Calvin flipped in-flight magazines. At least the third empty seat gave Panga a place to sit other than the wing, but even Panga seemed listless. Their threesome, once so jocular, had gone awkward.

A flier himself, Calvin was often uncomfortable as a passenger; this journey he was complacent, blithely taken for a ride. For his life was on auto-pilot. He was no more than obedient automaton, and that the orders came from himself was a technicality. His past was his master. An entire life demanded repudiation, from two billion others, perhaps, whose requirements dwarfed before the consuming agenda of one – this life that had to be finished, rounded; its insistence overwhelmed him. Calvin overwhelmed himself. He could claim he was in the grip of an obsession, but it was stranger than that. The obsession was old and in some ways even over, but not quite, and that he was no longer that interested did not pertain because he did what he was told. He wondered if he no longer really cared about population growth but he used to and that was enough. He followed through blindly and if it was folly from the start very well, for he felt to his marrow that the race itself was folly in the extreme, so that if he failed and was caught and jailed or killed it didn't matter, and if he succeeded and it was a horror and backfired it didn't matter, and if he succeeded and the reduction in human numbers was ever so beneficial in the long run *that* didn't matter either.

Arriving at Kenyatta Airport, they de-planed grubby, wrinkled and furry-toothed, with that classic anticlimax of arriving home: so much trouble simply to end up where you started. Oppressively *brown*, Kenyatta had the atmosphere of a bus station. Dawdling through immigration, Panga couldn't find her passport and had to slip through the back wall.

Gratefully as Calvin might have returned to his beloved conspiracy, Nairobi seemed in the distant past though they had only been gone a week, and whenever his mind turned to the object of his fixation, it went brown like the airport, as last week's newspapers will crêpe and ecru. How appalling that in matters affecting the future of the entire human race you could go rather off the idea; that enthusiasm for species salvation could come down to a question of mood. His office seemed an appealing prospect: the sealed room where he was safe and the atrocity photographs were cosily familiar. But the actual material on screen did not exult him. Calvin wanted to listen to Elgar.

'He didn't do it himself, did he?' asked Eleanor as they drove back to Karen, though neither had mentioned the shooting since the hotel.

'Of course not.'

'Is he dangerous? Physically?'

'Most leaders are only lethal by extension – because of what they think and say and because they're so persuasive. Only henchmen are literally dangerous. Charismatics tend to be lazy, on the ground, and their sensibilities are often – delicate.'

Out of the window, frazzled brush along Lang'ata recalled anaemic brochures for cut-rate safaris at Let's Go. The buffalo lolling morosely at the edge of the game park was not faintly exciting – that was what Africa did to you, it shabbied your own love for it, since nothing could remain exotic if you saw it every day. California time was ten hours behind and the blare of sun was horrible. Given a choice, Calvin preferred the dark, and since it should be midnight he felt cheated, overexposed.

'Might he have hit the wrong man?'

'Too accurate. Basengi was, if messy, just another envelope in the mail.'

'Why wasn't a contract put out on you?'

'Because then the game would be over. And he enjoys it.'

Calvin's voice, too, was faded, yellowed, his opinions pamphleted in a creaky wire rack and beginning to curl.

'You said he took you seriously.'

'Games are often serious.'

'But you're playing with an entire planet!'

'Great games have great stakes. Why do you think anyone bothers to go to war?'

'Personally,' said Eleanor, 'I haven't got the foggiest notion.'

On the answering machine back home was a veiled but urgent message from Norman: 'Pipe, it's your lucky day. Elephantine news. Swing by Pach, *toute suite*. Cheers.'

Though in an earlier era – that is, before two days ago – the message would have perked him up, this morning Calvin responded with a grunt.

'What's that about?' asked Eleanor.

'What do you think?' he snapped.

It was Eleanor's inspiration that they go to see Wallace Threadgill, though her reasons were weak: 'To let him know you know who did it,' when Wallace would be confident his envelope had been properly postmarked; 'to tell him to stop', when it was patently absurd to expect a man who had launched an assassination campaign to call it off because a family planning worker didn't think it was nice; 'to explain you've given up QUIETUS for good', which was a lie. The very futility of the trip guaranteed Calvin would go that very afternoon because futility was apropos. One more pointless trudge to Wallace's tent would match the insipid smily sun, the irrelevant animals nodding dully behind their fence, the newly arbitrary nature of night and day.

Wallace had returned from the conference early, skipping the final address, which he expected to be a bit eventful for the contemplative. Scanning the suitcaseful of photocopies he'd lugged back from San Francisco, he ate a chocolate bar. Wallace was in good humour, which took him by surprise, because Wallace was happy all the time. When Piper turned up with his cretinous sidekick late afternoon, although according to sources they'd been back in Nairobi a full six hours, Wallace was insulted at the delay.

Piper's aura had shrunk. His suit was crumpled, his hair

lank. The woman looked sleepy, and subsequently said nothing for the whole exchange. Wallace supposed getting that contorted every day must take a lot out of you.

Calvin squared himself on to a three-legged stool and lit a cigarette. Wallace knew for a fact that Piper didn't smoke, but had purchased a pack for the occasion. A tribute. The stale grey smell mingled with the demographer's dishevelled demeanour.

'Ordinarily you rather bore me, Threadgill,' said Calvin at last. 'But you've finally sparked my curiosity. Just how does a beneficent turn terrorist and still keep his puking sanctity intact?'

'Terrorists are the most self-righteous people on earth.' Wallace blew the rancid smoke back in Piper's direction.

'I've noticed that. How do they do it?'

'Well, what are you?'

'A terrorist. But I don't think I'm a saint. You do.'

'Human sacrifice is old as the hills, my child.'

The woman lay fatigued in her chair, fishing bits of crust from her eyes. Piper hadn't carted along a particularly captive audience. She aimlessly reset her watch. Her face was puffy and she looked ten years older.

'That's my line, human sacrifice,' Piper objected. 'I think we're getting our parts confused. I'm having a hard time keeping track of who's talking.'

Piper tossed the butt on the ground; Wallace extended a chubbly and crushed it. 'So how did it feel? Not a statistic, but the genuine article?'

'A bit tawdry. Ruined a good suit.'

'Try multiplying that by two billion.'

'Multiplied by two billion there would have been a point to it. I believe in population control, not petty vendetta.'

'Why, bless my mother's old boots! You're incensed! When you're after two billion and I take out one! Haven't I joined your side?'

'Quite. Hence my confusion.'

'I told you months ago – ' Wallace bounced his cane gamily in his palm. 'Goodness can be merciless.'

'Mmm,' Piper considered. 'I don't think so.'

Wallace smiled. 'I enjoy luring you into debates on the

nature of virtue when you deny its existence. Why so shocked when your enemy turns your own weapons against you?'

'I have never used a Barrett Light 50 in my life.'

'Death is death. Scrolling through your files, I couldn't understand why you were so fixated on its mechanics.'

'I could have you arrested.'

'You can't imagine the miserable Asian is traceable to me. And you must admit,' he added, 'he really wasn't a contented man.'

'He was better off dead?' asked Piper.

'It's instructive to hear one's own opinions in someone else's voice. One is often tempted to disagree.'

Eleanor had invited Oracle to her lap and the little mutt was frantically licking her chin. She looked hungry for animal warmth, stroking the dog and muttering something like, *I can't believe this.*

'As for turning me over to Interpol,' Wallace proceeded, 'should you try any such mischief, I will blow you and your poisonous project sky high.'

Calvin mashed another cigarette. *'Why haven't you already?'*

'In 1938,' said Wallace, 'two German diplomats went to Chamberlain and warned of the imminent invasion of Poland. They were accused of being treasonous to their own country and sent packing. All during the war, stragglers from camps tottered into Britain with stories so outlandish the government thought they were mad.'

'So no one would believe you now.'

'I do prefer to blow the whistle when I've got the goods. But if you force my hand, I will expose you now. You might not hang, but you'd have a poor time paying your phone bill.'

'Threadgill –' Piper leaned forward, and cast the rest of the pack in the fire. 'Why didn't you have me shot?'

'Because,' said Wallace, 'I think that's what you want.'

When Calvin returned from his flight to the lab the next evening, Eleanor noticed a blankness in his face right away. He said nothing, but unwrapped a package on the table – a stainless steel cylinder with a lot of clips and catches. It looked tightly sealed and all very high-tech, except for a sticker of Walt Disney's Dumbo on top, and an ad from an old conservation campaign during a drought, 'Buy an elephant a drink' taped around one side. In the little comic touches Eleanor immediately recognized: Norman. Calvin took a gingerly step back.

'What's that?' asked Eleanor.

'Pachyderm.'

It took her a minute, but gradually the hairs on her neck rose. 'No.'

Calvin made a sound of noncommittal confirmation in the back of his throat and sat down. He contemplated the object with his head cocked. 'It's not exactly a virus. A "prion"? A protein of some kind. It's tiny. Suspended in a solution hundreds of times more potent than botulism. Can be airborne or dissolved in water. Norman got word through his epidemiologist cronies of an AIDS vaccine that went wrong: some it immunized; others it destroyed overnight.'

'What about the parameters?'

'It strikes mostly children under five,' Calvin continued, moderately interested, 'about 60 per cent, and a progressively smaller percentage of older children and adults. The aged are susceptible – an economic plus.'

'How does he know?'

'Well, he was a bit apologetic – ' Calvin fished eight-by-tens from his briefcase. ' – Since I didn't give him the go-ahead. But he wanted to surprise me, and you know his position on a test.'

The photos were of an African village, with dozens of children sprawled on the ground, by women weeping. The *totos* looked strangely reposed.

'They used a low-flying crop dusting plane. Pachyderm works fast. Twelve hours or less. Norman claims there wasn't much evidence of agony, more the discomfiture of a tummy cramp. Some high fevers and delirium. And he was right, dying is never a bowl of cherries.'

'How many people did he kill?'

'The sample was about 400; of those, 137 were cropped. He's watching the village for longer-term attrition, but this organism can't live exposed to air for more than twenty-four hours, so secondary mortality shouldn't be significant.'

Eleanor let go of the photos; they stuck to her fingers. 'This is horrible.'

'The pathogen is cheap to manufacture. Norman claims we could organize within months.'

'What about 1999?'

'The Nostradamus angle always was a bit hokey.'

'So what are you going to do?'

'Basengi's work was nearly complete. Your research, you admitted last week, suggested HIV is no more than a modest assist, and Pachyderm functions doubly as a vaccine. The labour force calculations are in; the parameters are met. Except,' he noted sadly, 'the Jews.'

'What about wildlife?'

'Norman's tested an array of species and so far the only animals sensitive are roaches and rats, but not to an extent that will disturb the food chain. Norman thought a few less pests was swell.'

'Norman says. Norman thought. What do you think?'

'He wants to do more trials. But with Threadgill on our tail, haste is warranted; and the sooner we crop, the fewer we need to cull.' Calvin spoke with detached curiosity. Only a slight lilt, an upward tilt of his sentences, gave his monotone any topography at all.

'Why don't you kill Wallace?' asked Eleanor.

Calvin didn't look enthusiastic. 'I suppose we could. What a bother.' Calvin noticed the way she was looking at him and explained, 'Norman opened a bottle of champagne. I'm afraid it went rather to my head.'

'Champagne's not all that's gone to your head. Is this the only vial?'

'I don't know. He thought it would give me a kick to take it home with me. After seven years' research.'

'Calvin, bury it. Find a toxic waste barrel. Throw it in the sea.'

'That would be profligate. This is an expensive aperitif.' His tone was whimsical. 'Besides, Norman could make more.'

Eleanor threw up her hands. 'Shoot Norman!'

'Now,' he chided. 'You sound like Threadgill.'

'Or like you. What's the difference?'

Calvin asserted mechanically, 'I'm right.'

It was an old circle: so you say; so everyone says; wasn't the alternative to have no conviction. Eleanor skipped it.

'Can we go to bed?' he proposed. 'I know it's early, but I'm tired. Perhaps it was the flight.'

He stood, stretched and yawned, then nodded to Pachyderm. 'Take care of that. It's not coffee creamer.'

Calvin had worried that he'd roped himself with a single slip (under duress; hadn't she forced him?) into performing as a dutiful lover on a regular basis and had meant, if the future of the planet had not inconveniently intervened, to have a chat. (He hated chats. He hated *relationships*.) However, once next to her, his body had other ideas.

So he wanted her, but he did not want to want her, and consequently the act was savage because he was fighting himself. This time his visions were not oceanic, but thick and opaque. He saw pig's knuckles. When it was over he was hyperventilating. Eleanor held him lightly away from her, telling him to slow down, which he did only gradually, out of exhaustion.

Sleep, when it came, was more of the same. He dreamt of Lake Magadi. He had decided to go for a swim. Below the scabby pink crust, the water was crimson, like freshly cut meat, and though he knew that the soda would peel his skin he waded in. The lake stung his legs and clung to the hairs as he slogged on. Up to his neck, the red water filled his horizon. Insects swept the stagnant surface in black waves. The flamingos were ratty, their feathers matted, and they could not fly. His body was on fire and he could feel his skin moulting. If he kept walking he would sink, and he kept walking.

When Eleanor woke, Calvin was not in bed. She found him seated in the living room, and talked to the back of his chair. 'Don't you ever have sex like that with me again.'

'I won't.'

'It's better just to hold you, if the alternative is violence. I'm sore.'

Calvin sighed. 'I've always reviled animal lovers.'

'You revile anyone who loves anything.'

'Except demography.'

'Except demography.'

'You cannot always choose your passions.'

'You can choose to have more than one.'

'I am grateful for even one.' He let his head tip back over the chair.

'You're crying!'

'More,' he said, *'sentimentality.'*

She stepped into the room to discover he had Malthus on his lap. The monkey was limp.

'Clever bugger, wasn't he?' said Calvin.

The canister on the table was open. It exposed a thermosful of something like black bean soup. Calvin stayed her with a hand out. 'Don't go near it. Don't touch it or breathe it. You should leave the house.'

'Malthus got into that?'

'He was dextrous, if you'll remember.'

'You didn't even cry when Basengi died.'

'Please, Eleanor, go.'

'Then you should leave, too.'

'I will lock the creature back in its closet, but I don't want to upset it with you here.'

Eleanor dressed quickly and returned. 'Come with me. Call the WHO. Get someone in a suit to dispose of it.'

'No,' he said simply. 'Get out.'

There was no arguing. 'You won't – '

'What?'

'Take any yourself?'

He laughed drily. 'My dear, I wouldn't go to this much effort to concoct my own personal hemlock, I'm not that eccentric. Now please go.'

About an hour later, there was a knock on the door. It was not the postman.

19

Sprinkled with Vim
And Garnished with Doom

Calvin had always idealized prisons. To think in small, concrete terms, he had to be shackled in a small, concrete place. He required a world he could not escape. Behind bars there was no danger of intergalactic travel. He pictured days of horrid food you still looked forward to and work of uncreative drudgery at number plates as a kind of bliss. He revered a life where you were sufficiently uncomfortable that you thought of nothing but slop-outs and an extra blanket. He eagerly anticipated press-ups in exercise yards, crude male camaraderie, pin-ups over the bunk, wild fantasies about bust-outs that he would never attempt. So many people wished to burst their bonds; Calvin wanted to be locked up. He craved an orderly, mindless life run by someone else, where the universe never went funny on you and you could have discussions of the merits of this or that but never on whether there was such a thing as good and bad in the first place. He would love to feel passionately about Wednesday's cauliflower cheese. He had lived in a world without limits and it was frightful. Surely the answer was to get a strong-arm to build a wall around you and then you no longer had to worry about what you should and should not do because you could not.

Besides, what was the difference between prison and the world? You get up, eat breakfast, clean the wing, exercise, read, have problems with the neighbours, get raped, look for love . . . Sound familiar? Weren't you *sentenced to life* on both sides of the bars?

Of course, these fancies were all more abstracted waffle.

The holding cells in Nyayo House were themselves a study in over-population – there was no getting away. Detainees slept on the floor, and when all sixty were sandwiched side by side at night the whole row had to turn from their left to right sides at the same time. There were no toilets or even bedpans, and the place reeked of human effluence, the kind of smell so rank and constant you were supposed to get used to it; Calvin was waiting. Their only ration was *posho*, cooked into a stiff, lumpy *ugali* unseasoned with so much as salt, cold, and served in dog bowls. Calvin wouldn't touch it, though after two days passed into three he submitted to the diet of bathtub caulking.

Nyayo House was one of those edifying experiences only in the humblest sense, for it did not teach him fortitude, endurance, courage, his astonishing capacities of forbearance: Papillon. Instead Calvin realized within ten minutes of his stay that he was a panty-waist; that he'd led a pampered life and pampered was precisely the way he would like it to stay. Only the comfortable revere discomfort; only whisky-sippers in overstuffed armchairs can exalt suffering; only the free can construct elaborate and patently silly metaphors about prison life and its endearing capacity to keep your feet on the ground with chains. In short, like any normal person, as soon as he got in he wanted out, and though perhaps feeling like a normal person was this misadventure's only compensation, it wasn't sufficient by a long shot.

Calvin was the one *mzungu* in the cell, and hence something of a novelty. In keeping with this country's ambivalent relation to his colour, he drew both admiration and disdain; certainly dismay, since a European could bribe his way from jail. The white man's presence polarized the prisoners, since one lot were inclined to defecate on his feet and filch his watch, the other eager to shift him an extra handful of that terrifying *ugali* or lend him their wind-cheaters to cushion his head. In all, he was more mascot than kicked cat. He gave their cell distinction, especially once they asked, as all prisoners do, why he'd been lifted.

'Genocidal conspiracy,' he tried unsuccessfully with a

bloodied boy who'd been set upon by vigilante *wananchi* for stealing a pineapple.

'I was going to kill *mingi watu*,' he attempted next. 'As many as in China and India together.'

No one knew where, or what, China was, and Calvin was determined to communicate. 'I am a *mzungu* witchdoctor. I made a *dawa*, very strong. I was going to destroy my enemies by sprinkling them with dark dust.'

This version went down well. It was the best story in the cell by a yard. They laughed and retold it in their own fashion – better, Calvin thought. Some of these chaps would prove useful for a poetic touch in his posthumous biography.

He had prepared himself for standing achingly in waist-high cold water, but whether from superstition over his complexion or the 'Doctor' before his name, he was not tortured. Originally, Calvin might have been disappointed, but now he knew enough to be grateful.

It was five days before Calvin was dragged into a bleak room, whose guard sloped an automatic over one shoulder and wielded an electrified cattle prod. The warder's face was heavy and stupid, always petrifying in a man with a gun, and his helmet was too big, mushrooming to below his eyebrows; the guard kept his chin in the air to see. After ten minutes of his brutish silence, Eleanor Merritt was led to the opposite chair. It must have cost her pots of *chai* to arrange the meeting.

She looked terrible – thin, pale and haggard, and she'd gone back to her earlier schoolteacher clothes, with a high neck, sloped shoulders and a bow.

She said in a hoarse whisper, 'I was afraid you might be dead.'

'Oh, no,' he assured her. 'I've made my bed, now I'm lying in it. The mattress is concrete and shared with sixty other stinking Africans. Too perfect, don't you think?'

Eleanor drew back. 'I'm sorry, but you do smell.'

He chuckled. 'I expect something about QUIETUS has smelled from the beginning.'

'I've been trying to get you a lawyer. Imanyara won't touch it. There's a question about which country should try you. I'm negotiating with the embassy to get you extradited to the States. At least in Washington you'd get a bed, and there's no caning. With the stature of this case, you might even get yourself into one of those minimum security Howard Johnsons with a golf course.'

'I don't play golf. And don't go to any trouble. I want lots of publicity. That's all I care about.'

'Speaking of which, I brought you the papers.'

He had made the front page of the *Independent*, though he was insulted to note that because of another Eastern European country doing something cheerful he had not made the lead.

Former USAID Division Head
Arrested in Bizarre Depopulation Scandal

NAIROBI. Calvin Piper, until 1983 the controversial director of USAID's Population Division, was arrested by Kenya's Special Branch yesterday as the leader of an underground conspiracy to exterminate a third of the world's population in 1999. According to police reports, Dr Piper was discovered with a substance in his possession purported to be highly toxic, with which he planned to 'cull' humanity much as he once cropped elephants in Uganda in 1963. Experts from the World Health Organization have volunteered to analyse the suspicious liquid, and expect to report on their findings by the end of the week.

Dr Piper is being held in police custody in Nairobi.

The State Department has issued no comment, pending investigation. However, the current head of AID's population arm and Piper's successor, Dr Aaron Spring, was forthcoming. Asked if he found the charge incredible, Spring responded, 'Not in the least. Calvin Piper is a strange and dangerous man, perfectly capable of going off the deep end. He is obsessed with population, to the exclusion of every other issue. Population growth is a complex and culturally delicate issue in the Third World. At USAID, Piper was insensitive and simplistic. He was one step from a homicidal maniac in 1983.'

In his tenure at USAID, Piper was a successful lobbyist for population issues, and multiplied US funding for the field by several times. Caught shipping birth control pills, IUDs and vacuum aspirators to countries where they were illegal, he was replaced by the organization for violating USAID guidelines.

'Despite his crusading for population activities,' Spring noted, *'Piper turned back the contraceptive clock in developing countries. Our ground has been hard won, and the Dirty Harry of Demography only alienated local governments. It won't come as any surprise in Africa that Piper wants to march them all into gas chambers.'*

Active public support for family planning in Kenya, for example, has only come about in the last ten years. Spring fears this new turn of events will reflect badly on legitimate population programmes, and urged the Third World to regard Dr Piper as 'a renegade lunatic. Effectively, the man's insane'. Spring emphasized Piper's connections with USAID had been severed since his departure.

Kenyan officials have expressed their anger, condemning the plot as 'colonialist' and 'the devious scheming of foreign masters'. Distrust for the West's enthusiasm for family planning runs deep in African cultures.

Whether Piper will be tried in the US or in Kenya, where he has lived off and on for thirty years, is now being negotiated between the two governments. According to Dr Spring, 'Africa does odd things to white men. Ask Conrad. Piper's been there too long.' – UPI

'Aaron Spring is a tit,' Calvin commented, reading the article with a wide grin. 'Since he took over, Congress has cut his funding to the quick. He's a sad, tubby bureaucrat who's losing his hair, and he's *jealous*.'

'He has one point,' said Eleanor wearily. 'I'm not sure the publicity on your arrest is going to do the population lobby a world of good.'

'Publicity is publicity,' said Calvin merrily. 'Often, the worse the better. Scandal! This is cake. Let me see the rest.'

The tabloids were having a field day: 'Pop Expert Plans Baby Massacre; Deadly African Potion Could Destroy All Human Life . . .' However, these articles had a cry-wolf quality. QUIETUS was a real tabloid story, and if your papers always made mountains out of molehills, how did you write about real mountains? Calvin's story was impossible to sensationalize, and as a consequence the *Star*, the *Sunday World* and the *Daily Mail* were disappointingly staid.

'How are you?' asked Eleanor.

'Filthy, tired, hungry and pleased with myself.'

'I can't see why.'

'This press is unparalleled. Though I didn't get very far. I don't suppose they'll hang me,' he mourned. 'But how are you?'

'Not great.' Her eyes were twitching. 'Someone turned you in, didn't they?'

'You should know.'

'Why should *I* know?'

He shrugged.

'Well, it was obviously Wallace,' she said hurriedly.

'I disagree.' He eyed her. 'It was more likely an inside job. I doubt if Threadgill's intelligence was so good that he knew Pachyderm was already on the table. Only a handful of people knew we'd cracked the pathogen.'

Eleanor glanced at the guard. 'Shouldn't you watch what you say?'

'Why? I'm guilty. I intend to plead guilty. There's nothing to hide.'

'So who was the turncoat?'

'Eleanor, my poppet. Let's give each other a little more credit. I think we both know perfectly well.'

Calvin had been in Nyayo House three more days and had started to stomach the *ugali*. His spirits were high. He enjoyed his notoriety among his cell-mates. He lived for another instalment of newspapers. His greatest fear had been that the story would get hushed up, and those front pages reassured him.

Calvin spent much of his time fantasizing about his trial. He would contest nothing. They could bring in Norman, Bunny and Threadgill to testify. Maybe poor Eleanor could be left out on humanitarian grounds – too bad they weren't married. Calvin pictured himself with his hands clasped beside his useless lawyer, with a beatific smile and cool, photogenic eyes. The case would be followed closely by the press, day by day, and once the prosecution discovered the lab the evidence would be damning. Climactically, Calvin would at last take the stand himself. He would accost the world with the proliferation of its own demise. He organized his statistics during the long nights on cement. The illustration about the atomic bomb, he'd use that; it was graphic. The speech would be the most moving of his career. It would get quoted in full in the *New York Times*. No demographer in the history of the field would have organized a more spectacular cameo.

Therefore, imagine Calvin's surprise when a warder arrived to let him out. Surely Eleanor had bribed her way in for another visit, but there was no little room and she was nowhere in sight. They left him loitering in the hall, with no guard. He had to go and find one. 'Sorry,' said Calvin. 'Whom am I supposed to see? Where do I go?'

'You go home,' said the lump.

'I can't imagine anyone raised the bail for me. It must be astronomical.'

'No bail,' said the guard, bored. 'You are free. Get out.'

Mystified, Calvin wandered out into the smoggy, sunny glare of hideous downtown Nairobi, which he had hoped to have left behind for ever. Bereft, he wandered to a news-stand and bought the *Standard*.

Population Poison Revealed As Hoax

WHO *officials announced yesterday that the substance found with Dr Calvin Piper, ostensibly a toxin to depopulate the Third World, has been analysed as harmless. Lab technicians found traces of vinegar, pili-pili, sugar, flavourings and common household bleach. The conspiracy has been dismissed as a hoax, and some suspect Dr Piper has merely staged an elaborate publicity stunt. President Moi issued a statement that the Piper 'goo' was a 'sick joke'.*

Dr Piper has been released, as there is no evidence of wrong-doing besides, said the President, 'offending good taste and common decency, and wasting wananchi's time'. He had no wish to detain Dr Piper further, as the Kenyan justice system was reserved for prosecuting dangerous criminals, and not 'schoolboy pranksters'.

'Impossible!' cried Calvin on the street. He about-faced to Nyayo House and ran up the stairs (the elevators were broken again) to his QUIETUS office, which he feared had been looted for evidence. The door, however, was unharmed but padlocked, with a notice advising its tenants that entry was forbidden due to non-payment of rent.

Back on the street, he found a pay phone and, after dialling ten times with an irate queue forming behind him, he got through to Pachyderm. 'This is Piper. *Where's Norman?'*

The secretary was cool. 'Oh, Norman's been expecting you'd like to talk to him. He said he'd lunch at the Norfolk.' She hung up without saying goodbye.

Calvin scuttled towards the hotel lobby to wash up, but he reeked so much that security wouldn't let him in. He glanced in the door glass at his pilled beard and bath-mat hair. Decency be damned, he wanted some answers.

Norman was out on the terrace, with a dapper bow-tie. The microbiologist was munching buns with Campari and soda, perusing the Hot 'n' Snackies on which he rested his eye an extra beat before looking up.

Calvin threw the *Standard* on the table. 'What's this about *vinegar and bleach*? Did you suspend some shy little protein in that liquid they didn't find?'

'The only thing suspended in that salad dressing,' Norman purred, 'was your disbelief.' He took another nibble on his roll and dabbed his chin.

'But it killed Malthus.'

'I'm not surprised. We cooked up quite a porridge: Worcestershire, Peptang, mango chutney, Ribena and Marmite, dusted with a little Omo, sprinkled with Vim and garnished with a generous spray of Doom. I imagine such a breakfast would do in the heartiest monkey.'

'What about the photographs?'

'We found a little village not far from the lab. Told them we were making a movie. They were only too delighted to co-operate. Especially the kids. Dead sweet. Lolling on the ground with their tongues out – regular scene-stealers, every one. Then we threw a picnic. It was a hoot, Pipe, you should have been there.'

'I wasn't invited. You're going to explain to me, I hope, why I have spent eight days in the holding cells of Nyayo house so you could have a picnic?'

'We never expected you to get arrested,' said Norman,

sounding injured. 'All in good fun and that. Say, you couldn't sit in the next chair? You smell like a long drop.'

'I will not. I've suffered for your little joke, the least I can do is ruin your lunch.'

Norman kept a napkin over his nose. 'It wasn't just a joke, Pipe. It was research.'

'Into what?'

'Your character. See, Pachyderm's a bloody lot of work, my *mutu*. We've been putting in serious hours. We'd gotten somewhere, but we were still looking at five more years. Life's short. I've found the project theoretically enthralling, but I didn't want to waste my time if you were going to oo-worms in the eleventh hour. And I can't say what tipped me off, but I wasn't sure you'd follow through. They aren't obvious at first, but you've your soft spots.'

'You sound like Panga,' muttered Calvin.

'Now I suppose we'll never know,' Norman bemoaned. 'What we turned up instead was a nasty leak in QUIETUS. You should thank me. Better to find it now than later, when there's something spicier than Worcestershire in that sauce. And now you've learned something: next time you initiate an illegal international conspiracy, you'll find a girlfriend who keeps her mug shut.'

'I wish you wouldn't spread rumours about Eleanor being a grass.'

'It's common knowledge, boyo. And from what I hear, she's in no shape to worry about local gossip.'

'What do you mean?'

'Word's out she had a nervous breakdown – has been experiencing humours – whatever the latest lingo is for falling apart. Checked into Nairobi Hospital. Kept raving about how she was going to murder billions of people, so of course they put her on medication. I think your friend Wallie took her home with him.'

'If she wasn't ga-ga before,' Calvin grumbled, 'Threadgill should finish the job.'

'It's a pity about Pachyderm, though.' Norman reclined philosophically. 'I still think the idea was nifty. And what do you want me to do with the lab?'

'What else,' said Calvin blackly. 'Convert it to a summer camp for disadvantaged parking boys.'

After showering, Calvin went to retrieve Eleanor from Threadgill's ward. He approached the camp, diffident. Ducking his head under the tent flap, Calvin found Wallace sitting by the bed, murmuring over a thick black book. For Eleanor's sake, Calvin hoped it was Hans Christian Andersen, but when he crept nearer to the bed he saw the text was illustrated with spiritual diagrams of intersecting circles: WATER, WINDS OF VOID.

'Sh-sh.' Wallace held a finger to his lips and delicately led Calvin back outside. Calvin glanced at a chair, splayed with that morning's papers, his name on the front page. Neither he nor Threadgill mentioned it, decorously. So sententious when they'd last met, now Wallace was humble, soft spoken, polite.

'Is Eleanor all right?'

'She's heavily sedated.'

'No doubt by your bedtime stories,' said Calvin, but wryly, almost with affection. 'I want to take her home.'

He had expected resistance, but inexplicably their antagonism had collapsed. 'Yes,' said Wallace. 'I think you should.' He brought Eleanor's prescriptions, and went carefully through the dosages, counter-indications and side effects.

Back in the tent, threading his way between two dozen half-drunk mugs of cold tea, Calvin leaned beside Eleanor, who was sluggish and failed to recognize him. Calvin bundled her in his arms to the car.

For several days he fed her soup and the rest of the time she slept. She had moments of lucidity, when she would gasp with gratitude that he had rescued her from Threadgill's edifying lectures on the Orb of the Over-Conscious. 'Another week of Greater Galactic Love,' she confided, 'and I'd have founded a Pachyderm lab myself.'

Calvin waited until she was strong enough, and then slowly, carefully, explained that Norman had pulled their leg. Somehow the pathogen made of mango chutney did not pick her up much.

'You think I was the informer,' said Eleanor, dragging herself up on the pillow. She still had a complexion of boiled arrowroot.

'Is that what made you snap? That I didn't trust you?'

'No,' she sighed. 'I was mortified that I didn't turn you in. I should have. I couldn't forgive myself. Everyone in QUIE-TUS was convinced I rang Special Branch. Bunny started making threatening phone calls. But they gave me too much credit. If I had any integrity, I'd have handcuffed you person-ally. Do you believe me?'

'Yes.'

'You're sure, then, that I didn't go to the police?'

'Naturally.'

'So who do you think it was? It doesn't sound like Norman. Bunny?'

'Don't be silly,' said Calvin. 'I rang them myself.'

ENDPAPERS:

The Cool Rats

May you have as many children as possible until their
excrement buries you up to the neck.

TRADITIONAL KAMBA MARRIAGE BLESSING

There was talk in the Kenyan government of deporting Calvin
Piper for sedition, but the man had become such an international liability that both the British and the American
embassies went to lengths to keep him in his adoptive country
and out of theirs. Calvin himself was content to remain in
Africa because he hated it.

He and Eleanor refined a ritual argument: she pushing him
to admit why he'd rung Special Branch, when success, to all
appearances, was in reach. 'Because,' he explained, 'it would
have been too much trouble.'

One day she pushed him further. 'That's ridiculous. You'd
already gone to enormous trouble.'

'I was interested in the theory. I was interested in the computer model. I was interested in the economics, and even
in your AIDS research. But practically, QUIETUS seemed
laborious. I couldn't be bothered frankly.'

'Not even to *save the world*?'

'I keep telling you, "the world" does not require saving. the
little pear-shaped orb on which we spin will manage with
pond scum.' He dribbled lime juice over Eleanor's fresh
samosas; she had finally refused servants and was consequently becoming an excellent cook. 'It's only the human race
that needs saving, and I had to face the contradiction Thread-

gill astutely hung me on: I couldn't care less. Why should I rescue 5.3 billion wet-nosed, sticky-bummed whingers too pig thick to stop reproducing themselves like fruit flies? Let them rut, let them foul their own nest, let them starve. All a matter of sublime indifference to me.'

Eleanor was irked. 'Come on. Didn't you finally decide QUIETUS was repugnant?'

'I still think it was a laudable and logical plan of action. Furthermore, QUIETUS was intellectually courageous. It so happens that intellectual courage is the only kind I've got. On that score Panga had my number: in the field I'm a kitty cat. I'm a great tactician, but as a soldier I shoot myself in the foot.'

'You did cull elephants.'

Calvin confessed, 'It wasn't pleasant.'

'Somewhere in that concession lurks the nascent seeds of full-fledged moral revulsion.'

'Purely aesthetic. They stank,' said Calvin. 'But there was one more reason I wanted us stopped.'

'I'm on tenterhooks.'

'I don't believe in conspiracies. Not that they don't exist; more that they don't succeed. The CIA made a horlicks of Cuba, Argentina. How can we be dead sure that AIDS wasn't concocted by the Pentagon? Because it works. Pachyderm was inspired if all went according to plan, but I was gradually convinced that that was the one advent I could more or less discount. In short: Sod's Law.'

Calvin promptly lost all interest in population. He left his *Population and Development Reviews* in their mailing wrappers. In short order, he was in danger of having no interests at all. For someone who valued interest over love, demographic dispassion threatened personality collapse.

For Calvin refined a theory in relation to all the problems of the day which he called Muddling Through, a position somewhere between apathy and religious conviction: everything would sort out somehow. Population, after all, was self-correcting: if the earth could not support more people, then it would not. An orbiting voyeur, he would watch an unfolding wonder or imploding apocalypse with equal fascination. He continued to think the world was getting uglier, he continued to hum Mozart in preparation for a future without cellos, he continued to see Africa as he knew it in its paradisiacal days as spiralling down the toilet – but these were diverting opinions with no more consequence than the atrocities he still taped to his wall.

Moreover, Calvin theorized that because your projects never have the results you expect and because your reasons for executing them are never the ones you tell yourself they are, whatever you do it is critical to do it as little as possible.

For the removed, congenitally sardonic conclusion of his life, Calvin had a role model. When he and Norman conducted their density experiments with Norwegian rats, they had identified a variety of types, all adaptions to overcrowding: the hyper-sexed, the homosexual, the delinquent mother. The researchers discerned a small, discreet subsection of males, however, which Norman had christened the Cool Rats. These unruffled loners refused to take part in the struggle for dominance. They ignored all the other rats of both sexes, and all the other rats ignored them. They moved passively through the community like somnambulists. They were never attacked or approached for play. And these were the sleekest, healthiest animals in the pen, with thick, unmolested fur. The Cool Rats were pretending they weren't there. Calvin was suffering stress in density and Calvin bought sun-glasses.

It was necessary, however, to earn a living. Only a fraction of funds from QUIETUS remained, though donors were too embarrassed to demand them back. He still owned the NFD lab, now derelict, though the sale of the equipment barely covered some hefty chemical bills which piqued him, as Peptang was only forty-five shillings. Eleanor's salary was promptly withdrawn, for news of her link to Calvin had spread to Pathfinder, and that was the end of her family planning career for the next 5,000 years. Calvin's reputation was as biodegradable as egg-carton styrofoam.

With Eleanor's well-organized, brisk assistance, he cleared out Pachyderm and started a pottery. He was surprised to find he'd a knack. A natural mathematician, Calvin had a strong sense of symmetry and centred easily on the wheel. It was hard work which made his shoulders ache, but quiet, meditative and, most important, useless. There wasn't a soul who couldn't live without his silly pots. Consequently, he made lots of them. Besides, Panga was always trooping carelessly through and knocking over whole racks with her bayonet.

As for Eleanor, she gave her change to panhandlers when she felt like it; other afternoons she wasn't in the mood. Much as she might sometimes wish, and violently, that the huddled masses with their demands for glasses and basketball shoes would *go away*, they weren't going to. Their existence did not rely on her humour. She contented herself that their business in the NFD employed a dozen Turkana at good wages who could be proud of their work, and that was better for any country than hand-outs. She did sometimes miss her job, weary of delivering cartons of tacky tusk-handled coffee mugs to tourist traps, the same tiny Pachyderm stamp on the bottom of each cup, and resented Calvin for sabotaging her profession. Then, their arrangement came with its compensations: *small private happiness*, and she could always discuss with shopkeepers the benefits of smaller families, how much more feasible it was with fewer children to send them all to school. Ordinary economics was increasingly persuasive in East Africa, more so than 'development theory' or appeals to environmental preservation, and Kenya's fertility rate continued to drop.

She would occasionally stop by to see Peter Ndumba. He had learned to count on her for one birthday present, end of story, though jockeyed dates to celebrate twice a year; in return, she gladly accepted their meals of beans and corn, and took second helpings.

VISA at last caught the culprit with her credit card, and it wasn't Florence after all. The thief was from Pathfinder all right, but she was perfectly well off, and she was white.

Often on Saturday nights when Eleanor and Calvin returned from packing an exhausting order at Pachyderm, Wallace Threadgill would stop by for a nip. After the demise of QUIE-TUS, his vows had gradually slipped and, well, he was becoming a bit of a drunk. His contract had run out with the WHO, whose administrators had found his theories tiresome, and after a few whiskies the Orbs and Circles of Time and Fullnesses of Being would all start to reel in an incoherent, off-centre miasma. He was rather endearing, squiffy, though he and Calvin still got into ferocious arguments. On certain evenings Wallace would pull her aside and apologize with a maudlin droop on her shoulder, saying that he was 'very, very sorry, so very sorry', though he'd never say for what, and she wondered if he wasn't a trifle sweet on her. And he was awfully hard to get rid of when she and Calvin wanted to go to bed, with forty elephant-trunk candlesticks to glaze and fire the next day. Bunny Morton wanted a banquet set.

There we leave Calvin Piper, humming over his wheel, spattered in slip, easing the lip from humble clay. Eleanor wanted children. Well, he would reflect, sponging on more water, if the rest of these low-lifes could reiterate, maybe he should stick them with half a dozen little Calvins out of sheer spite. He moulded a handful of mud as it spun under his fingers, a turning, dirty globe, for according to the eminently sensible Ms Merritt, this was about as much of the earth as he should ever be entrusted with at one time.

EXCLUSIVE EXTRAS

❖ ❖ ❖

Meet Lionel Shriver

"If Only Poor People Would *Go Away*": Writing *Game Control*

Read an excerpt from *The Post-Birthday World*

Author's Picks

Have You Read?

MEET LIONEL SHRIVER

AH WAN OW! It took a while for my mother to decode the first words from my crib as "I want out." Since, *Ah wan ow* has become something of a running theme.

I wanted out of North Carolina, where I was born. I wanted out of my given name ("Margaret Ann"—the whole double-barrel; can you blame me?), and at fifteen chose another one. I wanted out of New York, where I went to university at Columbia. I wanted out of the United States.

In 1985, I cycled around Europe for six months; one hundred miles a day in wretched weather fortified a lifetime appetite for unnecessary suffering. The next year, I spent six months in Israel, including three on a kibbutz in the Galilee helping to manufacture waterproof plastic boots. Thereafter, I shifted "temporarily" to Belfast, where I remained based for twelve years. Within that time, I also spent a year in Nairobi, and several months in Bangkok. Yet only my partner's getting a job in London in 1999 tore me decisively from Belfast, a town that addictively commands equal parts love and loathing. As *We Need to Talk About Kevin* attests, I'm a sucker for ambivalence.

Though returning regularly to New York, I've lived in London ever since. I'm not sure if I've chosen this city so much as run out of wanderlust here. London is conventional for me, and I'm a bit disappointed in myself. But I've less appetite for travel than I once did. I'm not sure if this is from some larger grasp that people are the same everywhere and so why not save the plane fare, or from having just gotten lazy. My bets are on the latter.

At least the novels are still thematically peripatetic. Their disparate subject matter lines up like the fruit on slot machines when you do not win the jackpot: anthropology and a May-December love affair (*The Female of the Species*), rock-and-roll drumming and jealousy (*Checker and the Derailleurs*), the Northern Irish troubles and my once dreadful taste in men (*Ordinary Decent Criminals*), demography and AIDS in Africa (*Game Control*), inheritance (*A Perfectly Good Family*), professional tennis and career competition in marriage (*Double Fault*), terrorism and cults of personality (*The New Republic*, my *real* seventh novel, which has never seen the light of day), and high school massacres and motherhood (*We Need to Talk About Kevin*). My latest, *The Post-Birthday World*, is a romance—about the trade-offs of one man versus another and *snooker*, believe it or not—whose nature seems in context almost alarmingly innocent.

For the nosey: I am married, to an accomplished jazz drummer from New York. Perhaps mercifully for any prospective progeny, I have no children. I am confessedly and unashamedly fifty years old, and never lie about my age because I want credit for every damned year.

Lesser known facts:

I have sometimes been labeled a "feminist"—a term that never sits well with me, if only because connotatively you have no sense of humor. Nevertheless, I am an excellent cook, if one inclined to lace every dish with such a malice of fresh chilis that nobody but I can eat it. Indeed, I have been told more than once that I am "extreme." As I run through my preferences—for *dark* roast coffee, *dark* sesame oil, *dark* chocolate, *dark* meat chicken, even *dark* chili beans—a pattern emerges that, while it may not put me on the outer edges of human experience, does exude a faint whiff of the unsavory.

Illustrating the old saw that whatever doesn't kill you makes you stronger, I cycle everywhere, though I expect that eventually this perverse Luddite habit will kill me, period. I am a deplorable tennis player, which doesn't stop me from inflicting my crap net-game and cowardly refusal to play formal matches on anyone I can corner on a court.

I am a pedant. I insist that people pronounce "flaccid" *flak-sid*, which is dictionary-correct but defies onomatopoeic instinct; when I force them to look it up, they grow enraged and vow to keep saying *flassid* anyway. I never let anyone get away with using "enervated" to mean "energized," when the word means without energy, thank you very much. Not only am I, apparently, the last remaining American citizen who knows the difference between "like" and "as," but I freely alienate everyone in my surround by interrupting, "You mean, *as* I said." Or, "You mean, you gave it to *whom*," or "You mean, that's just between you and *me*." I am a lone champion of the accusative case, and so—obviously—have no friends.

I read every article I can find that commends the nutritional benefits of red wine; if they're right, I will live to 110. Though raised by

Adlai Stevenson Democrats, I have a violent, retrograde right-wing streak that alarms and horrifies my acquaintances in London and New York.

Those twelve years in Northern Ireland have left a peculiar residual warp in my accent—house = hyse, shower = shar; now = nye. Since an Ulster accent bears little relation to the more familiar mincing of a Dublin brogue, these aberrations are often misinterpreted as holdovers from my North Carolinian childhood. Because this handful of mangled vowels is one of the only souvenirs I took from Belfast, my wonky pronunciation is a point of pride (or, if you will, vanity), and when my "Hye nye bryne cye" (= how now brown cow) is mistaken for a bog-standard southern American drawl I get mad.

"IF ONLY POOR PEOPLE WOULD GO *AWAY*"

Writing *Game Control*

LIKE PARENTS, authors have favorites among their unruly broods, and *Game Control* is a favorite of mine. Of course, in fiction, effort and accomplishment can have an exasperatingly inverse relationship; nevertheless, I have never worked harder on any novel, before or since. I must have read enough seminal works in the field to have earned myself a de facto master's degree in demography. Indeed, every time *Game Control* arises in our conversation, a friend of mine in London chides that the novel's primary flaw is that it contains "too much research." (Last time I told her I'd got the message and to put a lid on it. Before publication, I culled out a good one hundred manuscript pages' worth of "research," so readers count your blessings.)

When I started this novel in the early 1990s, scientists were sending completely contradictory signals about Africa. (FYI: they still are.) Demographers were alarmed by the continent's soaring population; epidemiologists were alarmed by its prospectively plummeting population due to AIDS. So were Africans over-reproducing, or dying off? Surely you couldn't have it both ways. Hence I tracked down all seven of the studies then available on the projected interaction between Africa's AIDS mortality and population growth.

I was fascinated to uncover a pattern: Computer models by *demographers* predicted that AIDS would have a modest to negligible effect on population growth. Computer models by *epidemiologists* predicted that AIDS would eventually cause Africa's population to implode. In other words, however unconsciously, each scientific community managed to rig the results so that their problem of choice was the more dire—thus making their own field the more important. This confirmed what became a central thesis of the novel: that intellectual positions reliably arise from less rational, emotional wellsprings, and generally front for self-interest. The hidden motives and suspect desires teeming beneath the field of demography made it perfect material for fiction.

When I turned the finished manuscript in to my editor in New York, he rejected the novel, characterizing its content as addressing the same old "man versus woman" stand-off that he saw my previous books as having tackled. The novel's subsequent editor in the UK aired the view that *Game Control* was at core about "Eleanor and her relationship to her own fertility." Both these thumbnails are a load of hooey, and are typical—here's a real "man versus woman" gripe for you—of the intellectually reductive way that men in publishing often regard fiction by women. Certainly this novel is about Calvin Piper and Eleanor Merritt, temperamental opposites who desperately need each other. But it is also about *demography*.

I realize that for many readers that summation is a turn-off. I hasten to add that I have tried to tell a good story—a deliciously wicked story—with lively, distinctive characters. But demography is not just a dry, bean-counting subject. It's about people—whether they have children, and why. (In this sense, *Game Control* and my more widely read *We Need to Talk About Kevin* share a thematic thread.) Moreover, our relationship to demography tells much about our relationship to others, and to ourselves. I came to understand that I was drawn to this subject because I was raised in a guilt-ridden liberal household; my parents were always trying to make their children feel bad about being privileged (although we were merely middle-middle-class). I was eternally to bear in mind the starving Armenians or the starving Chinese or whoever it was who was starving that year. So I resented all those poor people, who were ruining my good time. Like Calvin, something in me wanted them to *go away*.

Runaway population growth—and in 2007 this issue has hardly vanished; a worldwide population of at least 9 billion is now a statistical certainty, and that is right around the point that we run out of fresh water—tempts us to blame suffering people for their own plight. If they just wouldn't have so many kids, they'd be better off by half. The perspective is a little mean-spirited, but secretly consoling. It lets us comfortable folks off the hook.

Thus while *Game Control* is often read as a satire, it isn't, quite. The premise may be outlandish, but as a fantasy—just making those pestersome poor people *go away*—it's serious as could be.

After the novel's UK release, one fan letter arrived that meant more to me than any other. The head of Rockefeller University's prestigious Laboratory of Populations admired the book not only as a story, but also as the product of impressive amateur research. I wrote back, and in time this connection led to my writing an essay on population in literature for Macmillan's 2003 *Encyclopedia of Population*. That essay in turn became the lead article in the June 2003 issue of *Population and Development Review*, a professional journal I had come greatly to admire while writing the novel. (*PDR* is more compelling and better written than the average *New Yorker*.) I relished having leapt from the dilettantish world of fiction writing into the scientifically exacting world of Calvin Piper, and still count that publication as one of the highlights of my career.

I moved to Nairobi for more than a year to set this book, dragging my demographic library in a massive leather case to the airport, where check-in dunned me $400 in overweight charges. Yet once the project came to fruition, this novel lost me my American publisher. I would be orphaned without a U.S. house for not only this novel but the next. *Game Control* netted a farcically tiny advance in the UK, until this American edition the only country in which this book has ever appeared, and there briefly. If critically a modest success, commercially the novel went nowhere, and most of the hardback run was pulped.

Therefore I might sensibly conclude that all that effort was wasted. But between reading dozens of books and moving to Africa, I got one of the great educations of my life. The vengeful misanthrope Calvin Piper and the guilty do-gooder Eleanor Merritt—Eleanor personifying that excuse-me-for-living sensibility I was pushed to embrace as a child—made for marvelous company over two very fine years, and I'd never wish to have spent them any other way.

READ AN EXCERPT FROM
THE POST-BIRTHDAY WORLD
(2007, HarperCollins)

Can the course of life hinge on a single kiss? That is the question that Lionel Shriver's The Post-Birthday World *seeks to answer with all the subtlety, perceptiveness, and drama that made her last novel,* We Need to Talk About Kevin, *an international bestseller and winner of the 2005 Orange Prize. Whether the American expatriate Irina McGovern does or doesn't lean into a certain pair of lips in London will determine whether she stays with her smart, disciplined, intellectual American partner, Lawrence, or runs off with Ramsey—a wild, exuberant British snooker star the couple has known for years. Employing a parallel-universe structure, Shriver follows Irina's life as it unfolds under the influence of two drastically different men. In a tour de force that, remarkably, has no villains, Shriver explores the implications, both large and small, of our choice of mate—a subject of timeless, universal fascination for both sexes.*

Chapter One

What began as coincidence had crystallized into tradition: on the sixth of July, they would have dinner with Ramsey Acton on his birthday.

Five years earlier, Irina had been collaborating with Ramsey's then-wife Jude Hartford on a children's book. Jude had made social overtures. Abjuring the airy we-really-must-get-together-sometime feints common to London, which can carry on indefinitely without threatening to clutter your diary with a real time and place, Jude had seemed driven to nail down a foursome so that her illustrator could meet her husband Ramsey. Or, no—she'd said, "My husband, Ramsey Acton." The locution had stood out. Irina assumed that Jude was prideful in that wearing feminist way about the fact that she'd not taken her husband's surname.

But then, it is always difficult to impress the ignorant. When negotiating with Lawrence over the prospective dinner back in 1992, Irina didn't know enough to mention, "Believe it or not, Jude's married to *Ramsey Acton*." For once Lawrence might have bolted for his *Economist* day-planner, instead of grumbling that if she had to schmooze for professional reasons, could she at least schedule an early dinner so that he could get back in time for *NYPD Blue*. Not realizing that she had been bequeathed two magic words that would vanquish Lawrence's broad hostility to social engagements, Irina had said instead, "Jude wants me to meet her husband, Raymond or something."

Yet when the date she proposed turned out to be *Raymond or something*'s birthday, Jude insisted that more would be merrier. Once returned to bachelorhood, Ramsey let slip enough details about his marriage for Irina to reconstruct: After a couple of years, they could not carry a conversation for longer than five minutes. Jude had leapt at the chance to avoid a sullen, silent dinner just the two of them.

Which Irina found baffling. Ramsey always seemed pleasant enough company, and the strange unease he always engendered in Irina herself would surely abate if you were married to the man.

Maybe Jude had loved dragging Ramsey out to impress colleagues, but was not sufficiently impressed on her own behalf. One-on-one he had bored her silly.

Besides, Jude's exhausting gaiety had a funny edge of hysteria about it, and simply wouldn't fly—would slide inevitably to the despair that lay beneath it—without that quorum of four. When you cocked only half an ear to her uproarious discourse, it was hard to tell if she was laughing or crying. Though she did laugh a great deal, including through most of her sentences, her voice rising in pitch as she drove herself into ever accelerating hilarity when nothing she had said was funny. It was a compulsive, deflective laughter, born of nerves more than humor, a masking device and therefore a little dishonest. Yet her impulse to put a brave, bearable face on what must have been a profound unhappiness was sympathetic. Her breathless mirth pushed Irina in the opposite direction—to speak soberly, to keep her voice deep and quiet, if only to demonstrate that it was acceptable to be serious. Thus if Irina was sometimes put off by Jude's manner, in the woman's presence she at least liked herself.

Irina hadn't been familiar with the name of Jude's husband, consciously. Nevertheless, that first birthday, when Jude had bounced into the Savoy Grill with Ramsey gliding beside her—it was already late enough in a marriage that was really just a big, well-meaning mistake that her clasp of his hand could only have been for show—Irina met the tall man's grey-blue eyes with a jolt, a tiny touching of live wires that she subsequently interpreted as visual recognition, and later—much later—as recognition of another kind. . . .

AUTHOR'S PICKS

THE AGE OF INNOCENCE, by Edith Wharton

I love virtually all of Edith Wharton, but this one's my favorite. Why Wharton, in general? I admire her prose style, which is lucid, intelligent, and artful rather than arty; she is eloquent but never fussy, and always clear. She never seems to be writing well to show off. As for *The Age of Innocence*, it's a poignant story that, typically for Wharton, illustrates the bind women found themselves in when trapped hazily between a demeaning if relaxing servitude and dignified if frightening independence, and that both sexes find themselves in when trapped between the demands of morality and the demands of the heart. The novel is romantic but not sentimental, and I'm a sucker for unhappy endings.

FLAG FOR SUNRISE, by Robert Stone

I'm a big fan of most of Stone's work. This one's the best, though—grim and brutal. Stone has a feel for politics in the gritty, ugly way they play out on the ground. His cynicism about what makes people tick, and his portrayal of how badly they behave when either desperate or given free rein to do what they like, jibes—alas—with my own experience of the species.

AS MEAT LOVES SALT, by Maria McCann

I include this more recent title if only because, especially in the U.S., it didn't get the attention it deserved. A historical novel—which I don't usually read—set in Cromwellian England, it's about a homosexual affair in the days when same-sex marriage was hardly in the headlines; rather, man-meets-man was a hanging offense. I relished the radical sexual tension McCann created, without ever becoming sordid or even very blow-by-blow (so to speak), and the story is sexy even for hetero readers like me. In fact, this riveting story works partly because it's told by a straight woman, and so isn't tainted by the faint self-justification of many gay authors' work.

PARIS TROUT, by Pete Dexter

I'd recommend all of Dexter's books, but he may never have topped this one. He writes about race and bigotry without the moral obviousness that this subject matter often elicits. His prose is terse and muscular, but not posy and tough-guy.

ATONEMENT, by Ian McEwan

A terrific examination of guilt and exculpation—or, as for the latter, lack thereof. He writes about childhood in a way that isn't white-washingly sweet, and he doesn't endorse cheap forgiveness, of yourself or anyone else. There's a powerful sense in this book that sometimes seemingly small sins have enormous and permanently dire consequences, with which you're condemned to live for the rest of your life. I read this while writing *Kevin*, and I think some of McEwan's and my themes must intersect.

ENGLISH PASSENGERS, by Matthew Kneale

Once again, I include this novel for its relative commercial obscurity in the U.S.—though it did, justly, win the Whitbread in the UK (and should have won the Booker). Seven years in the writing, *English Passengers* follows the hapless journey of a ship bound for Tasmania in the mid-nineteenth century to find the original Garden of Eden. The novel demonstrates the value of good research, which is seamlessly integrated into the text, and it's hilarious.

HAVE THE MEN HAD ENOUGH?, by Margaret Forster

Forster is underappreciated even in the UK, and shamefully neglected in the U.S. This book takes on subject matter from which most novelists have shied: the increasing decrepitude and dementia of an aging relative. Given the demographic future, this is material that most of us will soon have to contend with, like it or not.

REVOLUTIONARY ROAD, by Richard Yates

Yates was able to look at the disturbing underside of so-called ordinary life, and even more successfully than John Cheever exposed the angst and dissatisfaction that teem beneath the placid suburbs. I don't think anyone's life is simple or easy, even with enough food on the table, and Yates was depressive enough as a person to appreciate this fact.

THE IDIOT, by Fyodor Dostoevsky

Of Dostoevsky's novels, most writers would cite *The Brothers Karamazov*. Which I also adored in latter adolescence, but found I could not bear when I tried to read it again in my thirties. I hadn't the patience. By contrast, re-reading *The Idiot* as an adult rewarded the return. At that time, I was writing my second novel, *Checker and the Derailleurs*, and also grappling with how difficult it is to write about goodness. Virtue in literature, as it is often in real people, can be downright off-putting. The secret, I discovered, was to put virtue at risk—thus guaranteeing that our hero is misunderstood and persecuted. I preferred to confirm this with Dostoevsky, though if I hadn't acquired an allergy to all things religious during my Presbyterian childhood, I might also have located the same ingenious fictional strategy in the New Testament.

ALL THE KING'S MEN, by Robert Penn Warren

As I scan these (hopelessly arbitrary) selections, I note that a number of novels that have made a big impression on me have somehow managed to incorporate a political element—without being tiresome or polemical. In my own work, I've often tried to do the same. Penn Warren's loose fictionalized biography of Huey Long has stayed with me for so intertwining the personal and the political as to expose the distinction as artificial. Unfortunately, when I tracked down his other books—and there are not many—they were all disappointing in comparison. Read *All the King's Men* and forget the rest. Years hence folks may be dismissing most of my own novels in just this manner, but if they're still touting one title, and it's as good as this one, then I'll still be very lucky.

HAVE YOU READ?

**WE NEED TO TALK ABOUT KEVIN (winner of the 2005
Orange Prize for fiction)**

In this gripping novel of motherhood gone awry, Lionel Shriver
approaches the tragedy of a high-school massacre from the point
of view of the killer's mother. In letters written to the boy's father,
Eva probes the upbringing of this more-than-difficult child and
reveals herself to have been the reluctant mother of an unsavory
son. As the schisms in her family unfold, we draw closer to an
unexpected climax that holds breathtaking surprises and its own
hard-won redemption. In Eva, Shriver has created a narrator who
is touching, sad, funny, and reflective. A spellbinding read, *We
Need to Talk About Kevin* is as original as it is timely.

"Impossible to put down."

—*Boston Globe*

"In crisply crafted sentences that cut to the bone of her feelings
about motherhood, career, family, and what it is about American
culture that produces child killers, Shriver yanks the reader back
and forth between blame and empathy, retribution and forgiveness."
—*Booklist* (starred review)

A PERFECTLY GOOD FAMILY

Following the death of her worthy liberal parents, Corlis McCrea moves back into her family's grand Reconstruction mansion in North Carolina, willed to all three siblings. Her timid younger brother has never left home. When her bullying black-sheep older brother moves into "his" house as well, it's war.

Each heir wants the house. Yet to buy the other out, two siblings must team-up against one. Just as in girlhood, Corlis is torn between allying with the decent but fearful youngest and the iconoclastic eldest, who covets his legacy to destroy it. *A Perfectly Good Family* is a stunning examination of inheritance, literal and psychological: what we take from our parents, what we discard, and what we are stuck with, like it or not.

"Often funny and always intelligent, this is a sharply observed history of the redoubtable McCrea family, shot through with sardonic wit and black comedy."

—*The Independent* (London)